DECEIT

RUNS RED

Sierra Justice Series

Robert
Falkenberg

DECEIT RUNS RED

Falcon Mountain

Published by Falcon Mountain Publishing, LLC

This novel is a work of fiction. While certain locations mentioned may correspond to real places, all characters, events, and incidents are the product of the author's imagination. Any resemblance to actual persons, living or dead, is entirely coincidental.

ISBN 979-8-9924103-0-3 (paperback)
ISBN 979-8-9924103-1-0 (hardcover)
ISBN 979-8-218-56688-3 (ebook)

Cover by Bukovero

First Edition

DECEIT RUNS RED

Sierra Justice Series

For Faith. This book wouldn't exist without your sacrifices.

I love you like the stars.

Contents

BOOK THREE
Acceptance

Hobbes's Hand-Drawn Map

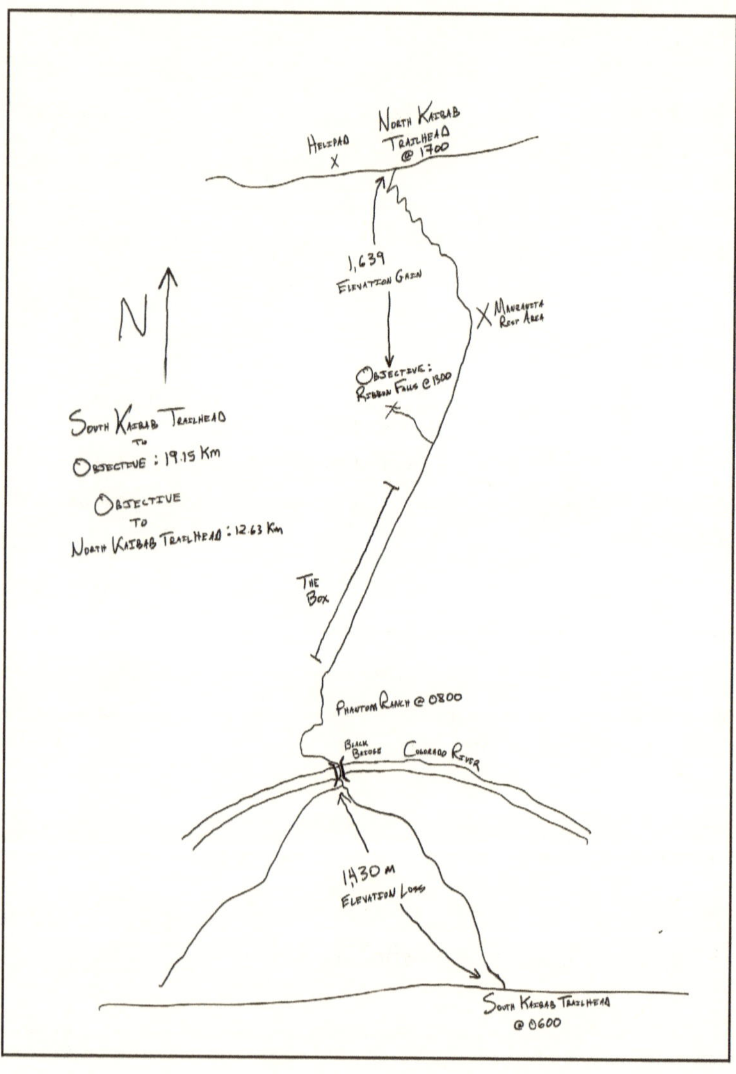

BOOK ONE

Offer

Chapter 1

Halloween Meeting

SHE FLICKED HER FINGERS BACK AND FORTH IN HER clutch as she watched the numbers light up and fade out in succession toward forty-two. Popped open her compact and twisted a silver tube and drew the rich rose petal hue across her cupid's bow. Snapped the compact shut. Her stomach churned as she fast ascended. After she flipped her shoulder-length blonde hair over the collar of her black jacket, she noticed that the top button of her white button-front blouse had popped open to expose cleavage that only a push-up bra could give her.

She closed her eyes and huffed.

After a moment she adjusted herself and rebuttoned her blouse. "At least if I die here, I'll have great boobs in the crime scene photos," she said aloud. After a beat, she curled her lip. "I guess that's not really funny, is it?" Deep breaths.

Through the elevator glass, she saw her aging and dented blue sedan parked like a forgotten toy under the lights below, set apart from the luxury and sports cars in the valet only parking garage. A jackass in a black EV had stolen her parking spot, eliciting from her an angry honk and a string of obscenities out her rolled-down window.

A raised middle finger shot back. She had endured a long, cold walk to the building in heels. A change in the light turned the glass from a window to a mirror. She glared at herself.

"This is stupid," she said. "What the hell am I doing here?"

The invitation had intrigued her. Who had scribbled the address that revealed only a company name: Ford Exploration and Developments, LLC? The Secretary of State website showed the registered agent was a paid service. No help.

Andrew would have insisted on coming—not something she could take right now. Leaving Benny with him right after trick-or-treating and lying about where she was going was easier. Benny would be six next year. When Sierra was that age, Mama's weakened resolve sent her down a path that would years later shatter Sierra's young life forever. At any cost, Sierra would never let Benny experience anything like that.

"You are my hope, Benny. I will do anything for you," she'd said to him before leaving the house. Words she had told him every day since his birth.

"I know, Mama," he always answered. She had tousled his curls, dark as a winter night and still as fine as baby's hair, and cupped a cheek ornamented with one irresistible dimple. His brown eyes connected with her blues in that fiery, deep place where the spark of motherhood lives.

How far would she go?

Her stomach was still swimming.

As far as it takes.

A digital woman announced the forty-second floor. Sierra put her finger on the trigger inside her clutch. The elevator opened to a graying man wearing a tie and holding a magnetic wand. In her modest business suit, she raised her arms, her right hand still in her clutch, her finger still on the trigger.

He scanned the contours of her slender body, nodded at the clutch. She lowered it and reluctantly let him shine a penlight on the contents. He chuckled, then beckoned her toward the smell of leather and tobacco. She followed him—he limped slightly—and put her finger back on the trigger.

A man in a sharp-cut gray suit, reminiscent of a spy from an old movie, occupied a plush leather club chair next to an octagonal brass-framed, glass-top coffee table. His debonair, clean-shaven face flushed a memory that flew away before Sierra could catch it. Neither he nor the obnoxious, gum-chewing man-child standing in a poorly cut suit behind him greeted her. The grandfather clock in the corner ticked away an awkward minute. Sierra took her finger off the trigger and pulled out the invitation. She cleared her throat and read aloud the handwritten, black-inked words.

"Dear Ms. Justice. I need to talk to you. Halloween. 8:00 p.m. Address on the envelope. Signed, WF." With a shaking hand, she returned the invitation to her purse and her finger went back on the trigger. "Here I am."

Massive windows revealed red-and-white lights passing like currents on the cold, dark Washington DC freeway below. Open veins exchanging old blood for new. The memory flew back. She realized with horror the identity of the man sitting before her.

"Wade Ford," they said in unison, he with a smile, Sierra with a recoil. He was just like he looked on TV. Early sixties. Stylish. The gray in his hair starting to win the battle.

"Is it a gimmick or your born surname?" Ford asked.

The man-child behind him snapped his gum in a quick three-pop succession. When Sierra busted him eyeing the V of her blouse, he averted his attention to some useless place on the wall, his face coloring in embarrassment. She glanced down and seethed. The damn button had popped open again and she was on ample display. She once again buttoned it back.

Sierra squinted, felt her lips turning into a snarl, tried to get her bearings. "I didn't become a lawyer because of my last name."

Ford nodded in understanding. "They were right on one count. You are striking, Ms. Justice. Only one way to find out if they were right about the other. Tell me how I can litigate a fight over a national park development in Sandstone County, Arizona." He tipped back a thick tumbler and sipped some amber liquid. "I intend to construct a five-star luxury resort in Grand Canyon National Park. The Peoples and Parks Coalition aren't going to be happy about it."

The churning feeling came back in a flood.

"Did you just say a five-star resort in Grand Canyon National Park?" Her face burned when she realized she hadn't connected his name to Ford Exploration and Developments, but then again, she'd never expected someone like Wade Ford to call. This was a business meeting and she likely wouldn't get assaulted, but she was still in the same room with him. His non-regional diction and well-educated eloquence made him no more tolerable. She took her finger off the pepper spray trigger and let her hand hang next to the black skirt ending just above her knee.

"Why would anyone build something so offensive in Grand Canyon National Park? Or try to litigate attacks from the Peoples and Parks Coalition in state court?" she said, glancing around the dark, spacious room. "Not gonna lie—I'm confused. And I brought pepper spray."

Without losing his smile, the older man shook his head. "Perhaps she's not the one, Billy."

"She just walked in, sir," said Gum Snapper, offering an identical tumbler of whiskey to Sierra. She shook her head. He raised his eyebrows and set it on the coffee table, glass against glass, with a satisfying, heavy clunk.

"William Clark, Ms. Justice. General counsel for Ford Exploration and Developments. I prefer Bill," he said, giving Ford a sideways glance. "We checked around DC. We want to talk to you about working for Mr. Ford."

Sierra cackled. "What? Are you fucking kidding me? You know who I am? What I do?"

Ford took over. "Precisely. It's why we summoned you, Ms. Justice." He sat forward and drew a dark cigar from the pocket of his gray jacket. "You're not allowing yourself a proper seat at the table." He clicked a silver butane lighter and rolled the cigar in his fingertips against the blue flame. He puffed smoke.

"One year of work. One year of your life. It'll be dangerous, but if you can hack it, I'll give you an unmitigated solution to your financial problems."

"My financial . . . what? How do you know anything about my finances?"

Ford took another puff.

Sierra's words to her son. The situation at home. The financial struggles. What would Mama have said to a man like Wade Ford?

Mama.

Did it even matter anymore?

Sierra gazed at the beckoning tumbler of whiskey. She knew better than to believe that it held any wisdom.

Chapter 2

Hostages

THAT SOUND. LIKE YOUR OWN NAME. NEVER FORGOTTEN. Again. Another blow to her ears and conscience. Another jolt to her body. Like some ghoulish purple-red octopus, a thick blood spatter ran in tendrils down the wall above the topless dead woman. Masked militants in black clothes held half-naked men and women at gunpoint against a gray wall, some type of huge machinery behind them. A loud pop. Screams. Accompanied by muffled thumps, the grainy image tumbled before leveling out again. A female's frantic voice, "No, no, please, no!" before there was another pop, another scream, followed by a jerky pan to a second topless woman with long brown hair and a vacant stare lying flat on her back. A masked man holding a machine gun approached the camera and shouted something inaudible as the screen went black.

Wearing a purple sports bra, gray yoga pants, and white trainers, her long dirty-blonde hair in a ponytail, Sierra stood unblinking in her kitchen. A solemn brunette anchor with eyes that had seen too much reported that at least three hostages were believed dead. The TV screen blurred. Sierra held her stomach. She dialed and snagged Bill on the third ring.

"Hello?"

"Bill, wake up."

"Does it sound like I'm still asleep?" he asked, his voice groggy.

"Turn on the news."

"Okay, okay. Slow down, Sierra. Which network?"

"Any of them."

Sierra grabbed the edge of the breakfast bar. She listened to him climb out of bed, turn on his TV.

"What's this?" he said.

"Know where that is? A couple hundred miles from Vista. They're killing people. Just . . . shooting them."

"Holy shit."

"There's only five days left in my contract, Bill."

"What?"

The sound of something crinkling, like foil. Then Bill chewing.

"Don't start snapping your gum."

He sighed. "Fine, I won't. Are you okay, Sierra?"

Maybe she was acting a bit hysterical.

The anchor interrupted them.

"Shocking footage taken from the cell phone of one of the hostages, shared seconds before the phone was taken. The crisis at Glen Canyon Dam that began Friday is still developing early this Saturday morning. Sources have confirmed that there are twenty-two hostages and at least three presumed dead. Nineteen of the hostages are Bureau of Reclamation workers or independent contractors who worked in the facility. The other three are private citizens, including a nine-year-old girl, who was part of a tour of the dam when the gunmen took control."

Sierra put her hand to her mouth.

"Who takes a dam hostage?" Bill asked.

Sierra, glued to the screen, couldn't answer.

"Reports suggest that the unfolding hostage crisis may have started as what officials are calling a protest against Ford Exploration and Developments' controversial Canyon's Dream luxury resort project in the heart of Grand Canyon National Park," the anchor stated.

"Oh, no, no, no, no," Sierra said, taking her hand from her mouth and backing up, each word louder than the next.

Three rapid-fire gum snaps shot through the line.

"Bill, I swear if you do that again—"

"Sorry, sorry. I'll reach out to Wade," said Bill. "You know you're gonna have to come in."

"And you're going to work your magic," she replied. "I'm not getting extended. This thing has to be over this week, Bill. One way or another."

"You know getting pushy never works with me. Why do you think I'm still single?"

"You don't want me to answer that."

"It was rhetorical," he said before hanging up.

Sierra watched the TV. Turned the sound down so she wouldn't have to hear the gunshots when they played the video again. The blood octopus on the wall leered back at her. She'd seen it before, in a different world, a different time. A bitter cold night. A falling body.

Wade Ford had told her a year ago that this would be dangerous. But she didn't expect anyone to get murdered.

———

The mercenary climbed onto a perch on the rim above the monstrous Glen Canyon Dam. His elevated heart rate, a resulting mix of excitement from the op and the ensuing terrifying climb, had dropped in the last few minutes. He shivered in the cold, soaked in sweat, waiting. Touched the growing knot in his neck and gritted his teeth. His mind jumped back to what had gone down in the power plant. How did it get out of control so fast?

The morning's peace rattled into deafening chaos. Three helos approached from different directions, drowning the dawn in vibrating thunder and gusting rotor wash. It was hard to tell location from the echoes, but his trained ear could decipher this in the din. He watched through the night vision goggles attached to his high-cut helmet.

Like a shark in dark water, a UH-60 Blackhawk faded in down

near the base of the dam. Two more pounded over the swollen lake. One MD 530 Little Bird buzzed in from the east and out over the highway bridge in front of the dam. Another flew in from the south over the dam toward the visitors' center, their angry miniguns covering the Blackhawks.

He looked up. He'd never be able to see it, but somewhere high above was an aircraft flying ISR—intelligence, surveillance, and reconnaissance. A crewed helo, plane, or unmanned drone? A mystery for now. He had to assume the ISR would see him.

He adjusted the dials on his two-way radio, trying the frequencies, listening for chatter, until he heard metallic voices.

"Thor, this is Odin, confirm tangos on target."

"Odin, this is Thor One, confirm multiple tangos. Out."

Automatic small arms fire rattled up in tracer-lit streams at each bird. Heavier machine guns rained orange bursts of fire down from the helos in response. The second and third Blackhawks hovered on opposite sides of the dam, one's rotor wash beating the immature commercial trees in front of the visitors' center, the other's swirling dust on the bare east side.

The chatter increased as door gunners in the choppers provided covering fire for several operators fast-roping to the dam's surface. They knelt in defensive positions, watching the perimeter through NVGs with their carbines at arms. The Little Birds' 7.62 x 51mm M134 miniguns burped bullet-filled flames on several men shooting at the helicopters.

In the bright floodlights at the base of the dam, black ropes fell from the first Blackhawk, slack at first, then taut with the weight of each sliding body. The mercenary flipped up his own NVGs to examine the chopper's sleek surface. Glossy black paint, meaning the FBI Hostage Rescue Team was working in conjunction with the military, most likely an Army Quick Reaction Force out of Yuma or a Special Operations Command—SOCOM—unit. Law enforcement alone would never use miniguns.

Several men roped onto the flat, green cooling grass platform between the dam and the humming rectangular power plant. Suppressed rifle flashes corresponded with the popping of shot-out floodlights. Darkness enveloped the complex.

The mercenary flipped the NVGs back over his eyes. Less than a minute after their arrival, all three Blackhawks retracted their ropes and disappeared. The Little Birds skirted the dam and were gone. A quiet peace returned to the dark canyon, the power plant's droning generators and rushing water far below the only sounds.

Small arms fire throughout the complex kicked off the ground assault. The goggles gave him the cinematography, while the two-way radio provided the soundtrack.

"Odin, this is Thor One, saber. Out."

"Odin, this is Thor Three, saber. Out."

A minute passed with no comms.

"Thor Two, this is Odin, status. Over."

Several seconds later, another voice said, "Odin, this is Thor Two, saber. Out."

They did it like he would have—converged from each side of the dam toward the elevators with small arms support, keeping men at each end for security.

"Contact right," a voice on the radio said.

A figure moved low near the west elevator. The forward two members of the team each punched two suppressed rounds into it. Another figure appeared. The next operator in line cut it down, the figure doing a silent jig. On the other side of the dam lay three disfigured lumps near the elevator shaft, the handiwork of the Little Birds' miniguns.

Just then the mercenary's eyes caught two squirters running away from the attack along the dam access road on the east side. "How'd we miss those little bastards?" he whispered.

The ISR platform would probably pick them up with thermal, but whether they tracked them any farther remained to be seen. Two groups of operators gathered around the elevator shafts and held defensive positions. The radio crackled back to life.

"Loki elements, this is Odin, phase three, go. Out."

A twelve-man team materialized from the shadows at the bottom of the dam. Two men guarding the main power plant entrance fired wild before they were slain by the operators. The team moved in.

"Loki elements, this is Odin, phase four, go. Out."

Minutes passed. A line of amber revealed itself over the rugged black eastern horizon.

The radio came to life again.

"This is a rescue. Get facedown on the floor with your hands empty and visible."

A moment passed. The same message, then a banging sound.

"Oh, God help them, no."

The next voice was low. Measured. "Odin, this is Loki One. Multiple confirmed dead. Over."

Less than ten minutes after the team's insertion, he watched through his NVGs as they emerged from the power plant. One operator leaned over and vomited on his boots. Another unslung his carbine and collapsed to his knees.

The mercenary checked his watch, did the math. If he left now, he might just make it. The sharp pain in his neck again. Maybe he deserved to let the disease run its course this time. But they'd discovered Amelia. It wouldn't be long before they used her against him. The only way out of Rev Six with his life was by following their orders. She was already grown and he'd missed all of it. He couldn't blame Amelia's mother—

"Stop thinking about it, idiot. Survive today. That's all there is," he said.

It was getting light. He flipped up the NVGs and knelt and turned off the radio.

The pills hardly did the trick. The VA shrink had said to find something stable, something calming. Silence was the only thing. Like the old wooden house in Detroit he had gone back to see during leave for his father's funeral. It had suffered the decay of time and neglect, white paint separating and curling up and flaking off gray boards, the ground beneath it bare dirt, the verdant grass of his youth long gone. The quiet was a friend. And an obstacle.

He jogged south through the desert morning using the scrub and rocks for cover, knowing it wasn't enough if ISR was overhead. He heard the chopping of returning helicopters.

"Good thing I left when I did," he muttered without looking back.

———

A nine-year-old girl.

Sierra felt Benny's warm breath tickle the back of her hand. She touched his forehead and pulled his thick, blue comforter tighter against his sleeping face. She watched him a minute. If anything ever happened to her six-year-old, they might as well kill her too.

"You are my hope, Benny. I will do anything for you," she whispered in his ear. She watched him a minute more, grateful he was warm, sheltered, secure.

Andrew snoozed in their bedroom down the hall, his long brown arms and legs reaching across the wrinkled depression where she'd been an hour ago. She wanted to talk, but he needed his sleep. Medical school was hard on them all.

Sierra put hip-hop in her ears and jogged in the cold garage on the whining treadmill that complained a bit more loudly with every step. After she was warm and stretched, she wrapped her hands and alternated punches and kicks at the heavy bag.

The gunshots from the newscast pulled her mind back to that dark night in that tiny Colorado house where Mama's resolve had changed everything. The frost on the open window pane. The cold hardwood under her bare feet. The shouting through the wall. Always the shouting. That night the shouts became screams.

Why did she do it? What did Mama know? Those two haunting questions refused to leave her alone no matter how much shame she carried or which therapist she saw. She pushed through her routine and went back upstairs and showered.

Sierra scrubbed and rinsed herself clean. She turned the water a little hotter. Put her head back and leaned against the hot tile. Let her hands wander and touch, rubbing, seeking that one familiar place, staying there, tuning out the noise, the reality, the burdens. A trick she had learned during her first year in the group home. Or a means to an end? It had been the first drug she knew, and after all these years, it was the only one left. She got herself there and rocked against the steaming tiles, her breathing coarse, her thoughts visceral. Those strange tears came. She shivered and caught her breath. Toweled off.

Hot vapor glistened against her tanned limbs and taut midsection. She began with the blow-dryer and ended with a sleek ponytail, a little makeup, jeans, a nice top, and heels. Saturday law office attire.

She put on the S-shaped gold scroll antique earrings with the pearl drops, the only earrings she ever wore. Some days they were heirlooms. Today they held the weight of chains.

She brushed. Flossed. Examined her teeth. Frowned as usual at that damn crooked right incisor that curved inward just enough to bother her. She had always told herself she'd get it fixed by her thirtieth birthday. Then Benny came and her late twenties and most of her early thirties passed her by in a haze of bottles and diapers, then sippy cups and pull-ups. Daycare and pre-school and kindergarten. He was in first grade. She'd finally made an appointment with an orthodontist.

Her nails. Yikes. While observing yesterday's remote pretrial, she noticed that the French glass nail on her right ring finger was cracked. She picked at it as she counted the number of hours left in her contract. The hearing ended. All ten nails were in a neat pile on her desk.

Because why not?

Sierra put another coffee pod in the machine downstairs and held her face in her hands. She smelled strong, fresh brew gurgling to the brim.

———

The mercenary stopped at the first motel off Highway 89 on the north side of Page. The Lazy Daze Inn. The maintenance crew, if they had one, lived up to the inn's name. Considering he was still dressed in sandy-colored tactical clothes and full kit, he moved behind cover. That it was still early morning helped.

Behind a rusting smelly dumpster in an alley between two low orange stucco buildings, he detached the NVGs and put them in their pouch. He pulled his gloves tight and donned the ballistic mask stowed in his front pouch. It was strange to wear, but things were different this time—he couldn't kill everybody, and there was no time to change. He didn't have any civilian clothes on him anyway.

During his three-mile jog through the cacti and scrub, he had repeated part of the creed he had lived by for almost two decades before the Army's physical evaluation board bastards kicked him to the curb: I know that I will be called upon to perform tasks in isolation, far from familiar faces and voices.

He was indebted to a different creed now. One of blood and deception, melded with the moon and collapsing stars. Either the ISR platform had missed him, or they were still watching. He'd seen nothing above, so his money was on it being a small drone. "If we gotta fight our way out, we gotta fight our way out," he grumbled.

The Lazy Daze was just the kind of dump where third-tier mercenaries could pay in cash and not be seen. It would be a mistake for them to check in here. If they'd made it, it would be their end. He'd find them later, if he had to. Someone had made decisions behind his back, and anyone who was part of what had gone down at the dam had to be eliminated. He entered the motel's low ramshackle office building—faded paint and replaced boards surrounded by rugged open desert and cacti.

The front-desk clerk was a plump, twenty-something white girl with blue hair and a ring looped through her nose. She didn't notice him lock the door behind him. "Help you?" she asked, not looking up from her magazine. Shitty electronica played from a speaker above his head.

"Did two men wearing black clothes check in?" he asked. The mask muffled his voice.

"Why you sound so—" Fear dissolved her composure when she saw his combat gear and full-coverage tan ballistic mask.

"Did two men in black clothes check in this morning?" he repeated, his voice cold and firm.

First her lip trembled. Then red rose in her cheeks and forehead. Tears threatened to spill.

"Yeah," she said, her voice thick.

"Give me the room number."

She was locked in a silent trance.

"C'mon . . . give it to me."

She blinked, then picked up a pencil and jotted a number down on a scrap of paper. Handed it to him. The tears made good on the threat.

"What's your name?"

"Heather," she said over a quivering chin.

"Heather, I'm sure they paid you extra to keep it a secret, but the men in that room deserve to die. Usually by now I'd have already shot you. But I'm trying not to be such an asshole these days. If you took that ring out of your nose and washed that shit from your hair, you might get a better job. But none of that will make a difference if you tell anyone I was here."

He pulled his Glock 19 from his thigh holster.

She jumped back with a squeal. Her body jiggled from her expansive chest to her thick haunches. She nodded, her voice hoarse with tears. "I never seen you. There ain't no cameras here. I won't never tell no one, I promise."

"Get in that office."

He followed her in, yanked the landline and Internet hardline from the wall. "Give me your cell phone."

She handed it to him, and he proceeded to stomp it. Heather squealed and jumped and jiggled some more.

"I won't hesitate to come back here and make you dead." He holstered the pistol and frowned behind his mask. "What are you listening to?"

Terror faded from her face and became confusion. "New Age? I-I dunno," she said, sniffling.

"You should listen to better music, Heather." He let the words sink in before realizing that all she could see was the faceless ballistic mask.

Muted bawling erupted after he closed the door. He swiped paper and office supplies and a giant printer that had to have been from the twentieth century from a low, heavy cabinet and shoved it in front of the door, trapping her inside.

He took his suppressor from a pouch and screwed it onto the Glock. He'd hit pay dirt on his first try, but again, Occam's Razor—the simplest explanation—and all that. He made his way down the covered walk to a door with peeling gray paint and the number Heather had written. There was a large rectangular window on his approach. He turned and walked back around the motel, scanning for onlookers. A few minutes later he stood fifteen feet from his original spot on the other side of the door. He checked his load and assumed his firing stance and listened. TV sounds. A muted voice.

An old woman wearing a black hijab appeared. Dueling braids of long graying hair protruded from her head covering. Her dark skin cracked like a sun-scorched lakebed and stretched over her high cheekbones and broad nose. Her face was solemn, her large owl-brown orbs holding him captive. They gawked at his mask, then the gun.

He motioned for her to keep walking.

She watched him instead. "I told you to stop following me," he said.

She didn't move or respond.

He ignored her and kicked the door open and dropped to one padded knee, gun raised. A naked man dived into the bathroom on the left. The mercenary fired five suppressed rounds into the wall and sliding mirrored door, shattering it. After the last shard tinkled against the tile, he heard whimpering. He judged the distance from his kneeling position to the bathroom to be roughly fifteen feet.

"I can't stand here. I'm bleeding real bad. I gotta come out now."

"Who gave the order at the dam?"

"I don't know what you're talking about," whined the wounded man in the bathroom.

"You don't, huh?"

"No, man, please," he begged.

"Did I get you?"

"No. The glass cut me. Please. I'm coming out." The man took a limping step out with his hands up. "We didn't know what—"

The mercenary fired as the man ducked, the shot missed, but the next struck him in the temple. The other side of his head, with blood and fragments of his skull and brain, splattered across the mirror and sink. The body fell in a wet, sloppy jumble on the tile. The mercenary looked around. No one else there. He ejected the nearly empty magazine and dropped it into his dump pouch, grabbed a full one from a mag pouch, and rammed it home. He policed his brass, dropping the spent casings in the dump pouch as well, and stepped inside. He closed the door, then pored through the dead man's clothes on the bed. No ID, but some cash in his pocket as instructed.

A woman's tinny voice repeated, "Hello" from something glowing faintly in the bathroom. He picked up the cell phone and put it near his ear. "Vince? Hello? What's that noise? Vince?" After he removed the battery, he stomped on the phone, picked up the pieces, and caught his masked reflection in the mirror.

Hell. He did look scary.

A vehicle started and revved up outside. He opened the door and checked left. The old woman in the black hijab was gone.

A late model red pickup with a white camper shell roared onto Highway 89 south from the lot. He put the broken phone in his dump pouch. Pulled the door shut. Observed the sky. Nothing visible. Scanned the parking lot.

A dark-skinned, dark-haired woman in a ball cap and hiking garb sat in an idling four-door silver sedan, scrolling on her phone. He approached and tapped the glass with his pistol, eliciting a muffled scream. He motioned for her to get out. She did, whining and hopping from foot to foot, wringing her hands.

"Keep your mouth shut, file your insurance claim, live," he said. He almost jumped in until he saw that the doorjamb would have taken his head off. Before getting in, he pushed the electric switch and waited for the seat to go down and back, shaking his leg and watching the pickup grow smaller in the distance. He slid in, adjusted the steering column back toward him, then floored it, causing the door to slam shut. The sedan fishtailed from the lot, and in the rearview mirror, the woman hit her knees.

———

Benny stumbled down the carpeted floating stairs like a tiny drunk. He made it to the first landing and stopped in a slow crumple. Sierra picked up the remote and paused the news. Unaware he was being watched, Benny stared into space. Sleepy brown eyes. Curly black hair. When he found her face, she smiled and held out her arms to him. He didn't budge and began nodding off again.

Andrew came down behind him, shirtless. The contrast between his dark skin and gray sweatpants caught her eye and held it a moment. He leaned down and kissed his son's forehead, waking him back up, then descended the rest of the stairs and took his turn at the coffeemaker before plopping onto the couch next to Sierra. They sipped coffee and watched Benny. Andrew went first.

"Those don't look like stay-at-home-on-Saturday clothes. I mean, don't get me wrong. Those jeans. Damn."

Sierra grinned her appreciation. "Have to go in, babe."

"Supposed to be off today, Sierra."

"Well . . . something came up, Andrew."

She motioned toward Benny and shook her head. Andrew took the hint. He sighed and softly brushed her cheek with his fingers, then walked to the kitchen and started clanging pans and utensils for breakfast. Benny shuffled to Sierra and snuggled in her lap. The refrigerator doors opened and closed a few times.

"Mama, what's Daddy making for breakfast?"

"Your VIP customer wants to know what's on the menu this morning," Sierra half shouted at Andrew with Benny's curls looped around her fingers.

"Waffles, Big B," Andrew said.

"Oooh, yummy waffles, Benny Boy," she whispered. He giggled

when her breath tickled his skin, exposing a missing front tooth. She hugged him tighter and sniffed his neck. A clean, warm scent of peace.

"Daddy woke you again, didn't he?" she said with a faux angry face. "Bad Daddy."

Benny nodded.

"Heard that," Andrew said.

"I know," Sierra replied. She glanced over and admired Andrew's bare muscular shoulders on his tall, dark frame. Friends often complimented their family, making her a bit sheepish.

Were they a family?

She was at peace with their cohabitation, despite the world around them being slow to catch up. Neither of Mama's marriages had made Sierra's childhood clan a family. The second had ripped them apart.

"Mama?"

"What, baby?" she asked, sipping from the mug she cradled.

"What's a prostitute?"

Between his youth and the missing tooth, he pronounced it *prossy-toot*.

Sierra almost spat out her coffee. She swallowed and lifted his chin with her finger.

"Where did you hear that word, Benjamin Riley Thomas?"

Benny's eyes turned from sleepy to frightened. He pouted, and his voice increased in fervor with each word. "Elijah said it." He sat up. "The other kids laughed, but I didn't know what it was." He was on the verge of tears.

Sierra set her coffee down and soothed him. "Shh . . . It's okay." She framed his face in her hands. "But now you know that's an adult word."

"Yes, Mama." A sniff.

She tilted her head. "Why did Elijah say it?"

Benny hid his face in his hands, refused to answer. Another sniff.

"Benny?" Sierra coaxed.

"His dad said that's what people on the internet call you."

"Oh."

Her reaction was one part understanding, two parts horror. She'd known the backlash would eventually reach Benny but never imagined what the reality would look like. Maybe she didn't ask for him, but the moment she learned she was pregnant, she committed to giving him the life she'd never had. But now her choice—*her* choice—had tarnished it. She was all over the Internet. They had to avoid certain places because she was getting recognized in public now. People weren't kind.

She put her mouth to his ear and said the same words she had whispered earlier as he slept. "You are my hope, Benny. I will do anything for you."

"I know, Mama." He snuggled closer in her arms. He was worth every disgusting meme. Every hate piece.

After devouring a giant waffle smothered in maple syrup and colored sprinkles, Benny padded to the couch, turned on his cartoon, and built a pillow fort. Sierra and Andrew finished their coffee at the breakfast bar as the morning sun lit up the room through the large windows on the back of the house.

"Shaking your leg again," Andrew observed.

"I'll give you one guess why."

———

The pickup screeched a left off of 89 onto eastbound Highway 98. The mercenary closed in, predator and prey weaving through a long line of traffic behind a tattered old motor home that had TRAVELING THROUGH SPACE AND TIME painted on its dusty rear end in red cursive.

"Some other space, some other time, you dumpy piece of shit!" he shouted as he floored it and drove around.

A few miles past the motor home, he pushed the sedan until the engine screamed under the hood. He nosed the left rear bumper of the pickup with the right front edge of the car. It swerved and swayed at speed, but the driver had skill and recovered.

The mercenary did it again with more speed and force. The pickup spun out and rolled across the highway, throwing the camper shell, tumbling to a dusty and debris-scattering stop in the roadside sage. He slowed and turned and pulled off the highway.

Flashes in the swirling dust.

He ducked a volley of supersonic bullets that raked the hood and fragmented the windshield. More rounds punched into the leather seats. He slid from his door to the back of the car.

The shooter in the pickup held suppressing fire on the sedan, rounds clanking and popping into metal as the mercenary crawled on his belly through the scrub around the shooter's left flank. Sage and the terrain obscured his vision, but he heard vehicles stop. Car doors opened and closed. Someone hollered, asking if everyone was all right, just before the gunman put another three-round burst into the sedan.

Screams. Doors slamming. Engines starting and rocks pinging off wheel wells.

He crawled and listened. Peeked at the overturned pickup. The shooter was on one knee, an M4 carbine with optical gunsight trained on the sedan. He held it with his right hand but used the turned wheel of the pickup to support the muzzle grip, his left arm bleeding from a jagged white bone piercing tattered red flesh. The mercenary saw that the rising sun and seat position made it appear as if a person was still in the sedan. The illusion wouldn't last.

He ignored the knot burning in his neck.

He crawled another few yards, then lifted his head again. Long shot. When he peeked again, the shooter had lowered the carbine. He popped up and fired three shots: one wild, another punching into the shooter's abdomen, and the third his shoulder. The man dropped the M4 and screamed something about a gut shot. He whined while the mercenary took a minute to find all three empty shells, then walked toward the man, the Glock trained on his wailing grimace.

"It is you. I knew even with the mask. You're so tall."

"Who gave the order?"

"What order?"

"You know."

"Why are you doing this, man? We did our jobs. Why did you kill—"

His forehead imploded and the contents of his skull hit the hot underbelly of the truck and started cooking with a hiss. The mercenary lowered his gun and listened, and over the sounds of sizzling blood and brains and dripping motor oil, he heard far-off sirens echoing through the canyon and the low brown hills to the east. He studied the roasting brain matter.

"Shit almost smells like a cookout," he said.

He was checking the man's clothes when the knot in his neck sparked another jolt of pain. He recovered, kneeling with his left hand braced against the dead man's chest. After dumping the last piece of brass, he unbuckled the mask and walked back to the sedan and grabbed his bag and moved south behind the cover of the drab sage, parallel to the road. Sirens howled to the north.

Ten minutes later he heard a car approach at a normal speed. He donned the mask and walked into the highway. Trained the Glock on the driver of a new black SUV. The elderly man, wearing a light-colored polo and a concerned expression, stopped. He and the woman in the passenger seat, herself wearing what appeared to be golf or tennis clothes, put their hands up.

"Get out," the mercenary commanded.

They complied in silence. Watched as he threw his pack in. Watched him adjust the seat. Watched as, with squealing tires, he turned the SUV back south, leaving them standing next to the road, hands raised. The mask was off again and he was driving the speed limit when two northbound Arizona state trooper cruisers met him with flashing lights. He lifted a finger at the first one.

The trooper raised a finger back.

———

"Watch," Sierra said, getting up. She put the news on the little kitchen TV and made sure Benny wasn't looking. Turned down the volume.

The cell phone video replayed, the woman's body and the blood octopus blurred this time. The brunette anchor from earlier that morning was back, looking more tired than before.

"Minutes ago the Federal Bureau of Investigation's crack Hostage Rescue Team and a United States Special Operations Command team, also known as USSOCOM, took back control of Glen Canyon Dam from a yet unidentified group. All twenty-two hostages were found dead in what the Department of Homeland Security has described as the worst domestic eco-terrorist event of the century. The victims include three private citizens on a tour of the dam, including a nine-year-old female."

"They killed the little girl?" Sierra asked in disbelief.

"Oh, damn," Andrew murmured.

The anchor continued. "Record-breaking snowfalls in the Rocky Mountains for the past five years have led to massive annual spring and summer runoff, filling Lake Powell, which had nearly dried up, to levels not seen in decades. Experts with the Bureau of Reclamation, the federal agency responsible for protecting and managing water resources, estimate the lake is at full pool, roughly twenty-six million acre-feet of water, or eight trillion gallons. Immediate upgrades to security are taking place as we report. Graffiti found in the dam confirms that the hostage crisis was directly connected to a protest against the controversial Canyon's Dream resort and Ribbon Falls gondola system, the luxury resort set to begin construction after Ford Exploration and Developments, owned by international developer Wade Ford, has its final hearing against the Peoples and Parks Coalition in the Sandstone County Courthouse on Monday."

Sierra put both hands on her head. "This is not happening. None of this is happening, right? I'm going to have to go to Arizona now. I know it. And he's gonna extend my contract."

"You don't have to go. That's in your contract too."

"No, Andrew. My contract says I don't do any in-court litigation. It doesn't say anything about me not having to go to Vista or Phoenix or any other place Wade wants me to go."

"I don't know what to tell you, Sierra. I wish I did."

She wiped her nose and eyes and swung her head toward him.

"Think about it. When my year is up, I'm out of a job. My salary, benefits, the car, all of it . . . *gone*. No one from the other side will ever hire me again. You're still in the thick of med school, Andrew. If I don't get that bonus . . ." She gestured with her hand. "Look at this frigging house. Remember the old apartment?"

"I don't need you to explain the money part to me, Sierra." He sipped his coffee.

"I folded Benny's thrift store clothes in his cramped little room. Wet them with my tears when you were working an odd job or studying. Then I'd go work for peanuts at Banks & Hardy. I believed in that work, I always did. I still do. But we both know that I can't ever go back. I have to get that bonus."

"The almighty bonus," Andrew said, singing the three words in a decent falsetto, miming a stroking motion with his closed fist, and letting his head roll back.

She slapped his arm and fought an unexpected urge to laugh. "Stop. Benny might see you. This is serious, Andrew."

"Just trying to help you relax. When do I get to find out how much this bonus is, anyway?"

"When I get it—like I've said a million times." Sierra put her fingers to her temples and moaned. "How did I get here?"

"We've been through this," Andrew said, rubbing her back. "Out of the blue you decided to work for Wade Ford." He pulled his hand back. "And hid it from me for weeks."

"You know why."

"Still can't believe you went to that building last Halloween by yourself. Didn't even watch Benny go through his candy bag. What if something bad had happened to you?"

"It didn't." She shrugged. "Or maybe it did and it's just a long, slow burn. Everything was off about that meeting. It all felt wrong. But I got here that night, looked at that contract while you and Benny were asleep, and signed it anyway."

He nodded at her suitcase against the kitchen wall. "You're gone all week?"

"Till Wednesday. I'm supposed to be out of the contract once this hearing is done. But with this tragedy, Judge Sumner may not want to proceed with the hearing. Not a great look when he's up for a federal bench appointment." Andrew touched her again, tickling both sides of her neck. She enjoyed the sensation and distracting shudder. "You think Benny will understand one day? All those AI-generated memes? The one where I'm on my knees in front of Wade? Benny's class already thinks I'm a prostitute."

"What?" Andrew asked. He broke into an involuntary laugh, covered his mouth.

"Some brat named Elijah said the internet called me a *prossy-toot*."

"I'm sorry, Sierra. Really." He started laughing again.

Despite her protest, Sierra caught the contagion. They shared shaking spasms of release. The laughter felt good. Comforting. A warm hand on her back. A blanket covering her legs on a chilly day. She put her head on his shoulder and opened her mouth to speak.

"What?"

She shook her head, the moment gone. "I have to go." She moved toward Benny to tell him goodbye.

From under the couch pillows, he said, "What's catering mean?" He struggled to pronounce "catering." A pause. "Oh. Do you have a dog that helps you take food to people?" Another pause. "What about a horse? I like horses."

"Who are you talking to?" Sierra demanded, pulling a pillow off Benny's head.

Benny's face froze when she took the phone. She put it to her ear. "Hello?"

"Yes, this is Ruth's Catering. Sounds like your little one has your phone, Mom."

"I'm sorry, he dials random numbers. Now and then, he calls a real person. Where's Ruth's Catering?"

"Des Moines."

"Sorry he bothered you. Thanks."

Sierra shoved her phone into her back jeans pocket and put her hands on her hips. Benny hid his face in his hands.

"I love you," she said, giving his tummy a soft poke with each word, causing him to squirm and brighten. "But you can't use my phone without permission, and dialing numbers and calling strange people is a big no-no. It's not safe. Do you want a bad man to come get you?"

He shook his head.

"Mama's going to work. We'll go to the farmers market this afternoon. Be good for Daddy. I love you sooo much."

"This came yesterday," said Andrew. "I forgot to tell you. Sorry." He grabbed an envelope from the stack of mail on the counter and held it out to her.

Sierra saw the unmistakable handwriting on the envelope. The return address and that familiar red stamp: INMATE MAIL. Had it already been another year? November was just around the corner. "Put it in the box, please," she said.

"I know you don't like to talk about it, Sierra. But why do you get one of these letters every year? Why won't you tell me?"

"You're right, I don't like to talk about it." She touched Andrew's lips and kissed Benny's syrupy cheek and walked out the front door.

———

A minute after she pulled away from the curb in her white luxury coupe, Sierra's phone rang. No Caller ID. With the issue at the dam, she couldn't ignore any calls.

"Hello?"

"Sierra. Come take a hop with me."

The East Texas accent. Her heart fluttered. "Eric? Wait—is that really you? How . . ." Her thoughts tumbled like shoes in a dryer.

"I'm in your neck of the woods. Let's go up, knock back a drink. Like old times."

She stared out at the road.

"Sierra?"

His voice saying her name brought her back to reality. "You call after all this time and expect me to get in a plane with you?"

"Whoa. Figured I'd give you a holler and see what's shaking. Don't be mad."

"I'm not mad. I'm—"

"You're what?"

She had a stranglehold on the coupe's steering wheel. She flashed back to five days in Cabo and a long kiss goodbye. Not a word since. "Did you seriously think I'd be living the same life?" Her voice rose. "Like you can drop in anytime? I'm hanging up now."

"Don't—"

She ended the call and focused back on the road. When the phone rang again, she was talking as soon as she answered. "There's somebody else in my life. Eric, I can't go with you like old times, whenever you think those were."

"Sierra. I know it's been a while—"

"A while?" She scoffed. "It's been years, Eric. I've . . ."

"You've what?"

"Nothing. My boyfriend wouldn't be happy about me seeing you."

"Boyfriend?"

"Yeah. Imagine that, huh?" Sierra put her hand to her lips. Her nose stung. "I'm not going with you." She hung up again. Pulled the car onto the shoulder and jumped out and vomited her breakfast on the near-frozen roadside grass. Passing cars buffeted her hair and clothes in gusty roars as she wiped her mouth with the back of her sleeve. She stared into the overcast sky. Her throat locked up. That sting in her nose increased with the blurring of her vision. She held it together until a tsunami of grief and nostalgia billowed over her, the sobs in her chest like heavy knocks against an old wooden door.

"Why now?" she asked aloud. She slumped back into her car and wiped her eyes and nose. Saw Eric's face. For so long she had yearned for him to call, willed it come, needed to hear his voice. But it never came until now, at the worst time possible. She caught her wild eyes in the rearview mirror. If he'd known what happened in the years after their last kiss, would he have had the nerve to call? A text vibrated her phone. She ignored it.

———

The mercenary sat in a comfortable black chair in the empty boardroom at the top of a Phoenix high-rise, hands flat on his knees, watching his glass of ice water bead condensation. He'd changed into clothes that his Rev Six contact had provided him with at their meet-and-debrief just before coming here. The Glock was in his waistband holster under his black jacket. The old woman in the black hijab pervaded his mind. When was the last time he'd seen her?

Three people entered the room: two men in black suits, one short and stocky, the other tall and thin. He knew their names, but he preferred calling them Philly and Ichabod. The third was an elegant woman with graying black hair who was wearing an expensive-looking camel-colored business suit. Even after six years of working with her in her role as the director of Rev Six's North American high office, he was still enamored with Senator Pace's natural elegance. She was an astonishing seventy-one. Miss Arizona. Lawyer. Businesswoman. Arizona State Senator. United States Senator.

"You're late," he said to them.

Senator Pace stared at him in angry surprise. "What happened this morning, Hobbes?" she asked him. None of them sat.

"I could ask you the same question," he replied. "Who gave the order?"

"Order? What do you mean?" she asked.

He thought he saw a flash of recognition, but she was a politician who had survived years of putting on faces in Washington. Hobbes shook his head and chuckled. "Right. Never mind." It was the wrong time. Maybe it was a mystery he'd never solve.

"You said the hostage situation would last until our demands to postpone Ford's hearing on Monday were met. This was supposed to be a protest. Spray paint and graffiti. A computer hack. Instead, all twenty-two hostages were killed. No one told you to do that," Senator Pace said, her voice measured, holding a trace of suspicion. She scrutinized Hobbes. "This went terribly off the rails."

Hobbes frowned. "Because someone on the team of amateurs you assembled made a really, really bad decision. I barely made it out." He recalled the scene in the power plant.

"You expected me to hire mercenaries with real-world special ops experience for a peaceful protest? Would have been a hard sell, don't you think?" asked Senator Pace. She squinted. "How *did* you get out?"

"I have real-world special ops experience."

She sat in the rolling black boardroom chair Ichabod pulled out for her. "My contact said they had a Raven drone in the air. Did you go underground before you came here?"

"What do you think Rev Six pays me for?"

Yet Hobbes wasn't positive that the Raven crew hadn't caught him on camera or that he wasn't being tracked. He'd taken several precautionary measures, switching routes and using buildings and covered walkways to avoid detection.

"The Peoples and Parks Coalition shit the bed," Senator Pace said. "Experts keep saying they've already lost. But that dead little girl and her grandfather might still make Gerry Sumner pass on the hearing on Monday. He's slated for a federal bench. Regardless, we shift protocol now. I need those signatures on the documents before Sumner signs Ford's order. If Ford gets that order to start construction without my name on the lease, I won't have any other chance to stop him. Grand Canyon National Park is in my state. I can't let him desecrate it like this."

The stocky man looked at Hobbes and in a thick Philadelphia accent asked, "Where will you execute this?"

"In Arizona."

"Cute, Cowboy. Where?" Philly asked again.

"His hotel room," Hobbes said, staring Philly down. He turned back to Senator Pace. "If the hearing goes forward, how long will I have?"

"You need to get it done by Monday," Senator Pace said. "Study that script, Hobbes. You're no lawyer, but you're smart. Memorize the words."

Ichabod, the taller, skinny man, set an inconspicuous black leather duffle bag on the table. "Dossiers and the script. That's half in there. You'll get the rest after it's done and Senator Pace has the paperwork in hand," he said, his voice soft and his speech enunciated. His cheekbones were pronounced on his slender face, the skin stretched like the canvas of a wind-taut sail. "A car will be waiting for you at an abandoned airstrip outside Phoenix. Coordinates for the airstrip are in this bag. Everything you requisitioned will be in the car, as well as the documents. Do not fail to get the legal documents signed, Hobbes."

Philly pulled a chair close. His grating voice entered Hobbes's ear on an evil grin.

"I feel the need to remind you after last night that this is the highest profile op you're ever gonna do. No more screwups, eh, Cowboy?"

Hobbes smirked at Philly. Nodded at the money in the duffel. "Is that Rev Six's cash or yours, Senator Pace? Or does it belong to United States taxpayers?"

She leaned in over the table. Her blouse dropped to expose her neckline, and her graying hair swung in front of her still glamorous face. That radiance. Perhaps that was how he'd missed all the clues. She possessed a distracting energy.

"What are you not telling me?" she asked.

"Do you remember, Senator Pace, why Rev Six exists?"

"Enough melodrama, Hobbes." Senator Pace shot Ichabod a face filled with concern, then looked back at Hobbes. "What do you know about an op called Cygnus?"

Hobbes shook his head, put up his hands in a confused gesture. "No idea, Senator."

Ichabod stepped forward, his voice again delicate, almost wistful. "We can send assassins anywhere you go."

"With liberty and justice for all," Hobbes said.

Senator Pace shook her head. "Cut it out. You haven't heard anything about something called Cygnus?"

"No, ma'am."

Her gaze was hard. "We're heading back to Washington this afternoon. Contact me there when it's done. I won't be back in Arizona anytime soon. Monday, Hobbes." She walked out with Philly and Ichabod trailing behind.

Hobbes watched them stooge after her until he broke into a slow rolling chuckle. Pace was the real deal—how had she ever selected Ichabod and Philly? He hoped Pace didn't catch wind of him making his own Rev Six-financed flight back to Washington that evening. Outside the building he pulled out his burner and called Pieter in The Hague. Pieter picked up.

"Are you free?" Hobbes said.

"Oh, my boy, this is just the voice I wanted to hear today," Pieter said, his Dutch accenting otherwise perfect English, TH coming off as D, and W as a slight V. His voice was melodic, his emphasis skipping every third word or so.

"You'll have no problem moving that much on short notice?"

"Daddy, please. I told you I can have everything set to start the transfers on short notice. It will take a few days for them to close, though."

"Shell companies?" Hobbes asked.

"Done. I told you—I have all the rizz."

Hobbes grimaced. "This'll be our last deal."

"That's ass. Why, my boy?"

"Don't miss my next call."

He removed the battery and broke the burner into pieces. Tossed one piece into the nearest trash can. When he reached the rendezvous with his Rev Six contact to debrief, he threw another piece into a dumpster. He had already ditched the newer SUV for a ratty all-wheel-drive midsize utility vehicle and parked it in an alley. When he returned to it, he tossed the last piece of the phone into a drain and checked his watch. He had time to nap before his next meeting. He performed a brass and load check on the Glock, set his watch alarm, and closed his eyes.

CHAPTER 3

Occupational Hazards

IF TAKING COMMAND OF GLEN CANYON DAM IMMEDIATELY after the hostage situation hadn't been enough to boil Fred Goodnight's nerves, the water this sunny Saturday was.

"This is called seepage, Chief." Miller, the aging Bureau of Reclamation engineer appointed to give Goodnight his inaugural tour, pointed to a spot where the cold concrete of the abutment tunnel dribbled a stream of water. They both wore goggles and white hard hats.

"That happen regularly?" Goodnight asked.

"As vegetarian shit." Miller's experienced, good-natured voice was peppered with gravel. "Every dam seeps from cracks or joints. This one about twenty-six hundred gallons per minute."

"You're shittin' me."

"Nope. She's a lot spongier than she lets on. But she's healthy. No worries, Chief."

"Except for that trickling water, it's like a tomb in here," Goodnight observed.

Miller chuckled. "Unsettling, ain't it? But as we go lower, you'll start to hear the power plant. Penstocks over the turbines. The water comes from high in the lake and flows down a tunnel that gets smaller and smaller, and that's what turns the turbines. Wear your ear protection down there."

Amid the federal investigators and extra armed security members clamoring over the premises, a team of Bureau of Reclamation engineers and dam workers were set to open the left spillway because the penstocks and outlet works weren't keeping up with the flow of water coming into Lake Powell.

"I can't believe the lake is that high already," Goodnight said.

"Mother Nature," Miller replied, smoothing his gray beard. "Before all this snow, the lake was in a decades-long drought. No one thought she'd ever come up again. I told all of 'em 'bout a bad couple thunderstorms in Utah one summer. Lake Powell went up four feet in one day. And they didn't think she could come up fifty feet in several years?" He patted the concrete next to his head. "Now here she is lappin' the top like a thirsty dog."

Miller stopped walking and turned to Goodnight.

"I hope you're more alert than Bob was. You folks in that ivory tower up there on the cliff need to be careful. Bob got himself and a lot of other people killed this morning. I've been an engineer here a long time. Good friends died. Poor Pete and his granddaughter." He stared at his feet. "Damn shame."

"Ivory tower?"

"That's what us BOR peons down here in the dam call that office up in the visitors' center."

"I see. I thought all major dams were off-limits to civilians to prevent terrorism. What was that tour about?"

Miller shrugged. "Once in a blue moon, Bob let a few people in. Friday morning was bad timing. Crazy protestors. I don't want a resort in Grand Canyon either, but it ain't worth anyone's life."

Goodnight nodded. "You weren't here?"

"Wife found a leak under the kitchen sink." He gave Goodnight a pensive stare. "Time it took me to find a set of channel locks, fix the leak, and put 'em back saved my life. Got here fifteen minutes after the mess started and the bad guys had locked us out. Lucky."

Goodnight grunted. "I intend to keep this placed buttoned up tight, Mr. Miller."

They moved through the dank concrete tunnel under fluorescent lights.

"Go on, feel it," said Miller. "Eight trillion gallons of trapped Rocky Mountain snowmelt keeps the concrete cool to the touch."

Goodnight reached out. "Cold."

Minutes later he stood with Miller and other operations control staff in front of the dam, monitoring the release. Another group gathered high up on the red and rocky canyon lip, watching from above.

"How can they tell it's working right?" Goodnight hollered over the roar of the water. A fine spray met his face and arms. The smell of lake water permeated his nostrils.

"If it comes out and shoots up in a nice arc, everything's A-okay," Miller shouted, touching his thumb and forefinger and smiling. "But if it starts comin' out choppy and red, the concrete has breached again, and the whole tube could be kaput. That's what happened before. Cost BOR millions to get it fixed before the spring thaw."

Goodnight watched and listened, hoping to learn something more. Another crew member standing near something that looked like a giant breaker box picked up his radio. "Six-Oh-Three, this is Six-Oh-Four, all clear in the power plant?"

A voice came across. "Copy, Six-Oh-Four, all clear."

"Six-Oh-Five, this is Six-Oh-Four, all set upstairs for observation?"

"Roger, Six-Oh-Four, all set," said a third voice.

"Copy, proceed to ten thousand, Six-Oh-Three."

Through his earmuffs Goodnight heard a low buzz, then a muted roar as ice-cold lake water burst from the spillway and shot high into the air.

"Looks good up here, nice flow, Six-Oh-Four. Increase to fifteen thousand."

The roar grew louder, and the stream of water shot higher and farther from the spillway. The engineers and crew watched for several minutes before erupting in a cheer, clapping and whooping their elation.

"That's good?" Goodnight asked.

Miller hooted and clapped Goodnight on the back. "Damn right."

Goodnight watched the swollen river below the dam as it swirled angrier. Bureau of Reclamation officials had put the public on two weeks' notice that the flow downstream would increase to over ninety thousand cubic feet per second.

Miller laughed. "It's going to be a heyday for the whitewater folks."

"Nut jobs, if you ask me," Goodnight muttered. When he heard his name on the radio clipped to his belt, he grabbed it and put it to his mouth. "Goodnight," he shouted, sticking a pinky in one ear.

"They're ready for you, sir. And the team's here too."

"Be up soon. Anxious to meet 'em." He nodded at Miller. "Looks like I'm needed in the ivory tower."

Miller winked.

———

The chatter stopped and the staff and a few associates slipped into cubicles when she entered. Did they really think she never noticed? She shut the door and fell onto her office couch, doing her best to put Eric's reemergence out of her mind.

His face. His smile. His wit. All those late mornings in twisted sheets where he'd made her laugh so easily. His intentional eye contact when he listened to her, drawing his fingers lazily across her ticklish back, reading her mind when she needed it most. Their passion had made her ache then. His image made her ache now. A yearning. Something dangerous.

He had, after all, disappeared.

So why did she want to call him so bad?

She stared at the frames on her office wall. Anything to stop thinking about Eric. A bachelor's degree. A law school diploma. A law license. Awards. Blah, blah, blah.

Too bad she was terrified of courtrooms.

Her attention shifted to the only photo she had of Mama. The blue knit scarf around her neck. The gray jacket. A mountainous landscape rising behind light brown hair that cascaded like a waterfall from under a hiking hat, which shaded a toothy smile curtained by the same high cheekbones she'd passed down to Sierra. The S-shaped gold scroll antique earrings with the pearl drops adorning her ears. *No matter what happens, Sierra, no matter how bad things ever get, don't hock or sell these earrings*, Mama had always told her.

She shook her head at the photo and wondered yet again, why? Why did she do it? What did she know?

Sierra remembered hoarding stolen food under her bed. Mama heating water in the fireplace when the power was turned off. Mama's sweet voice saying, *I'm sorry, kiddos, the car's broken down again.* Mama marrying *him* so they wouldn't be poor anymore.

All her years in the group home, Sierra vowed to never end up like Mama.

Yet she almost had. Those days before Wade Ford's mysterious offer, she lived a bare existence. Why had he called her and offered a solution? And a title: deputy general counsel for Ford Exploration and Developments, LLC.

She had spent a year trying to swallow his explanation that she had valuable knowledge akin to priceless trade secrets. Well, so did several other environmental attorneys. So why her? How many times over the last year had she taken off her reading glasses and closed her eyes to the case law and statutes in front of her to pinch the bridge of her nose and ask that question? Through all the pages and hours and research, the answer never came.

And there was the other pounding question crashing around her head since the night of that meeting last Halloween: What would Mama have thought about all this?

———

Goodnight hated interviews almost as much as the tie choking him. He had switched to T-shirts right around the time the world went crazy. The world was sorta back to normal now, but he was still wearing T-shirts on the reg.

Last night he'd been chuckling at *Catch-22* for the umpteenth time when the phone rang, bringing an official request like something from a fever dream. He'd think about it, he said. Then he'd watched the news this morning. The topless lady's blood running down the wall. A dead girl. A child. A grandchild.

He accepted. They stuck the title of interim security chief on him, emailed him a plane ticket, and told him he had to pass a confirmation interview. The boardroom they were using for the interview had a brilliant view of the dam and the lake behind it from a wall of floor-to-ceiling windows. Natural light reflected across the polished boardroom table. A young man with dark hair and a clean shave identified himself as Special Agent Lynch.

"Your military and police records speak volumes, Lieutenant Colonel Goodnight. Decades of public service. Several citations and medals. Bravery in action. Fast mover in the Arizona Department of Public Safety ranks. But we're most interested in your experience as the head of the Counter Terrorism Information Center," said Lynch.

"We did a lot of good there."

A long and awkward silence. The four interviewers swiveled their heads. "Forgive me," Goodnight said. "I haven't interviewed in years. My last three commands were shoo-in promotions. I should be sitting with my Blanche near a mountain stream somewhere up in the Northwest catching trout and making her laugh. She had such a great laugh." He trailed off and stared at the table. Looked back up. "But she's dead and I'm here."

He realized that two of them were pretty wet behind the ears, and only one of them wore a wedding band.

"I want to help. I don't scare easy. I've commanded men and women for decades. I've fired my duty weapon in cleared shoots. I've choppered over search and rescues in tandem with the National Park Service and county and state agencies. I can use a computer. Hell, I can even watch the tic-tacky videos my grandkids send me."

One of the young women sitting across from him laughed, then covered her mouth.

Lynch gave her the side-eye and continued. "The private security contract is terminated effective immediately. The FBI, in conjunction with the Department of Homeland Security and the United States Army, are taking over dam security control for the time being."

"I don't know anything about dams or hydroelectric power plants," said Goodnight.

"BOR, the Bureau of Reclamation, takes care of all that. Your sole responsibility is security. You have a good budget and the full support of the president. Under the Homeland Security Presidential Directive, because you'll be here at least a year, you and your people will have special access cards to restricted areas. Make no mistake: This is a military operation. Yes, there's a lot of anti-Ford Exploration and Developments graffiti in the facility, but these weren't run-of-the-mill environmental protestors. There were killers here yesterday and this morning, Lieutenant Colonel Goodnight," Lynch said. The young man let that sit. "We suspect the protester angle might be a front for real terrorism. You're getting a full team of United States Special Operations Command operators. You're familiar with SOCOM?"

"SOCOM? Why? Isn't this situation what the Joint Terrorism Task Forces are for?"

Lynch cleared his throat, adjusted his tie, and sat up.

"Of course, JTTF is involved, but someone in Washington felt that we needed a bit more help." He smiled.

"Special forces operators?" Goodnight asked. "Who exactly do you all think is responsible for the attack?"

"You start today as interim security chief, the equivalent of a colonel, of the Glen Canyon facility. We're putting you in special joint-operation command of the SOCOM operators and FBI special agents. Once we complete all the paperwork, you'll be named permanent security chief. This is quite a task, sir. Are you up for it?"

Goodnight frowned. Special Agent Lynch had avoided his question.

———

He met his executive officer ten minutes later. An early-forties fellow with a stout conformation, salt-and-pepper hair, and a face and mustache that screamed military regs. "Lieutenant Mark Jones. Good morning, Colonel Goodnight," he said, standing at attention.

Goodnight laughed. "Relax, Jones," he said, sticking his hand out. "Chief Goodnight will do just fine, I reckon."

Jones melted a bit and engaged in the handshake, then handed Goodnight a paper roster.

"So you're my XO. You were here last night?"

"Yes, sir. I was in command of the power plant assault, attached to the FBI Hostage Rescue Team. It was a mix of HRT and Special Operations Command elements from Yuma. Some members of your new team were with me," he said, pointing at the roster.

"That must have been tough to see."

"Sir."

"Where'd you serve before SOCOM?"

"Naval Special Warfare, sir."

Goodnight squinted at Jones. "You kill any important bad guys?" he said in jest.

"They gave the credit to some other dick cheese."

Goodnight chuckled. "You're all right by me, Lieutenant. Let's go meet our people."

They entered a briefing room where thirty-six SOCOM or FBI Hostage Rescue Team men and women waited. Their dress and appearance exuded professionalism. Everyone, including Jones, had been called up in a hurry and was subject to the same confirmation process. Goodnight looked at the roster in his hand and wondered again where the Joint Terrorism Task Forces were on this.

"You'll work in teams of twelve," Jones stated. "Each team will have three up on the dam covering down to the center. One in the visitors' center. Six will patrol the power plant, inspection tunnels, elevators, and outbuildings. The other two will monitor the spiral staircases on both sides of the dam, and Two-Mile Tunnel on the west side. One team on, the other two off until shift change, which is every eight hours. You'll all get a rotating forty-eight-hour pass. Every inch of the dam has to be under constant armed surveillance."

Goodnight turned a chair backwards and sat, leaning forward to address his team. "The White House, the FBI, and the Bureau of Reclamation are pretty embarrassed about this morning's tragedy. The intelligence community doesn't think this was the work of a bunch of people upset about Ford's development downriver in the park. They think this was terrorism, and that maybe the terrorists were using the national protests against Ford Exploration and Developments as a cover. We will be sharp, folks." He let that hang before continuing.

"No family, no friends, no visitors. You'll be sleeping two to each CONEX they've brought in and lined up behind the visitors' center. They're not five-star hotels, but they are custom units that include electrical and a sink and toilet. You'll all use the employee showers in the visitors' center." He paused and considered that he had a co-ed crew. "We're all adults here, but let's remember, we're under observation. Please don't cause a stir by . . . showering together."

Some snickering erupted.

"When you're not on shift, you can go off-site for visits, but no more than ten miles in any direction. There are a few hotels within that radius for family time. Uncle Sam will cover the tab. This is a joint operation, what you could call a very special assignment. We're all military or former military here, but if you look around, you'll see some FBI Hostage Rescue Team folks too. After last night, this area of operations is considered hazardous, and by order of the president, a domestic deployment. Your pay reflects that, so treat it like one."

Someone piped up from the back, "Will there be hookers like on deployment?"

Laughter.

Goodnight suppressed a smile. "Dismissed."

That afternoon he watched the water blow out the bottom of the dam far below. In less than twenty-four hours, he had been put in charge of protecting a volatile natural resource with a group of folks he'd had no time to vet. Why was SOCOM here? Where was the JTTF? Was he up to the task? He wondered if he should have said no.

———

Sierra, Bill, and eight others waited, watching the big screen at the head of the table. Sierra fought the urge to open the unread text from Eric. She muted their microphone and tugged Bill's sleeve as she gestured at the screen. "Where is he?" she whispered. "I told Benny we'd go to the farmers market this afternoon."

Bill rubbed his hands together.

"Ooh . . . let's see. He's down the street at the Hotel Maryland, drinking by the indoor pool, maybe getting a rubdown under the table, probably spending a million here, a couple hundred million there—" He noticed Sierra's stone face and lowered his hands. "You know he hates our office, Sierra. We should be done early afternoon—I hope. This protest-hostage debacle has him more than a wee bit miffed. I actually heard him use the F-word this morning." He pretended to be concerned, making her giggle.

"You still going to Maine when this is all over?" Sierra asked.

"Oh, yeah. When you're the only child, it's all on you to take care of the octogenarians."

Sierra looked at him. "Don't ever take that for granted, Bill. You're lucky."

He leaned back and raised his brow. "Noted, Sierra."

She found Bill delightful and funny, despite his gum snapping and awkward wardrobe choices. Sierra felt he had a probable life sentence as a bachelor, so she was always on the lookout for his match.

Scarlett O'Neill, the trusted paralegal and close friend Sierra had brought with her from Banks & Hardy, handed her a folder with meeting notes.

"Thanks, Scarlett," Sierra said. She pulled her close. "You sure you don't want to sit up here with me and Bill?"

Scarlett fake-gagged as she looked at the back of Bill's head. Sierra scowled. Scarlett couldn't get past Bill's hairline, spare tire, and gum snapping. Sierra couldn't blame her for the last one.

Wade was a tougher nut. Sierra had to admire a man who'd come from meager Midwest beginnings and worked his way into financial aristocracy. And he was forever a topic of discussion among the legal team.

Bill leaned back over. "I heard a few of the young associates talking in the bathroom yesterday. Like straight-out-of-law-school young. They didn't know I was occupying a stall."

"Thanks for that tidbit of unnecessary information," said Sierra.

"It's an important detail for my story. Anyway, one of them asks the other if they'd ever seen Wade in person. The other says, 'Yeah, I met him once.' The first one asks, 'Well, what'd you think?' Second one says, 'I feel like he watched nothing but hokey British films for culture,'" Bill said, breaking out in a laugh.

Sierra snickered too.

"Then this motherfu—sorry, Sierra—this kid says, 'Thank God he doesn't try the accent too. Can you imagine?'" Bill started giggling harder. "And then he breaks into this awful British accent, says, ''ello love, would you like to see my billionaire balls? Just had 'em shined this morning. Give us a look, eh?' Then the other associate says, 'Bro, put your nasty balls away.' I was trying so hard not to laugh out loud that I . . . that I . . ." Bill caught his breath. "The echo, Sierra." He reached out and touched her arm, shaking. "It was so loud."

Bill was crying, holding his stomach, trying to keep it together. Sierra slapped his arm. "*Ew.* You are so disgusting."

"Those two guys had their hands washed in seconds and got the hell outta there. I'm never gonna tell them it was me."

Sierra sighed. "Half the world loves Wade for his business savvy and good looks. The other half hates him because he has the environmental ethics of a cyborg. I doubt the accent would make a difference."

Bill shook his head. "I've been on more blind dates and online first dates than every man in Washington. Still single. Then you got a guy like Wade. Think about it . . . Wade could have married any number of well-pedigreed women, but he goes through these young unattached beauties like toilet paper." He turned to Sierra. "Toilet paper," he said, and lost it again.

Sierra remembered Wade looking her up and down the night she met him. Whatever his intentions, she'd never let herself be alone with him for longer than a minute.

Despite that, he still managed to disarm her in their interactions. When they'd won their final constitutional battle earlier that month, paving the way for the project to move forward with the state court details in Sandstone County, she had sulked into the mandatory after-party. Wade pulled her close amid the cheers and popping champagne bottles and loud classic rock. He smelled fresh, with just the right dose of some expensive cologne, like always.

"I knew hiring you was the right thing when you walked into that first meeting, Sierra." His expression had been genuine, heartfelt. "Marvelous job."

She smiled and nodded, blushing. But when he walked away, she felt violated.

Now Wade appeared on the screen and sat. His head consumed most of the giant display, some of a turquoise indoor pool visible behind him. Victor Rivera, Wade's kind security guard who had wanded Sierra a year ago, appeared at various times, walking with his peculiar gait as he performed his duties. Like always, classic rock played in the background.

Two tanned, bikini-clad women, one a platinum blonde, the other a brunette, slipped into the water holding umbrella drinks.

A pasty man in his mid-fifties, wearing only a red thong and thick body hair, screamed as he jumped off the diving board, then hit the water with a splash. The Washington legal team was salty after several weeks of long days in the office. They snickered at the scene.

Sierra whispered to Bill, "These people need some R&R before Monday morning. Look at them. All they need right now is a tub of popcorn."

"Or a tub of lube," Bill replied. "Look at those two cuties. And that guy in the skimpy swim briefs? What a freakshow."

"You pig. And that's a thong, not swim briefs."

"Does it make a difference?"

Wade broke his silence. "Billy, I read your memo. Pardon, but when have I ever delayed business because of my public image?"

Bill's voice and diction flipped from joking to the seriousness of a consummate professional.

"Mr. Ford, the protests in Vista and Phoenix are already bad, and you won't even be in Arizona for another twenty-four hours. The president had barely ordered the flags at half-staff before the talking heads started pointing fingers at you. They're suggesting crazy things, like you ultimately being responsible for the deaths. That idea would never fly in court, but we'd sure have to deal with more lawsuits."

"You're muted, Billy," Wade grumbled.

Bill gave Sierra an embarrassed look, unmuted, and then repeated himself.

Wade sat back and lit a cigar. Most days he was in Italian tailored suits—slim fitting, impeccable, impressive. Today, however, the top three buttons of his cabana-style shirt were undone, exposing a thick gold necklace snaking through the graying forest on his chest. He used the cigar between his thumb and index finger as a pointer.

"We'll fly the flags at half-staff, of course," Wade said. "But don't think I'm going to pack up my toys without a fight. Sierra, what have you to say?"

She shook her head. "Litigation and appearances aren't my arena, Mr. Ford." She refused to step on a land mine and unintentionally trigger the ninety-day contingency in her contract.

"Mr. Ford, we've got an idea. But we might still take everyone to Arizona to get poured out Monday morning," said Bill.

Another scream. Thong Man jackknifed off the diving platform and splashed water over the two women. They covered their drinks and cackled in feigned outrage behind oversized sunglasses. Sierra marveled at how the .001 percent lived. The reality of how her family's life was about to change entered her mind again. She only had to be Wade's clown for a few more days.

Wade puffed and sat in the cigar's haze. "We break ground as soon as this hearing is over, Billy. I've advanced millions to deploy construction units outside Fredonia. You say neither the court nor Peoples and Parks have reached out about a reset, so why should we?" He shoved the cigar between his teeth.

Bill's puffy face made him look as if he'd just walked out of a sauna. The past twelve months had been hard on them all, but Sierra knew that Bill's weight gain was a direct result of using fast food and booze as coping mechanisms.

"On Monday we should ask for an in-chambers conference with Judge Sumner and opposing counsel. Offer our condolences to the people of Arizona," Bill said.

Sierra looked at her hands. She'd already told Bill this was a bad idea. Judge Sumner might see it as a cheap ploy. Bill had overruled her.

"We soften the blow, save time," Bill continued. He paused before delivering the next part. "We stipulate to Items 1–22."

Wade sat up. "Pardon?"

"We stipulate to Items 1—"

"I heard you, Billy. No. I made myself clear last week," Wade complained.

The two pool goddesses glanced at Wade, whispering. The platinum blonde handed her drink to the brunette.

"You did, Mr. Ford. But this new develop—"

"We should be breaking ground whether these people are dead or alive." A taupe bikini top landed on Wade's head, one cup and a strap hanging down his face like a folded napkin containing a single limp spaghetti noodle. His head jerked a bit in reaction, and then he pulled it off and studied it. He turned red and hid it from the camera's view, then stared back at the screen, puffing.

Behind Sierra, more stifled laughter. Bill shushed the legal team with a glare, then turned back to Wade.

"Mr. Ford, respectfully, I disagree," Bill said. "Twenty-two people were murdered. One of the dead was a nine-year-old girl. Your name was spray-painted all over the Glen Canyon facilities."

"I agree it's unpleasant, Billy," he said. "Victor, my tablet, please?"

Victor's encumbered hand entered the screen. Wade put on his readers. Tapped the screen. Read a portion with disdain. "'*Stipulation No. 15, A National Park Service Environmental Professional selected by the National Park Service, Department of the Interior, shall observe the daily progress of the Work . . .*' and blah blah blah, bloody blah."

Sierra and Bill followed along on their own screens. Wade held his tablet up and Victor's hand took it.

"Atrocious legalese, borderline offensive. They'd stop us every five minutes to save a lizard or an endangered cactus. The bill the president signed contained none of this," said Wade.

Bill then did the thing that always impressed Sierra. She'd seen skillful lawyers with tactile client control, but Bill had a way with Wade Ford the Billionaire.

"Mr. Ford, I'm listening to you, and . . . I'm concerned."

"Why, Billy?"

"I'm not sure you know your own case, Mr. Ford."

"How's that?" Wade asked, turning and politely waving away the now topless platinum blonde bimbo in the pool. With a generous flash of bare boob, she pouted and moved out of view.

Wade's face turned red again.

More sniggering from the eight people behind them in the boardroom. Sierra hid her smile. Bill gave everyone, her included, a more severe glare this time.

"You've got the chance of a lifetime here, Mr. Ford," Bill said.

"Do I?"

"Peoples and Parks knows we intend to call three experts. To save time in light of the dam incident, we proffer the witness testimony in a summation instead," Bill said, gesturing to Sierra.

"How so?" Wade asked.

Bill raised his eyebrows and paused, a little dramatic flair Sierra appreciated. Then he leaned forward. Made a show of exhaling hard.

"Put yourself in Judge Sumner's place, Mr. Ford. Everyone knows he's up for a federal bench. If this hearing is contested, you're asking him to approve construction of a private luxury resort, not to mention a massive gondola and tram system, in the heart of Arizona's prize national park. This after a year of public protests while the state is busy mourning twenty-two lost citizens. It's a publicity nightmare for him. If you don't have an agreement, you're looking at a reset. Another six months probably. By then Sumner may be in the federal courthouse and you'll have to start all over with a new judge."

It wasn't lost on Sierra that Bill had timed his attack when Wade was distracted by Pool Bimbo's naked boobs.

Bill leaned back. "If there's no agreement on Monday morning, Sumner will punt to his successor. But with an agreement, you get what you want. All they get are a few measly conditions."

Wade was quiet. Sierra watched him. When it came to business and developments, he was sophisticated. Ruthless. However, when it came to legal strategy, he employed an unrestrained reliance on his attorneys. He put down his cigar. Sipped his drink.

"All right. We stipulate. But should I get delayed for weeks so an 'Environmental Professional' can watch an endangered baby bird do a poo and take wing, you'll answer for it. I'll see you all tomorrow morning at the hangar. Good evening."

Thong Man's fleshy rump rose from the water as he turned a flip. One of the women squealed. Wade tapped the screen and the image went black.

"If you only could have convinced him to let me stay in DC, I wouldn't have to go home and pack," said Sierra.

"How about you kiss my ass?" Bill quipped. "You still have time for the farmers market," he said, then snapped his gum. "See the set on that blonde?"

Sierra glared back at him. "You have got to break that habit, Bill." Her cell buzzed in her hand. No Caller ID again. She ignored it.

———

An outfitted forest-green SUV with dark-tinted windows and a matte black snorkel entered the warehouse. Hobbes flipped through the photos again. The dossiers were thorough, but he lingered on the lawyer's picture. Her file revealed useful vulnerabilities. But her face held another appeal. Beauty, sure. Yet something else was there. He blinked and returned everything to the file and closed it. He exited his vehicle, put on the mask, pulled out the Glock, and stood behind the door. The SUV's big mud tires crunched the red gravel.

The driver shifted, killed the engine, but kept the parking lights glowing.

"Hands," Hobbes said.

Three men stepped out and held their hands at waist level. A bearded Caucasian man dressed in black with a giant tattoo of Mjölnir on his left forearm exited the front passenger side. A thin black man also wearing dark clothes exited the rear driver's-side door. The driver, another Caucasian, wore varying shades of olive and gray and sported a regulation mustache. They approached Hobbes's all-wheel-drive vehicle and stopped.

Hobbes tossed a white towel onto the hood and raised the Glock. "Put your pieces on the towel—knives, too."

Jackets were unzipped, Velcro was peeled, and pockets emptied. Two full-size Glocks, a SIG Sauer P227, a compact Walther PPS M2, three tactical knives, and a set of brass knuckles lay on the fabric.

"Back up."

Hobbes folded the corners of the towel and placed the makeshift basket on the front seat. He stood over all three of them, the black bag from Ichabod in his right hand and his Glock in his left.

The bearded man hadn't backed up and stood scrutinizing Hobbes. "Southpaw, huh? Sweet mask, bro." He nodded toward the SUV. "Seat go back far enough in that thing for you?"

Hobbes dropped the bag and took two nimble steps toward him and threw a fist into his gut. The big man leaned over and gasped. Hobbes stood over him and waited. "Anything else you want to say?"

He stood and caught his breath. "No."

"Now back up."

He complied, holding his stomach.

Mustache Man pointed to his jacket. "Take my tablet out?"

"Slowly."

Mustache Man set the device on the all-wheel-drive's hood, his face illuminated in the screen's dim blue glow as he studied Hobbes. "With a few keystrokes into the hardline, everything will be operational. When you call, I'll activate." He gestured at the other two men. "They'll have the devices you stowed deployed by then. Fully automated to use the host's power and software against itself."

He held out a cell phone-sized metal device with buttons on it to Hobbes, who took it and examined it. "Are you confident in the execution? Range?" Hobbes asked, turning the device over in his hand. "I'm supposed to be near Page when it goes down, but things could change."

"It's satellite based. Solid. We tested it last week on a dummy system like you asked. Should work from anywhere."

"What? I told you no satellite-based tech."

"No other way, bro. A radio signal is too short of range. Plus obstructions block radio signals."

Hobbes frowned and sighed. "No other way. Right. How's the new interim head of security?"

"Goodnight? He's experienced. Watching closely, but we'll achieve the objective."

"You'll remain on the premises after this meeting. Be ready any time."

"Hell, we're breaking Goodnight's rules by meeting you now. Did you know two of those amateurs got out this morning and ran across the desert?"

"Yes."

Hobbes set the black bag that Ichabod had given him on the hood and opened it. They leaned in as if trying to catch a glimpse of a peep show. "There's no final payment unless this is done," he said. "Split this however you want." He laid the towel on the asphalt at his feet and winced with a grunt when a stinging pain radiated through his neck.

"You all right there?" Mustache Man asked.

Hobbes took a moment to wait for the pain to subside. "When I'm gone you can pick up your gear. He pointed at Bearded Man. "Don't fuck up my operation."

CHAPTER 4

Proximity and Reciprocity

Y OU STILL WANT TO GO FOR A RUN?" SIERRA ASKED. "Yep. Just preparing for my new rotation on Monday. Who knew there were so many different words for feces?" Andrew replied.

"Gross. Let me see if Scarlett's busy." Sierra dialed, thinking for the millionth time it was insulting to ask Scarlett to double as a nanny, then remembering that she always said it wasn't. She had never missed any of Benny's birthday parties, and like Sierra, doted on the boy as if he was the future of mankind. They embraced fifteen minutes later when Scarlett walked in without knocking or ringing the doorbell.

"Sorry for the short notice. He'll be easy—the farmers market wore him out," said Sierra.

Scarlett furrowed her lightly freckled forehead, looking pensive behind her oversized round glasses. "You know, besides all the dorky lawyers at the office and my cat, Benny is the only male in my life. More of a man than most of them. Come to think of it, so is Smiles, and he's neutered."

"There's a man out there who loves sarcastic wit and head full of long red hair," said Sierra. "And cats. And true crime docs. And flannel. Bill Clark is just that—"

"Blech . . . Stop pushing Bill on me. Besides, we both know I'm the quintessential old biddy in training. I'm wearing pajama pants right now that I wore all week after work without washing. When you find a tall, handsome, successful-but-might-choke-me-a-little non-lawyer who likes redheads prone to asthma attacks, let me know."

"After Arizona we're going out. I'll be your wingman. Woman. Person. Whatever."

"I'm wearing my freakin' pajamas and I'm bringing Smiles."

"Get rid of Smiles, and maybe you won't be so prone to asthma attacks."

"Yeah, but no. I'll suffocate to death before I live without my cat."

"That's redundant."

"No one except other nerds like you would ever say that."

After Benny's hugs and kisses, Sierra did her best to act normal on the way to the park. Eric's reemergence made her feel alive but edgy. Like a triple espresso or a silent quickie against the counter with Andrew in the locked bathroom while Benny watched TV.

After they parked, she walked in the brisk late-afternoon air to where Andrew sat on the coupe's open liftgate, wrapping his left ankle.

"You'd think rupturing an Achilles in college wouldn't be such a pain in the ass after all these years," he said.

"You're still faster than I'll ever be. All those surgeries made you bionic," she answered, donning her ear warmers, running gloves, and light jacket.

"I seem to remember you were once a track star yourself."

"I ran track in high school, Andrew, not college. I wasn't a star, either. Not one that anyone would have cared about, anyway."

Andrew ran with her a bit on the concrete sidewalk before bounding away. An occasional bird or squirrel chittered in the leafless trees around her. Sierra's mind wandered back to Eric. It was her fault, letting him back in that one last time years ago. She'd be damned before she let that happen again. Benny deserved better. Andrew deserved better. Hell, she deserved better. At the end of the loop, she was shocked to see her best 5k time in years. Andrew clapped. She bent over to catch her breath, wishing she could tell him what had pushed her so hard.

"I need to stretch," she said, handing him her phone. "Will you make sure my app logged my mileage and time, please?"

"Sure," he said, taking it from her.

Sierra was in a deep runner's lunge when Andrew whispered, "What the hell?" He held the phone up for her to see. "Who's Eric?"

She blinked and felt her stomach drop. The text she never read. If she played this poorly, Andrew might suspect things that had never happened. "I got that earlier today. I don't even know what it says."

"Is he one of your recovery people?" Andrew asked as he showed her the phone. "He got the hots for you? 'Hey, it's Eric again, gorgeous. Sure you don't wanna get high with me? Is dinner with an old friend tonight ok?' The hell, Sierra?"

She panicked.

"Get high?"

"He's a pilot. He means take a flight with him. He's an old . . . friend. He wanted to take me up for a flight, catch up," she answered.

Andrew gave her a blank stare. "Then let's go to dinner."

"What? The three of us?"

"If he's a guy you've known since high school and he's texting you, probably best I meet him," Andrew said.

"Oh, perfect. You wanna piss all over me before we go so he knows I belong to you?"

"Maybe. You didn't seem to think I needed to know an old boyfriend was texting you."

"I never said he was a boyfriend."

"I'll text him back the place and time." Andrew picked up her phone and tapped the screen. "Done."

They bickered some more. Sierra tried to hide her terror, but also attempted to put the shoe on the other foot. Maybe Andrew wasn't marking territory so much as trying to protect it, but whatever the case, this was going to be a train wreck.

______

Scarlett had no plans and wanted to catch up on some work. Her faux protest against staying longer to sit Benny was half-hearted. She pulled her laptop from her purse and waved her hand as if she were Marie Antoinette. "Go enjoy life, be merry, all the things people in relationships do," she said with a good-natured smirk and eye roll.

Sierra grabbed her arm and pulled her into the half bath next to the kitchen. They stared at each other, Sierra breathing hard, unable to speak.

Scarlett finally shrugged. "What are we doing, Sierra?"

"Shh . . . keep your voice down," Sierra whispered. "Eric is back."

"I'm sorry, but I seem to be missing a ton of context clues," Scarlett replied in a flat whisper. "Why are we whispering? Why am I locked in a bathroom with you?"

"Eric, Scarlett. Eric. The Eric," Sierra said, shaking her hands in front of her.

Scarlett thought for a second and then her face lit up and her eyes popped. "Oh, shit, Eric," she nearly shouted.

"Keep your voice down," Sierra said. "He texted me today. Andrew found the text. We're going to some sort of twisted dinner with him right now." She shrugged and held out her hands, imploring Scarlett to offer some sort of wisdom.

"Girl, I don't even know. Like . . . I need some time with this."

"So do I," Sierra said. "But we don't have any."

Scarlett shook her head. Sierra mirrored her. They exited the bathroom, Sierra looking for Andrew, wondering if he'd heard anything.

She read Benny a quick bedtime story and tucked him in. On her way out the door, she waved at Scarlett, who sat with her laptop on the couch. Scarlett pretended to hang herself, her tongue lolling. Sierra flipped her the bird.

They arrived at the restaurant five minutes early. Andrew brought drinks from the bar.

"Were you close?" he asked.

"He was my boyfriend. I haven't talked to him in years." She sipped her martini and grimaced.

"So he was your boyfriend?"

Sierra met Andrew's eyes.

"Eric's a part of my past I'm not ready to explain. You should respect that."

Andrew scratched his neck. "Something's been up with you for months. I pushed for this weird-ass dinner because I wanted to know if this guy is that something. I need to know for myself."

She scoffed and fumbled for what to say, then blurted out what she'd almost said that morning. "I need a change, Andrew." She saw the worry on his face. Her phone buzzed and she checked it.

"Eric's here. Don't say anything about Benny to him."

———

"Evening, Ranger Moore," Goodnight said into his cell phone.

"Good evening, Chief Goodnight," Judy replied. "How's the new job at the reservoir?"

"Wet. A little scary."

"All those climate experts said it would never happen again. Turns out never was only five years of heavy snowpack."

"It leaks. They call it seepage. It's like a mausoleum when you're inside it. This old bitch—sorry, Judy—this old dam is eerie."

"It's trying to convince you it still serves a purpose. Don't believe it. And how many times do I have to tell you that while I appreciate chivalry, you can swear in my presence, Fred. I won't die."

Goodnight realized on his first day of his new job that he'd called Judy because he was nervous. It made him feel guilty to need someone other than Blanche.

"They've got investigators and bureaucrats all over the place, huh?" Judy asked.

"Yep. I met my XO, guy named Jones. He was actually here last night in the raid. He's squared away. We also met the team they called up. There's a lot of work to be done, a lot for me to learn," he said. "I wonder if I'm too old to take this on. During that interview this morning, I felt like they were speaking another language at times."

"Enough, Fred. They called the right man for the job," Judy replied. "When do I get another apple pie?"

"I don't think that's funny."

"Oh, I thought it was cute, this silver fox walking up to my door with a white box full of apple pie, getting mauled by my Chihuahuas."

"Yeah, then you asked me if I baked it when they were ripping my leg off. I thought you were serious for a minute there. You love puttin' me on, don't you?"

Judy laughed. "I've never seen a grown man so scared of three tiny dogs. And nervous to talk to a woman. Like a middle school boy at a dance with his first girl. I think you stared out the back door at my plants for a good minute before you thawed out."

"I couldn't do anything until you put the hounds from hell up in the bedroom."

"Be nice to my babies."

"Babies? I still don't know what to do, Judy," Goodnight said. "Seems like I was just telling Blanche I was ready to retire. Now it's been years since she died. Seemed like no matter what I ever said, she'd nod her head with that same sweet smile she gave me the night we met."

Judy let him talk. He'd appreciated that about her from the start.

"I guess it got to where I could tell that my kids were tired of me. Grandkids, too, I reckon. I tried to spend a week in Yellowstone. When Old Faithful erupted, I looked over to see Blanche's reaction. I forgot. Do I sound crazy? I guess I'm just not over her yet."

Judy tsk-tsked into the phone. "You don't have to be. Before you came along, I had resigned myself to turning into dust and blowing into the canyon one day. You're a treat, Fred. And you're gonna do just fine running things at Glen Canyon."

"I appreciate your vote," he said. "My concern is that I don't know if . . . well . . . I don't even want to say it."

"Say what?"

"I think maybe I have half an idea what Daniel felt like when they threw him in that pit."

———

Eric wore the same type of blue jeans and untucked pearl snap cowboy shirts he'd always worn. Cowboy boots and a matching worn brown leather jacket. Stubble beard. Hair longer than Sierra remembered. The same toothy grin she'd always liked. Symmetrical face. In a word, handsome.

They embraced too long, he smelling of the brisk air outside and faint cologne and the old leather jacket. She pulled away. Eric appraised her. "You don't ever disappoint, Ms. Justice," he said.

She blushed and held her hand out toward Andrew. "Eric, Andrew. Andrew, Eric. Eric stopped as if shot. His eyes pleaded with Sierra's. Andrew held out his hand.

To her relief Eric adjusted fast and pumped it. "Andy, good to know you."

"Andrew."

Eric held up his hands. "Andrew. No offense." He looked around. "What is this place? Y'all live near here?"

"No. We try to avoid places close to home these days," said Sierra. Eric nodded.

They were seated in a large booth when Eric called the server over. "Can we please get a round of drinks over here? My treat. Sierra?"

When she asked for water, Eric dropped his menu. "We haven't seen each other in years and you're gonna celebrate with water? I won't allow it, Ms. Justice."

"She doesn't drink," Andrew said.

Eric laughed. "Since when? What about you, Andrew?"

Andrew raised his brow at Sierra, who nodded. "It's fine," she said.

"Merlot, please," Andrew said.

Eric grinned at Andrew, shook his head, then ordered for himself. "Gunner's Mate whiskey, neat, and make it a double, would you?"

"You're back out of the blue after all this time, Eric?" Andrew asked.

"Yessir. Just retired from the Marines. Up until then I was at Uncle Sam's mercy. Now I get to make my own big boy choices," he said, slowly dancing from syllable to syllable as he spoke each word.

"Like calling old girlfriends?"

Sierra kicked Andrew under the table. Their drinks came with a basket of warm, sweet rolls and they ordered their entrees. Old Italian music played faintly over the silence.

"What are you doing now?" Sierra asked Eric.

"Still flying. Private work. Got a damn good gig, and the pay kicks ass," Eric said as he tore apart a roll and slathered it with butter.

"You have a dirty mouth," Andrew said.

Sierra put her hand on Andrew's. "Andrew, I have a dirty mouth. Eric's been this way since I met him. I'm not offended."

"Well, Andy—sorry, Andrew—I went straight from high school into the Marines. Got my college degree on active duty and became a pilot. So it's like I've been in high school for two decades," Eric said. "We sorta say whatever the fuck we want when we're keeping you and your family safe."

Sierra cringed, worrying that a real confrontation might unfold, but she'd allowed Andrew to ambush Eric, so she endured it. The arrival of their entrees lifted the mood. She took a bite of lasagna and noticed Eric watching her. Their eyes locked as a long-forgotten surge shot through her. The moment held, however briefly, until Eric turned his smile to Andrew.

"Andrew," Eric said. "I just wanted to say hello to my friend and catch up. No worries, all right? How's that salmon?"

"The L is silent and the A is short. It's not pronounced like 'almond.'"

Sierra caught Eric's scowl. "What sort of work are you doing for your client, Eric?" she asked.

"Glorified air taxi." He took a bite and continued talking with a mouth full of food, somehow pulling it off without being disgusting. "He's more like my boss, though. The flying's great, aircraft's state of the art. He takes care of his people. I went from base housing to satin sheets."

She watched him again. She'd always liked the way his lips complemented his teeth, the way his mouth moved when he spoke. His accent. She realized she was gawking and stopped.

"How long you had this job?" Sierra asked.

"Long enough. By the way, saw your pretty face on TV."

She cringed. "I was only on TV because I was standing behind our general counsel, Bill. I guess you've seen all the hit pieces on my boss and me, too, huh? The protests against Canyon's Dream, the hostage situation this morning?"

Eric waved his hand. "I don't pay attention to all that crap, Sierra." He pointed with his fork at Andrew and asked, "What do you do for a living?"

"I was a phlebotomist. Now I'm in med school," Andrew said.

"Med school at your age? Sheesh. Hats off."

"I'm thirty-five" came Andrew's annoyed reply.

"What kind of doctor?"

"Cardiologist."

"Good luck. I hated every school I had to go to from kindergarten to college, up to flight school, and every damn thing in between," Eric said.

Dinner never improved. Sierra couldn't talk to Eric about anything she wanted to discuss, and the men were behaving like roosters sharing a henhouse. She took her last bite and swallowed some water and was ready to leave. The check came, and she slipped the server her card before the men could fight over that too.

"Time to go, boys," she said, getting up with a smile. Both men looked at Sierra, confused.

They talked in the parking lot.

"Wish we could have taken that hop," Eric said to Sierra. He smiled at Andrew. "All three of us."

Before Andrew could respond, Sierra jumped in with, "Me too, Eric. Maybe don't wait another century to call."

They embraced again. In the dark of the snow-lined parking lot, Sierra felt his splayed fingers against her lower back. A gentle but intentional push. Even in the low light, she recognized the same look he'd given her that night on the beach in Cabo.

"You still got the earrings, huh?" He reached out and fingered one of the pearl drops. "That's something else, Sierra."

Andrew cleared his throat. Neither man spoke when they squeezed the life from each other's palms. Sierra waited for Eric to look back before getting into his car. He didn't.

————

Not long after he landed in Washington, exhausted and irritated, Hobbes watched from across the street the trio leaving the restaurant. His own love life might have consisted of meaningless hookups and fake names, but he wasn't blind.

"Boyfriend better watch out. Blondie likes the flyboy," he muttered as he monitored their movements. After a long, tight hug, the lady lawyer lingered and watched Samuels walk to his car. Hobbes gave the pilot a conservative tail to his hotel.

He parked, slipped on the ballistic mask, and went up the back entrance to the room number that Rev Six's Second Seal intelligence had provided. When the pilot held his key card next to his door lock, Hobbes made a hard line for him. Samuels heard him and turned at the last second with a wild swing that hit only air.

Hobbes threw his right hand over Samuels's left shoulder and pushed his left arm up under the pilot's right. He clasped his hands behind Samuels's back and stepped across with his right leg. When Samuels was off balance, Hobbes pulled him over his leg, throwing Samuels down and knocking his head against the doorjamb. He picked up the key card Samuels dropped and held it to the lock. Once the door was open, he dragged Samuels into the room by his waistband. The door shut behind him as he kicked Samuels in the stomach to make sure he stayed down.

He sat on one of the queen-sized beds and pulled out his pistol. Samuels heaved and gagged until the acidic smell of vomit forced Hobbes to move to the other bed.

Samuels sat up against the first bed, coughed, and looked up at him. "Killed my buzz, dickhead. Nice mask. Can you even see?" he said, wheezing and wiping blood from the cut on his hairline, a little clump of hair already stained crimson. "Glad this ain't my first time. Might think you were going to take advantage of me."

"Shut up. Listen to my proposition, Major Samuels."

"I don't swing that way, buddy," Samuels said. "Not even at gunpoint. But if we're going to be this intimate, you should call me Eric. How the hell do you know me?"

"I know a lot about you. I give you tasks, you give me information," Hobbes said.

Eric pushed his fingertips into his ribs and groaned. "Thank God you didn't break one. Sounds like a shitty deal for me. Why would I do anything for you?"

Hobbes reached into his jacket and tossed a folded piece of paper to Samuels, who unfolded and read it. Samuels's face went slack and he looked up in surprise. "This is legit?"

"I have access to his email."

"I don't even want to know how."

"No, you don't."

"So I might be out of a job, huh?" He looked at Hobbes. "You think just because you have this email I'm gonna screw him over? Who the hell are you?" asked Samuels, holding up the paper.

"I need you to help me get somewhere with him. You'll make more money with me than you do flying for him. Here's a little start-up capital." Hobbes pulled two wrapped stacks of cash from the other side of his jacket and tossed them on the floor.

Samuels eyed them, then picked them up and ran his thumb along their edges. He tossed them back. "I'm not helping you, bro."

Hobbes smirked. Time for plan B. "Yes, you will. Pay close attention, Major Samuels."

"Why do men think women need them so bad?" Sierra blurted out during the ride home under a bleary sky. Headlights lit their faces from time to time.

"I don't need a crossing guard, Andrew."

She changed her voice to a goofy, deep mocking tone and said, "Careful, Sierra, here comes a car. Whoa, look out, Sierra, your ex-boyfriend is trying to stick his pee-pee in you."

"What the hell?" Andrew said, glancing over at her. "This Eric guy trigger you?"

"I told you I wanted something else," she muttered, knowing full well that Eric had triggered her, just as Andrew had by insisting on that awful dinner.

"A change. That's what you said earlier. By the way, your boy Eric talks like he escaped a damn carnival."

"There's that crossing guard again. And he doesn't talk like that."

"Now you're defending him?"

Sierra let out something like a growl.

Andrew exhaled. "How many times we gotta go through this?" he asked, frustration rising in his voice. "We worked so hard to get you past it, you know?"

"It?" She glared at him, breathing harder.

Andrew groaned. "You need to read what's in those envelopes in that box, Sierra. I learned to stop asking what happened to you as a child, but the answers you need might be in there."

"Look at me," she said.

Andrew did.

"Shut up about the box, Andrew."

The rest of the drive was silent. Later they watched an approaching storm from the fireplace on the back patio, a united effort to dissolve the tension. Lightning flickered high above the heavy flakes falling over the Washington suburbs. Sierra warmed one hand near the gas-fueled fire as she cradled a mug of hot chocolate in the other.

"You can have another drink, Andrew. Don't make it a thing."

"I always wonder if I'll be the cause of a relapse."

"If I was going to relapse, I would have done it a long time ago. I turned that corner when I found out I was pregnant. I'd never do that to Benny, and I'd never do that to you. So, please."

Andrew returned a few minutes later with a soft gray throw blanket, a bottle of whiskey, and a glass. He put the blanket over Sierra's shoulders, then poured a finger of the amber bourbon into it and downed the shot before immediately pouring another.

"Thank you for the blanket," she said.

"Welcome. I've never seen lightning in a snowstorm."

"It's called thundersnow. I saw it once as a girl in Colorado," Sierra said. "Mama was so excited."

"Can I ask you a question?"

"Sure."

"Will you tell me one memory of your mom?"

"Andrew . . ."

"Just one."

Sierra leaned her head back and watched the lightning illuminate the snowfall. Her mind wandered through a foggy hall of shelves containing colors and feelings. She'd settle on one, fight it, then move to another, fuzzy though they were. Then . . . a feeling and a color she could stomach. One that wouldn't lead to Andrew's further exploration. She felt the tug of a smile against her lips.

"One Saturday she dragged my sister and my brother and me out to some town—I don't remember the name. It was the summer after my real dad died, I think. Everything was green. There was a protest that day against a power company. She packed us a lunch. Paper bags, everything wrapped in cloth, no plastic." Sierra took a deep breath. Felt the heat of her mug in her hand. Appreciated Andrew giving her the space.

"We were just kids. We had no idea what we were yelling, but we raised our fists and chanted along with Mama. I felt so big, you know? Then she took us to the park. We ate our turkey sandwiches and pickle spears and fruit. I remember how cool the grass was, even under the sun. I remember Mama's laugh. Her hugs. Her smell. She pointed at the mountains in the distance and said, 'It'll be up to all of you to protect them.'"

"Sounds like a great day," Andrew said.

Sierra's voice grew thick. "Mama refused to use paper towels or disposable diapers. She drove across state lines to picket against builders and oil companies and the government. She could lie on the cool grass of a summer alpine meadow and fall asleep like she was in a four-poster bed. She fought for pine trees and rainbow trout. And we were always broke. Always hungry. Then she married him."

"Who?"

She wiped her eye and shook her head at Andrew. "Say what you want to say."

Andrew sighed. "I'm glad we went to dinner. It helped to meet the guy. But Eric—he's an ex. It needs to end there."

Sierra took in the falling snow and heard the faint rumble of thunder.

———

Goodnight stood outside in front of FBI Assistant Director Hayes from the bureau's Counterterrorism Division. Hayes had intense gray eyes, a narrow nose, and a strong jawline. He lit a cigarette. In the lighter's glow, the man's face was tight, his jaw clenched.

"What I'm about to tell you is classified. Tired cliché, but true. There's no press allowed in the dam area right now, and part of the president's order was for the entire area to be a no-fly zone. We're not even letting private citizens on the lake hang out or fish within five hundred yards of the bomb barrier."

"That's a good start," Goodnight said.

Hayes sucked on his cigarette, the smoke from his mouth whipping away in the wind. Under the waning gibbous moon, Goodnight saw a swollen, ink-colored mass, its tentacles reaching into side canyons and ending at the dam's abrupt stop, silver moonlight reflecting down the center. The floating aluminum bomb barrier etched a thin perpendicular line from one side of the lake to the other.

Hayes continued. "Whether you believe in climate change or any of that stuff I don't pretend to understand, we've had multiple straight years of solid winter snowpack in the Upper Colorado River Basin. More damn snow than Christmas."

Hayes took a final drag and dropped and covered the smoldering cigarette butt with his shoe. Goodnight noticed Hayes didn't pick it back up. The wind blew it away before Goodnight could do it for him.

"The lake is almost sloshing over the top like when they put plywood up there decades ago. Tomorrow the engineers are going to open the other spillway. Another fifteen thousand cubic feet per second added to the river flow."

Goodnight whistled.

"More water means a greater threat level. More folks in and out. More tests, more experts. And we still have no idea who hit us."

"A bunch of amateur protestors with more balls and guns than experience," Goodnight said sarcastically.

"That's what someone wanted us to think, and that's what we're telling the American public. But the intelligence community is looking at Revelation Six. Ever heard of them?"

"Nope."

"They're an international non-government organization. They do all sorts of humanitarian good. Been around for ages. But for years Washington has suspected Revelation Six could be conducting deep state operations around the globe."

"Like what?"

"Like orchestrating major world events to control sovereign nations. You've heard all those wackos talk about how some secret organization controls the world, uses everyone else for their own good? Illuminati?"

"Yep."

"The theory is like that, but reversed. It's for the greater good. Our intelligence community has worked on it for a long time but never come up with anything concrete. Those people are ghosts."

"Ghosts?" Goodnight chuckled. "Or something else the American public doesn't need to know about?"

Hayes glanced around, then leaned in and whispered, "Officials who have brought it up on recorded phone calls or in writing have been known to have fatal car accidents. Commit suicide in motel rooms. Disappear." He put a hand on Goodnight's shoulder. "You sure you want to hear this, Chief?"

Goodnight swallowed. "Shoot."

"Whoever took the dam had the opportunity to do whatever they wanted for twenty-four hours. But they didn't damage anything except spray paint their decoy anti-Ford graffiti. They left nothing but dead bodies. Someone wanted no witnesses. My theory? They're coming back."

"Why?"

"That I don't know."

"Why not beef up security with more than just my thirty-six people? Bring the Army down here now?" Goodnight asked, shaking his head. "And where the hell are the Joint Terrorism Task Forces on this? Everyone is either FBI or SOCOM."

"The president doesn't want photos of a major military presence all over the internet and cable news. As far as JTTF, let's just say they're fighting a very public battle over Freedom of Information Act requests right now." Hayes gave Goodnight a knowing stare.

"Oh," Goodnight. "So it's like that? Shit."

Hayes raised an eyebrow. "It's like that. If anything goes down, it's you and your boys for at least the first half hour, Fred."

Goodnight scratched his head, reeling. "You think they're gonna try to destroy it?"

"No. They'd lose all their leverage. I think they want to hold the resource itself hostage from the United States. But if they did somehow destroy it"—Hayes gave Goodnight a dark look—"that would be a massive disaster. Massive."

The men stared out at the lake.

"Why would they come again after they saw how easy it was for you all to take it back?" Goodnight asked.

"I think someone was gathering intel. If they come back, they'll know how to seal themselves up in the dam. That would make any attack to remove them impossible because it might kill more hostages or damage the integrity of the structure. Power and water for millions of people. That might seem like a ransom worth paying."

"Or a deal worth making," Goodnight said.

Hayes squared up to Goodnight. "No deals. You know that. If they come back, you have to win, Fred. Because if you don't, you're all going to die in the fight to take it, or the fight to get it back."

"You said they killed most of their own team. What did you mean by most?"

Hayes leaned closer. "You never heard this from me. Intelligence, surveillance, and reconnaissance." He pointed up into the sky. "They picked up three squirters during the HRT and SOCOM assault this morning. The chase team found one of them shot dead in a motel and another dead execution-style just off the highway. They tracked the third to Phoenix, but they lost him."

Hayes fumbled with and lit another cigarette. Inhaled when the tip turned cherry red and blew out the smoke.

"This dude ghosted some very high-level contractors and special operators. No one knows who he was, who he worked for, or where he went. Watch your six."

After Hayes took his leave, Goodnight walked to the downriver side of the dam. There was so much going on. So much to consider. He looked down the dark canyon and thought of Judy downstream under the same moon. The water connected them, in a way. That gave him some peace.

Chapter 5

Arizona

THE STATE-OF-THE-ART BLACK PRIVATE JET GLEAMED IN the bright morning sun. A flight attendant adorned the bottom of the stairs and another decorated the top, both dressed in sleek black thigh-high skirts, black stiletto heels, white button-front blouses, and little black ties. Both stunners. The platinum blonde was unmistakable. Pool Bimbo. Sierra assumed the brunette flight attendant was the other woman from the pool.

"Wow. He has no shame. I swear I'll never understand this old man, Andrew."

"What?"

"Nothing."

A cheery young man in a snappy pilot's uniform appeared from nowhere and whisked her bags to the aircraft. A black luxury limousine rolled up and Wade popped out, not waiting for Victor to open his door. He greeted Sierra and Andrew. "Ready to knock 'em dead?" he asked Sierra, fixing his scarf and donning his old-school fedora. She gave him the obligatory smile and nod she'd perfected over the last year.

"How do you do, Anton? Been quite some time. Corporate counsel spring retreat, correct?" Wade asked.

Andrew shook his outstretched hand. "Yes, sir. And it's Andrew. Nice to see you again, Mr. Ford."

"Apologies, Andy," Wade said, returning a vigorous shake. He marched to the jet, Victor trotting behind in his awkward gait.

Andrew turned to Sierra, his brow raised. She giggled.

"Be good to Scarlett. She's pissed she wasn't included in this one," Sierra said. "Give Benny extra love. I don't want him worrying anymore." Benny had grown accustomed to Sierra being gone more, but this time he'd cried real tears.

"Don't go, Mama," he'd whimpered, standing in the doorway in his baggy blue pajamas.

"I'm sorry, baby, I have to." The guilt made her tear up too. "You'll have fun with Daddy and Aunt Scarlett."

Scarlett had just arrived, still half asleep with coffee in hand and a purple beanie covering her red locks. "You bet—so much freaking fun," she mumbled. Sierra shot her a scowl. Scarlett was still peeved that Sierra wouldn't share the details about dinner with Eric on the phone earlier.

"Are you going to that dam?" Benny asked. "Where the bad men hurt those people?" Sierra and Andrew exchanged knowing glances.

She cradled her son's moon-shaped face in her hands. "No. I don't have to go there. It's all safe now. They got the bad men," she said, pulling him close. She whispered in his ear, "You are my hope, Benny. I will do anything for you."

He let out a sob. "I know, Ma—" His tears cut off his words. Sierra squeezed him tight. Soothed him. Focused on his heart beating against hers.

"It's all good, Ben," Andrew said. "There's no bad guys where Mama's going. Give her a kiss." Benny's puffy little lips had caressed Sierra's cheek. She missed him already.

"Enjoy that warm weather," Andrew said, shivering. When she reached the staircase, the brunette flight attendant welcomed her and told her to watch her step. Sierra turned to wave at Andrew one more time. His smile disintegrated.

A voice behind her. "Time to go, ladies. Boss is ready to be wheels up."

Sierra knew the voice but for a moment couldn't place it. Then her worlds collided. She turned in horror to find Eric in his white pilot's shirt and black pants.

"No worries, Andy, I'll bring her home safe," Eric shouted across the tarmac, waving big at Andrew. He smiled at Sierra and disappeared into the fuselage.

Andrew's face gave her the impression that he was about to go full caveman for the first time in his life. Storm the jet. Kill Eric. Blow up the plane. Drag Sierra home by her hair. Burn the damn house down. Instead, he restrained himself. The last thing she saw before she stumbled into the fuselage was him standing alone in the cold, shaking his head, his fists by his sides. He might have been crying.

———

Hobbes woke up handcuffed and groggy in a chair in his Washington hotel room.

The interrogator's stubble-bearded face was an inch away from Hobbes's. Just like the first time, he wore all black. Slicked-back dark hair. A voice rich and full of power. Another male voice was singing opera over a symphony from a stereo the interrogator had put next to the TV.

Hobbes squirmed in pain, his hands bound behind his back. "What?" Then he realized what he was in for. His stomach dropped. "Aw, not again, man. You Second Seal pukes told me all this weeks ago. Everything's set up. Please don't do this again."

"So you do remember me? Ooh, baby. Time to go to work, 451588." He pronounced it four-fifty-one, five-eighty-eight. "You want out? You play her little game, but you bring the documents back to us, right?"

"I got it, man. Please, don't do this."

"Ooh, baby, baby. This is the beginning of the new campaign, 451588. A next-level op, and you have the privilege of being the first," the interrogator shouted, dancing around.

He went quiet and waved his hand along with the opera music, eyes shut, smiling. He sneered at Hobbes.

"Puccini. Can't go wrong." He leaned in again. "Folks upstairs thought you could use a reminder. 009853 has been the Rev Six North American high office director for a long, long time. She's got friends in Washington, friends in every Rev Six high office in every major country."

"Jesus, man, I got it!" Hobbes screamed as he slammed both feet on the floor.

The interrogator whispered, "But she made us all look bad. Broke the rules, 451588. You made us look bad. We can't move on our own director here in North America without an international proceeding. Without that evidence, Rev Six will put us all on the chopping block."

He jumped up and shouted, "Ooh, baby. They won't let me hit you in the face. Say you gotta keep up appearances." He smiled. "But nobody ever pays much attention to ears."

The interrogator grabbed the lobe of Hobbes's right ear and twisted it until it felt as if it was ripping. Simultaneously, he drove a wet fingertip into Hobbes's left ear. Hobbes's protest morphed into a scream at the intense pressure and blinding pain shooting through his head. It felt as though the fingertip was in the middle of his head, worming, snaking. He screamed until he was hoarse.

Someone else entered the room.

The interrogator stood behind Hobbes with his hands on his shoulders. Squeezing. Relaxing. Squeezing. Breathing. Hobbes smelled dried spit on the man's finger. His ears throbbed with each heartbeat.

A small fastidious-looking man sat across from Hobbes in another chair wearing a simple black-and-white suit.

Hobbes moaned. "Who the hell are you? I know my objective."

The man's eyes were as calculating and cold as those of a circling shark. "I'm a director. And you only know part of your objective. This operation runs deep, as you now well understand from the packages you delivered for us yesterday. But we still don't trust—"

"I still don't know the plan for the packages. Shouldn't I know that by now?" Hobbes asked, grimacing and having a hard time hearing.

Shark Eyes reacted as if he smelled something putrid. He paused for a long time. He looked at the floor, then around the hotel room, then at the interrogator.

Wet finger. Twisted earlobe. That intense pressure, that shooting, shocking pain. More screams. A few minutes later, Hobbes had settled down.

The director continued. "009853 thought she could make deals for her own gain under our nose. She thought she could lie to America. Lie to the world. Lie to Revelation Six. The murders at the dam were . . . unauthorized. 009853 needs redirection. The United States needs redirection. You will execute Operation Cygnus. You will deliver . . . redirection."

"Told you, 451588," said the interrogator from behind him, squeezing Hobbes's shoulders tight. "Next-level op."

"Are you lying to us, too, 451588? Or will you accomplish your mission?" asked the director. "Operation Cygnus is your lifeline. And hers." He dropped a color photo of Amelia walking alone down the street, oblivious to Second Seal surveillance, into Hobbes's lap. The director's bland expression didn't change at all when Hobbes's face broke up. The photo was taken the day they'd met for coffee—Amelia was dressed in the same clothes she wore that day.

There it was. Suspecting that they'd use her to control him didn't make it any less shocking to find out they were.

"Understand, 451588? No one ever leaves Rev Six alive. We're making you a deal."

"Fuck you," Hobbes snapped. His head rocked from a hard slap to one ear, then another twist of the other. He screamed again.

They gave him more orders. The kind no one, not even the cruelest mercenary, ever wanted. The interrogator uncuffed him, handed him something in a box, and they left. He sat on the couch with his ears throbbing and swigged cheap whiskey from the bottle, zoning out to some adult-themed cartoon on mute, Amelia's photo in his hand.

———

Sierra sat in the rear of the plane as panic, a feeling like fizzy champagne bubbles, rose in her chest. Her eyes were open, but nothing registered. Not only was he back, but Eric was also taking her away. Sierra had been too busy paying attention to his mouth at dinner to comprehend what he'd said: Glorified air taxi. Aircraft's state of the art. He takes care of his people.

His lazy drawl filled the plane.

"Good morning, Mr. Ford, ladies and gentlemen. This is Captain Eric Samuels, along with First Officer Mike Richards. This is a nonstop flight from Washington, DC, to Phoenix. Our cruising altitude will be forty-one thousand feet, at a speed of approximately five hundred knots. The weather in Phoenix is a sunny seventy degrees. As we prepare for departure, please make sure your seat belt is buckled and your favorite drink is full."

Sierra's phone vibrated. Three unread text messages from Andrew.

"Did you decide on a drink, ma'am?" asked Pool Bimbo.

Sierra sized her up. Yes, definitely her. Same platinum blonde hair, same gorgeous face. Sierra had to assume the same great boobs were filling out her uniform.

"Water, please," Sierra said.

Pool Bimbo brought the water, then disappeared.

She wanted to go full cavewoman and storm the cabin and grab Eric's throat. There was no way this was coincidence.

The nimble aircraft screamed down the runway and up into the blue at a surprising speed, and soon Eric interrupted the vanilla-flavored soft rock. "Ladies and gentlemen, we've reached our cruising altitude and speed. You are free to move about the cabin. Enjoy your flight."

Pool Bimbo resumed moving around. Wade said to her, "Let's put on something a little more fun, shall we, sugar?"

She turned and flashed a dazzling smile. "What would you like to hear, Mr. Ford?"

"Whatever you like," Wade said, leafing through a magazine. "Thank you, sugar." His head tracked Pool Bimbo's every move. After changing the music, she returned and refilled Sierra's water glass.

"You let him call you sugar? A little demeaning, huh?" Sierra whispered.

"It's our joke. My real name is Candi," Pool Bimbo whispered back.

Sierra covered her mouth. "I'm sorry."

"No worries, darlin'. Need anything else? Wi-Fi password is jdrock1916. All lowercase. Those earrings are gorgeous, by the way. Vintage?"

"They were my mama's," Sierra said, touching the right earring.

"Aww," Candi cooed.

Sierra noticed how good Candi smelled, how her uniform was tailored and creased and pressed around her curves, how immaculate her hair and makeup were. There was a strength in her demeanor and voice. Sierra had been wrong about her; Candi was working her gifts with a billionaire and doing a damn good job of it. "The pilot, Eric Samuels. Know him?" Sierra asked.

Candi shot her a furtive glance. "Maybe."

Sierra's jaw dropped. "Well . . . ummm . . . can you please tell him I need to speak with him?"

Candi's eyes flashed. "Scandalous. I'll see what I can do. No promises." She nodded her head toward Victor.

Sierra realized that her mouth was still hanging open. Eric might be double-dipping with the same flight attendant as Wade. And Eric was her . . . coworker. No, it was worse. She was jealous that Candi might be getting Eric's attention. She watched white puffs of cloud pass under the wing and decided to read Andrew's texts. She entered the Wi-Fi password and waited for them to load.

Did you know Eric worked for Ford?

Was this planned?

How long you been talking to this POS behind my back?

She slid the phone into her purse and stared at it, an old familiar weight on her chest.

Candi came from the cockpit and whispered with Victor. He smiled at Sierra as Candi walked back toward her.

"When you see the first officer come out, go in. My colleague will hold the door for you. Victor's allowing you five minutes. He said don't touch anything," Candi said. "That includes Captain Samuels." She winked.

Sierra scoffed.

A minute later the young first officer exited the cockpit. The brunette flight attendant, herself worthy of a Miss Universe slot, held the door. Eric slumped in the pilot's seat like a tired little boy who'd been playing outside all day. Sierra made her way into the copilot's chair behind a bank of colorful computer screens. His eyes were closed behind his sunglasses.

"Eric," she said, sitting forward on the edge of the seat. He didn't respond. She threw up her hands. "Congratulations, Andrew's convinced we're screwing."

He startled and removed his sunglasses. "Was I sleeping again?"

"Imagine that—all these years and that joke still isn't funny," she said, punching him in the arm. "How could you get all the way through dinner without telling me you worked for the same man as me?"

"Ouch," Eric said, rubbing the spot where she hit him.

"Shut up. Start talking."

He raised his eyebrows.

Sierra huffed. "Talk."

"We work for the same boss, Sierra. Big deal." Eric said.

"Honesty is a big issue for Andrew," she replied. "Me too."

"Honesty, huh? That's interesting, Sierra."

"What's that supposed to mean?"

Eric opened his mouth to answer, but stopped short. He sighed. "Forget it. You cheat on him?" he asked, checking his instruments.

"No, I did not cheat on him. I had . . . other issues."

A brief silence. "Ah. No drink last night. You're on the wagon."

"I prefer saying in recovery. Andrew watches out for me."

"Lucky you."

She looked out the window. "Last time I saw the air from this seat was Cabo," she said. "Does Candi sit up here now?"

He sat up and seemed alarmed, losing his calm. "What?"

Sierra realized she had tapped into something but felt it wasn't the right time to pursue it. "Nothing. That blonde flight attendant says she knows you."

"Knows me how?"

"Jesus, Eric. I don't know. Why are you so worried about it?"

His shoulders relaxed, but Sierra saw strain on his face. "I'm not," he said.

"What happened to your head?"

"What do you mean?"

She pointed at his hairline. "Your head, Eric. There's a fresh cut there."

He touched it. "Oh yeah. Slipped on the wet floor this morning. Caught the edge of the shower door. My fault. Should have put the little bathmat down."

"You feeling all right? We're not going to go down, are we?"

"Hope not."

Tufts of white sped toward them over a vast expanse of green and yellow patchwork below.

"Remember what we used to say to each other, Eric?"

He smiled. "Maybe."

"There's a reason I drank."

"You had a rough childhood."

"That's half of it."

"What's the other half?"

"You."

He grimaced. "Sorry I disappeared."

"Part of me wants to know why. Another part wants to erase you," Sierra said. They sat for a moment listening to the cockpit's soft noise.

"Then why'd you text me back yesterday?"

"I didn't. Andrew did that to find out who you were. How long have you known we both worked for Wade, Eric? How did I not know?"

"I can't leave Richards out there long. Victor will get upset," he said. "So will the Federal Aviation Administration. Not sure which one scares me more."

"You're really going to dodge my question?"

"We have the same boss. Sierra, he's a billionaire with a lot of employees. Call it a coincidence. What's that phrase? A God wink? Anyway, why does it matter?" Eric asked, shaking his head.

"Why people do what they do always matters," she said. "Like, why did you ghost me? Why did you choose not to tell me last night you were Wade's pilot? Why have I decided to quit the law after this trip?"

She gasped. "I can't believe I just said that."

"Whoops," Eric said, smiling at her. "You don't have to quit the law because of Wade Ford."

"I've wanted to tell Andrew that for almost a year. I almost did yesterday, but I chickened out."

"Uh-oh."

"Yeah. Uh-oh. Things at home haven't been great," said Sierra. "I was frustrated with my career. We were broke. Then Wade offered me this job. Fell from the sky. That made me feel wanted. I should have seen right through him, but I was impressed. Swanky high-rise office, sitting there in his expensive suit talking about putting my work in front of the Supreme Court, throwing money at me. I didn't tell Andrew I'd taken it until almost a month later."

Eric said nothing.

"I'm at this new job listening to Wade talk about paying for Congress and the president to pass his pet legislation for Canyon's Dream like he was making dinner plans, wondering how I'm going to tell my boyfriend I've sold my soul." She sighed. "Even with my share, I'm still a mess."

"You said why people do things matters. Money's why Wade is public enemy number one. Money's why I fly for him. Money's why you're on this plane."

"Is money also why you're an asshole?"

"I deserve that," he said.

Like a child, she touched the yoke in front of her.

"Remember when I was bussing tables at that diner? You were in your uniform and you kept checking me out. I was seventeen but I lied and said I was nineteen. You asked where I lived, remember? I blurted out that I lived at the jailhouse. That was so embarrassing."

Eric laughed. "I remember. Then I said I hope there's room for one more at that jailhouse, because you already have my heart in custody."

Sierra snorted, then made herself stop. "I'm not laughing at you or your terrible pickup line again. It wasn't funny then. You're still not funny."

"Okay, Sierra. I'm still not funny."

"You're not." She smirked at him, then took a breath. "The jailhouse. That's what we called it. All the motherless and fatherless girls who lived there. It really felt like a jail. But I ran from every foster home they put me in. All those people trying to play mom and dad were worse than the jailhouse. Eventually they stopped trying. I ran to books. Books were the only thing that kept me going until I was old enough to work. Until I met you."

"Sorry you grew up like that, Sierra."

"Everybody's always sorry," she muttered. "All you wanted was to go fast. All I wanted was to honor Mama's wishes. Remember?"

He tapped a screen and studied the gauges.

"I did go fast. Too fast in the wrong direction," he said, holding her gaze.

A knock on the door. Eric sat up and said, "Time's up. Give 'em hell tomorrow."

She shrugged. "I'll probably lock myself in my hotel room."

"What? You still get those jitters after everything? I've always wondered, Sierra. Why law school? After everything that happened?"

"I don't know. All the tuition was free because I was a child of the system. Maybe I was intrigued by it? I just decided to go. And then I was determined to finish."

"That's one theory, I suppose."

"The worst irony of it all is that I went to college and law school for free, but then I had a child with a guy who decided to go to medical school and bury us in debt."

"It'll pay off one day."

She focused on nothing but him for a moment. "You were the only one who believed me when I said I was going to be a lawyer. The only one who watched me graduate from law school."

Eric grabbed her hand and squeezed it.

"Don't go. Stay here with me forever," Sierra said.

"Forever doesn't pay the bills."

"That's not how the saying goes," she replied.

Eric leaned over and kissed her. Before Sierra could react, his tongue engaged hers in a brief dance. She grabbed a handful of his hair and kissed him back. The jet screamed high above the earth. Then she pulled away, touched her lips, and walked out. She fell into her seat. Touched her lips again.

Candi was at her side. "Enjoy yourself up there?"

Sierra failed to compose herself.

Candi touched her arm. "Careful with Eric. He doesn't call back."

Sierra bemoaned what she had in common with Candi with the perfect boobs. She pulled her phone out of her purse.

Another text from Andrew:

Gonna ignore me?

She tapped her response.

Composed. Revised. Composed more, revised again, sent. *Andrew, I'm sorry. I had no idea Eric worked for Wade. I can't imagine how this makes you feel. I'll call you when I get settled into my room.*

———

Hobbes opened a large black waterproof utility case. He pulled out the suppressed desert-colored special operations forces combat assault rifle—SCAR—chambered in 7.62 x 51mm and worked the action, inspecting the ambidextrous weapon. He put on earmuffs as if his head might burst and winced at the lingering pain. He grabbed one of several loaded mags, inserted it, charged the bolt. He pulverized a barrel cactus, emptying the entire twenty-round magazine. The gunfire pummeled his tender ears before fading into the desert air.

"That'll work," he said, grimacing as he inspected the smoking SCAR.

He removed the mag and set the gun down. Another Glock 19, along with a smaller frame Glock 26, both chambered in 9mm Luger, both with threaded barrel and accompanying suppressors, were in the case with plenty of interchangeable mags and ammo. He took turns terrorizing the destroyed leaning cactus with a full mag through each pistol.

In a separate case was an M24 rifle, also ambidextrous, with H-S Precision stock and Zeiss glass as he'd requested, chambered in .300 Win Mag. Considering he had the SCAR, he'd debated whether to bother with the M24 for this op but requisitioned it anyway. There was an old windsock pole with an illegible, rusty metal sign attached. He put three rounds through it with the M24.

"Not your best, Snake Eater, but close enough."

He inventoried the rest of the gear in the trunk of the matte gray sports car. He messed with the desert-toned plate carrier that held several gear and magazine pouches. Looked over an assortment of survival gear. Some C-4 and detonators. Gadgets, including a lock-picking kit. A medical kit and syringes full of tranquilizers and antibiotics. A combat application tourniquet. He stared at it a moment; after what had happened to Johnson, he hadn't gone on any ops for Rev Six without a CAT. He pushed the memory away.

"If all goes well, I'll only need the Glocks and the lock-picking set. And this damn thing is too flashy," he said, looking at the car.

Senator Pace's goons didn't understand staying invisible. He'd have to ditch the new sports car and find something else quick because the computer inside could be hacked or tracked. It was also clear from the packing job that they'd used Rev Six resources to outfit his assignment. "How ironic," he said.

The dull and non-conversational Rev Six pilot from Washington hadn't reacted when Hobbes had jerked awake on the plane, shouting.

It was the nightmare about Johnson and the old lady again, the one the VA shrink had tried to help him forget, the one he would never forget, no matter how much therapy, no matter how many pills.

He'd slept for most of Sunday in Washington and nearly the whole flight too, but he was still hungover. Two back-to-back flights across the country in less than twenty-four hours used to be all in a day's work. These days, he felt the weight of gravity increasing. Plenty of sleep, lots of naps, constant training, detailed planning. Discipline made the difference when it came to functioning as a special operator.

"Who are you kidding? You're not a special operator anymore. You're a mercenary," he said.

A rusty door squeaked open and closed on the collapsing shell of a crumbling wooden building. A shattered, dusty window gaped at him below a sign that stated OFFICE in fading black block letters. How many deserted airstrips just like this?

"You're wasting time," he said.

He rifled through two travel duffels, each containing the items he'd requested in anticipation of any possible scenarios. In one were two sets of discreet street clothes and shoes, a jacket, socks, and underwear. In the other was tactical clothing including jogging pants, one set monochrome, the other tan and brown. There was a pair of brown trail runners next to the desert hybrid combat boots in the trunk. All one size bigger, as he'd requested.

He tossed in the plastic grocery bag he'd brought onto the plane. It held jeans, flip-flops, a black concert T-shirt, plain black ball cap, and other assorted items. His just-in-case bag.

It also included the powered-down two-way satellite radio from the box that the interrogator had shoved in Hobbes's face before he departed. It worked almost like a phone and allowed him to call anywhere. First the satellite transmitter his team leader had given him. Now this. Footprints. Evidence. Hobbes had called and coded in to ask about it.

"You're gonna need it," the interrogator had said.

"We never use sat radios in the field," he replied. "Anyone can find me with this."

"Director thought you'd need it for this op, 451588. Doesn't want a regular radio to tank the mission. You'll have to do a better job of not being found, won't you?" The interrogator's words and his chuckle still rumbled around in Hobbes's head.

A black Faraday bag containing four basic burner flip phones was stashed under the driver's seat, batteries removed. He kept them in the bag to later power on only as needed. GPS, smartphones, watches, artificial intelligence, machines tracking him, even thinking for him—Rev Six avoided them except as a last resort. Rev Six fieldwork was old-school maps and flip phones, and two-way radios. Except, of course, for the damned two-way satellite radio for this op.

There was an envelope full of cash in multiple denominations. It was probably marked, so he'd exchange it at a local bank in Phoenix. He also inspected the fake Arizona driver's license in the envelope bearing his photo under the name "Larry Woods."

"Larry Woods? I don't look anything like a Larry."

A credit card under the same name was clipped to the license. It was obviously Rev Six work, and although they'd never failed him before, using fakes was also a last resort.

There was one thing he hadn't found. He searched the car more and noticed the corner of a thin metal lockbox protruding from under the front passenger seat. He grabbed it and saw that the combination was set to his Rev Six ID number, 451588. It opened with a click, and he pulled the documents out. Flipped through them. Shook his head. Put them back and scrambled the combo.

"Of everything in this damn trunk, those papers are the most valuable?" Rev Six and Senator Pace and Hobbes had all been on the same team once. Or at least he had thought so.

He leaned on the car and watched the sun sink into the desert. The disease being back should have been enough, but it was Amelia's face that made him decide against having the cigarette he craved. There was a cracking sound, then a crash. The barrel cactus was dead.

Part of him wished she'd never reached out. Then again, it had been his decision to meet for coffee. She was beautiful. Articulate. He saw things in her he recognized. He could tell she'd been sizing him up, figuring him out. Whatever happened, he couldn't let Rev Six harm her.

He turned to settle into the sports car and realized he was about to sardine himself. He cursed, wondering what goddamn hobbit had driven the car there. He adjusted the seat. After he started the engine and connected his ancient non-networked MP3 player, he scrolled until he found a dark, tortured rock song. He cranked the volume and stomped on the gas, turning three full donuts with the music blaring, throwing a plume of dust, working the wheel and pedals as he'd been trained. He fishtailed once, then straightened out and headed toward civilization.

———

Sierra kicked off her heels and let her hair down, trying to forget the strained call with Andrew. More of his questions. More of her dodging the real answers. At least Benny's voice and laugh when she told him goodnight had made her smile. Imagining his sweet smell and warm jammies made her desperate for a hug. A few days more and she'd be able to hold him again.

She was in the process of unzipping her gray skirt when she heard a knock. Who was it? Victor? Wade? Housekeeping? No. She rezipped her skirt and smoothed it and straightened her light blue blouse and moved toward the door.

Hesitation slowed her steps. She could ignore it. She should ignore it. Halfway across the suite she stopped when another knock came. It was a soft rap, suggesting the person tapping their knuckles against the wood knew better.

She took a deep breath before the last few steps. Unlocked the bolt, but left the latch secured. When she opened the door, the little brass chain grew taut.

Eric's face. A welcome sight. An adrenaline pill. An old, begging addiction.

"Evening," he said.

"You shouldn't have kissed me."

"You kissed me back."

"How'd you get my room number?"

"I have my ways."

"We have a conversation to finish."

"Let's finish it."

She thought about her last text to Andrew. Eric's eyes simmered with something wild. Her breath was haggard. "Don't open the door for him," she whispered to herself.

Eric reached through the crack for her hand. She let him take it. He squeezed it. Seconds passed as she savored his firm touch. This was safe. No lines crossed.

"Open up. We can talk."

She had told herself not to open the door. Her own words.

Yet, in a fog, Sierra reached up and released the latch. He entered and shut the door behind him. They stood looking at each other, suddenly not touching. He had changed out of his uniform into his boots and blue jeans and a navy t-shirt that accentuated his athletic build.

"I want to know what else you have to say," Sierra said, backing away.

"You know I'm not here to talk." He moved toward her.

"What do you think is going to happen here, Eric?"

"What do you want to happen here, Sierra?"

Her lips parted. Her head felt like it might explode. She thought of Benny and Andrew. This was the moment where she could tell Eric to leave or let the past suck her back in. She thought about who she once was. Wondered who she was now.

He moved closer. She let him. Eric removed his shirt. His body was still strong, angular but not without the rounded shapes of his shoulders and chest descending into the faint lines of his abdominals. She smelled him. Felt a twinge.

He put his hand in the small of her back and pulled her to him. She grabbed his face.

Their tongues resumed the dance they had started in the plane.

———

The morning news showed a photo of Glen Canyon Dam with photos of the victims superimposed upon it. The little girl and her grandfather appeared on the screen, their images magnified. Her name was Emma Reynolds. Her brown hair was in pigtails, her smile was missing a front tooth, and her T-shirt said CERTIFIED TROUBLEMAKER.

Sierra bit her lip. She pictured Benny's face on that screen and groaned aloud. She dialed Andrew's cell and peeked out the curtain. No protesters or news vans. Wade's tight-lipped entourage had at least managed to keep their hotel location a secret.

"Yeah," Andrew answered.

"Hmm. Good morning to you too."

"Rough night. Benny wouldn't sleep, and I have to hurry."

"Is he okay?"

"We're all fine."

"Andrew." She hesitated. "Eric working for Wade—"

"—is something else you didn't know. Right. Reminds me of the time you didn't tell me you were working for Wade for several weeks. We're gonna talk about this, Sierra."

"What's all that noise?"

"Uhh . . . running some water, got the microwave on."

"Can I talk to Benny?"

"Hang on," Andrew said, grunting for some reason. Sierra heard him whispering to Benny.

"Hi, Mama."

She smiled. "Hi, Benny Boy. How are you? Daddy making you breakfast?"

There was a pause. Andrew whispered and then Benny came back. "Yeah, Mama. We gonna eat breakfast."

"Well, enjoy it, Benny Boy. I love you sooo much," she said. "You are my hope, Benny. I will do anything for you."

"I know, Mama. Love you," Benny said in a little voice that made Sierra homesick. Andrew came back on.

"Good luck today. Get some sleep." she said.

"Thank you. Got it. See you." He hung up.

Sierra sat on the bed wearing only panties and the earrings. She lay back and toyed with regret. Eric had wanted to stay the night, and he kept fishing for details about her life. He seemed shocked that she gave him none and had made him leave. The bedsheet was cool against her skin. She recalled other nights they had spent together years before. She had told him so much. Eric knew that the last time she had seen Mama was also the last day she'd ever been in a courtroom.

The frost on the window. The cold floor. Shouting. Screaming. A falling body. What did Mama know? Why did she do it?

She put two fingers against the pulse in her neck. Faster than it should be. Maybe the regret *was* there. Or maybe the burning was a rekindled flame? She needed to calm down. Focus. No alcohol. No drugs. Only one way. Even after last night? Who was she? Her hands moved. She found the spot, licked her lips, raised her hips. Ten minutes later she was curled up, shaking, sweat dampening her back. She wiped her tears. The burning question was still there.

Book Two

Consideration

Chapter 6

Vertigo

THE HOLLANDAISE SAUCE CONGEALED. ITS GLOSSY surface faded as the thick liquid cooled on the poached eggs and seared ham atop an English muffin. She couldn't eat the eggs Benedict. The only smell she could stomach was that of the robust coffee steaming into her nose. It was barely 8:00 a.m. and the bright Arizona sun had been up for hours.

"I need you in the courtroom," Bill said, dabbing his napkin at his mouth.

"I can't go in there," said Sierra.

"Stephanie is the only other woman on the team. Not to be sexist, but two women will soften the blow."

"Nice, Billy. You don't want to sound sexist, but you want to show the judge you're soft by bringing along two women?"

"I meant that a bunch of men going in there trying to violate a national park after a tragedy might go over better with more gender diversity." He sighed and folded his arms. "I sound like a jackass, don't I? Please don't call me Billy."

"At least you're finally telling it like it is."

"A lot of lawyers get nervous in court," Bill said. "Hell, I still do."

"You still think this is about me getting nervous?"

"All you have to do is sit there."

"I'm not going."

"You won't have to say a word."

"I had a bad experience in a courtroom as a child," Sierra blurted out.

A long pause. "I had no idea," Bill said. "Something to do with the whole orphan thing?"

She nodded, her lips sealed tight like a vault. "Yeah. Bad memories from my 'orphanage days.'" The last two words in air quotes.

"I guess that word is a bit out of date."

Sierra pushed her forehead against the heel of her hand. "Bill, I hate to let you down, but I hate the thought of Judge Sumner resetting even more. That means a ninety-day extension on my contract I'd like to avoid. How far is Vista from here?"

"Ninety minutes by car. You want that bonus and to get the hell outta Dodge, huh?"

"Wouldn't you? Why'd we stay in Phoenix?"

Bill's face went wooden. "Yeah . . . right. Wade Ford, billionaire, holing up in Vista, Arizona."

Sierra rolled her eyes. "All I have to do is sit there?"

He nodded. "I'll handle opening, evidence, and closing. Stephanie's got demonstratives." He coughed into his hand, then rubbed his chest behind his loud orange-and-blue-striped tie.

"Cold? Keep it over there, please," said Sierra.

"Flying gives me indigestion."

"See the news? Lots of protesters at the courthouse in Vista."

"Plenty of cops to make them behave," Bill said. He stifled a burp, signed for the meal, then put a piece of gum in his mouth. "See you out front in ten."

"I'm getting out of here before you start snapping that damn gum," Sierra said, then headed up to her room.

A silver limousine picked up the important players from the hotel. A black SUV brought along the supporting members. A Sandstone County sheriff's deputy detail of two motorcycle cops and two Arizona state police cruisers enveloped both vehicles on the sunny drive to Vista. Sierra was too nervous to enjoy the expansive desert views and tall saguaro cacti jutting up from the rock-crusted cliffs. She looked up from her notes to find Wade watching her from across the limousine's aisle.

"You thought my invitation was cryptic. And said that you had pepper spray in your purse." He nudged Bill, smiling. Bill met her eyes, chuckled, then went back to his own notes.

Sierra was loath to reminisce. "I wondered for a week if I was going to get propositioned or assaulted. I almost didn't come to that first meeting."

"I suppose the last year hasn't made you any more open to the idea of my project, eh? You wake up in a king-size bed with a view overlooking the canyon through giant windows. You're out there enjoying nature while a server brings you a hot latte to sip as you ride down the gondola to see the magnificent Ribbon Falls. You come back up for a massage in the spa followed by a five-course dinner. What's not to like, Sierra?"

Sierra forced a smile. He didn't get it. He never would.

"I really wondered if your name was a gimmick, you know."

"Everybody thinks that because of my profession."

"You must know by now that the whole meeting was carefully designed, of course."

"What?"

"The cryptic invitation. The whiskey. The fact that neither Bill nor I offered you a seat. Hitting you over the head with something I knew you'd find offensive."

Sierra squinted at him.

"I wanted to see if you'd shoot that glass of expensive bourbon, Sierra. If you had, someone else would be sitting in your seat right now." He settled himself and closed his eyes.

Bill offered her a consoling smile. She found no comfort in it.

———

The rush of a hundred thousand cubic feet of water per second coursing through and around both sides of the dam Monday morning was exciting, but if Goodnight was being honest, it gave him anxiety. The Lower Colorado River was at its highest flood stage in years.

He watched the security crew do their classroom training in a conference room next to the command post in the visitors' center, including crash courses on eco-terrorists, dam-specific defensive combat training, and the basic functions of the dam and its engineering. Yesterday morning had started a bit rough—their first hiccup in operations—when he had Jones initiate a simple radio check.

"Let's see how they are on response time, Jones. Request a status update on all sectors," Goodnight had ordered.

"All units radio in for sector status," Jones said.

All but two voices affirmed their sectors were clear. A minute passed. Jones gave Goodnight a concerned look. "Sector Three, Sector Five, this is Deputy Chief Jones, sound off."

"Sector Three, clear," said a voice.

"Sector Five, what is your status?"

"Yeah. Clear," a second voice responded.

"Who's manning those sectors?" Goodnight asked.

Jones checked the monitor. "Let me see . . . Three is Jackson at Two-Mile Tunnel. Anderson has Five—he's in the power plant."

Goodnight frowned. Sergeant Daniel Anderson had come to SOCOM from Delta. Big beard, bigger chest and arms, big hammer tattoo on one arm, cold eyes. Goodnight had been in the service long enough to recognize a killer. You had to give killers some slack. They performed well when it mattered, so busting their balls over minutiae was counterproductive. But a simple missed radio check on the first shift? The other guy, Darell Jackson, was FBI Hostage Rescue Team. He seemed like a good enough guy, but Goodnight noticed he spoke to Anderson more than anyone else on the team. Goodnight pressed the talk button. "Ladies and gents, be quicker on the sector checks. This channel is subject to monitoring from the brass. Look and act sharp."

"You hear what I heard, Chief?"

"Yep. That's their one freebie."

"I meant the attitude."

"So did I," said Goodnight, watching the steam waft from his lidless Styrofoam cup like a meandering distant river on a cold winter day.

"If we need to pull the plug on anyone, I suggest we tell SOCOM sooner than later, sir. Before the operators get close."

Goodnight nodded.

"Lot of water coming out of the dam, isn't there?"

Goodnight gazed out the massive windows at the blue expanse of the lake. "There is, Jones. A lot of water."

———

The limo slowed. Sierra heard bodies shifting on the leather seats. "Good grief," Wade muttered.

Sierra sat up. A busy hive of protesters and several reporters covered the courthouse lawn and staircase. News vans. Bouncing posterboards on sticks. Sandwich boards bobbing, arms and legs and heads sticking out of them. Indigenous peoples in ceremonial dress chanting and dancing. Food trucks. Loud rock music. Bill had another coughing fit.

"You okay?" Sierra asked.

He smiled at her, red-faced. "Right as rain."

"Remain in the vehicle until the officers come," Victor said. "People here want to harm us." He drove into the barricaded lot. Cups and liquids and assorted objects flew from the crowd and struck the limo. The raucous protesters screamed insults and profanities. Sierra saw a sign that read FIRST MY UTERUS, NOW MY PARKS. Another stated HEY, FORD DEVELOPMENTS, DEVELOP A FUCKING CONSCIENCE.

Then a third. SIERRA JUSTICE: DEPUTY GENERAL WHORE.

Below the words was that same AI-generated photo of Sierra on her knees, Wade standing over her, hands on his hips, his head lolling back.

She clasped her hands in her lap. Thought of last night.

"I'm sorry, Sierra," said Wade, then changed the subject. "Why is America only capitalist for the poor? Once you achieve significant wealth, you're not allowed to keep going?"

Sierra opened her mouth, but Bill touched her arm.

Several SWAT team members approached with opaque plastic riot shields labeled Police. Under their protection the group exited the car in front of a roaring crowd and walked up the steps of the Sandstone County Courthouse, objects thumping off the shields. Bill stopped in front of Sierra, coughing.

"Keep it moving, sir," one of the SWAT officers shouted.

Bill clutched his chest and crumpled on the stairs. Sierra screamed.

"Victor," Wade hollered over the crowd noise and blaring rock music as he knelt over Bill.

"God, it hurts," Bill said, writhing next to the metal banister.

Victor squeezed Bill's hand. "Breathe, Bill. Breathe through it."

Two officers ripped open Bill's shirt, popping off white buttons. "It's so damn heavy," Bill cried through gritted teeth.

The crowd shouted awful things. A fast-food cup landed next to Bill's head, splashing thick light brown sludge across his face, which Victor wiped away with his bare hand. Sierra caught a whiff of the milkshake Bill was blinking away from his left eye.

Medics appeared and produced an automated external defibrillator as officers escorted Sierra and the rest of the team into the courthouse. The protesters cheered as if they'd won a great victory against worldwide evil. Through the courthouse window, Sierra watched the medics strap Bill, who'd been fitted with an oxygen mask, to the stretcher, load him into the ambulance, and disappear, sirens wailing into the muted throng. Wade and the rest of the legal team gathered around.

"He had milkshake in his eye," Sierra said.

"Awful shame," Wade murmured.

"Who's going to the hospital?" Stephanie asked.

"You are," Wade said without looking at the young lawyer.

"What?" Sierra snapped out of her trance. "Stephanie is the only other prepped litigator here. We have to announce not ready."

"Billy informed me that Stephanie was here to present photos. He said you were the brains behind our case, Sierra," Wade said.

"No, I can't. I-I . . . I haven't done any trial advocacy since law school," she stammered. Her face felt numb.

"Billy's briefcase is right there. Open it and begin reading. You have thirty minutes." With coffee breath, Wade whispered into her ear, "What is it about courtrooms, Sierra?"

"My contract is for out-of-court work only."

Wade's face reflected pity. She'd seen him use contrived sympathy as a tactic in business deals and hallway negotiations for a year. "Look around you. The federal legislation that put us here for Canyon's Dream? My progress that everybody hates? That came from a United States president and Congress that know me by my first name. How many days remain in our arrangement?"

"Three."

"Correct. Unless we're still involved in litigation. Then you'll be extended. But if you don't comply, I'll have no alternative but to consider you in breach. Less than complete performance. I'll have to take away your bonus."

"Complete performance doesn't mean you can override other provisions in the contract. I'm protected from litigating in a courtroom. You'd lose," she said.

The disappointment in Wade's eyes was part of his natural charm. "Sierra, the night I offered you this job, your looks alone were impressive. But then you showed me that what everyone said about you, that you were the best with constitutional issues, was true. Your research and arguments got us here. Beauty and a spectacular brain. Knowing what I know now, I'd have paid you double."

She raised an eyebrow.

He shrugged. "We had a deal for your bonus. The best chance you have is getting this thing done today. Besides, I could lose millions fighting you in court and absorb the impact quite comfortably. What can you afford to lose? Certainly not that bonus."

He nodded toward the protesters outside. "Look at them. Think about what some of them did to those poor hostages at Glen Canyon Dam. They hate you just as much as they hate me. More, perhaps. Better make this worth the risks."

———

Sierra vomited to the point of dry heaves. Her knees against the cold tile in the stall. That musty smell of an old bathroom. Even in her $800 taupe pantsuit, it still felt like her first night in the jailhouse after they took her from Mama. Hardened teenage girls glaring at her. Whispers and taunts in the dark. The first of several beatings. No one had checked on terrified twelve-year-old Sierra when she cried herself to sleep. The older girls had laughed.

The knock on the bathroom door broke her trance. Made her get up.

She ran through the procedure as she washed her hands. Introduce herself, her client. Address the court. Arguments. Objections. Presenting evidence. Bill had made them all complete pro hac vice forms for the Arizona state bar, but she knew nothing about Arizona procedure. Another dry heave hit her. She checked her hair. Opened her purse and touched up her makeup. Fake-smiled to make sure there wasn't any lipstick or wayward coffee grounds in her teeth. Damn crooked tooth.

She found Victor waiting outside the door. "You all right, Ms. Justice?"

"No. But I don't have a choice," she said. "This is so unfair."

"Fair isn't part of the equation. Forget fair. But you always have a choice." He opened the vestibule door but waited to open the court-room door when Sierra stopped and held her stomach.

"The first time I jumped out of an airplane, I shit my pants," Victor said.

"What? Gross."

"I know." Victor chuckled. "But I still had a choice. Refuse to jump and get kicked out of the Airborne, or jump. Know which one I picked?"

"You jumped."

"No. I fell. Como un estupido. Right out of the C-130. I had decided not to jump. Then the crap in my pants itched something terrible. I went to scratch it right when the plane lurched. I lost my balance and fell out. No one ever knew I meant to quit that day," Victor said. "You know what you need to do here, Ms. Justice?"

"Shit my pants?" Sierra quipped.

Victor grimaced and swore under his breath. "Aye Dios mio. Get in there and lose your balance a little. Live your life. Falling out of the plane was the greatest thing that ever happened to me. I became a man. Jumped out of planes for years."

Sierra pointed at his leg. "Your limp."

"Yes, ma'am."

"Okay, Victor. Let's go lose our balance."

"Just don't shit your pants," he whispered.

She stifled a nervous hoot. The door swung open.

The last time she had made this walk, she was twelve. In the silence of the high ceiling and tall white walls, her footfalls competed against the creak of her leather bag. The swinging waist-high door that separated the gallery from the courtroom well squeaked in undulating protest after she passed through it. A male paralegal stood and stopped it. Wade tapped his watch. Her body felt cold despite the sweat accumulating on her brow and in the small of her back. She sensed ten thousand faces looming from opposing counsel's table but dared not look.

The paralegals had arranged Bill's notes, the exhibit list, and the trial notebook in front of her. She had seen these things before, even prepared some of them, but using them in real time in a courtroom was a different story.

"All rise. The 362nd District Court of Sandstone County, Arizona, is now in session, the Honorable Gerald Sumner presiding. God Bless the United States, the State of Arizona, and this honorable court," the bailiff said. "Turn off all cell phones now."

Sierra stood so fast that her knee bumped the table. Its legs sounded like an obnoxious bulb horn on the finished wooden floor. Her face flushed.

Tall gray-haired Judge Sumner appeared in his black robe and examined the room as if he was some sort of demigod. "Please be seated," he said in a clear and poised voice.

The room echoed with the sounds of people situating themselves in chairs and turning off their phones. A cough. A cleared throat. A sickening bouquet of cologne, perfume, aftershave, mints, and bad breath.

Wade leaned over. "Stop shaking, Sierra."

Judge Sumner said, "The court calls the matter of the Peoples and Parks Coalition versus Ford Exploration and Developments, LLC, Wade Ford, et al. What say the parties? Ms. Justice? Is that your real name or some stunt?"

Sierra stood. Opened her mouth. Closed it. Cleared her throat. "No stunt, Your Honor. I became an attorney for other reasons."

"Terrific surname for an attorney," Judge Sumner said, shrugging. "Counselors, I'm leaning hard toward a reset. With the protest and the hostage tragedy, today feels . . . icky. Ms. Justice, you better have a convincing argument to change my mind."

Wade tapped her leg. Sierra knew that Sumner's feelings weren't based on ick as much as they were on negative press hurting his pending federal bench appointment. She glanced at Bill's notes.

"Your Honor," she said, her vision blurred as she blundered through the notebook, "Mr. Ford requests an in-chambers conference."

"For what?" asked the lead counsel for the Peoples and Parks Coalition. The dapper middle-aged man wearing a navy suit complete with white pocket square, stood and said, "Edwin Muse, lead counsel for Peoples and Parks." He buttoned his jacket.

Judge Sumner waited.

Bill had wanted the in-chambers conference to express condolences to the people of Arizona to curry favor with Sumner. Sierra knew it was a bad idea then. She remembered Wade's words from earlier. Her best chance, he had said. The bonus. Freedom.

"Ms. Justice, we had a preliminary hearing by Zoom last week—"

"Strike that, Your Honor," Sierra blurted out, interrupting Judge Sumner. She covered her mouth as if she had burped.

"What are you doing?" Wade whispered.

Sierra swatted the air next to her leg as she often did to Benny when he nagged her while she was talking to another adult.

Sumner's throat cleared. "Ms. Justice."

Her words came as if they were fed to her from somewhere else, bubbling up like water from a spring. "The protest and tragedy at the dam were very . . . er . . . unfortunate, Your Honor. But justice . . . uh . . . justice must carry on. When the Framers of the Constitution designed our judicial system, they did so after inciting a rebellion where they could have been shot or hanged for being traitors, for . . . treason. They meant for justice to prevail in all situations. In the same spirit, courts across the nation have carried on with hearings and trials throughout every major conflict, including mass loss of life, over the last two hundred-plus years."

She wondered whether she sounded like an idiot or a real lawyer.

"Although the dam protest and tragedy hit close to home for this court and the people of Arizona, it can't stop my client from having his scheduled day in court to get the final construction approvals for the Canyon's Dream resort and Ribbon Falls gondola system."

As her words echoed from the high ceilings, something stirred within her. For the first time as a lawyer, she had the attention of the person in the black robe. Years of reading the arguments of other lawyers had taught her more than she realized.

"Your Honor, Mr. Ford initially intended to call three witnesses in response to the Peoples and Parks Coalition requested conditions. In light of the tragedy this weekend, I propose—excuse me—the respondent proposes to proffer the main points of the testimony and stipulates to Items 1–22."

Judge Sumner cocked his head at Muse. "Any objection?"

Muse smirked. "No objection, Your Honor, subject to the right to cross. We'll stipulate. They were our requests to this legislation that Mr. Ford purchased and forced on American taxpayers," he said, glancing sideways at Sierra.

To her horror Wade responded directly to Muse.

"I didn't do anything that big pharmaceutical companies don't do every day in Washington. What do you think lobbying is, sir?"

"Mr. Muse," said Judge Sumner sternly, "I'll not have such sidebar comments in this court. I may have my own thoughts about hearing the federal government's problems in my courtroom, but the Supreme Court of the United States said I have to hear it, and I intend to follow the law." He pointed at Wade. "And you, Mr. Ford—don't speak unless either I or one of the attorneys ask you to speak. Understood?" Like an angry dog, he alternated between glaring at Muse and Wade, then offered a pleasant smile to Sierra.

"Compromise is always welcome in this court. Ms. Justice, proffer away," said Judge Sumner.

She considered Bill's words in the trial notebook. Took a breath. "May it please the court. Your Honor, the fate of Canyon's Dream, not to mention the pilot program enacted by Congress and signed into law by the president of the United States, lies in the hands of this honorable court."

Judge Sumner watched her with a calm intensity.

"As this honorable court knows, throughout the history of our nation, national park issues have been reserved to the federal courts. However, the Supreme Court of the United States made their landmark decision of overturning a reproductive rights case several years ago and started a trickle-down effect—"

"Yes, Ms. Justice," said Judge Sumner, "But I'm also aware that the Supreme Court made it clear that only reproductive rights cases were affected by that ruling."

"Correct, Your Honor. Nevertheless . . . er . . . under this states' rights attitude, the pilot-program legislation for Canyon's Dream and the Ribbon Falls gondola system was introduced in Congress. Due to the recession, Congress solicited research on whether the Department of the Interior could profit by putting an environmentally friendly luxury resort directly in a national park. As you pointed out, the federal legislation put all construction-based oversight and litigation in the hands of the state court in the largest county in which the national park sits."

"Pardon, Ms. Justice, but I'd just like to hear you say it. Why didn't Congress vote in a private inholding? Why all this new legislation and fuss in the courts?" asked Judge Sumner.

Wade squirmed in his seat a bit, cleared his throat.

Sierra swallowed. "Due to the size of the development, Judge Sumner."

With a grim smile, the old jurist nodded. "Because forty thousand pristine acres of Grand Canyon National Park, from the North Rim down to the Ribbon Falls area, had to be the guinea pig, huh? Lucky Arizona. Lucky me."

Sierra waited a beat, unsure how to respond.

"After . . . uh . . . the president signed the law into effect, Mr. Ford put in his bid to win the ten-year contract and was successful. In addition to countless special interests groups, the Indigenous peoples, other states, and governmental entities, Mr. Ford and his legal teams have fought the Property Clause of Article 4 of the Constitution and the Supremacy Clause of Article 6. He finally convinced the United States Supreme Court that an Arizona state court has a more penetrating, justiciable interest in the land, and also has an open door to a more educated presence on the ground—the people of Arizona."

Muse laughed. Judge Sumner appeared grim. Sierra felt the urge to pause again before continuing.

"Mr. Ford argues that the bill the president signed includes congressional research-based and expert-driven conditions and requirements. The legislation survived scrutiny from the Supreme Court of the United States without modification and—"

Muse stood and buttoned his coat again. "Your Honor, is she going to make her proffer or argue all day? If so, Peoples and Parks has their counterargument."

"Begin your proffer, Ms. Justice," Sumner said, writing something.

She delved into the first witness's proffer. She was shaky but delivered. When she was into her summation of the third and final witness's testimony, a young woman entered the courtroom and whispered to the bailiff, who then whispered to Judge Sumner.

He leaned back in his chair and sighed. "Counsel, please approach," he said.

Sierra and Muse did so in tandem. She concentrated so as not to trip in her heels. Up close Judge Sumner channeled a kind and thoughtful grandpa figure, something she had never known. An American flag pinned to his collar protruded from his robe. Silver cufflinks adorned his exposed white shirtsleeves.

He leaned forward and covered his microphone. "You're getting that conference after all, Ms. Justice," he whispered. "I'll need the attorneys and Mr. Ford to join me in chambers. Mr. Muse, designate one plaintiff to join us." He stood and disappeared behind the bench.

The spartan desk in Sumner's modest office held a laptop and a photo of the judge with a woman Sierra presumed was his wife. The judge's vanity wall boasted only his law license. The head of a large stuffed deer protruded from the opposite wall. A folded American flag and the Arizona state seal hung on another, the latter bearing two Latin words.

"Nice trip in, Mr. Ford?" Muse asked as they settled into wooden chairs.

"Perfect," Wade answered.

"Can't imagine what could go wrong on a brand-new private jet," Muse said, chuckling with his co-counsel and winking at Sierra.

"It could crash," Wade said without taking his focus off the Arizona state seal. "'Ditat deus,'" he read.

"I'm not well-versed in Latin," Muse said, obviously thrown off by Wade's nonchalance at the thought of aviation disasters. "Afraid I don't know what it means."

"God enriches," said Wade. "That's one way to look at it."

Judge Sumner entered wearing gray slacks, his white button-front shirt, and a blue tie. He sat and gave Sierra and Wade a somber nod. A long silence held the room. Sierra leaned forward in her chair. Judge Sumner spoke. "Your lead attorney, Mr. Clark, has passed away. The young lawyer you sent with him called from the hospital. She's pretty shaken up. You have my sincere condolences."

Sierra gasped. Wade sat up.

"Our condolences as well," Muse said.

"We'll provide you with an escort back to Phoenix. We'll also assist with arrangements across state lines," Judge Sumner said.

Sierra recalled poor Bill dying on the courthouse steps with milkshake in his eye. She thought about who would give the news to his parents. About how she'd been mean to him for snapping his gum. She sniffed and took two tissues from the box Judge Sumner handed her from his desk.

"I'll have my coordinator check the docket for a date to resume," he said, putting the tissue box back on his desk.

Wade turned his head toward the window. "It's quite a shame. Bill Clark was a Harvard graduate. Such a nice fellow. Good to his mother and father."

"I imagine this will be a big loss for his family, your company, and his community," Judge Sumner said.

Wade turned his head to Sumner. "Judge, I hate to be crass, and Bill was a dear friend, but he's . . . well, dead."

Judge Sumner gawked at him. He addressed Muse and his team. "Would you all please excuse us?"

Muse blinked. "You're going to meet with opposing counsel and her client without us?"

"Relax. I'm going to chat with Mr. Ford about compassion in times of grief." He gestured at the door. After Muse left with his co-counsel and designated client, Sumner and Wade stared at the closed door for a moment, then at each other.

Sierra grasped the arms of her chair. "What's going on?"

Judge Sumner pointed at her. "Is she privy?"

"She was just promoted to general counsel."

Sierra's stomach lurched.

"Sorry about your man, Wade," Judge Sumner said.

"Thank you, Gerry. However, this puts quite the damper on our plan."

A shock ran down Sierra's spine.

"And I'm sure your dearly departed friend would agree. Do you really think we could finish this case today? A little girl got killed, for God's sake, by bad actors protesting your Canyon's Dream case. I was up there wringing my hands."

"That whole thing out there was an act?" Sierra asked.

"No," Judge Sumner said, chortling. "Not all of it."

For a second Sierra forgot that Bill was dead. She stared open-mouthed at the judge.

Wade leaned forward. "Gerry, might you have any idea how much money and equipment and people I have sitting out there in the desert waiting for the word? I'll lose millions if you postpone Canyon's Dream. And months, maybe years of time."

"That's the thing about you, Wade. For all your fancy speech and clothes, you never could figure out the people part of business or politics, or anything, really. Some things are meant to stay wild."

"Please don't pretend you're a saint."

"Keep your voice down," Judge Sumner said irritably. "The media already blasted me for closing this proceeding. Half the people in Sandstone County, not to mention every state legislator and justice, hate me for hearing it at all. What if they found out that we proceeded after your lead attorney died? You don't think some investigative journalist would start digging?"

"They'd be hard-pressed to find anything on paper," Wade said.

"Wade, you could lose a billion dollars out there today and still sip whiskey with one of your trollops this evening."

Wade stood. "I'm not wealthy because I throw money away, sir." He pointed at Sierra. "She's a primary reason this plan came to fruition. I hired her. Paid for the legal brain that created the constitutional arguments to get us here. I spent the money. I delivered at the cost of some burned bridges. If I leave here without an order, perhaps I should make some calls to Washington and repair those bridges, eh, Gerry?"

The judge's face turned to red stone. There was a knock at the door.

"Come," Judge Sumner commanded. He leaned over the desk and grabbed Sierra's hand with both of his for Muse and his team to see. "Again, Ms. Justice, I'm sorry for your loss." He glowered at Wade. "I'll see you at the next hearing, Mr. Ford," he said, his words stabbing the air.

Red-faced himself, Wade took a deep breath and buttoned his jacket. When they stepped out into the main hall, he turned to Sierra.

"For all the good you did in the courtroom, you failed miserably in his office."

She took a menacing step toward him. "'Tell me how I can litigate a fight over a national park development in Sandstone County, Arizona.' One of the first things you ever said to me after you looked me up and down in your fancy clothes in your fancy office."

Wade stiffened. "Careful, Sierra."

She controlled her voice. "Is there anyone in the legal system, federal or state, you haven't bought or who isn't your friend? I've wondered for a year—why Grand Canyon? Why Sandstone County? You could have picked any national park. But you had a crony here in Arizona, huh? There's a ninety-day extension on my year, remember? We can get one of the other litigators up to speed and come back, but really, sounds like you've got it in the bag, don't you? You're not taking away my bonus."

She tried to calm herself. Wade remained silent.

"You chose me. There were better candidates. You never needed my brain. You needed another blonde bimbo to fill a seat. A mouthpiece in an office writing Bill's scripts." She stared at the floor. "Did the Supreme Court even care about my arguments?"

Wade softened. "Oh, Sierra. Whatever you think went on in there with Gerry, I promise you, I have no influence on the Supreme Court. You're no bimbo, Sierra Justice."

She glared at him and walked back into the courtroom. She had just told off Wade Ford when she had no real proof that he'd actually influenced Judge Sumner. Maybe they were just acquaintances.

The rowdy crowd had drawn more uniformed officers and SWAT team members in riot gear. They drove out in the limo, facing another hail of drinks and eggs and spit, plus a few rocks knocking against the riot shields this time. Victor asked Wade if he wanted to go to the hospital or the hotel first.

"I'm going to make arrangements to get Billy home to his parents, and then we'll have a meeting in my suite in Phoenix. I didn't make the trip out here for nothing."

———

Eric watched her buck and moan against him, her excitement growing in intensity. Although he admired the little connected triangles of her tan lines and her perfect mouth as she cried out, she wasn't Sierra. Her wavy platinum tresses swung above him, cascading down to pink nipples swaying on exquisite medium-sized breasts. Getting it up for her had been more of an effort than usual, so he was grateful when she yelled her crescendo in time with the rhythm of her hips, finally sending him over the edge. She lay on top of him for a moment before rolling over to grab her purse off the nightstand. Lit up a joint. Leaned over and kissed him. "This is a non-smoking room," he said.

She stared at him for a moment, then burst out laughing.

As good as she was, Candi hadn't been worth risking his job for. But this morning he had lay in bed thinking of his time with Sierra and what Hobbes wanted from him. Candi's text had at first irritated him, and he had known better than to answer her after last night with Sierra, but he figured giving her what she wanted would prevent another potential problem for him. Candi, being Candi, had of course helped him forget it all for a bit. He grabbed the remote and flipped channels while she smoked her joint.

It wasn't 1030 yet. He guessed they had until 1730 before everyone returned. How did Wade find out about them? The old buzzard was using him for this last trip without giving him any warning that he was letting him go.

"I like that show," Candi said. She inhaled deeply, sitting up against the headboard, her long legs folded.

"It's stupid. None of those people are in love," Eric said, staring at the twisty floral tattoo inked down the side of Candi's waist to the top of her right leg.

"What would you know about love?"

He thought of how disgusted Sierra would be if she knew he was in here with Candi. He was pondering how to get rid of her when Victor buzzed his cell. "Yeah, Vic?"

"We're headed back in a hurry. Boss wants you to charter a helicopter for the next three days."

"What?"

"Bill's dead. Heart attack."

Eric sat up and swung his naked legs off the side of the bed. "When?"

"About an hour ago."

"Damn." Eric stood to dress. "Why am I chartering a bird?"

"We're going to the jobsite."

"The jobsite? Who?"

"Wade, me, you, and Sierra."

"Why?"

"Publicity. I have to find a photographer willing to go down in the canyon tomorrow."

"This is nuts. I can understand you, but why me? And Sierra?"

"Que chingadera . . . We're veterans, Eric. Wade Ford is our CO now. We follow orders or we fall out," Victor said. "He wants the chopper at the hangar within the next few hours." Then his voice changed a bit. "And it's none of my business, Eric, but you might want to be more careful about your comings and goings. Now get it done." Victor hung up.

Eric hung up and stared at the wall. What the hell did he just say? Victor knew. Knew what? About Candi or . . . Sierra? Had to be Candi. That's how Wade found out. Which meant Victor was watching him. What else does Victor know?

He put his head in his hands. He had to put it out of his mind. He had work to do, and there was a lot more riding on it than a paycheck.

"What's wrong, baby?" Candi asked.

Eric groaned. She went away after some convincing and a deep kiss. He went with it but avoided eye contact. He watched her saunter toward the elevator and sighed.

Five minutes later he was at a red light belting out the lyrics to a classic country song when Hobbes opened the door and slid into the backseat.

"Whoa," Eric yelled, jumping. "You got any people skills at all, man? Don't you think it's time you take off the stupid mask in front of me?"

"Turn that shit down and drive around the block," Hobbes said. "Where's Ford going?"

"One of the lawyers died at the court—"

"I know. Get in the game, Samuels. Where?"

"The Grand Canyon. To the jobsite."

"The jobsite? Why?"

"I don't know, man. He wants to get some press, take a photo down there."

Hobbes growled. "How many of you?"

"Four. No, five. Wade, Victor, me, Sierra, and a photographer."

"When?"

"Man, figure it out yourself."

Hobbes grabbed Eric's neck in a vice grip. Eric grunted and swerved in his lane. "You really wanna do this with me, Samuels?"

Eric shook him off. "Fuck's sake," he shouted. "We leave this afternoon to be at a place called Ribbon Falls tomorrow afternoon for a photo op."

Hobbes leaned back. "It's miles down into the canyon to get there. No roads. A photo op?" He shook his head in the rearview mirror. "What were you listening to?"

"Country music. That a problem, Your Highness?"

Hobbes was quiet a moment, then dropped one of his flip phones into Eric's lap. "Call me with the details when you know them. Don't leave a message. After we talk, remove the battery, destroy that phone, and trash it in different places. Let me off here. You should listen to better music, Samuels. You can't sing either."

Eric stopped the car and Hobbes exited. He rubbed his neck. "Told you to call me Eric, bitch," he muttered, turning his music back up.

———

Wade ordered Sierra to send the legal team home on a commercial flight. Rich but not wasteful, he saw no point in feeding and lodging them anymore. The private jet and the supermodel flight attendants would remain in Phoenix. Sierra wondered what next lay in store. She sat with Eric, Wade, and Victor in Wade's elaborate penthouse suite. Wade held a crystal glass containing a sliver of scotch. Eric's eyes pleaded with her for some sort of acknowledgment. Sierra ignored him.

"The bird's ready when you are, Mr. Ford," Eric said.

"How long is the flight to the canyon?" Wade asked.

"An hour, maybe a shade over."

"The canyon?" Sierra asked, sitting up.

"And the flight time down into the canyon to the jobsite?"

Eric looked at Victor. Victor swallowed and said, "Mr. Ford, I learned from the NPS that helicopter flights into that part of the canyon are emergency only."

"Excuse me?"

"The canyon?" Sierra repeated.

"Only government agencies involved in search and rescues can fly into that part of the canyon," Victor said.

"What's happening in the canyon?" Sierra asked, holding her hand out.

"Did you tell them I have federal clearance to be on the North Rim with nearly a billion dollars' worth of men and materials and equipment?"

Victor nodded. "I did, sir."

"And?"

"They said you don't have a court order with clearance yet, Mr. Ford."

Wade raised his glass to throw it but instead grimaced and set it down hard on the end table, splashing scotch onto the floor.

He grimaced at it, then at his guests. "That's a hundred-dollar spill." No one reacted. He paced and cursed. "I need to place some calls. We will land by helicopter in the canyon tomorrow to take our photos at my jobsite."

Sierra stood with her hands on her hips and asked, "What the hell is going on in the canyon?"

"I'm afraid not, Mr. Ford," Eric said. "I made calls too. The Department of the Interior holds the cards on this one. I can't fly you down there. They could take my license—"

Wade held up his hand. He dialed a number and began griping at someone as he pounded his steps to the bedroom.

"Someone better answer me. What's this about the damn canyon?" Sierra snapped.

Victor put a light hand on her shoulder. "He's worried about the project. He wants his own press. Photos of you and him down at Ribbon Falls. A write-up about how environmentally friendly Canyon's Dream will be above the falls, and with the gondola system down below."

Sierra glared at Victor, then at Eric. She opened her mouth to speak, but the anger was too thick. They waited. Eric continued staring at Sierra. She fumed with her arms crossed, refusing to return his gaze. Victor stood silent. Wade returned, grumbling.

"I guess the president wasn't available?" Eric asked.

Wade glared at him for a long time before looking at Victor. "What do you suppose we do, Vic? I'm not exactly up for a thirty-mile hike."

"Mules, sir."

"Mules? Do you mean something that defecates and walks on four hooves, or an all-terrain vehicle with tires?"

"The defecating kind, sir. With the hooves." Victor paused, scrutinizing Wade before he continued. "A mule train leaves every morning. I've already made contact with the wrangler. He named his price to take us down and avoid the crowds. I wired him the funds. We're set."

Wade sat down hard on the couch. Chuckled without humor and shook his head. "Mules? That's our only option?"

"Yes, sir. He'll only take us as far as a place called Phantom Ranch. That's still almost eight miles from the site, but that part of the walk is mostly flat. After the photos there's a campground about a mile and a half from the falls where we can sleep, and then it's a steep hike up to the North Rim the next day to get to the helipad with the chopper."

Eric nodded. "The service will fly the Da Vinci to the North Rim helipad and have it waiting for us," he added. "I set that up too."

"I've not camped since I was in the scouts," Wade said. "It is what it is. Vic, get sizes from these two. You know mine. Have clothes and hiking boots and any necessary gear in the helicopter by three p.m. Please find me a comfortable blow-up mattress I can sleep on. And get that photographer on the phone and squared away."

Sierra held up her hand like a fifth grader. "Mr. Ford, I'm not riding a horse or hiking down into the Grand Canyon."

Wade's hard face settled on hers. "You'll be riding a mule, not a horse. Your contract is now in a ninety-day extension. Complete performance means you ride the mule, make the hike, and smile for the damn photo." He stood and pulled up close to her ear and whispered, "Where would you go, Sierra? Your old friends won't hire you. You're stuck with me until this is done. Or at least another ninety days, perhaps. You won't see that bonus until then. And don't forget, you're still my attorney and I hold the privilege. You're also subject to our nondisclosure agreement. So if you think you'll be talking to anyone about me or Judge Sumner or your bonus, think again." He wheeled around and made for his bedroom.

She ignored Eric and Victor's confused faces, stormed from the penthouse, and took the elevator down to her room, stomping hard enough in her heels to punch holes in the plush carpet. When she pulled her key card from her purse, she saw a figure near her door. When he turned toward her, she gasped. She put a hand against the wall.

He wore a corny smile. "Surprise."

"What are you doing here, Andrew? Where's Benny?"

Andrew huffed. "With Scarlett. Don't waste time acknowledging the gesture, Sierra."

She closed the distance and hugged him. "I'm sorry—it's just that you're the last person I expected."

"That . . . doesn't make me feel any better."

She pulled back. "Is this really a surprise, or are you checking up on me?"

"Both."

She groaned. "I had no idea he was going to be flying that plane, Andrew." She was terrified that Eric might choose this moment to come rehash last night.

"Can we go in, or do we need to have this conversation in the hall? You left Benny with Scarlett? He's safe?" she asked as she waved her key card in front of the door lock.

"And sound."

Inside the room, she stopped. "Wait—your rotation. You missed the first day to come out here? How did you get here so fast? How could you possibly arrange flights and pack bags to be here already?"

"I wasn't totally honest with you this morning, Sierra. I booked flights yesterday. I managed to find one headed to Phoenix but had to go through Vegas first. Just got to Phoenix forty-five minutes ago. Took the airport shuttle here. Been a crazy morning. We aren't used to running through airports."

"I can't believe you found a flight. What about school, your rotation?"

"I'll get it figured out. This was—"

"Wait . . . You just said 'we.'" She leaned back. "You didn't. Did you?"

"Come with me."

They walked down the hall and Andrew pulled out a key card, which Sierra ripped from his hand and swiped. She threw open the door.

Benny jumped off the bed and ran to her. "Surprise, Mama!" he cried out.

Scarlett slid off the same bed and came to the door.

"Oh my God, Benny!" Sierra squealed. He jumped and she caught him in a hug, kissing his cheek, holding him tight.

"Surprise," Scarlett echoed, smiling as she held a scrunchy in her teeth and put up her hair.

Sierra finally put Benny down and hugged Scarlett.

"We all wanted to come," said Andrew. "Even if it was just for the night."

Sierra tousled Benny's hair and smiled at all of them.

"Caught someone dialing numbers again," Scarlett said. "He just had a man on the line speaking a foreign language. Sounded Asian."

"Benny, what is it with you?" Sierra asked.

He hid behind Scarlett and peeked around.

"We'll talk about this some more later, Little Mister," Sierra said, goosing him.

Benny giggled.

"So what happened in court this morning?" Scarlett asked.

Sierra was excited to share her experience in the courtroom, clouded though it was by Bill's death. She didn't mention anything about Wade and Judge Sumner other than the reset.

Andrew whistled.

Scarlett's face registered the shock of hearing about Bill's death and the delay. "That's a lot of damn news to absorb."

"Little ears, please."

"Sorry," Scarlett said. "I'm just a little blown away here."

"I haven't even had time to process it yet," said Sierra.

Andrew touched Sierra's shoulders. "I'm sorry about Bill. But I'm proud of you, girl. Really, I am. You finally got over that courtroom thing." He hugged her. "But another three months of this a-hole?"

"Looking like it."

"I'm sorry about Bill too," Scarlett said, pulling out her inhaler and taking a hit. She held it up with a frown. "This higher elevation is kicking my ass."

"Take it easy, then," Sierra said, touching Scarlett's shoulder. "I'm sorry as well. He was your friend too."

"I made it to sunny Arizona anyway," Scarlett said, pocketing her inhaler.

Sierra laughed.

"What?"

Sierra laughed harder. Scarlett and Andrew giggled nervously along with her, waiting for her to spill. Sierra finally calmed down. She sighed. "We're leaving soon to go to the Grand Canyon. And we're riding mules down into it."

CHAPTER 7

Shift Change

HOBBES PICKED UP ON THE SECOND RING. ERIC HATED THIS cloak-and-dagger crap—burner phones, the mask. Who was this guy? "La Placita Lodge, Grand Canyon Village, South Rim. Room 7. Seventeen hundred hours," Eric grumbled into the phone. He hung it up and crushed it under his boot. Stared at the pieces on the concrete hangar floor as if they were some sort of poison he couldn't touch. He eventually picked them up and threw them in the hangar trash can and walked out to the Da Vinci. He scanned for prying eyes. Looked for Victor. Didn't see him.

The weight hit him during preflight. It was true. Sierra had a kid. Andrew's kid. What the hell was last night, then? Why did she hide her son from him? He realized he'd been staring at the same sentence in the pilot's operating handbook for several minutes. He should probably have a copilot for this aircraft, but he was planning to go solo. Sometimes he hated his inclination to go his own way.

After he had inspected the helicopter, stowed the bags and gear, and boarded his passengers, they were cleared for takeoff. Eric turned and winked at Sierra through the narrow doorway. She smiled back, but it seemed strained.

"They all squared away on a car?" he asked.

"They'll be there a few hours after us," she said, shooting a sideways glance at Wade. He'd had the audacity to invite Andrew on the trip for his medical knowledge but refused him and Benny a flight, despite empty seats. Liability issues, he'd said. He made it worse when he insisted Sierra fly in the helicopter so they could discuss the legal implications of the reset hearing. The kid had stayed with Andrew and the cute redhead.

Eric looked at his boss, not missing Victor's hard face staring back at him next to Wade. "You ready, Mr. Ford?" Wade shot him a thumbs-up. Eric went to work on the Da Vinci's collective and cyclic pitch controls and pedals, and the helicopter rose from the tarmac in that magical feat of human aeronautics he had always loved.

———

Hobbes scowled as he surveilled Samuels's movements through binoculars at a hangar with a sign that read Luxury Helos of Phoenix in big blue block letters. He'd traded the sports car for a less conspicuous four-cylinder commuter car that had seen better days. When he moved everything over, he parked the sports car on a busy street, unlocked with the keys on the seat, hoping it would be stolen fast.

He had put great care into his plan to take care of business with Ford and the lawyer Monday night at the hotel in Phoenix. Rev Six had made it clear to him that he was to execute Senator Pace's plan in Arizona, her backyard. Now his Phoenix plans were scrapped, and against his training he had to make a new operation plan on short notice.

But there was a plus side. His primary target was a billionaire power player in a civilized world. To force Ford's cooperation in Senator Pace's objective, Hobbes had known that he needed to sweep the old man's legs out from under him. Perhaps this was how: Get Ford on the ground in his world, rather than do the deal in a swanky hotel.

"Old bastard just handed himself to us on a platter, didn't he?" Hobbes said.

Indeed, the billionaire had decided to put himself in the middle of nowhere with few witnesses. The question was whether the equipment and systems Hobbes already had in place for Rev Six's assignment would work at a longer range. His team had assured him they were solid. His anger subsided into acceptance.

"I guess I should be thanking you, Mr. Ford," Hobbes said, staring through the binos at Samuels moving around in the helicopter.

When he'd checked in with the Second Seal, Rev Six offered a chopper ride to the canyon. Hobbes declined. It would cause unnecessary attention, and the commuter would get him to the South Rim in plenty of time. He called Pieter in The Hague again, suffering through the Dutchman's enthusiastic and awkward attempts at being hip. Everything was set. He confirmed wiring instructions with the banks, pretending to be the real estate broker they'd come to know and love. There was nothing to do but drive.

He considered calling Amelia. No. Their mutual survival depended on his being a cold operator for at least another forty-eight hours, but every time he tried to forget the image of that little girl at the dam, he came up short. He needed to focus, finish the job, and get clear physically and mentally before he talked to Amelia again.

The helicopter rose and faded into the distance. He made his way to the interstate in the commuter car. For a few hours he put himself on autopilot, pushed it all away. He didn't think of Rev Six's threat to Amelia. He didn't think of the old woman in the black hijab. And the lump in his neck didn't hurt.

———

"Mama wanted to bring us here," said Sierra. "She said it was impossible to describe. I understand now."

"Real," said Andrew, gazing out at the gaping canyon, his eyebrows raised.

Benny stood between them. "Mama, Daddy. Look how big," he said in awe, pointing and looking up at both of them.

"We see it, baby. Isn't it cool?" Sierra replied.

The canyon was miles across. She had read a sign that stated it was a mile deep. Expansive shadows moved across the rock pillars and slot canyons from clouds above, ships sailing across the sky, outrunning imaginary pursuers. Layers of the earth, stripped away over eons, revealed deep reds, flames of orange, and browns. Yellows of every shade. The brisk air fragrant of nature, space, and pine trees. Sierra's vision dazzled with colors and dizzying heights. Her stomach lurched when she peered over the edge from the safety behind the low rock wall, even more than when Eric had flown the helicopter through unrestricted airspace over a portion of the canyon on their way here.

The vertical face of the cliff in front of her was only yards from where small children ran and shouted and laughed at each other in front of the only restaurant. There was no ranger or other person policing how close people got to the edge. How many kids had fallen over the side? What a wild place.

She grabbed Benny and Andrew's hands. Benny looked up at her to speak, but she put her finger to her lips. She knelt and held him tight. They listened to the breeze whir through the scrubby pines alongside the canyon. A small bird flew up to the edge and lit upon a branch. It sat there a moment before hovering over the thousand-foot drop, as if taunting them, then flitted somewhere down below the rim.

"I wish I could do that!" Benny exclaimed.

"We all do, son," Andrew said.

Behind them stood Grand Canyon Village, consisting of a stretched-out line of rustic wood-beam-and-rock lodges, a towering hotel, and shops clustered on the canyon's South Rim. Sierra heard a loud whistle, like something from another century. Snaking behind the buildings lay the Grand Canyon Railway tracks, which held the thrumming silver Grand Canyon train. Passengers were boarding.

She hugged Andrew's arm. "Let's go get a table."

"What did you ever see in that guy?" he whispered.

Sierra fell taciturn. Andrew gave her a dismissive nod and moved with Benny to another vantage point. She stood alone. Scarlett rested back in her room. To her right Eric was on a call, standing in the sun's golden hour, his tanned face meeting his wild hair, his eyes hidden behind aviators.

The Eric conundrum. The dead, stupid weight of some clumsy beast lumbering behind on a leash, begging to be fed. So why did she keep feeding it? What did she see in him?

She turned. A tall man watched her from near the dark wood beams of the A-frame Grand Canyon ice cream shop. Something seemed off about him. Maybe it was the black medical mask; most people had stopped wearing them long ago. Perhaps it was the way he held Sierra's gaze before disappearing around the corner of the building like mist in a breeze. She puzzled over it for a moment, then blew it off and moved to rejoin Benny and Andrew for dinner.

———

At dusk Eric watched tourists walking along the rim's deadly edge, resting their asses on the rock wall, eating their ice cream, snapping their stupid selfies. Satisfied that Victor nor none of the rest of his group was close, he walked through a heavy wooden door into a lounge and sat at the bar.

"Gunner's Mate, neat," he said, and the young bartender poured two fingers of light gold whiskey into a glass and set it atop a white cocktail napkin in front of Eric. He quaffed it and savored the sweet fire that went from his tongue, down his throat, and into his stomach. Asked for another. When he ordered the fifth, Hobbes appeared wearing the medical mask, which set off his penetrating blue eyes.

"Come with me," he said.

They walked under high ceilings, past large bay windows, and over the cool Saltillo tile of the elegant Southwestern-themed lobby down to a wood-paneled, plush-carpeted hallway that expanded into a bright open room with magnificent vistas of the canyon. They sat in large leather chairs near a crackling fireplace. From above the mantel, President Theodore Roosevelt's black-and-white portrait sized them up, his stern face and his mustache conveying confidence and authority.

"Roosevelt had a meeting in this room a long time ago," Hobbes said.

Eric gave Hobbes a slow, silent, whiskey-warmed nod.

"'The Grand Canyon fills me with awe. It is beyond comparison—beyond description; absolutely unparalleled throughout the wide world . . . Let this great wonder of nature remain as it now is. Do nothing to mar its grandeur, sublimity and loveliness.' President Theodore Roosevelt," Hobbes recited.

"Real purdy," Eric said. "Guess that's why he made president. You actually memorized that?"

Hobbes gestured to the speech framed on the wall.

"There a point?" Eric asked.

"The lawyer has to be there when I deal with Ford."

Eric sat up. "Like hell she does."

Hobbes leaned forward. "Keep your voice down," he said, looking at the few other patrons sitting in chairs and conversing over drinks.

"Longer I'm in here, bigger the chance someone's gonna come looking for me," Eric said.

"Is everything arranged?"

"Yep. Even the mules."

"Mules?"

"Mules. Victor was throwing a fit about Wade keeling over walking the whole way. He chartered a mule train."

Hobbes grumbled and sat back in thought. "If you leave early enough on the mules, he can walk the rest and still make it in time."

"I hope you have a plan for dealing with Victor. He's always packing and he's watching me. How you gonna do this without violence?"

"I'll handle it."

"Something I have to know. Why here?" Eric jerked a thumb over his shoulder. "He's in his room right now. You could have had him in DC or Phoenix. But you came all the way out here. Doesn't make sense."

Hobbes didn't answer.

Eric narrowed his eyes. "I don't understand why Sierra has to be a part of it."

"Just do your job. Get paid."

"When do I get paid?"

"When we land abroad. I've arranged for the wire."

"You gotta make it look like I'm your hostage."

"Done."

"I'm still not sure I'm willing to do this for you, man."

With shocking speed, Hobbes moved to the seat next to Eric. Dark energy oozed from his pores. His teeth clenched, and the cords popped out from his slim but muscular neck. Eric couldn't maintain eye contact with him; it was too visceral. Below Hobbes's mask he noticed a slight bulge protruding from the left side of his neck.

"Do you remember what I told you will happen if you don't?" Hobbes asked.

Eric huffed. He caught a man and woman watching them from chairs nearby. "Yeah, man." He stood and rushed out.

In his room, Eric saw himself in the low mirror attached to the dresser. "Why couldn't you settle down, idiot?" he asked aloud. Sierra was the only woman worth chasing, and even after their night together, maybe too far out of reach. She was slipping away, and he was out of a job.

He lay down. Searched the textured patterns of the low white ceiling for any solutions that would allow him to avoid what he knew would happen the next day. When he finally accepted there were none, he sank into a fitful sleep.

———

One hand on her hip, Sierra stood in nothing but her towel in their TV-less little room, discussing the next morning with Andrew before her shower. All their clothes and gear for the next morning were laid out on the extra bed. He stood from his chair and kissed her in mid-sentence. She hesitated when the guilty images of Eric filled her mind. But when Andrew held her in his big hands and wrapped her in his arms, she gave herself over to him.

One hand ran up her leg, stopping at the curve of her ass, then searched, raising her skin. She moaned when his mouth found her neck. Gasped when he gave a fistful of her hair a gentle tug. The towel fell. Her breath grew ragged as he worked his way down, squeezing, touching, tasting.

She worked Andrew's belt and pants open and stroked him until he was rigid. She threw her head back when he entered her, wincing. In the strange bed, their rhythm was off at first. When they found it, they kissed deeply through their moans. She imagined she was with Eric again. In her fiction, his thrusts were more fulfilling, and she groaned and shut her eyes. Eric's hand on her neck, Eric's body in her arms. They finished together in collapsing limbs and shuddering grunts, panting, sweating. Through the wall they heard muted giggling and half-hearted clapping.

"Good thing Scarlett and Benny are down the hall," Andrew said. "Thank you," he shouted. Sierra covered her mouth. They snickered along with their unseen neighbors. She traced the nail marks she'd made on his back.

"Sorry if I hurt you," she whispered, knowing she could never tell Andrew why it had been so intense.

"Badges of honor."

Andrew leaned over and kissed her. They took a cramped shower together, then lay down, exhausted.

———

Fresh from a few hours of hard sleep, Goodnight came in early to read Fitzgerald's *The Last Tycoon*. The plush ergonomic command post chairs were much more comfortable than that folding crap in his CONEX. He pulled the paperback from his cargo pants pocket, and in between pages he watched the shift change on the new camera monitor bank. They entered in ones and twos. He focused on Anderson and Jackson. Something about their interactions was familiar.

"Those two serve together?" he asked, pointing at the screen.

Jones put on his jacket to leave and squinted. "Let me check, Chief." He perused both their dossiers, then checked their electronic files in the system. He shrugged. "Nothing in their history matches. Anderson spent time in Delta. Jackson was . . . er . . . regular army. But he's got computer skills, so he wound up in the HRT through the FBI Cyber Division. I only met him a few weeks ago."

"Hmm," Goodnight said. "Maybe it's just me."

Jones grabbed his belongings. Petty Officer First Class Patrick Harris, another Naval Special Warfare Command operator who almost could have passed for Jones's brother, stayed at his terminal.

"Harris? Ain't you tired?" Goodnight asked.

"One minute, Chief," Harris said. "Need to run a few systems checks on the alarms, check all the cameras before you and Maguire take over." A minute later, Staff Sergeant John Maguire, a lean Force Reconnaissance Marine, walked in and took up his chair near Harris.

Jones stood at the door. "It's been over forty-eight hours since you took command, Chief. No incidents. We've got a few loose ends, but nothing we can't tie down."

"Thanks, Jones. Everyone finish their initial training course?"

"Yes, sir."

"Where are we with the perimeter alarm?"

"They're working around the clock. Their head honcho said they'll be operational tonight and work on customization throughout the week."

"Cameras?"

"Everything's online." Jones pointed to the bank of monitors in front of Harris. "It's all touch screen. You can toggle between any camera with a tap."

"Outstanding. I'll play around with it. See you, Jones."

"Oh, one more thing. The secondary command post you requested in the dam? There's a decent-sized room inside below the west elevator.

It's been wired up with computers and systems capabilities almost as good as the ones here. The floor has some electrical access panels the BOR folks might have to access at some point, but they covered those up with desk chair mats. We can start manning it tomorrow. The BOR guys named it the dungeon."

Goodnight smiled. "I like it."

"What are you reading this morning, sir?"

Goodnight held up the paperback. "Taking another crack at Fitzgerald's last work. Didn't quite finish it before a heart attack got him. It's time to get down to business, though," he said, putting the book down.

Jones departed.

Thirty minutes passed. Goodnight frowned at Harris. "You still here? Maguire and I got it. Get some rest, Petty Officer."

"Two minutes, Chief, then I'm done," Harris said.

"Save some work for me," Maguire joked. "It gets boring up here."

Five minutes later Harris was still at it. Goodnight stood over him. "Your two minutes were up three minutes ago," he said. "I appreciate the dedication, but I want you all to stick to the shifts so everyone gets plenty of rest."

Harris slid the mouse around and clicked a few things, then stood and pulled the chair out for Goodnight. "All yours, Chief," he said, and took his leave.

Goodnight switched between views. He tapped on one of the power plant's interior cameras and frowned. "Anderson," he grumbled.

Maguire looked at the screen. Anderson sat on top of a table in the turbine hall near one of the huge generators, his carbine slung over his shoulder, eating. A female Bureau of Reclamation employee sat in a chair at the same table. Even with the time lapse, it was clear they were chatting.

"Want me to call him up, Chief?" Maguire asked.

"No. I'm going to him. No one gets in here but me, Sergeant."

He made his way down the ivory tower elevator. Took the golf cart onto the dam and parked near the west dam elevator. He donned his hardhat and goggles and began the minutes-long trip down through five hundred feet of concrete. At the bottom, he exited the elevator and put up his collar against the fifty-degree temperature inside the dam. He touched the wall in wonder at the seeping water, still amazed it was so soggy.

He resumed his trek, remembering he had his own leaks to plug. Goodnight enjoyed the open air along the path next to the manicured Bermuda grass between the dam and the power plant. He turned and stared up in awe at the massive wall of concrete looming over him as the sound of the released water roared behind him.

The black female operator standing guard swiped the door open for him.

"Morning, Sergeant Epps. Looking for Anderson," Goodnight said.

"Morning, sir. He's down there," she said. "On roving patrols around the turbine hall, Chief."

Several Bureau of Reclamation employees and contractors moved around the thrumming generators.

Goodnight didn't pretend to understand how it all worked, but he remembered that Miller said that with the water so high, the dam could produce over a thousand megawatts. The eight yellow generators stood in a line like massive robots tasked with guarding the dam. He stuck his earplugs in against the noise.

As he made his way down, he spied Anderson still sitting on the table. Fresh spackling covered several holes in the wall under the catwalk. A haunting reminder of why Goodnight had accepted the job.

"Don't you have a perimeter to sweep, Sergeant Anderson?" Goodnight asked from behind him.

The brunette sitting at the table turned red, grabbed her food, and escaped the situation.

Anderson turned to him, taking the last bite of his apple. "Snack break, Chief."

"Say again?"

"Snack break."

"We don't have breaks, Sergeant. This is an active area of operation, and you're on duty in a combat zone. I don't care if you eat now and then, but this ain't a union job. You're a SOCOM operator. No more fraternizing with the BOR people or any of the contractors. Understood?"

Anderson stood and nodded with a weak smile. "Got it, Chief."

Goodnight didn't miss the mocking. "I won't let this happen again, Sergeant."

Anderson squared up to him. "It won't happen again."

"Dismissed," Goodnight said. Whether the man with the big beard and arms was a killer or not, Goodnight showed him no weakness.

Anderson didn't move.

"Did you hear me, Sergeant?"

The two men faced off eyeball to eyeball. Goodnight swallowed.

Anderson smirked. "Yes, sir." He turned and went back to his patrol, and Goodnight let out his breath.

Back in the control room, Goodnight leaned over Maguire's shoulder and toggled back to the power plant cameras. Anderson walked the inside perimeter. Goodnight sat in his chair, grateful the incident hadn't escalated. "Well, Maguire, I guess we better lean hard into the deep night watch."

"Yes, sir."

Chapter 8

Descent

THE NIGHTMARE SNAPPED HIS EYES OPEN. ALWAYS HIS LAST op as a Green Beret. Johnson. The old woman with the braids in the black hijab. Like all the other times, Hobbes woke up sweating and shouting, wishing he could go back and do it differently. His watch alarm had twelve minutes to go. He'd caught up on his sleep, which he'd need for this op. He switched off the alarm as the burner phone lit up on the nightstand with an incoming text. He read it, squinting at the screen, which was as bright as halogen lights on a midnight road.

He swore, gripped the phone, tapped it against his head.

It wasn't a mission critical development, but it was a concern. Maybe they should have picked a better hiding spot?

Nothing he could do about it now. He was more pissed that his contact had burned the phone. He took out the battery. Used the hinged side of the bathroom door against the jamb to break it into several pieces. Put them in the Faraday bag for later disposal.

He dressed in his running clothes and trail runners. He removed the plates from the plate carrier and rearranged the Velcro pouches to conceal essentials like full mags as much as possible. Between all the veterans and fitness freaks running around, nobody looked twice at folks wearing plate carriers on a workout, but he'd still need to blend in as a civilian. He kept the flat pack for food, medical supplies, and for storing the metal lockbox with the documents. The Glock 26 and silencer would stay hidden in his fanny pack, along with his thigh holster, until he needed them. He had a topographical map and had studied the distances and elevations, but he had also drawn a crude map on the hotel stationary with the major checkpoints for his op and the times he needed to reach each one. He folded it and placed it in a pouch on the plate carrier.

The roar of a cold-started engine made him look out the window into the dark. Ford's entourage was getting into a black luxury SUV, Samuels driving. "Through it all we remain the hidden defenders," Hobbes mumbled, letting go of the curtain.

He donned his medical mask and secured his fixed blade knife. Walked down the hall. Checked both directions before using his lock-picking tools to open the door. A nightlight in the bathroom cast a faint blue glow. He slipped in and waited for his vision to adjust, listening over the humming fan from the HVAC unit below the window. Waited until he could make out the lumps, one much smaller than the other, in the two full-sized beds. Their torsos rose and fell in offbeat rhythms.

He approached the nanny and watched her breathing in the fuzzy darkness. She slept on her left side, facing the entry door, her long red hair covering her pillow and most of her back. He mimed putting his hand over her mouth and bringing the knife up into her back below her rib cage. Quick and quiet. He practiced the positioning twice, then pulled her covers down a few inches. She was a petite woman, not much bigger than a child herself.

Taking the boy alive was crucial to his new plan. The nanny, not so much. However, the second his hand gripped her mouth, his right knee pinning her almost waif-like torso just above her hip, she let out a whimper. If she fought to escape him, he couldn't feel it, so small was her stature. Their eyes connected in the dim light. Hers held the same confusion he'd seen in the eyes of the little girl from the dam. He tightened his grip. The boy stirred.

"There's a big-ass sign back there that says we're not supposed to park in here," Andrew said.

"Some people spend their whole lives following rules," Eric shot back.

"Right," Andrew muttered. "What if they tow the car?"

"See, Andy, you already think you've lost. Why not believe you might win?"

"Enough," said Sierra.

"Where are the mules, Victor?" Wade asked.

"They'll be here, sir. Folks, riding an animal down steep terrain is hard work. I suggest stretching and loosening up just as if you'll be hiking down."

They milled around the lit-up trailhead parking lot, checking packs, filling water bladders at the public spigot, and tightening straps. Eric sensed a difference in the air out in the darkness before them, the great chasm descending into falling shadow, outside the reach and safety of the lights. A smell. A feeling. Anticipation? Foreboding? He couldn't put a word to it. A weight upon him.

Wade checked his phone, and at Victor's encouragement did the occasional uncoordinated squat or lunge. Eric hadn't noticed Victor giving him anymore funny looks. It had to have only been Candi that Victor knew about, and to Eric's misfortune, that had been handled. It seemed that Victor didn't know about Eric and Sierra, and definitely not Eric's contact with Hobbes. Victor would have taken action already. The fit, dark-haired photographer, Miles Nguyen, had joined them at the lot on time. He seemed all right to Eric, and from their little bit of conversation, also experienced with photography and the Grand Canyon.

Speaking of fit, Eric tried not to stare at Sierra as she bent over in her black leggings and stretched her shapely glutes and hamstrings. It proved difficult, especially when she raised her arms overhead and exposed the sculpted midriff and defined hips he had finally touched again in Phoenix.

Andrew was chatting up Victor over calisthenics, so Eric took advantage. "How you feeling about things?" he asked Sierra.

She popped up from stretching and, with a sarcastic smile, tossed her blonde hair.

"My son and my legal assistant-slash-nanny are in a motel room with no TV near a giant child death trap. My boss is forcing me to follow him into the Grand Canyon for a freaking picture nobody wants to see. I'm about to get on a live mule for the first time in my life and ride it down a bunch of cliffs. I'm feeling great. How the hell are you?"

"Just making conversation. Think Wade really understands how far this is?"

Sierra shrugged. "Conversation. Yeah, sure. Victor told Wade what he's getting into. About thirteen miles to Ribbon Falls. Another eight miles up the other side. At least he'll be on a mule for the first seven or eight miles. Sleeping down there for a night should help."

"It's not the distance that gets you, it's the elevation. Down this side, five thousand feet. Up the other side, another six thousand."

"The tension between you and Andrew will kill me first," she said, her face hard. "It never should have happened, Eric."

Before he could respond, the headlights of an approaching car caught his eye. The driver parked at the other end. Given the man was so tall, there was no mistaking Hobbes. Eric tried to be nonchalant about watching him. Hobbes took some gear out of the car's trunk before making his way to the trailhead. When he disappeared into the darkness, Eric again felt that heavy, nauseous weight upon him. Dread. That was the word he couldn't find earlier. The sounds of metal horseshoes on pavement distracted him. "Here come our rides," he said.

A stocky young woman in blue jeans, brown riding boots, a red plaid button-front western shirt, and a dirty, silver felt cowboy hat rode up on a tall brown mule leading a string of six more. With a cascade of loud footfalls, they clopped into the parking lot. When she stopped, Eric heard the animals breathing, smelled their tang in the air, and saw their bodies steaming in the cool early morning, their large ears turning at every sound.

"Who's Victor?" The woman spat a brown stream of tobacco juice right after she asked, splattering the pavement near Eric's foot. Her cabbage-shaped face held two large dark orbs that surveyed them all. Brown hair descended from her hat onto her shoulders.

"That's me, ma'am," Victor said, making his way to her and reaching up to shake her hand. "I'm sorry, but I spoke with a Mr. Chatrie about guiding us down."

"Mr. Chatrie is my daddy. I'm Melanie Chatrie. The mules and everybody else know me as Mel. That goddamn bright light's blindin' me, Victor." Her voice was raspy, her drawl thick. Eric was amazed that her ability to drop consonants was far more powerful than his own.

Victor examined her with suspicion, then nodded and flipped off his headlamp. "Well, Mel, we're ready."

She slid off her mount and held the reins. "Hold up, now. I gotta give you all the skinny. Anyone ever ride?" Everyone gathered around. When no one answered, Mel raised an eyebrow and frowned.

"First things first—turn down them headlamps. Any other day the mules go down Bright Angel Trail over at the main lodge. We usually come up South Kai. But you got a supposed celebrity in your midst." She paused and glared at Wade. "Victor here paid extry to avoid the tourists, so everybody gotta do just like I say. Hear?"

The group nodded and grunted their confirmation.

"I ride point on Gomer. Long as Gomer's happy, all your mules are happy, 'cause to them, Gomer's the leader, not Mel. Hear?"

More grunts to confirm.

"Give the mules their head. Don't yank the reins like you're gonna fall off the dang trail. Don't squeeze or kick the mules with your feet. Don't do nothin' stupid like whistle or slap a mule's ass. Don't stop unless Gomer stops. Don't go unless Gomer goes. Don't lean over the side tryin' ta get a dang selfie with your fancy phone. Dammit ta hell, this trail is dangerous. Hear?"

Another round of grunts.

"Some of these trails are an eight-hundred-foot clean-ass drop over the side, some more. The mules are trained and steady, long as you let them do their job. You upset the mules, you could fall and drop a thousand feet. You ain't gonna fall and just die."

She spat tobacco juice before delivering her next sentence. "You fall that far . . . you bust into a million juicy watermelon pieces." She stared them down. "Now you gonna mind what I'm sayin'?"

A tense silence, then a much more enthusiastic round of grunts to confirm. "Heat is the biggest killer out here. This year's hotter than most, 'specially for October. Drink your water and keep your hats and long sleeves on. No cell service down there. Don't plan on makin' calls or doin' some stupid-ass live stream, dammit ta hell."

Sierra raised her hand. "Are there bears? What about cougars?" Eric snickered. Sierra shot him a disgusted scowl.

"We got mountain lions, but they won't eat you. Biggest thing to watch out for is rattlers. And don't feed the squirrels. Little sons o' bitches bite more people round here than anything else. Don't get in the river. You'll drown. Most the time it's blue. Right now it's brown and red. Anyone know why?"

"Flood stage?" Sierra asked.

"Right you are, pretty lady. You guys ready?"

"Quite ready," Wade said. "We're wasting time."

Mel gave him the stink eye. "I know you, Mr. Kajillionaire. I watch the news. I don't care for what you're doin' to our canyon with your big fancy resort. People like you are why nobody trusts the government. I'm only helpin' you 'cause me and Daddy need the money. Got me?"

Eric found the awkward moment amusing. He noticed Sierra hiding a smirk.

"Let's get you guys mounted," Mel said.

Ten minutes later, everyone was ready. Eric noticed the sun's soft orange glow, which betrayed the horizon's craggy black lines. When Mel was satisfied with the light, she rode Gomer to the trailhead.

Riding down the South Kaibab Trail was a steep and dusty affair hemmed by the occasional black abyss of shadows that remained untouched by the dawn. Water bars made of rocks or wood cut into the trail to prevent erosion—Mel explained—existed every four to six feet. Many of the water bars were over a foot tall, sometimes almost two.

Eric couldn't figure out how to protect his manhood each time his mule, Omar, stepped down a water bar. The plodding mule hooves sent up a thick dust cloud that tickled his throat. The salty-sweet smell of mule sweat and dung, and the sound of creaking leather—strangers to his senses—were a far cry from the sleek, technical avionics of an aircraft.

The mule train descended the switchbacks as the rising sun exposed more and more of the tremendous landscape plunging down to the river.

Mel stopped the train, dismounted Gomer at a place called Ooh Aah Point, and instructed them to admire the view as she tightened the cinches on all their saddles. "Wouldn't want no one to slide off a cliff on account of these sneaky mules takin' a big breath when I saddled 'em earlier," she said.

Miles snapped a string of silhouette shots of Wade staring out at the canyon.

Almost two hours later, they approached the Colorado River ahead of schedule. Eric watched Sierra from the switchback above. She beamed, her hips in tune with the animal's rhythm, her long blonde ponytail rocking like a pendulum from under her hat, her laugh sweetening the air.

Andrew caught Eric watching her. He didn't return Eric's wave.

———

There was a rap on his CONEX door. Goodnight wiped his sleepy face. "Yeah?"

"It's Jones, sir. Hate to wake you, but you ordered me to. Brought you coffee."

Goodnight unlocked the door. "Come in, Jones."

"You should sleep more, sir."

"I got a few hours. What do you want me to do, get in a coffin and die?"

They sipped coffee, saying little. Although all the other members of the team had several hours between shifts, Goodnight and Jones were on shorter, more sporadic rotations until Goodnight felt more comfortable with operations. He could see that both he and Jones were suffering for it. He went behind the curtain to dress.

"Need you to help me keep an eye on Anderson today. Jackson, too," Goodnight said as he buttoned his shirt.

"Will do, Chief."

"Anderson's a hard case. I know the type. Jackson seems mostly all right, but I've seen them together."

"Understood, sir."

"How you feeling about things?"

"Tight ship so far, Chief."

Goodnight came out from behind the curtain and sat in the folding chair next to Jones. Sipped his coffee. "Hayes gave me an earful the other day."

"About?"

"They've staged reserve infantry, FBI Hostage Rescue Team, and lots of state and county law enforcement out in the desert under restricted federal airspace. They're expecting company again. Said if we don't hold this place by the time the cavalry gets here, we're dead either way."

Jones considered it. Took a deep breath. "Damn. Looks like we better hang on, then. Bright side? If they're anything like the guys from Friday night, that won't be hard. Bunch of limp-dick peckerwoods. They weren't pros, that's for sure."

Goodnight leaned in. "What exactly happened in the power plant?"

Jones studied his coffee. "I've seen a lot of death, Chief. Dealt a lot of it. I've seen dead civilians. But what they did in the power plant was . . ."

Goodnight let the moment sit, knowing he couldn't share most of what Hayes had told him with Jones. "I'm only asking because I need to know what kind of sons of bitches we're up against."

Jones's voice grew thick. "They made them all undress to their skivvies. Even that little girl." He swallowed hard. "Lined 'em up against the wall under the catwalk. All twenty-two of them just standing in a line. You'd think an execution by firing squad would be twenty-two head shots." Jones choked up. "I'm sorry, Chief."

"You're alright, Jones."

"Limp-dick amateurs shot them all in the chest, Chief. I keep thinking about how long it took them to bleed out."

Goodnight knew better than to respond.

"The coroner said that the little girl was still warm when the medics arrived. Said she died at least an hour, maybe longer, after everyone else. That poor little girl had to watch it, Chief. All those people shot and bleeding out, crying and pissing and shitting themselves, dying around her."

Goodnight stared at his shoes.

Jones took another deep breath.

"Then they shot her too."

———

Beth's twitching ears on her bobbing head. The click-clack of her hooves against the rocks. The gentle rocking of her gait. At first, Sierra was terrified that Beth might stumble and send them both hurtling into eternity, but she remembered Mel's words: *Give the mules their head*. Once Sierra did that, she could relax a little, let her mind drift.

She'd relished Eric ogling her in the parking lot this morning. The uninvited kiss in the plane, the scruff of his stubble against the back of her neck in her room. The way he'd always been able to—

She needed to stop. She thought about Benny instead.

He had begged for a pony when he turned four. Considering they were still broke then and their neighborhood wasn't exactly horse appropriate, his consolation prize had been a twenty-minute ride on a grumpy little pony around a corral at a farm outside the city. On the way home, Benny had grinned out the car's open window at the trees lining the little country road, singing "Old MacDonald" from his booster seat, letting his hand ride the wind. That smile was worth every dollar Sierra had scraped together. His requests for a pony increased tenfold after that.

She shifted her pack on her shoulders. It was stuffed with two liters of water, about four thousand calories in quick trail snacks like nuts and energy bars, a little candy, electrolyte powder, and salt packets. One change of clothes. Andrew carried their two-man tent. The National Park Service website showed all the water spigots operational, so no more than two liters at a time were necessary once they left Phantom Ranch for the hiking portion of the trip. As such, Victor had decided they didn't need water filters, and he told them not to drink the creek water because it could make them sick.

As they approached the tunnel leading to what Mel called the Black Bridge, Victor unfolded his map with one hand, held his reins in the other.

"How far?" Wade asked.

"Bit over six miles," answered Victor.

"The mules did better down South Kai than I expected. Proud of 'em," Mel said, spitting tobacco juice and patting Gomer's neck as they headed toward the mouth of the tunnel.

Eric chimed in. "They slowed down on that steep stretch over the last mile or so. We need to be at Ribbon Falls by thirteen hundred hours, Victor."

"Why a specific time?" Andrew asked.

"Because Victor and I don't want Wade walking this trail in the dark," he lied. "We need to be done with the photos and setting up camp at Cottonwood before then."

"We have headlamps," Andrew said. "It might be better for him to spend a little time in the dark rather than push too hard in the heat."

"When you're running things, I'll take your advice," Eric said, grunting as Omar stepped off a water bar.

"Guys," Sierra cautioned, "I'm enjoying my ride. Don't."

"He's right," Wade said over his shoulder toward them. "I don't mind being out here in the dark. He is the doctor."

Eric groaned.

"He's a med student, Mr. Ford. If that bird isn't in the air on schedule tomorrow, they'll come get it. We had to pull strings with NPS for AirOps to land it on the North Rim. It's not like parking a commuter in the carpool lot. It's a six-million-dollar aircraft," he said.

"We should have just brought mine," said Wade.

"Why can't it stay another night on the North Rim?" Sierra asked, ignoring Wade's arrogant sidebar.

Eric shook his head and snapped, "Am I the only one here who wants to stick to the damn schedule?"

Everyone, even Mel, turned to look at him.

"Easy, Eric," Victor said. "It'll all work out all right."

Sierra searched Eric's eyes, but this time he didn't reciprocate.

———

From behind a boulder on the north side, Hobbes checked the mule train's progress as they entered the tunnel. He navigated back to the trail, careful to remain unseen.

He jogged the half mile into Phantom Ranch and put the medical mask back on. One thing about the post-pandemic world—no one questioned a mask anymore. A veneer of sweat coated his body when he stopped at a wood and rock structure, the Phantom Ranch CANTEEN. The rich aroma of coffee, bacon, and pancakes wafted from the elevated wooden porch. Campers milled around, eating breakfast, murmuring their morning conversations. He moved his head around, touched the lump, and cursed it.

A jovial man watched him from the top of the canteen's steps. "Will you be having breakfast with us this morning, sir?" he asked. Hobbes stared at him. The man appeared uncomfortable and stepped back inside.

Five young women wearing sweats and beanies sat at a picnic table near where Hobbes stood, giggling over their coffee about the man who'd snored all night who turned out to be a woman and could be heard throughout the camp. Their giggles morphed into uncontrolled snorting and wheezing laughter behind their hands.

Did Amelia have friends like these? Did she grow up having sleepovers? Did she ever have braces? Play sports? He ruminated on the lost years as he filled his water bottles and ate an energy bar. Back on the trail, he walked a bit to conserve energy.

Shark Eyes, the cold Rev Six director, had ordered Hobbes to demand $100 million from Senator Pace, despite knowing of her control of the defense appropriations committee's accounts and her access to billions of dollars in obscure funds with no congressional oversight. Dark, untraceable money. The reason for the menial demand was obvious.

To make it look real. To make it work.

Cygnus was a high-level, deep-cover sting. Senator Pace's staff would open their mail soon. Between the photos and the written instructions Hobbes had his Nevada lawyer send overnight, the message was simple: Pay. Shark Eyes had been clear. If Senator Pace refused, the next stage of Cygnus, a darker stage, would begin. Hobbes's stomach knotted at the thought.

He took his hand-drawn map out and compared his checkpoint time with his watch. He was on schedule. Just before he resumed running, he saw the old woman again. She knelt on a massive boulder above the North Kaibab Trail, watching him. There was no mistaking her dueling braids, the leathered skin, the black hijab.

"How did you get down here?" he mumbled, the words leaving his mouth in slow motion.

"You better hope the canyon lets you out, Snake Eater. They don't let everyone out," she said, speaking Dari, pursing her wrinkled lips.

Startled and dumbfounded, he stepped back. She had never spoken. Her voice was a low croak.

"Who?" Hobbes asked, struggling to remember the basic Dari he'd learned in the qualification course. Her eyes were like an owl's. Deep unmoving browns reaching into his soul.

"The spirits that let you come down here," she said. "I hope you prayed before you came down. If they let you out, you must pray then too."

"You can't be here," Hobbes said in her dialect. He wasn't sure the words came out right. He squeezed his eyes shut. Opened them.

A big raven stood where the old woman had been. It called out in a gruff croak, then flew from the boulder in a whoosh of large wings. His thoughts wouldn't settle. He resigned himself to running and began the gradual ascent through the Box.

———

The river raged below. Something resonated in Eric when he saw the tunnel leading to the bridge. The pre-dawn landscape as he was coming down South Kaibab had been lunar, pale rocks and powdery dust. As the sun rose, the colors moved from neutral tones to hues of pink and orange and red. He was meant for climbs, turns, and rolls in a fighter cockpit, not down here a mile below the earth's surface. He was a trespasser in a giant scar, a wound, meddling in something he couldn't control.

Omar entered a passageway of uneven, blasted angles of orange and red sedimentary rock. After twenty yards the light from the other side opened to the surprising expanse of the Black Bridge and the river's deafening roar.

Eric guessed that the bridge spanned at least the length of a football field, maybe a shade longer. The swift red-brown waters flowed southwest under graying boards that mule hooves and thousands of trekking poles had chipped. He had the sensation of floating upriver. The expanse of the pool below tapered to a V as it descended into crashing whitewater. The crescendo filled his ears, swells beating against the canyon walls, muting the plodding of twenty-four shod hooves in Eric's ears. The huge cable suspension system pulled tight against itself between the looming cliffs.

In the middle of the bridge, he broke Mel's rule and pulled Omar to a stop. Checked his six. For that moment, it was just him and Omar at the bottom of Grand Canyon. A strange feeling, as if he'd been here before. In a dream, perhaps.

He remembered how a few weeks before Phoenix, over scotch and cigars in a rooftop hot tub filled with nameless, scantily clad women, Wade had asked him why he insisted that Sierra not know he was flying for her boss. It was stupid, now that Eric thought about it, to have kept that secret from her. Wade being Wade, he had no problem carrying on the deception.

That stung. Not only because of how it affected Sierra, but also because Eric realized that based on the date he'd seen on the email Hobbes had shown him in Washington, Wade had already made the decision to fire him before that night, never letting on that he knew about Eric and Candi. Eric became expendable, and Wade took full advantage. Now he was in a position to press his own advantage, and there was nothing Wade Ford could do to keep Eric from getting on his six.

The unforgiving knife-edge of wasted time sliced into his thoughts. He had followed a dream and seen it to fruition. The dream had been full of adventure, but devoid of love. And it had recently turned into a nightmare.

Nightmare.

From Eric's perspective, Sierra's life had been one for a long time. A lawyer terrified of courtrooms? Wearing her mother's earrings every day? He wondered if she still kept that box of unopened letters.

Maybe Sierra had never needed his help. Maybe the truth deep inside her was waiting for something else. It terrified him that perhaps her life would never again include Major Eric Samuels.

Chapter 9

Unforeseeable

GOODNIGHT SIPPED HIS COFFEE AND GAVE THE DUNGEON'S monitor bank a blank stare. He preferred the dungeon's quicker access to the elevators over the detached command post in the ivory tower. Plus, it got him away from the Bureau of Reclamation suits' unsolicited opinions on how he should be doing things. Though the gray concrete walls were a far cry from the panorama of the lake and the expansive facility, he felt more part of the action. Less exposed. Someone had found some cheap carpet and rolled it out over the plastic floor protectors covering the electrical access panels. It was just fine as far as Goodnight was concerned.

Jones entered looking concerned. "Chief, there's no sign of Anderson anywhere."

"This isn't his forty-eight off?"

"No, sir. He's got one more shift. He's gone," Jones said. "Not in his CONEX. Not in mess, not on any cameras. Not in the head."

"Who's in reserve?" Goodnight checked the list. "Send Rollins, Zachery, and Purtill to search."

"Something else, Chief."

"Of course there is. What?"

"Jackson still hasn't responded from Sector Three."

"What, again? Give me your radio." Goodnight took it from Jones and put it to his mouth. "Sector Three, radio check, come back." He waited. "Sector Three, are you receiving?" Nothing. Goodnight swallowed and looked at Jones. "Give the entire facility the white glove."

"Roger that, sir."

"I have to call this in," Goodnight blurted out.

Jones stared at him, waiting.

"We didn't have enough time to vet these guys, Jones. I have to call the ivory tower." He walked to the phone and dialed the number. "Chief Goodnight here. I need Director Perkins, please. No, dammit, I won't hold," he said grumbled. He felt weak in the knees when a voice answered. His voice cracked. "We got a problem, sir. Two men are AWOL."

"How hard have you searched, Chief?" Perkins asked.

Goodnight raised his eyebrows. "Hard enough to know I have a problem, sir."

"We can't jump the gun on this, Chief. Look again, be thorough, then call me back." Perkins hung up. Goodnight stared at the phone, shaking his head.

"Chief?"

"He wants us to look again. This smells real bad." Goodnight said, recalling everything Hayes had said the other day.

"We'll keep looking."

"No need," said Harris, pushing back from his terminal. "They're gone. About a half hour ago."

Goodnight swore under his breath. "How do you know?"

Harris held a tablet up for Goodnight. Grainy surveillance footage showed one figure approaching another, both clothed in black, near the twelve-foot metal security gate at Two-Mile Tunnel. As one figure approached, the other one near the gate pulled a device from their belt that emitted a bright flash. When the other figure reached the gate, they did the same.

"Vapor torches," Jones said.

Less than a minute later, the gate lock was disabled, the cut ends glowing. Both figures moved through the service tunnel gate and disappeared.

"Jackson was posted at that gate," Goodnight said. "And that sure looks like Anderson's build to me."

Jones nodded. "Yes, sir."

Goodnight's face felt hot. "Why wouldn't Jackson just open the gate with his access card? Why cut it like that?" Jones and Harris gazed back at him. Goodnight studied their faces and got distracted. "You two could be brothers with those regulation haircuts and mustaches, you know that?"

Jones and Harris gave each other a wary once-over, then focused back on Goodnight.

"Jones, get a team out to Two-Mile Tunnel and secure the area for clues. Call up everyone who's off shift and mobilize them to start scouring the facility and grounds for irregularities." Goodnight picked up the phone and looked at Harris. "Get that footage to BOR and make sure it doesn't get leaked. I can't stress that enough, Harris."

"Yes, sir."

"Jones, let's not get compartmentalized. Three things. One, there's no positive ID on those two figures. Maybe it's Anderson and Jackson, maybe it ain't. We need to operate as if we have two missing crew and we've been breached by two enemy combatants. Two, we don't know what they have planned. They may be coming back in numbers. Get the team ready for battle conditions. And three . . ."

"Chief?" Jones asked.

"The security perimeter alarm," Goodnight said, smiling and nodding in a sort of frustrated realization. "They cut the gate so there'd be no record of a swiped badge. But dammit, that expensive thing was supposed to be tamper-proof. Alarm should have sounded if it was cut, right?"

"Yes, sir."

"We either die fighting to keep it, or we die in the fight to take it back," Goodnight said.

"Pardon, sir?"

"Never mind."

Reports chittered in over the dungeon's radio as the morning grew long. All other operators and dam personnel were eventually accounted for and their whereabouts confirmed.

"Jones, what did you say they used to cut the gate?" Goodnight asked.

"Vapor torches. Very expensive on the black market. But military or police tactical can get one with the proper clearance. They fry through metal quick."

Goodnight scolded himself for being a stupid old man.

Sometime later, a solemn-faced Jones appeared at his side. Goodnight waited. "Well, spit it out, Jones."

"The perimeter alarm. It's off, sir. Several critical systems were shut off at the terminal right before those two cut through the fence."

Goodnight rocked back in his chair. "How? No one had access to the terminals during that time frame but me, Harris, and . . . you," he said, making eye contact with Jones.

Neither he nor Jones moved.

———

Despite her ass hurting after the long, sunny descent, Sierra admired the tall cottonwoods standing like gentle giants welcoming their mule train into shady Phantom Ranch. With their fluttering yellow and orange fall leaves, they towered over the picturesque creek rushing down toward the Colorado River.

They said goodbye to Mel at the camp corral. When Sierra gave Beth's hot sweaty neck a hug, the mule snorted out a nose full of dust in gratitude before reaching out to nibble on the corral piping in front of her.

A few other trekkers passed through, but most of the numerous people she saw were campers dressed in a mix of hiking gear and pajamas and lounging near the creek or chatting around a building that said Canteen on the front, drinking coffee or what appeared to be lemonade. Sierra wanted to bring Benny down here and camp for a few days. He'd enjoy getting to ride a mule into the Grand Canyon. How many kids could say they'd done that?

A friendly lady wearing a volunteer vest noticed them refilling their water. "You guys are part of that mule train that came down the wrong way, huh? Not sure how you convinced Mel. You must be important."

Wade snorted, but to Sierra's relief, didn't answer.

"Can we interest you all in breakfast before you get under way again? Coffee?"

"Coffee would be awesome," said Sierra.

"No thank you," Victor said. He pulled Sierra close. "We need to get Mr. Ford out of here before he gets recognized."

"Nonsense, Vic. I'd love a cup, ma'am. Two, please," Wade said, winking at Sierra.

Victor frowned. The woman returned with two coffees. Wade pulled out a twenty and told her to keep the change. While the rest of the group ate an energy bar or banana and filled their water bladders, Wade and Sierra stood sipping from steaming paper cups.

"Extraordinary coffee for the bottom of the Grand Canyon, isn't it?" he said.

She nodded, still astonished by his kind gesture. "Yes, Mr. Ford. Extraordinary."

He gazed back at her. "I'm grateful you're here, Sierra. After Bill passed, I . . . well, I felt lost. Thank you for not walking out on me."

She met his smile with her own conflicted one. "You're welcome, Mr. Ford."

The group peed before moving out of Phantom Ranch toward the Box. Miles told them that this stretch would be like hiking in an oven. Hydration was key, as shade was almost nonexistent for the next several miles.

A few minutes later, Sierra missed a wayward rock in the trail and went sprawling, grunting hard when she hit the ground. Andrew and Victor were at her side in a second.

"Anything hurt, babe?" Andrew asked.

"Just wounded pride." Sierra stood and dusted herself off.

"Be careful," Wade said. "Injuries are a liability we don't need."

"It was an accident," said Andrew.

"Accidents cost time and money."

Sierra saw Andrew about to respond and touched his arm. "I'm fine, Andrew," she said. "Let's go."

Then she saw it. Her body buzzed with fear. "Mr. Ford, don't move."

"Pardon?"

"Don't move."

Everyone froze.

"There's a snake coiled behind your boot."

"What kind of snake?" Wade asked.

"Like I would know?" she snapped. "Far as I'm concerned, they all need to die."

The group moved away from Wade as if he were a leper. Victor peered at the serpent.

"Can you tell what it is?" Eric asked Victor.

Victor shook his head, then turned to Wade. "Mr. Ford, think you can jump?"

"Are you joking? Right now I could fly," Wade murmured, his jaw tightening. He held his water bottle in one hand, the fingers of his other hand in a claw-like pose. Even with her fear of the snake, Sierra stifled a laugh. He resembled an Egyptian hieroglyphic. Wade Ford, billionaire developer, playing freeze tag with a snake.

"Mr. Ford, on three, jump with everything you've got," Victor said.

"What do you plan to do on three?" Wade asked, exasperated.

"Hit it with this." Victor held up a softball-sized river rock.

Miles snorted. "You have any idea how fast a snake can strike?"

"Quiet, please, Mr. Photographer," Wade said, almost yelping. "I'm ready, Vic."

Sierra and Andrew backed off to watch the show. Eric joined them. Miles shared a snarky look with the group.

Victor counted. "One . . . two . . . three."

Wade jumped with a loud grunt, lost his balance on the landing, and fell flat on his face. Victor threw the rock, hitting the snake dead center, then ran to Wade and helped him up. The whole process seemed to play out in slow motion. Unable to hold it any longer, Sierra snorted and cackled. The two men shuffled away from the snake and turned around to find the rest of the group laughing.

"You find it funny when someone falls?" Wade yelled.

It took them a moment to catch their breath. Eric walked over and picked up the snake for all to see. It was only an old piece of coiled, rotting water hose. "We're safe. It's dead."

The group fell into another round of hysterics. For a moment, Wade did nothing. Then, to Sierra's surprise, he started in too. He looked at her in a silent red-faced convulsion that ended in a long wheeze. After a year in his employ, she'd never seen Wade laugh like that.

Down the trail they drank from their water bottles and admired the cold clear flow of Bright Angel Creek. A group of female athletes wearing University of Arizona apparel, including scant shorts, bounded past them on toned legs, all bouncing ponytails and indefatigable youth.

Eric said hello to each of them, one after another, eliciting energetic responses from all. Victor and the rest of their group stopped and stared down the line at Eric. "What?" he asked, throwing up his hands.

They eventually spread out over a quarter mile, Andrew leading, Miles close behind. Andrew was a fierce competitor on foot, not to be outdone by anyone. Wade and Victor plodded along in the middle. Eric was just ahead of Sierra. She had hung back to enjoy the solitude. Apparently, Eric wasn't going to squander the opportunity to talk. He slowed enough for her to catch up.

"He won't like you being back here with me."

"I just want to ask you something?" Eric said.

"Go ahead, if you must," she said between deep breaths up a steep incline. She felt her shoulders tense.

"What happened after Cabo?"

Her shoulders relaxed. "Oh. Well, you ghosted me."

"I get that you're pissed about that. But that's not really what I'm asking. Back in the plane you said you were in recovery. You used to drink with the best of us. How exactly am I responsible for that?"

Sierra sighed. "I guess now is as good a time as any. So here goes, Eric. I drank a lot after Cabo. After you disappeared. One morning I was hungover and had fifteen missed calls from Scarlett."

"You mean that cute redhead watching the kid that you didn't tell me about?"

"I had my reasons for not telling you, Eric. I guess they don't matter much now. And stay away from Scarlett. Anyway, a senior partner had gone into my office looking for some briefs. They found a bottle in my desk. Fired me. A week later Scarlett came over, saw my apartment was a disaster. I was broke. 'How did this happen, Sierra?' she asked me. The look on her face broke my heart. But I took a drag of my cigarette and followed it with a big gulp of vodka anyway. Stared her right in the eye while I did it."

"Hard-core," Eric mumbled.

"I guess. Scarlett's like a sister. She convinced the firm to get me into rehab. After my thirty days were up, the partners put me on probation with a handler. I worked my way out of it."

"I had no idea."

"Why would you?" she said, scoffing. "Anyway, I stayed sober, but I was still messed up." She stopped and faced Eric, her voice hot. "I waited so long for you to call. Even after I had Benny with Andrew, I waited on your call. You were the only person I ever told about my childhood. About Mama. Remember dropping in from time to time to see me during my college years? You know what I loved the most back then, Eric? I loved the way you ran your fingers through my hair when I told you my darkest secrets. I loved it that I could trust you. That I had someone to trust. Then you abandoned me, Eric. I was lost. After I got sober, I still felt alone. So I tried something else." She turned and resumed walking.

"Drugs?"

"No, dummy. Sex. Lots and lots of sex."

"Really? You?"

"Oh yeah. Did it so much that I got bored and started doing weird stuff. One night I was in a nice hotel with a man Wade's age. After, he asked me if I knew why I was doing it to myself. He said it was because I was angry."

"How kind of him."

"Yep. He nailed me."

"Interesting choice of words."

Sierra snickered. "A week later I went in for a checkup and blood work. A handsome black phlebotomist drew my blood. He was kind. Put me at ease, made me laugh."

"Andrew."

"Yep. The fog lifted. I'm an addict, Eric. With unresolved issues, as Andrew likes to remind me. He's right, though. He's a good judge of character too. Sniffed you out right away."

"That's not nice."

She whirled on him. "Was he wrong?" She took a deep breath and let it out. "You leaving was a trigger that needed pulling. But even after all that—when I heard your voice on the phone the other day—I felt, I don't know, something. I was glad you came to my room. But now . . ." She turned away again.

They walked in silence. "Can I tell you a story, Sierra?" Eric asked.

"I don't know—should you?"

Eric chuckled. "On my last deployment I had a conversation with a buddy in my squadron. Old Man Traeger. He was only six years older than the next-oldest pilot in the squadron, still in his thirties, but he smoked a pipe like a weirdo, so the call sign stuck. I was with him for years. One day we were on an Alert 30 on the carrier, ready to jump in the F-18s when we got the call."

"Alert 30?"

"It means we had to be ready in thirty minutes for action."

"Oh."

"Anyway, my call sign was Blue Collar. Give you one guess why."

Sierra giggled.

"I told him all about you. How we met. Our long-distance

relationship. Cabo. How I disappeared on you. He asked me, 'Blue Collar, why didn't you ever commit to this girl?'"

Sierra's pace slowed a bit.

"I told him that I wanted to fly fighters. Said that if I'd married or committed to you, I'd never have made it inside an F-18."

"How do you know that?"

"That's exactly what Old Man asked me."

"He sounds like a smart guy."

"He was." Eric took a breath. "That wasn't the truth, though. The truth is, I was afraid."

Once again, she stopped and turned, her face twisted.

"Of what?"

He hesitated. "That I couldn't take care of you. You lost everything, Sierra. It was awful, what happened to you. Maybe I thought I was too selfish to be there for you." They stood face-to-face on the trail.

"But maybe that wasn't true either. Old Man called it right there on that aircraft carrier in the Indian Ocean. He told me that as ballsy as I was in the air, I was scared to death of commitment. He was right. I'm sorry, Sierra. Sorry for all the lost time."

She wiped her unwanted tears, pivoted, and started moving again.

Eric changed the subject. "Still got that box of letters?"

"One for every year since I was twelve. Get one every fall."

"Ever open 'em?"

"I don't want to talk about that."

"Okee doke. Another question, then. Why aren't you and Andrew married? You got a kid. What's the hold up?"

Sierra didn't respond and picked up her pace.

———

Jones stood in front of Goodnight. "I can't find Harris now, Chief."

"You're joking." Goodnight had found Jones to be beyond reproach. But two men were AWOL, and someone had turned off the alarm. Now this?

"No, sir. He's gone."

Goodnight put his head in his hands. A noose was tightening around his neck. The phone rang and he snatched it up. "Goodnight."

"This is Hayes, Chief Goodnight. Is this line secure? Are you alone?"

"Yes, sir." He motioned for Jones to step out.

"Perkins called. I've got BOR Chief Engineer Bartles and General Foster of the 3rd Infantry Division here with me. How long ago did they leave?"

Goodnight swallowed. "A few hours ago. I had a feeling about these two, so I told my XO to keep an eye on 'em. I called you soon as they turned up missing. We checked the entire facility again as ordered. One of the two missing men was posted at Two-Mile gate."

"How sure are you this is a breach and not just two flakes going AWOL?" Hayes asked.

"They're on camera cutting through Two-Mile's security gate with vapor torches. And someone turned off the brand-new perimeter detection system from the terminal in my command post," Goodnight said.

"What?" Hayes asked with more urgency. "Where's Two-Mile? What is that?"

"It's a tunnel that runs from the bottom of the dam all the way to the top of the canyon. It's for heavy equipment. That's how they got out without anyone noticing. It gets worse. Now another man, Harris, one of my computer techs, is missing."

General Foster spoke. "Chief, are saying you have not two, but three men AWOL?"

"Yes, sir—General. I only had one morning to vet the crew," Goodnight said, grimacing. "It gets worse. My XO also had access to the alarm system controls. I have no idea who turned it off."

It sounded like Hayes covered the phone and murmured indistinctly. His hand must have slipped a bit, because Goodnight heard Foster say in a forceful whisper, "Do not tell him anything about Cygnus or the sunny day breach protocol, Hayes."

Hayes came back. "Chief, we're going to deploy and reinforce you. The HRT will be on standby from the visitors' center parking lot. We'll set up a command post there. The general says the 3rd will stage and set up roadblocks on all roadways to the dam. We'll have an ISR platform, some helos on overwatch, and a full company to assist with security all over the facility and grounds."

"What about my people?"

"Keep them posted and call up anyone who's off to bolster your ranks. Find that other mole. Detain your XO. Don't let him out of your sight," Hayes said.

Goodnight hung up. He opened the door and let Jones back in. "I'm only going to ask you this once, Lieutenant. Do you know anything about how that alarm got turned off?"

The man deflated. "Chief, I . . . I'd die before I dishonored my oath."

Jones's expression told Goodnight all he needed to know. He wasn't locking Jones up today or any other day.

"Find Harris. I don't know what Anderson and Jackson were up to, but we have to suspect Harris was in on it."

He scratched his head. "You know something? They told me Saturday morning that we fall under proprietary jurisdiction. That means I can call in local law enforcement. Page PD, Sandstone County, Coconino County, Arizona Highway Patrol."

Goodnight dialed the phone and got a dispatcher. "This is Glen Canyon Dam Security Chief Fred Goodnight. I'm calling for air support and ground support with a K-9 unit on the east Glen Canyon Dam access road and Highway 89 down into Page. Suspects are three males dressed in black fatigues and full military kit. Suspects are considered armed and extremely dangerous. Suspect one is Daniel Anderson, thirty-nine, Caucasian, six foot two, two hundred and twenty pounds, black hair, green eyes, full beard, tattoos covering both arms, SOCOM operator. Suspect two is Darell Jackson, forty-one, African American, five foot eleven, a hundred and eighty-five pounds, shaved head, brown eyes. No visible tattoos. FBI Hostage Rescue Team assault team member. Suspect three is Dominick Harris, thirty-six, Caucasian, six feet, one hundred and seventy pounds, brown hair, blue eyes, regulation mustache. No visible tattoos. SOCOM operator. Proceed with all haste and caution."

———

Hobbes woke up from the nightmare, gasping for air and shouting.

He sat against a boulder hidden from the trail, listening to his watch alarm beep. He had budgeted time for a fifteen-minute nap. He turned off the alarm and stood and peeked around, making sure no one was close, then got back on the trail.

Doubt infested him. If he'd put that knife to the nanny before receiving Amelia's letter, before they met for that awkward cup of coffee, he wouldn't have hesitated. Despite knowing that Rev Six would kill him if he failed Cygnus, he struggled more knowing they'd kill Amelia too. There could be no more hesitation, no matter how brutal the task, no matter who the victim was.

He found the concept of the documents absurd. But Senator Pace, a former lawyer herself, had insisted on it. Before Rev Six had gotten wise to her plans, Senator Pace had given Hobbes the false impression that her goal, both as a senator and a Rev Six high office director, was to save the Grand Canyon from Ford's project, in turn exposing more Washington corruption. Unfortunately for her, she'd tasked Hobbes with this project after the Second Seal had already filled his ears.

"Filled my ears." He chuckled. "Damn, I'm losing it."

But after all this time being Senator Pace's blunt yet effective tool, he now had the edge, even if it came at a high price. Hobbes kept moving.

———

"Sir, we found demo. It's a device attached to the base of the dam behind the power plant. Someone hid it pretty good. It's a small gray box with an antenna and a sensor. Little green light. Looks like it's sitting on a couple pounds of C-4," said one of the operators on patrol.

"Did they move it?" Goodnight asked Jones, who repeated the question into the radio.

"No, sir," said the operator.

Jones nodded. "I'll be down in five."

Goodnight shook his head. "I'll go. You keep the boys looking for Harris, and whatever happens, do not leave the dungeon. Keep the door locked."

Goodnight descended the elevator and found Purtill and Rollins standing near the device in the abutment tunnel. It was stuck to the side of the dam behind an electrical box, neatly tucked away. He plucked his radio from his belt. "Jones, call BOR and tell them we need that FBI explosives team now."

"Roger, Chief. There's another one. Smith was on his way to meet you and found it," Jones said. "Small box, gray like the walls, has an antenna, looks like a sensor. Green blinking light. Says it's sitting on what looks like a hunk of plastic," Jones said.

Goodnight cursed. "Start a mandatory evac of all non-security personnel." He double-timed it back to the dungeon, barking orders into the radio as he went. "I want every able body looking for more of these things. Mark any you find and block all access to those areas. Get the BOR people and all civilians out."

He was shooting from the hip. They had considered multiple scenarios in the last few days, but not a security breach with explosives already inside the dam. Goodnight pulled out his flashlight and performed his own search.

Fifteen minutes later he checked in with Jones. "Any trace of Harris? Status on evac?"

"There's no one in the power plant, all systems are on auto, and the last of the workers are headed to the visitors' center for lockdown and debriefing," reported Jones. "No sign of Harris."

"What's the ETA on the explosive ordnance disposal team?" asked Goodnight.

"Any second, Chief."

"How many have we found so far? And how did no one see these earlier when we were looking for Anderson and Jackson?"

"Three more. We were looking for men, not bombs, Chief."

Goodnight exited the dam elevator and was headed to the ivory tower elevator when he encountered a landing Blackhawk. A group of men exited the glossy black aircraft and made their way to Goodnight and Jones, who'd followed Goodnight up to the surface.

A short, muscular man trotted up and spoke. "Assistant Special Agent in Charge Dick Parker, bomb technicians team leader. We're attached to the HRT down the road," he shouted over the departing helicopter. He gestured at his team, several of them carrying machines, two of them in bomb disposal suits, and the rest carrying carbines and dressed in full combat kit. "These are some of my guys, a few HRT folks, and a few SWAT guys. You have everyone out of the structure, Chief?"

"Working on it. I've got two AWOL operators who we caught leaving on surveillance. I've got another missing operator who had access to our critical security and information systems. Might have hacked us."

Parker grimaced.

Goodnight offered a sheepish shake of the head. "I know. It's bad. We're breached, and I'm certain it was two, maybe three of my very own men."

"Let's go take a look," shouted Parker above the fading staccato of the helicopter blades, clapping Goodnight on the shoulder and nodding at Jones. "The 3rd, the HRT, and a Quick Reaction Force out of Yuma are on the way, too. Uncle Sam's not taking any chances since the takeover."

Goodnight dreaded the nightmare headed his way. "You need me to show you around?"

"We've studied files since Friday night when they put us on alert," said Parker. "But a schematic wouldn't hurt."

Goodnight took him to the dungeon and showed him digital schematics and the surveillance footage, and then Parker deployed with his team.

Minutes later Goodnight and Jones listened to Parker on the radio. "We found fourteen so far, Chief. Inside the tunnels, specific rooms, and on the surface of the dam itself. Each one small, with the same setup as the initial two, each one near communication or electrical boxes. We tested one—it's C-4. Not sure which one's dominant, but either the antenna or the sensor are the primary trigger, and the other one's either a backup or a dummy. Then again, the sensor could be a fail-safe trigger."

"Meaning?" Jones asked, his brow furrowed.

"We move the device, the sensor trips, and it explodes. Maybe it sets them all off. They're all hardwired in. That's why we found them all near electrical and communication lines."

"Can't you just cut the main signal to the lines they're connected to?" Goodnight asked.

"Sure," Parker replied, chuckling. "And then we might all go boom, Chief. It's a fail-safe most sophisticated terrorists use. Besides, we don't have time."

"How do you know that?" asked Goodnight.

"From the surveillance footage you showed me, I'd bet those two worked as a team to place and hide the bombs over the last few days."

Goodnight frowned.

"We've got cameras everywhere with someone sitting in front of a computer monitoring it all. How could they have pulled that off?"

"Pretty simple to wire them in, Chief. Probably only took a few minutes at a time—nothing major anyone would notice on camera unless they were looking for it. Once they were done, they booked it. It's showtime. I've already got a guy on your computer system trying to find clues to a possible detonation signal to all these bad boys."

Goodnight groaned and squinted at Jones. "The missed radio checks. Jackson. Anderson. One causing a diversion for the other. Harris watched me go check on Anderson, and I'll bet that's when Jackson was setting a bomb or two."

Goodnight heard Parker ordering his men to move out. "Chief, the rest of us are going to position ourselves on as many known devices as possible. I'll try to figure out how to disarm one, then radio that information to the other teams. With any luck we'll have them disarmed and removed within the next several minutes."

"How much explosive is attached to each one?"

"A couple pounds. That much plastique is only enough to destroy or kill anything within twenty meters or so. But I don't think that's the point."

Jones broke the silence. "So what do we do?"

For the first time since Goodnight had met him, Jones seemed edgy.

Parker let out a crazy laugh. "Evac. This dam has never been popular with the domestic population. Then you figure in international terrorists."

"What about warning people downstream?" Goodnight asked.

Parker was silent.

"Oh. So that's . . . that, then?" Goodnight said.

"Let our superiors figure out how to handle publicity, Chief," Parker said. "There could be something bigger hidden somewhere else. We have to assume this facility, plus—hell, I don't know—another mile in any direction, is a kill zone. Anyone inside that circle is at risk. Let's go to work. We're out, Chief."

"Jones," said Goodnight, "the dam's running on autopilot. No one needs to risk getting blown up. Get our team out."

"What about you, sir?" Jones asked.

"I'm staying with Parker. Have to make a call, Jones. If I don't see you when I get off the phone, there's no shame." Goodnight nodded at Jones and walked down the tunnel to the door. He took the elevator up to the top and stared out at the lake as the phone rang.

"What's shakin', Chief Goodnight? The dam still holding water?" Judy giggled and waited for him to respond.

"Judy . . ." He groaned into the phone.

"Fred? What's wrong?"

"Something's happening. You can't share this with anyone but folks you trust."

Her cheery voice turned solemn in an instant. "Tell me."

Goodnight laid it all down. When he finished, he heard nothing but her light breathing.

When she spoke, she was calm. "What do we do?"

Goodnight cleared his throat. "I've got an idea."

CHAPTER 10

Theory of Mind

A CRYSTALLINE SKY OVER THE OPENING CANYON WAS A NICE break from the dark, steep walls of the Box. The towering canyon walls were enthralling at first. Sierra had craned her neck more than once to appreciate their height and splendor, but after several miles they had morphed into faceless rock enclosures, concealing their trapping movements, as if pushed toward her by some invisible force intent on throwing her into Bright Angel Creek and mincing her in its cold water. As the massive walls retreated and allowed their group to escape the Box, her sense of claustrophobia waned.

They hiked to the Ribbon Falls turnoff on schedule and picked their way down the steep incline to the creek crossing below the scrubby flat. Sierra felt a creeping fatigue from the trail miles in the bones and tissues of her feet.

Wade had forced her to come on this ridiculous publicity stunt for her bonus, so Sierra was having some fun with him. "But don't you think that preventing anarchy is what defines the concept of record ownership?" she asked.

"No. That's what the police are for," Wade answered. "Ownership is freedom."

She shook her head, her blonde hair bouncing under her hat, her feet crunching gravel and sand. "What happens in two hundred years when no one can find the records that you ever owned the land?"

"Two hundred years?"

"It's probably closer to a hundred." she said. "But who would care? There'd be no memory or concept of Wade Ford or Sierra Justice. Maybe a photo, but probably not. No nostalgia. No matter what a piece of paper says, ownership eventually becomes meaningless. Ask the ancient Romans."

"What if I'm a billionaire and they're my heirs?"

Sierra snorted. She started to respond to him when she rounded a squatty boulder the height and width of a mature tree just before the creek crossing.

She saw a tall man wearing a black medical mask. He stood in an alcove between the first boulder and a second equally large one. He was dressed in earth-toned clothes, a boonie hat, some sort of military-looking vest, and trail running shoes. He held a pistol with a long round barrel in his hand. There was a holster strapped to his left leg.

He seemed familiar. Something about him. But how?

She stopped cold. Eric slammed into her with a grunt, and Wade smacked into both of them. The trio went down like football players swarming a tackle and let out a collective grunt as they hit the ground. Andrew and Miles managed to avoid tripping over them and helped each of them get to their feet. Victor stepped around them and pulled out his pistol, placing his body out front.

As Victor brandished his gun, the tall man held up one hand in a gesture of peace. His expression was flat. "Interesting conversation, from the bit I heard. I didn't mean to startle you," he said with a wave of his hand to Victor. He slowly slipped his pistol into the holster. Victor remained in a firing stance, but after a moment he lowered his gun. Sierra could barely think after seeing the guns, much less move.

"What are you doing out here with a firearm?" Victor asked Tall Man.

"What are you doing out here with one?"

Used to confrontation, Wade broke in. "Well, now that we've all had a good scare, we need to get going," he said to Tall Man. "If you'll excuse us, please, we'll leave you to your business. Thank you." He walked on the trail in the man's direction.

Victor turned to Wade and held his right hand up to stop him. That's when Tall Man pulled out his pistol again.

Three quick pops, quieter than what Sierra remembered a gun sounding like. Victor's body tensed, then fell. The thinnest trace of pink vapor hung for a second in the air. She screamed.

In almost the same instant, Miles made the mistake of moving. Tall Man pivoted and shot him three times as well.

Andrew called out to her. She stared into space, breathing, not seeing. Her insides queased into darkness.

Someone grabbed her shoulders and put her on her knees. Everything was fuzzy. She flashed to Benny's tender little face that morning as he slept peacefully in the room with Scarlett. She had kissed his cheek.

She remembered to say the words, right? Yes? No?

Her thoughts wouldn't come into focus. She gasped when she remembered where she was. Tall Man had her, Eric, and Andrew kneeling, holding out their hands. With the exception of Wade, Tall Man zip-tied their wrists behind them. The gravel under Sierra's knees pinched her skin. Tall Man pulled something metal from his gun, put it into his vest, then put another similar metal thing in, and with a clicking sound, snapped the top of the gun shut. Then he picked up the little brass-colored shells from the ground and walked to Wade. He spoke to him in hushed tones near a big rock, explaining something. To her right, Eric spat out blood.

"What . . . is . . . happening?" she asked in a gasp.

Victor lay dead not ten feet away, arms and legs sprawled, staring into the sky, his mouth open. Miles lay next to him in a fetal position. But for the blood soaking the trail under his body, his frowning face suggested he might have been in a fitful sleep. Sierra wondered if he still had a mother somewhere, and in that instant, she felt an aching sorrow for her.

Eric interrupted her thoughts with his usual sarcastic twangy delivery. "We stumbled down the wrong—"

"Shut up," Tall Man said in a calm voice. He walked over and slammed his fist into Eric's stomach with a sick whump sound. Eric vomited. The sound and sour smell caused Sierra to lean over and vomit too. The man went back to Wade.

She tasted acid and watched Tall Man unbuckle a pack from his vest, open it, and remove a slim metal box. He took out documents wrapped in plastic. He produced a pen from the box and then presented it and the documents to Wade, who removed the plastic, examined them, then looked back at Tall Man.

"You want me to do what?" he asked. He shook his head, uttering a nervous laugh. "Sign over fifty percent of my interests in Canyon's Dream? Out here? In the wilderness? Who in the hell is Lucinda Pace?"

Sierra screamed again when Tall Man pointed the pistol at Wade's head. The man turned and approached her in a slow walk, his eyes like a hyena stumbling upon a wounded animal. He knelt in front of her and raised her chin with his fingers. He took off his mask. He smelled of mint gum, sweat, and something sterile like bleach in his clothes.

———

Hobbes saw her make the connection.

"The ice cream shop. You were watching me yesterday," she said, breathless.

Hobbes smirked. "Attorney Justice is astute, isn't she, Major Samuels? Fitting name for a lawyer."

Sierra stared wide-eyed at Hobbes.

He faced her down until she looked away. "Call me Hobbes. Your client, Mr. Ford, is going to sign these documents, which transfer half of his leasehold interests in the Canyon's Dream and Ribbon Falls gondola system development bid to my employer."

Ford chuckled. "You must be the worst terrorist ever. You take us hostage in the Grand Canyon so I'll sign documents that steal from me?"

Sierra's voice was ragged and out of breath. "Whatever you have there for him to sign, he'd be doing it under duress. It's no good. Let us go."

"But you're here, Ms. Justice."

"Here? Nobody knew we would be out here. Who are you? How did you know?"

"Mr. Ford will sign these documents," Hobbes said. "No duress."

"You have a gun to his head. He's tied up. That's textbook duress."

"But you're his legal counsel, and you will advise him to sign the documents," Hobbes said, doing his best to remember his lines from the script Ichabod and Senator Pace had given him.

Her eyes bugged out. "How crazy are you?"

Hobbes noticed that one of her teeth curved inward, unsettling the symmetry of a mouthful of otherwise straight teeth. Her passion and something about that crooked tooth appealed to him. He put his mouth to her ear and whispered, "Your son and his nanny are gagged and tied up in my room back on the rim. If you scream or tell anyone else, I'll kill Baby-Daddy first."

Hobbes saw the air leave Sierra's body. She slumped from an alert kneeling position down to a sitting one, limp. Her expression went blank. Her mouth stayed open. The vibrance seemed to leave her like water from a drain when a stopper is pulled, as if she had somehow departed the present for some other place. After a moment, her swimming eyes connected again with his, the right one pooling a single large tear. She blinked and it rolled away, cutting a tiny clear path through the dust over her cheekbone down into the corner of her mouth.

Her face remained vacant for a long time before she squeezed her eyes shut and spoke, her voice raw with emotion. Hobbes found her words puzzling.

"You are my hope, Benny. I will do anything for you."

"Sierra," Samuels said in a raspy, breathless voice from beside her, "I need to tell—"

"Shut up, Samuels," Hobbes said, shoving the barrel of his pistol up under Samuels's chin.

———

A swing of Hobbes's pistol raked Eric's face, bloodied his cheek, and shut him up.

Something similar to what Sierra had felt in the courtroom in Phoenix took hold of her. Life had become primordially simple. This man had her son. She would do anything to get Benny back. Hobbes's attention fell upon her face again. She couldn't look away from the gun in his hand.

"Fair enough," Hobbes said, holstering the pistol. "Get up, go over there, and advise your client to sign the documents." He grabbed her arm and helped her up off her knees.

Sierra, still zip-tied, dirty, and shaking, stumbled toward Wade and opened her mouth to instruct him to sign, but a jarring thought, an epiphany amid the pain and gritty reality, stopped her cold.

Wade cleared his throat. "Mr. Hobbes, sir. What is your price? Whatever they're paying you to do this, let me pay you more. We can arrange a wire transfer for today. Name your price, please, sir."

Hobbes glared at him. "Try not to be so predictable, Mr. Ford. Offer me money again, I'll kill Sierra first. Then you."

The color drained from Wade's face.

"What do I do, Sierra?" She wanted to cry. To scream. To run. Instead, she had to be rational in a world gone crazy. Wade made high-stakes business decisions that made or lost truckloads of dollars, but he leaned heavily on his legions of lawyers to guide him through his legal troubles. Whether it was intentional or by accident, Hobbes had made this look more like a legal problem for Wade than a life-or-death one.

The answer was obvious, but anguishing. "Don't sign, Wade," said Sierra. "That's my legal advice."

———

"You understand that if I tell the higher-ups that we need to evac the corridor based on my boyfriend's hunch, if I can call you that, I'm risking a thirty-year career and my retirement, right, Fred?"

"So am I. But I'm not asking you to do anything yet. And maybe don't refer to me as your boyfriend when you call it in," said Goodnight.

"NPS pilots don't fly at night. We'd have to call in state and county pilots if it happens after dark. Even if we rally every chopper pilot Sentinel Air or HeliFlight have out of Page or St. George, some won't fly into government-restricted areas. The ones who can will charge Uncle Sam up the wazoo for it to risk their pilot's license."

"I get it."

"October is one of the most popular months in the canyon. The Bright Angel and Havasupai Gardens campgrounds are both full. There are hundreds of people. Plus, the high water has all the crazy whitewater people on the river. Outfitters, rafters. Dozens of them. Not even twenty helicopters carrying ten people at a time could get them all out that fast. Not to mention the hikers and runners out on the trails—"

Judy started talking to someone else. Papers rustling.

When she came back, her voice carried a trace of fear. "Fred, we just got orders for radio silence. Rumor is it's from Washington. Only authorized personnel can communicate with any other stations or rangers right now." Her voice turned thoughtful. "If I radio down to Phantom or Bright Angel or Havasupai Gardens, I'll be the one getting locked up. Plausible deniability," she said, her voice turning hard. "This pisses me off."

"Judy, please know that—"

"Fred, I'll do it."

"Not yet. This whole thing could still blow over." He frowned. "But why not just send a chopper or a fast runner down now and alert someone in charge?"

"Oh, Fred. Bless your heart. You're lucky you don't have to think about federal air regulations and park visitors and NPS orders."

"Not even in an emergency?"

"It's not an emergency here yet. If I send a helicopter down into the inner canyon corridor to do a checkup, NPS will never hear the end of it about violating air restrictions. And I'll never hear the end of it for letting it happen. I don't have any fast runners on staff and I can't go recruiting civilians. That's a chief ranger or park superintendent decision."

"If I give you the green light, what will you tell these pilots?"

"What the hell can I tell them? They gotta trust me like I'm trusting you."

"Judy, I have no words."

"Thank you works."

"Thank you, Judy."

"I'll wait for your call."

"By the way, the answer is yes."

"Yes to what?"

"You can call me your boyfriend." He hung up the phone. Paced. Blackhawks and Little Birds buzzed around the dam facility, evacuating stragglers. He raised Jones on the walkie-talkie. "Everyone out?" he asked.

"Everyone but EOD and their crew, Chief. I practically had to make our people leave at gunpoint. They all wanted to stay."

"Where'd you send 'em?"

"Staging area where the 3rd and the HRT are. They're taking everyone into custody, Chief."

"Get on a bird, Jones. I'll see you when I'm done here."

Judy called back.

"What happened?" Goodnight asked.

"Something's up for sure," Judy said, new excitement in her voice. "My boss is Stan Carpenter, the district ranger. I've known Stan twenty years. He's buttoned up. Nervous."

"What did you say? We have to keep our stories straight," said Goodnight.

"Told him we had an anonymous tip that people in the inner canyon corridor might be in danger. He said there were no reports of anything out of the ordinary. I told him the tip was about something uplake at Glen Canyon. He got real quiet, Fred, then started going on about how since the hostage takeover the dam has been under tight surveillance. Security, drones, satellite imagery. How the Army and the FBI are on standby minutes away, and to let them do their jobs, keep my head down, and get this, to ignore the tip," Judy said. "And he wasn't the friendly Stan I've always known."

"What do you think?"

"I'd have to get the folder out, but we've got a whole standard operating procedure on what to do if there's a dam breach at Glen Canyon. Stan said if we start evacuating people in the corridor, we'll set off a chain of events that can't be stopped. Best he could do is make his superiors aware that I called," Judy said. "Said when Bureau of Rec or NPS tells him to evacuate, he'll do it. I said by that time the people in the canyon might be dead, and . . . well . . . I kinda hung up on him."

"What now?"

"When you say when, I'll start calling in favors. I don't know what's going on uplake or if you're a crazy old man, Fred Goodnight. If you're wrong, only you and I lose. But if you're right, we could save a lot of lives."

———

Hobbes smirked and his breathing quickened. "Not the answer I expected, Ms. Justice. I'm giving you two minutes. I suggest you reconsider your counsel."

Wade had the same look of expectation she had seen many times before. If his style and charm and charisma had taught her anything, it was that aggressive billionaire or not, Wade Ford placed great value on his life. "Sierra, I realize I spent a year fighting legal battles that cost me millions. I bargained in money and stocks and promises to congressmen to get the legislation from committee to the president's desk," Wade whispered, his face covered in shame and exasperation. "But I'm not dying for it."

Sierra had never seen Wade squirm. She recalled how Bill had handled client control with him. "Wade, let me help you," she whispered. A glint of deference marked his expression.

"I know what we've been through to get here. You may have

spent the money, but I've put a year of my life into it. I put my family through it." Saying that made her sick all over again. "If you sign, the litigation surrounding those documents, even if we can prove fraud and duress, will stall the development for months. Maybe forever." Sierra let that soak in.

"But that's not your real problem here, Wade." She leaned in and met his eyes. "He took off his mask. We've all seen his face. If you sign those documents, you'll never walk out of this canyon. We're the only witnesses to the fraud. Wake up, Wade. None of us will leave here alive." Wade bowed his head. Sierra saw Victor and Miles again and fought another urge to vomit.

Clicking sounds and static interrupted her thoughts.

Hobbes punched buttons on something like a really thick cell phone with a long black antenna. He held it to his mouth. "In position," he said. As he returned it to his vest and closed the Velcro pouch, he grabbed his neck, sucked in air through his teeth. He caught Sierra watching him and acted as if nothing was wrong.

At the same time, a twenty-something man and woman, their hands all over each other, walked around the big boulder. Their giggling and touching stopped when they saw the gun in Hobbes's hand and the bodies on the ground. Sierra's throat locked up and she tried to make eye contact with either of them, but Hobbes put his pistol away, pulled his black medical mask back up, and stepped in front of her.

He held up his hands in a friendly gesture. "I'm sorry, folks. This is an official national park law enforcement operation. I'm Ranger Brian Taylor, and this is a crime scene. I need you to turn around and go back."

They nodded in obvious terror and turned back in a hurry.

Sierra let her breath out, grateful not to have to watch more people die. Her relief was short-lived.

"Help us!" Andrew screamed. "He's a murderer."

More popping sounds. Both hikers fell. The male was crying and struggling to get up when Hobbes put a bullet in each of their heads. Sierra threw up again. She wiped her mouth and stifled sobs of terror. Hobbes searched for and picked up the brass shells as he had before.

Hobbes approached Andrew and stared at him for a long time, nudging the gun against his head a few times. Sierra fought not to scream again. Hobbes pulled the mask back down. "I wanted to let them live," he said as Andrew hung his head. "You die next time."

"Really jacked up their quickie, didn't you? Who'd you just radio? What's in position?" Eric asked Hobbes. His smirk disappeared when Hobbes whispered something in his ear.

Andrew perked up. "Wait, what'd he say?"

Sierra wondered the same thing. Who is Hobbes? Victor had kept a tight lid on all their travel. Even the press had missed their leaving Phoenix for the Grand Canyon. How could Hobbes have coordinated this?

"Have you changed the nature of your legal advice, Ms. Justice?"

Sierra opened her mouth, but Wade interrupted her. "I'll sign. My apologies, Sierra, but I've decided not to accept your legal advice."

"Wade, please."

He lost his composure and eyed her like she was crazy. "Are you trying to get me killed? He just murdered those two hikers."

Sierra moved close to his ear. "No, Wade, I'm trying to save your life," she whispered. "I have no idea what this lunatic's plan is. I just know that the only chance of us staying alive is if you don't sign."

Hobbes stepped in. "I guess I haven't made myself clear. If you don't pick up the papers and started signing, I'll kill Sierra." He put the pistol's tip next to her mouth. Wade's eyes flew open. Sierra trembled. The cold metal against her lip. She tasted bitterness.

"Hobbes!" Eric shouted.

"You've got three seconds, Mr. Ford. Then she dies."

Sierra's knees buckled. Wade's face dissolved as her vision tunneled. The sound in her ears faded. Two words, distant.

"Time's up."

———

"Better get your dudes outta here, Chief," Parker's surfer voice squawked through Goodnight's radio.

Goodnight pressed the send button and held the radio to his mouth. "Say again?"

"The lights on our little friends just went from green to red."

Goodnight looked at Jones. "You sure everyone's out?"

"Everyone except for Harris, sir. Never found him."

"Get yourself out, Jones."

"Negative, Chief. I'll wait for you. Orders?"

Goodnight grabbed Jones's shoulders. "Those are your orders. I've spent my entire life fighting the bad guys. I let three of them in right under my nose. It's on me to stay and fix this."

"But, sir, you—"

"Go, Lieutenant. Those EOD guys might need me anyway," he shouted. "I'm not asking."

Goodnight saw the anguish in Jones's face as he stood ramrod straight and snapped a crisp salute. Goodnight smiled at the gesture but reciprocated. With that, Jones turned an about-face and trotted down the tunnel.

Goodnight grabbed his radio. "Where are you, Parker?"

Static crackled. "I'm on top of the dam right in the middle of no place you ever want to be. Whoever designed this was a real one. Never seen anything like it."

"I'm coming to you," Goodnight said.

"Negative, get out of here, Chief."

———

"I'll sign, dammit!" Wade screamed. "Please stop shooting people."

Sierra wobbled on her feet. Hobbes surprised her when he reached out and saved her from falling.

Wade's disappointment showed through every scribbled signature he wrote against his raised knee. Hope was all Sierra had now. He was signing their death warrants. Wade executed the last document and handed it over to Hobbes, who was in the middle of putting more bullets into another one of those metal things from his vest. He took the one in the gun out and put the full one in. Put the other back in a pouch on his vest. Pulled his knife and cut Sierra's zip tie. Held the documents out to her. She shook her head.

Hobbes raised the pistol and ran the tip of it across her cheek, stopping on her nose. "No counting this time, Ms. Justice."

The scenario had flipped. Against her advice, once again Wade had compromised her life. Now Sierra had to sign too, if she was to have any chance of living to save Benny.

The question she'd been asking herself rose to the surface again. "Why all this trouble?" Sierra asked Hobbes. "This makes no sense. Why not just forge the docs? Kill us all back in DC?"

Hobbes acted as if he wanted to answer, but then, as if he was considering otherwise, he didn't. "Do it now," he said, pushing the gun against her nose again.

She grabbed the documents and the pen. Skimmed the language, words and concepts with which she was all too familiar. Wade was signing over half his leasehold interest in the Canyon's Dream and Ribbon Falls gondola system project to a United States senator from Arizona named Lucinda Pace. Sierra might've laughed had she not been so terrified. Wade had used his cronies to grab a leasehold interest in national park land, and now someone else's crony was stealing half of it away from him. Andrew and Eric watched her. In their own way, each of their faces encouraged her to sign.

How could they not see this was game over?

She penned her signature and initialed where indicated. She handed the documents back to Hobbes. Her neck was tight, her brain thrummed, and her chest felt heavy. Fear gave way to despair. How could this awful violence be happening in her life again? That deep pain of loss she'd known since she was twelve filled her being. Because she chose this. She *deserved* this. A sob broke out as she covered her mouth.

Hobbes holstered his pistol. He examined the papers, then rewrapped them in the plastic. After he slipped them and the pen back into the box, he turned the combination lock, put the box into the pack, put the pack back on, then buckled it to his vest.

"Thank you, both," he said. He pulled out another zip tie and restrained Sierra's hands again.

Then he drew his pistol and shot Wade above the left eye.

Sierra heard Wade's final grunt as the back of his head splashed the boulder behind him in a red splat. Blood misted her face and arms. What remained of Wade's head above his deformed nose wobbled on his neck. His knees buckled. His body crumpled in a heap next to her. Blue smoke wafted from the gun's barrel.

Sierra stared down at Wade's arm lying across her bloodied hiking boot.

She was next.

"I'm sorry, Benny. I love you."

Chapter 11

Politicians and Generals, Chief

GOODNIGHT EXITED THE DOORS TO THE DAM'S SURFACE. More helicopters and flashing lights occupied the highway bridge. The military, Bureau of Reclamation, civilian officials, and several law enforcement agencies had convened for a front row seat. They had road-blocked the Highway 89 bridge at both ends with vehicles and flares.

"You seen the crowd up there?" Goodnight asked Parker and one of his crew as he squatted in the center of the dam.

"Yup. I told 'em to get the hell out of Dodge, but they won't listen. If this dam rocks, that bridge is in the kill radius. The concussions might even bring down the cliffs holding the bridge up. Politicians and generals, Chief," Parker said. With a pair of wire cutters, he bent over one of the devices attached to the underside of a drainage grate.

"Can I help?" Goodnight asked.

"Nope. Alice has taken me down a rabbit hole I don't think I'll ever escape," Parker said.

He touched his throat mike. "This is Milkman. Bonsai One and Two, hold your positions. All other units, exfiltrate pronto. Get off the dam and order everyone you make contact with to evacuate the area a minimum of one mile. Over."

Parker and his comrade trotted toward the edge of the dam. Goodnight jogged to keep up. "You said these were little bombs, Parker."

"These charges are small, Chief, but I can't say they don't have a big one in there somewhere." Parker's radio chirped and he stopped. "Go for Milkman," he said.

"This is Ground." It was a woman's voice. "Do you copy?"

Parker looked at Goodnight and nodded. "Roger, Ground. Are you ready to receive?"

"Go ahead, Milkman" came her reply.

"Cygnus confirmed. Repeat. Cygnus confirmed. Do you copy?"

"Good copy, Milkman. Cygnus confirmed. Hang one," she said.

"Wilco," Parker replied. He shrugged at his teammate and Goodnight, waiting.

Goodnight threw up his hands. "What the hell is Cygnus?"

Parker held up a finger as he waited for a reply.

The radio crackled and the woman came back on the other end. "Milkman, Raptor Two. Say again, Raptor Two. Are you receiving?"

Parker's face dropped. He took in a strained breath and replied, "Good copy. Raptor Two, confirmed."

"Ground, out."

"Milkman, out." Parker frowned at Goodnight. "I'll need your sidearm, Chief." Goodnight was speechless when Parker pulled Goodnight's weapon from his holster. They grabbed his arms, zip-tied his hands, and marched him off the dam.

———

Blood and gore covered Sierra. Their hands still bound, Eric and Andrew ran to where she lay. Eric leaned over her.

"Get away, asshole!" Andrew screamed. "Get off my girl. He shot her."

Eric ignored him and examined Sierra. With a choking sound, Andrew flew backwards onto the sandy ground; Hobbes's foot, in a desert-colored trail runner, had landed hard on his chest.

"Don't move again," Hobbes said, stooping to pick up the shell from the bullet that killed Wade.

"She's fainted, not shot," Eric said.

Hobbes pointed the pistol at him. "She'll live, Major. Move away."

Eric looked up at Hobbes. "You ain't gonna shoot me."

"No?"

They faced each other down, Hobbes wearing the faintest of smiles.

Andrew rubbed his throat. "Is there something I need to know?" he asked Eric, his voice raspy.

"Keep quiet, Andy," said Eric.

"What'd you get us into, man?"

"He's right. Shut up or you won't need to worry about what you know. She's the only reason I'm keeping you alive," Hobbes said to Andrew.

"Man, that's the woman I love. She's the mother of my child." Tears streaked Andrew's dusty face. For a second, Eric wondered if Andrew might piss Hobbes off enough to . . . To what?

"How can you be such a psycho?" Andrew asked. "You already killed five people."

Eric's pulse quickened when Hobbes marched over and held the pistol up to Andrew's face.

Instead of cowering, Andrew sat up tall. "You're just a psycho with a gun. You wanna be a man? Save lives, bitch. That's what I do. Even if you shoot me dead, I'll always be better than you."

Eric's mouth stretched into a bloody grin. Andrew was more of a hard-ass than he thought. But he lost the smile when Hobbes raised the pistol.

———

"I didn't see this coming. This is on me," Goodnight said. He stopped walking and leaned over and vomited. They gave him a moment.

"All right, all right, let's not start kicking ourselves in the dick just yet, just keep moving, Chief," Parker said. They reached the end of the dam and rode the ivory tower elevator up to where Parker's explosive ordnance disposal team and other military and law enforcement officials waited in the visitors' center parking lot.

"That him?" asked a striking woman in combat uniform with a star on her helmet, nodding at Goodnight.

"Roger, General Tanaka," said Parker. "The rest of his crew are under MP guard. Two unaccounted for. Chief says he saw them on surveillance video leaving earlier this morning."

"Three of my men are missing," Goodnight said. "Two went AWOL, yes, but there's a third, Sergeant Dominick Harris. You find him, you'll get the intel you're looking for."

"We'll get intel from you, too, Chief," said General Tanaka, fire in her dark brown almond-shaped eyes. "You better be thinking about what you want to tell me." She looked at two men behind her in military police uniforms. "No one but me talks to him until the investigators arrive." She turned her head toward Parker.

"All your men out? Did you get a confirmation that all the civilians were evacuated?"

"Affirmative."

"Give him his hands," General Tanaka said.

One of the military police cut Goodnight's zip tie. He rubbed his wrists. The general removed her helmet, revealing a stylish shock of gray that streamed from the left side of her forehead through her pinned-up jet-black hair.

"I'm General Lisa Tanaka. Smoke?"

Her staff officer held out a pack of cigarettes, lit one, and handed it to her. She nodded to Goodnight.

Goodnight hadn't smoked in decades but took the cigarette. The staff officer clicked the lighter for him. General Tanaka took a deep drag and looked back at Goodnight.

"Anything else you want to tell me?"

It was an old trick he'd used long ago himself. Make the detainee feel a connection. Offer them a smoke. Create common ground to get them talking. A ruse, Goodnight knew, but the cigarette tasted good and the almost instant nicotine high calmed his nerves.

"What was it Oscar Wilde said about devils and hell? Something about how we make hell? Or we are the devil? That's what I think this is, General," Goodnight said.

"I'm serious, Chief," Tanaka said.

"So am I. Tell me what Cygnus means, I'll tell you what I think."

"You're not calling the shots anymore."

"I'm not talking until I know what Cygnus means."

Tanaka eyed Goodnight over another long drag and blew out the smoke.

"You really don't know, do you?" She looked him up and down. "Can you keep a secret?"

"Wasn't ever good at it, but I'll try."

Tanaka smiled. "Last week intelligence intercepted a transmission. No IDs on the source or recipient, just an uncoded conversation about an attack using bombs. They mentioned the words Glen Canyon and Cygnus a few times." She took a drag. "We weren't sure if Cygnus was the attack from a few days ago, something different, or nothing at all. A red herring, perhaps? We adopted the word Cygnus as our command code for the response. Part of the Cygnus response plan if there's another attack is a population-dense protocol. Avoid public panic, divert all evacuation resources to heavily populated areas."

"What? How many people won't get the message? Thousands?"

"You expect us to evacuate entire cities downstream and destroy lives and businesses and economies over a radio transmission? We had to wait for something concrete."

"What else does the Cygnus response plan mean?" Goodnight asked.

"Sunny day breach. Structural failure. That's the public face of it."

"How many, General?"

"Fifty percent. We hope."

Goodnight groaned. "So if this thing blows, you're not going to tell most of the people downstream, you're going to get half out, and you're going to lie?"

She eyed him. "It's obvious we're both like mushrooms, Chief.

In the dark. I hoped you could tell me something else, but maybe you can't. Radio," Tanaka said without looking away from Goodnight. "Sergeant, make sure Chief Goodnight doesn't wander off."

"Yes, ma'am," a young sergeant in a military police uniform said, handing her the radio.

She raised it to her mouth and said, "This is Ground, calling with Security Clearance Code 66812 Alpha. Copy?"

"Copy, Ground, 66812 Alpha, Over," said an unidentified voice.

"Cygnus confirmed. Facility secure. Raptor Two. Anderson, Jackson, and Harris MIA. No further intel to report. Ground, out."

Goodnight could relate to the strain on General Tanaka's face.

"How much time you think we have, Chief?" she asked, her voice softer and pensive.

"There ain't a soul on the planet can answer you that."

She turned to him with a wry smile. "At least we got good seats, huh?" She raised the radio to her lips. "All Viking ships, commence evac of all military personnel, out." The sound of approaching rotors filled the air. "With me, Chief." She raised the radio again and said, "Command, we need to evac the bridge immediately, sir, over."

Goodnight heard General Foster's voice. "Ground, I've got a lot of stars and pissed-off state officials up here. They just arrived on a scrambled bird from Phoenix. And local media is at the roadblock, sniffing around, over."

Goodnight wondered if he had waited too long to tell Judy to pull the trigger.

———

Instead of shooting Andrew, Hobbes whacked him with the pistol, sending him down groaning. He stepped toward Sierra and produced a vial from his pocket. Popped the top. Put it under one of her nostrils and pinched the other shut.

She awoke with a shriek. "Andrew? Eric? What's happening? Did he really shoot Wade? Is he dead?" Sierra asked, panting.

"Quiet," Hobbes ordered. He pulled the two-way satellite radio from its pouch, walked a little distance away, and dialed. Tried to calm his nerves. He stared at his captives as it rang. Wondered if everything was still in place with his team. Thought about the text he'd received that morning. Considered how Sierra was the only one to have figured out how to save Ford's life. Something about her.

Philly answered. "Oh, you're in it now, ain't you, Cowboy?"

"Put her on, you fat tub of shit," Hobbes demanded.

Silence. Philly came back. Less enthusiasm. "Wait."

Senator Pace's vinegar-filled voice came on next. "I hope you can get out of that canyon faster than my assassin can get to you. Dumb move, using a sat phone."

She hesitated. "Is this line secure?"

"My instructions were clear. One hundred million. You have the account numbers and the wiring instructions. Initiate the transfers now."

"Any idea what the Second Seal does to people who go rogue, Hobbes? Have you forgotten who you're speaking to?"

"No. That's how I know you're good for the money."

"It's barbaric, what they do. I don't fold to this sort of thing."

"There are copies of everything I sent to you, Senator. Think about it. If you don't cooperate, they'll get leaked. I don't think that'll be very good for you."

She didn't speak for a moment. "What are you doing, Hobbes? Does this have anything to do with that Cygnus rumor I asked you about Saturday?"

Hobbes cracked, his voice suddenly angry and sharp. "All these years, Senator—I was with you. Force for the greater good. But you lied to me. Now you're trying to get a half interest in Ford's project. I know why. You don't need the money. No—you want to broker deals to gain power. Maybe become Madam President. If you control half the interest in this Canyon's Dream project, you can wheel and deal, push it, shut it down, do whatever you see fit so you can play the Washington game, right?"

"Who've you been talking to?" Genuine concern was in her voice.

"Six years of service to your high office, Senator. I would have died for you. Does that even matter?"

"What happens if you don't get your hundred million?"

"Something the whole world will feel."

She cursed, played tough, but he had her. He needed to be quick. No doubt her assassin had already boarded a helicopter.

"Enough with the cat and mouse. What are you going to do?"

"I've left all the clues to point the finger at you. An Arizona senator who staged a violent protest to get her greedy name on some documents. Who didn't get her way. Who blew up a dam in her own state."

Sierra's head snapped up, confusion and surprise on her face. He stared back at her as he spoke.

Senator Pace's voice lost steam. "Hobbes, you're no player, and this isn't your game. You're Rev Six's garbageman. My garbageman."

"Fifteen minutes—I'll check with my contact then. If the transfers of all one hundred million aren't initiated and confirmed with the listed accounts, you'll finally learn what Cygnus means. You saw the photos I sent. You know what's in Glen Canyon Dam."

———

Goodnight stood mired in guilt, watching helicopters land at intervals and whisk personnel away. Most of his crew were already at the staging area down the road. He followed Tanaka's brisk pace as she directed orders at her staff and into the radio.

Parker set up a computer and monitor with a glare shield on the hood of a Humvee.

"Take a look, Chief," Tanaka shouted.

The screen flipped between a few different images. One was of the interior of the power plant. Another showed the inside of one of the tunnels. The feeds were blurry and shook with interference, but clear enough. The third was inside the dungeon.

Parker yelled over the din of the helicopters, "I wasn't sure the timing would allow us to tap into the dam security feeds, so we put cameras near two of the devices, and stuck one in your command post, Chief. Hopefully the cameras don't get blown to hell if things go south. From here we can monitor at least three areas for damage. After the raid the other night, the bureau hacked into all of the cameras, so they're watching too, for now."

Goodnight shouted back, "They've been watching us the last three days? No one thought I should know?"

Parker shrugged. "Now you know."

"Hell, if they've been watching me since Saturday, why am I being detained? How did they not see the moles on my team planting bombs?"

Parker raised an eyebrow at Goodnight. "Same reason your guys missed 'em too, Chief."

"It was protocol to detain you," Tanaka hollered. "We also figured that with three missing men, this could be some kind of a ruse. How long will this thing hold power, Parker?"

"A few hours."

Goodnight squinted through dusty rotor wash and saw movement in the image of the dungeon. He peered closer. "There's somebody in there. Look, right there," he shouted, pointing.

A shadowy figure entered the dungeon and walked to one of the computer terminals. The feed shook with interference, but when it came back, the monitor's light illuminated the face.

"I'll be damned," Goodnight yelled. "That's Mark Jones."

CHAPTER 12

Cognitive Dissonance

THE ARIZONA SUN BAKED WADE'S BLOOD SPATTERS ONTO Sierra's skin. When her face moved, she felt the dried fluid crack. The dead man's warming gore filled her nostrils with the scent of pennies. She looked at him by accident. His once handsome face was deformed and bloody, his lips and teeth baring a sinister grin. The urge to vomit again. She tried to think of some other smell. Benny's hair in the morning after a bath the night before. A dripping mountain forest after a summer rain. Warmed sweet rolls.

Her knees and wrists hurt. Andrew groaned next to her, one side of his face swollen. Eric knelt to her left, watching Hobbes's every move. She was obsessed with what Hobbes had said about blowing the dam. Was he serious? She didn't have to wait long.

Hobbes pulled another black rectangular device from a pouch on the front of his vest and held it up for them to see. Something in his voice was different. "This is a satellite uplink transmitter. If I press this button, a timer starts inside a worm I planted in Glen Canyon Dam's security system. When the timer runs out, several Composition C-4 explosives will detonate on Glen Canyon Dam. Each explosion will damage crucial weight-bearing points."

Sierra heard Hobbes speaking but only saw Benny's face. What did Wade's money matter now?

"Around four hours after the dam breaks, the wall of water will reach the bridge we all crossed this morning, eighty-seven miles downstream from the dam. It'll be anywhere between three hundred to five hundred feet high. Nothing will sur—"

"Horseshit," Eric said. "Wade spent a day on the phone after that hostage fiasco the other day. People in Washington assured him that placed was buttoned up. Your toy doesn't connect to anything."

Hobbes ignored him. "The bottom three hundred to five hundred feet of the canyon will be erased. Everything gone. Gravel, dirt, rocks, plants, trees, animals. Humans. They couldn't tell me how far up north the water would go, but it's gotta be pretty far. I'll bet that Phantom Ranch area gets wiped out. Told me to move north out of the canyon, fast."

Something was different in Hobbes's face too.

"Sierra," Eric said, "don't listen to this nut."

Hobbes held the device in one hand and the Glock in the other. "It'll be the biggest flood the world has ever seen. After it leaves the canyon, the flood surge will hit Lake Mead. The Hoover Dam will fail. All the cities and towns below, flooded, destroyed. Then millions will be without water or power for . . . who knows how long?"

His face and voice sent dread into Sierra's chest. The same lurking horror she had felt as a child. The terror that sometimes woke her from a deep sleep and made her sit up with relief that it wasn't real, merely part of her history unleashed to terrorize her mind.

"Please let us get back to our son," she pleaded. "We won't say anything to anyone. Please."

"Ignore him, Sierra. Look at me," Eric said. She turned to him. He nodded at Hobbes. "He doesn't do emotion."

Andrew sniffled. "I was so stupid, bringing Benny out here. It was my insecurity, Sierra. I'm sorry."

"It'll be okay, Andrew," she said, not believing herself but following Eric's lead.

Hobbes again knelt beside her. Looked at his watch. "Ten minutes. Now we wait."

"And what happens after the ten minutes are up?" Sierra asked him.

He didn't answer. He seemed to stare at nothing for several seconds. Then he said, "They say the mountain lions down here don't see people as food. Wasn't that long ago humans had to run from lions to avoid getting eaten. What's scarier? Getting eaten by something or getting washed away?"

Was he trying to connect with her? Should she engage with him? Would he stop? "People still run from predators," she said. "But they look like you now. You don't have to be one."

"I read about this young woman dying of cancer. She said the little stuff didn't matter when you knew you were out of time. She described the day she had that final realization as something like a burning feeling in her heart. I can't remember the exact word she used," Hobbes said.

He looked skyward and touched the lump in his neck absently, as if unaware he was doing it. "I'm interested in what happens after a crisis. You know what that usually is?"

"Tell me," Sierra said, her voice shaking.

"People make their deals with God. The crisis ends. They go back to what they were. What if that girl hadn't been dying of cancer? Would she still have seen things the same?" He stared out at the canyon. "They all think I killed them."

"Killed who?" Sierra asked.

"The hostages at the dam."

Eric's voice. "You were there?"

Hobbes ignored him and looked at Sierra. "My initial orders were to take hostages. Stage a protest to stop the late Wade Ford's hearing." He took a breath, released a sigh. "My orders changed substantially to bringing explosives. We took the dam. My team split up. Some sprayed graffiti, others guarded the hostages. We planted the worm in the computer system and hid the bombs in a staging area. I went down the elevator and walked into the power plant right as they shot that little girl in the chest."

Even if he was her enemy, it was disconcerting to watch him coming unhinged.

"They aren't like us. Children, I mean. The light in their eyes is different. I've seen the light fade out of a lot of adult eyes. Some I put out myself. Others were brothers I lost. But the kind of light in that little girl's eyes was . . . different. Innocent. Scared. Beautiful."

"Emma."

"What?"

"Her name was Emma," Sierra said. Maybe she could get him to stop.

"Emma," Hobbes repeated. "I lost it. I shot all four of my guys in the power plant. I got out right before the feds and SOCOM came and killed everyone else."

Sierra felt time slipping away, knowing that with every second she was here, she had less of a chance to get back to Benny, get him to safety, hold him close to her breast.

"Hobbes."

"Sierra?"

"What happens next here?"

His expression showed no emotion. "You're all going to die."

A silence fell. Sierra's thoughts ranged from accepting her fate to believing Hobbes and feeling like she deserved this. She checked on Eric and Andrew. She loved both of them and they were hurting. Because of her. She thought of Benny and Scarlett wearing gags. Crying. Confused. Scared.

This had to stop. She had to stop him. "Look at me, Hobbes."

He did. Sierra locked eyes with him.

"When I found out I was pregnant, I made my first promise to my unborn child. The one promise I'll keep no matter what. When he was born I named him Benjamin and held him close while he nursed. He wasn't an hour old yet. I didn't know what I was doing. I told him my promise. 'You are my hope, Benny. I will do anything for you.' Now I say it to him every day. I whispered it in his ear this morning when he was asleep. I'm going to keep my promise, Hobbes." She clenched her jaw, spoke through her teeth. "If I have to kill you, I will."

Hobbes studied her, then said, "Scientists say the earth is 4.5 billion years old. Entire worlds evolved from microbes. A civilization is born, dies, disappears. Everything we are will one day be a band of ancient rock. And in all of humanity that's evolved to not care, there's you."

"You'll never understand a mother's love."

"Loving something doesn't mean it's safe."

"He's not an 'it'. His name is Benny. He's my son. It's obvious you don't have children."

His face held surprise. "Maybe I understand you more than you know." He rubbed his stubbled chin, then held up his finger. "Caustic. That's the word the dying woman used." Hobbes smiled, but Sierra saw no joy in it.

He stood and looked at the device in his hand. "I read up on you, Sierra. An environmental lawyer who wanted change. But instead, you changed. For your son. I see that now. I'm trying to change too, but this life I chose..." He looked back at her. "I still have one bad dream I can't shake. And I keep seeing things."

———

"How does this work out for you?" Sierra asked.

"This is bigger than me," Hobbes said.

"You can stop it."

He laughed. Stared at her. "You worked for years trying to help environmental groups 'save the planet,'" he said, using air quotes. "You honestly think that the human race, which can't even preserve itself, can dictate the course of a 4.5-billion-year-old rock?"

He paused to check on Samuels and Andrew. Looked back at Sierra.

"We have power hungry, wannabe autocrats working clandestine social media campaigns with artificial intelligence to hijack and rewire the thoughts of entire generations. People fight online about meaningless things. Most of that bullshit is posted by bots. These people hate each other and don't even know why."

He took a breath. "We worry about dictators or egotistical presidents having the power of the nuke at their fingertips. What about exploiting advanced technology to control the very humans who created it? How much longer do we have, Sierra? Look around you. You think this canyon needs you? We can abuse it for a thousand years, and a thousand years after we're gone, it'll look like we were never here. The earth doesn't need us. The human race does."

He saw a trace of something, understanding perhaps, in her face. "I think Rev Six is done pondering. Done observing—"

"Cancer?" Sierra interrupted. "You have it your neck?"

Hobbes felt a flash of anger. "That's none of your business." He glared at her. "But since we're sharing, what kind of person sells out everything they believe in to get rich?"

"What? What the hell are you doing right now?" she snapped.

"What kind of mother shows that example to her child?"

"Leave her alone," Andrew yelled.

Hobbes leaned into Sierra. "You'll feel better if you admit you sold out," he said, goading her. "That's why you're down here, right? That's why your son is in danger. It's your fault."

She held his gaze, fighting back tears, starting to rock back-and-forth.

He nodded at her, knowing he'd hit a nerve. "Go on. Say it. Why'd you sell out? And what other kind of work did you do for Wade Ford?" Air quotes again around "work."

Sierra opened her mouth and made a croaking noise. "The clock said three minutes to midnight," she said, gritting her teeth. "Mama . . ."

Hobbes froze. "What are you talking about, Sierra?"

Her breathing grew rapid.

Samuels and Andrew shouted at Hobbes in protest.

"Mama—"

The ringing two-way satellite radio startled them. He rose and moved away to answer the call as Sierra broke down. It was Pieter.

"Can you confirm all the transfers were initiated?" Hobbes asked.

"Confirmed," said the happy-game-show-host Dutch voice on the other end.

"You're sure?"

"Positive. What is with you today, anyway, my boy?" he asked. "Who shit in your Cheerios?"

Hobbes groaned. "It's *pissed* in your Cheerios. They can't reverse the payments?"

A laugh. "Nee, my boy. You are golden. It will take a few days, but they are all in progress. Where the hell are you? Sounds like you are on the moon."

"Might as well be," said Hobbes. He hung up the satellite phone and dialed. Sweat flooded his vision. He trembled. The line opened.

"Code in." There was no mistaking the cold voice of Shark Eyes, the director from the interrogation room.

Hobbes thought for a second. Today's code-in language was Italian. "L'inganno puó far sanguinare la luna," he said. Deceit may bleed the moon.

The response came. "E far cadere le stelle." And cause the stars to fall. "Pale Horse One. Go."

"This is ID number 451588 to Pale Horse One," Hobbes said. "Packages received. ID number 009853 complied. Request permission to execute diversion and abort Cygnus, over."

"Stand by, 451588."

A minute ticked by. Hobbes felt sweat pouring down his back. Sierra was watching him, panting. Yes. There was something about her. Something drawing him in. Distracting.

"451588 to Pale Horse One, say again, request permission to execute diversion and abort Cygnus, over," Hobbes repeated. He swore through gritted teeth.

His captives watched him. The roar of the creek was like blood in his ears.

Shark Eyes came back on the line. "Execute diversion. Proceed with Cygnus."

Hobbes's lowered the radio. Swallowed. Raised it back up. "Bad copy, Pale Horse One. Interrogative: My orders are to execute diversion and Cygnus? Say again, 009853 complied. Packages received. Do you confirm?"

"Affirmative. Proceed with diversion and Cygnus. Deliver packages as ordered. Complete the assignment, 451588."

"Wait . . ." Hobbes said, almost in awe. Thoughts flashed like strobe lights. "Did you play me?"

"Don't break radio protocol. You know what's on the table. We're watching her. And watch your six, 451588. 009853 contacted US intelligence. An assassin is en route."

A click sounded.

Hobbes's mouth filled with acid.

He puked up what little was in his stomach but recovered fast. Sierra and Andrew hadn't moved, but Samuels was already on one knee, his stance revealing his intentions. Hobbes wiped his mouth. Remembered what he'd told them about the flood. What he had thought was a lie. Instead, what Rev Six intended with Cygnus was real.

He raised the pistol at Andrew first.

For all her stoicism, Sierra crumbled and became hysterical. "Please, no, please let us go. We won't tell anyone anything. Please don't kill him."

Andrew's eyes were warm above his slight smile. "I've loved you, Sierra. I hope you felt that. Having Benny with you was my greatest accomplishment. Don't watch, baby."

Hobbes felt the Glock's weight in his hand. Pictured it being Amelia bound and gagged in that room. He let out his breath to squeeze the trigger. The chances of Sierra and Andrew escaping the canyon alive were nil. There was no way they'd make it out in time.

Life. Death. A new start. More nightmares.

Caustic.

All three of them breathed out a heavy sigh of relief when Hobbes lowered the gun. He pulled the key card from his pocket and tossed it on the ground in front of Sierra.

"That's the key I found in their room."

"Whose room?" asked Andrew.

Hobbes checked his watch. "They've probably pissed themselves by now. They're hungry. Breathing is harder with a gag. You're over fifteen miles away, most of it on foot through the canyon. You won't make it."

"Sierra? Whose room?" Andrew pleaded. "Does he have our son?" He became frantic, his voice shrill. "Does he have our son?"

Hobbes walked to Andrew and put the gun to his head. "Don't make me change my mind."

Andrew stayed quiet, but his chest heaved and his wild expression searched Sierra and Hobbes for answers.

Hobbes stepped up on a flat boulder. Raised the arm that held the transmitter. Wondered if it would work from this distance. He wasn't near Page. He was in the bottom of nowhere, surrounded by walls. Maybe it wouldn't work. Maybe nothing would happen at all.

"Wait," Sierra shouted. "They paid you. I heard you say it. Why are you still doing this?"

Looking up at the sky he said, "Violence may shake the earth and turn the sun black." A long pause. "Deceit may bleed the moon and . . . and . . . cause the stars to fall. Though the heavens may diminish, and the mountains move, through it all we . . . we remain the hidden defenders. The sworn protectors. The chosen crusaders." He looked at her. "I can usually say it perfectly."

"Say what perfectly?" she pleaded.

"They made me their fall guy. If I fail or get caught, I'm just another environmental terrorist in Senator Pace's arsenal. No link back to Rev Six either way. And they still get her. How did I not sniff it out sooner?"

"What are you talking about?" she said gasping, shaking her head.

Could he explain it to Sierra? Should he? He had only one overpowering thought: Amelia's life depended on his going through with something the American public had never seen.

"I believed my superiors. They told me it had to be a credible threat or she'd never pay. We set the small bombs to make sure she knew we meant business. To keep the bomb squad busy. A classic diversion. If she refused, I was supposed to blow the little ones, let her freak out, then tell her the bigger bombs were hidden in the middle of the dam. They told me those big ones were an insurance policy to remind the United States that Rev Six could do whatever we wanted. She pays, it's over. That was my objective. But now . . . now . . ." Hobbes touched his neck.

He gave Sierra a long, sincere look. "I don't know why I'm telling you all this. Sometimes you have to dance with death to know what kind of party it is." He returned his gaze to the sky and muttered, "I'm sorry, Amelia."

He flipped the plastic cover on the transmitter and pressed a button. The controller made a beeping sound, then a long, haunting tone, then another beeping sound. He pressed the second button, the one he thought he'd never press. He had been naïve. Another beep. Another haunting tone. Then the final, confirming beep. Hobbes would never be sure, but he thought he heard an old woman calling in distress, as if something was attacking her. Or was it a raven? He jerked his head toward the sound but didn't hear it again. He wondered if he had heard it at all.

Chapter 13

Operation Cygnus

ONE AFTER ANOTHER, HELICOPTERS SWARMED IN THE evacuation. Goodnight marveled at Jones's brilliant acting. In the monitor, Jones moved around the command center, typing on a keyboard, moving a mouse, negotiating the machines with a familiarity Goodnight hadn't seen in their three days of working together.

"Hell of an actor, ain't he? What's he doing?" Goodnight asked. Then it hit him. "Harris."

"What?" Tanaka asked.

"Harris. You haven't found him because he's still in there. Jones must have done something with him. I guess that whenever Jones was manning the observation terminal over the last few days, he was covering Anderson and Jackson while they hid their bombs. Had all of us fooled, the son of a bitch."

"I'm pretty pissed about it, too, dude," Parker said.

"Don't get any ideas, Colonel Parker," Tanaka said. "That thing could blow at any time. It's a suicide mission."

Parker smiled. "I haven't been called colonel in a long time, General. In and out, ma'am. We still don't know for sure if it's going to blow. Or when. But our superiors are going to want this guy bad. What'll happen to us if this thing doesn't blow and they find out we let him go? Or that we didn't work harder to stop it? I'm sure Chief here wants some payback. My guys are up for a party anytime. In and out, ma'am."

Goodnight gave Tanaka an eager nod. He remembered all that malarkey Jones had told him about the hostages being executed. It'd be good to finish that conversation with Jones in an interrogation room.

Tanaka looked at the group of men before her. "Negative. Absolutely not."

Goodnight, Parker, and the other men didn't give an inch.

She scoffed, saying, "You all realize what you're asking? What's at stake?" The men nodded.

Tanaka glared at Goodnight. "Chief, if you lead these men into a trap, you better die in there. Parker, it's a snatch-and-grab only. You get your ass back here on the double. I'm putting mine on the line for you."

"Hooah, ma'am. Gear up, Chief," Parker said. "We leave in ninety seconds."

There was one more thing Goodnight needed to do. He walked around the Humvee and hunkered down, then dialed.

Judy picked up. "Fred, what's going on? The big cheeses are running around like Chicken Little, but no one's squawking. What's all that noise?"

Goodnight shouted over the helicopters while trying to be discreet. "Judy, telling you this might get me thrown in prison or worse. If you don't figure out how to get people out of the canyon, it's going to be bad."

"You're scaring me."

"Fear is a helluva motivator." He turned to see if he was being watched. The military police had their backs turned. Tanaka was griping at someone on the radio. He plugged his other ear with his pinky. "We've evacuated the structure. The 3rd Infantry, National Guard, the FBI Hostage Rescue Team, explosive ordnance disposal, Sandstone County, Coconino County, everyone. They're all here."

"EOD? Explosives?" There was a long silence on the other end. "Oh God. Tell me this isn't what I think it is."

"Guys went rogue on me, Judy. We found bombs all over the facility. The lights on those things turned from green to red."

"I can't believe this is real."

"We have to assume so. If so, there'll be a wall of water coming down the canyon that will . . . well, you know." Goodnight's voice was full of shame. "This is on me. They beat me. But we might still be able to stop it."

"Focus, Fred. I'm working on flight crews, but it's slow-going. It's taking me longer because I have to keep all this secret and I can't tell any of the pilots why I might need them. Everyone I've talked to so far has cold feet about flying into restricted federal airspace without clearance."

"Tell 'em what's coming."

"You said not to tell anyone."

"Aw, screw it. The government's only handling high population density areas. They'll tell everyone it was a 'sunny day breach,' whatever that is. No mention of bombs or terrorists. No press allowed. They don't plan to save all the little communities downriver, so a few hundred people down in the canyon aren't enough to spare time and resources for either. They don't want a panic. You got any communications with the rangers down there?"

Judy was quiet for a few beats.

"Four hours, Judy."

"Four hours what?"

"If the dam blows, the engineers said the flood will hit the Black Bridge three or four hours later. Where the hell is the Black Bridge?"

"It's the main crossing right in the middle of the corridor, not far from Phantom Ranch and Bright Angel Campground. Lots of folks down there. The extreme rafters are on the river in the dozens for the high water."

Goodnight closed his eyes. "Two feet of water can float a car. Five hundred feet will destroy everything in its path. Stay by the phone."

"What are you going to do?"

"Something stupid. Talk to you soon."

"Fred?"

Eric listened to the beeps and tones. The beeps reminded him of the sound the buttons on the microwave in his apartment made. Was Hobbes telling the truth? Did those beeps mean death out here? Hobbes stepped off the boulder, dropped the transmitter, stomped on it, and picked up the pieces. Then he startled, as if something had scared him, and looked off into the distance. Eric noticed the sweat beading on Hobbes's colorless face. Hobbes addressed Sierra and Andrew.

"Go north, Benny and the nanny die bound and gagged. You might not make the climb up the north rim, anyway. I hear it's a real bitch. Go south, you have a chance to save them. But you won't make it in time to beat the flood." He turned to Eric. "We have a helicopter to steal."

"I'm not leaving my baby!" Sierra screamed as she struggled to get at Hobbes.

He pointed the gun at her. Eric was afraid of what either of them might do next. Sierra's body hitched, her face dirty, her teeth bared. Hobbes stared back at her, waiting.

"Sierra," Eric said. "We're almost out of this. Hang on."

She looked like something possessed, but she stayed put. Hobbes lowered the gun. He went to each of their packs and poured out their water, taking some for himself. He did the same with Victor and Wade's packs. He flicked open a tactical knife and cut Sierra's zip tie.

"After I leave with Samuels, you let your boyfriend loose. If you do it before I'm out of sight, I'll shoot Samuels."

"Where are you taking him?" she asked.

"Yeah, what's your plan, asshole?" Eric asked.

Hobbes didn't answer. He grabbed Eric's elbow and helped him up, then turned to address Sierra and Andrew. "Stay here for ten minutes. If I see you behind me, I'll kill you."

They hadn't made it far down the trail when Eric, still zip-tied, made his move. Hobbes had the pistol stuck in Eric's back, but a tall water bar gave Eric an opening. When Hobbes stepped down, balanced on one leg as the other negotiated the drop, Eric pivoted and rammed his head into Hobbes's abdomen. They fell onto the trail, Hobbes coughing and sucking air. Eric fought to stand and kicked him twice, his adrenaline pumping.

At the second kick, Hobbes's two-way satellite radio fell from the pouch on his plate carrier. Eric looked for the pistol but didn't see it. Hobbes lay on his side, still coughing. It was now or never.

He remembered his survival and escape training. Eric leaned over, raised his arms behind him as far as he could, and slammed them down onto his lower back. Something in his right thumb popped. He cried out from the pain. The zip tie held. He repeated the process. It snapped on the third attempt. He picked up the two-way satellite radio and shoved it into his cargo pocket. Scanned for the pistol again. Had to be under Hobbes's writhing body. He looked for the knife Hobbes had used earlier but couldn't find it. When he raised his foot over Hobbes's head to heel-crush his skull, the man's eyes opened. He grabbed Eric's foot and twisted it. Eric lost his balance and stumbled but ran back toward Sierra and Andrew.

He'd made it thirty feet when it felt like a fire broke out on his lower back. He fell and rolled hard to a stop. There was a crack near his ear, then a zing above his head. Eric scrambled behind a boulder as a chunk of it exploded into dusty red fragments. He crouched for a moment, panting and hurting, then peered around the boulder. Waited. Touched his back under his shirt. Blood on his fingers.

He checked the trail. No sign of Hobbes.

Eric ran, grunting from the pain in his back. He entered the alcove where Sierra and Andrew were hiding behind one of the two big boulders and collapsed. She ran to him and landed on her knees. Andrew screamed at her to get back behind the rock.

"Andrew, help me," Sierra begged.

"He might still be shooting, Sierra!" Andrew shouted.

They pulled Eric back to their hiding spot behind the boulder. "Hobbes didn't follow me," he said, gasping. Tunnel vision closed in on him. His hearing faded. His fighter pilot training reminded him he was losing consciousness. Someone lifted his shirt.

"Entry wound in his lower back. No exit wound," Andrew said, his voice muddled.

Before his vision went black, Eric saw Andrew pull off his own long-sleeved shirt. Felt Andrew shove it under his back where the pain burned hot. "Hold that tight on the wound, Sierra."

From somewhere far away, Sierra shouted, "You're the doctor. Help him."

Then Andrew, even farther away. "I'm not a doctor, Sierra. I'm a med student."

Sierra again, almost inaudible. "What are we supposed to do?"

———

Goodnight felt like an interloper; Parker's team moved as one, as if by telepathy, stopping, moving, aiming their carbines, advancing through the facility. He didn't belong with them, and worse, the dam felt different now. Less mystical, more macabre. Goodnight remembered his conversation with Miller about it sounding like a tomb inside. He gritted his teeth at the thought.

"Parker," Goodnight shouted as they ran, "we can take the elevator and get there faster. Or we can take the spiral staircase. I don't know if there's a bomb in that elevator shaft."

"How long will it take us to get down the staircase?"

"To the dungeon's level? About ten, fifteen minutes in quick time."

"Seriously? What about back up?"

"Thirty. Forty-five, maybe."

"We don't have that kinda time. We'll take our chances."

They rode the elevator down to the dungeon. Conversation was terse. The men's faces were solemn. Parker asked Goodnight, "Do we take him dead or alive?"

"Alive," Goodnight answered. "So you're Colonel Parker now, huh? What happened to Milkman?"

Parker's team members snickered and exchanged glances.

"Just assistant special agent in charge now. Milkman on ops," he said, shaking his head. "Which is a long, stupid story." He sneered at his team before he addressed them. "Lieutenant Mark Jones is a combat veteran, fellas. SEAL Team Six. Don't underestimate him, and don't assume he's alone. Chief, stay in the back."

Goodnight nodded, accepting his limits.

Exiting the elevator, one of the operators looked at Goodnight. "None of ASAC Parker's kids look like him."

Goodnight squinted, confused. Then it hit him. "Oh. Milkman." Despite himself and the situation, he let out a laugh.

Within minutes they stood outside the dungeon. One of the men peeked into the door's tiny window and nodded at Parker. Goodnight scowled. The idea that Jones was a bad guy was still alien to him. The idea that the dam might explode with them in it wasn't any easier to swallow.

———

Andrew stopped rifling through Victor's pack and asked Sierra, "When were you going to tell me that psycho kidnapped our son?"

"Andrew, we have to get to Benny." She looked around for answers as if someone might be holding them on cue cards.

"I asked you a question. How long did you know?"

"Can we beat eight trillion gallons of water to that bridge we crossed this morning?"

"Sierra."

"Fine," she snapped. "He told me when he took us hostage. Said if I told any of you, he'd start killing people. Satisfied? Or do you think I'm lying again? And how the hell are you so calm right now?"

"Because I have to be. The thought of our child being kidnapped and tied up freaks me out more than this supposed flood coming. But we have to solve this problem. Getting worked up won't do it. I'm sorry I got emotional earlier—I thought he shot you." He knelt and tapped her hand, pointing at Eric. "Something else. He was in on it."

"What?"

"He was in on it. When you passed out, Hobbes talked to Eric like they both knew something we didn't."

Sierra gawked at Andrew, then looked back at Eric, her mouth wide open.

"Told you I didn't trust this dude."

She took a deep breath and glared at Andrew. "You really think this is a good time for your crossing guard act again? I know you don't like him." Then again, it had been years since she'd known Eric. All of a sudden, Andrew had her wondering. It made her question herself. Which made her bristle.

"What you're saying is nuts. Especially now when he's lying here shot. When our lives are stake." Her anger and frustration took over. Sierra stood and shouted, "Benny's in danger! The water might drown all of us. So just shut up, Andrew." She broke down crying. "I thought I said the words this morning to Benny. I did, right? Didn't I say them?"

"Easy, Sierra. Easy." He remained quiet, staring at her. "Help me lift him, and I'll work on him." He was quiet until she knelt back down. "Victor had a trauma kit in his pack. One thing he did right."

Sierra breathed, hating herself for projecting her anger and fear and doubt onto Andrew. Hating herself even more for doubling down on him after what she had done with the very man he was treating.

Grunting, they pulled Eric over. He was unconscious, moaning as Andrew tended the wound.

"The bullet's still in there. We have some bandages and scissors, your basic pack-and-wrap kit," Andrew said as he placed the items neatly on a flat rock near Eric's torso. "Let me see what I can do."

He used scissors from the kit to cut Eric's shirt away. Cleaned the wound. Ripped open a packet of bright white gauze and stuffed it into the bloody bullet hole. Sierra felt helpless. Her mind raced. Andrew tore open another gauze packet and shoved it into the wound too, pressing down again, applying more pressure. Then he bound the bandages tight with cloth wraps around Eric's torso.

"Wait. He has a knife," Sierra said, panting as she pulled out the folding knife Eric had clipped to his pocket. "Can you get the bullet out with this?"

Andrew looked stunned. "Are you kidding? I have no way to sterilize it. Taking a bullet out is surgical, not something I'd try out here, even if I had a shaver or hemostats. It's not like the movies, Sierra. If I try to get that bullet out, I might kill him."

He'd grabbed whatever he thought was helpful from all the packs and stuffed it into his. They tried every cell phone Andrew had found in his grim search of the bodies, hoping that one might pick up a signal. Nothing worked. He crouched down beside her and Eric. "I think the bleeding has slowed. Eric, can you hear me?" he said, tapping Eric's cheek. Eric stirred. Sierra helped Andrew coax him up. He looked at them, dazed.

"I found this in Victor's pack," Andrew said, holding up a sleek gadget that looked expensive. "Sat phone." He held up another gadget. "This is some kind of locator device. You push this button."

"What are you waiting for? Turn it on, call 911. Push the damn button," Sierra exclaimed.

———

The team set up on both sides of the door, guns ready. Parker nodded at a burly man who, with the force of a mule, kicked the door off the hinges. The men poured through the doorway like water. Goodnight heard screaming and yelling and fists striking flesh, but no gunfire. A second later, there was a shriek.

Several voices yelled, "Clear."

"Chief," Parker hollered, "we gotta be snappy about this."

Jones stood pinned against the wall behind the computer bank. Blood streamed from both nostrils and the corner of his mouth. His head lolled. When he opened his mouth to talk, they punched him again.

"Wait!" Goodnight shouted. He worked his way past the men and to Jones. "Why, Jones? What'd you give it all up for? Why blow up the dam?"

Jones caught his breath and sniffled through the blood. His head rolled and he tried to focus on Goodnight. "Rev . . . rev . . . sss . . ."

"What? C'mon, Jones!" Goodnight yelled.

"Reve . . . Revelations . . ." Jones said.

"Revelations? Is he talking about the Bible?" Parker asked Goodnight. "We gotta go, Chief."

"Hell, I don't know," Goodnight said. "Start making sense, Jones. These guys are ready to eat you up and shit you out. What are you up to?"

"Revelation . . . S-Six. H-Hobbes."

"Wait—Revelation Six."

Goodnight looked at Parker. "That's what Hayes with the FBI mentioned the other day." He looked back at Jones. "Who is Hobbes?"

Jones's head swung toward him again, his lolling eyes focusing on Goodnight. "I was sent here to . . . to . . ."

———

Andrew stood and dialed. Sierra saw his face light up when someone answered.

"Yes, ma'am, my name is Andrew Thomas. I'm in Grand Canyon National Park near— what's this place called?"

"Ribbon Falls," she answered with a grin, looking around for where the rescue helicopter would land. "Andrew, tell them about Benny and Scarlett. Give them the room number."

Andrew continued. "Ribbon Falls. A man has been shot. Our son has been kidnapped." He nodded at Sierra, smiling, then looked puzzled and pulled the phone away from his ear. "Said they were dispatch and were getting me to the rangers, but then the line went dead." Andrew repeated the process with the same result.

Sierra grabbed the phone and tried herself, this time talking over the dispatcher when they answered. "We have an emergency down here near Ribbon Falls, and our son has been kidnapped—" She pulled the phone away from her ear. "The line went dead again." She kept trying to no avail.

"Why the hell would it keep cutting off like that?" Andrew asked.

Puzzled, Sierra sank back to her knees next to Eric. Then she noticed something hanging out of the side pocket on his right pant leg. It looked like the same sort of antenna she'd seen on Hobbes's phone. She pulled it out, unable contain her surprise when she recognized it. "Andrew," she said, "this is the phone Hobbes had. Eric must have stolen it. It looks . . . complicated. There's a button on the side. It's like a walkie-talkie, maybe? You push this button to talk?"

"Try 911 again."

"I don't know how to dial out on this thing."

Andrew looked at it. "It'll take us a while to figure it out."

Sierra examined the phone, hoping something would make sense. Four buttons surrounded a square navigation pad. She pressed the one on the top left and the digital screen displayed SELECT. She navigated through the screen but found several more functions she didn't understand. She was about to give up when she saw a setting that said PRESET. She selected it. The screen flashed PRESET SELECT 1–99. She looked at Andrew.

"I think it's got a speed dial function." She selected number one and shrugged at Andrew.

The phone beeped out ten numbers in quick succession and started ringing.

———

". . . to stop Hobbes. To stop Cygnus," Jones said.

Goodnight's blood went icy. "Cygnus," he said, looking at Parker, then back at Jones. "You were sent here to stop who, Jones?"

"Hobbes. S-sorry, Chief. You were right. Anderson. Jackson. Harris."

"How can I believe you? Was any of what you told me about the little girl the other day true?"

Jones looked Goodnight in the eye. "W-wouldn't lie about something like that."

"Who are you, Jones? Where's Harris?"

Jones chuckled through the blood. "I'm nobody, Chief. I had a real n-name once. Mark Jones now. Pretty damn anonymous, isn't it? Harris is in the closet."

One of Parker's men opened the closet door, and Harris's sitting body fell over. A large splotch of blood covered his lower back and the closet floor.

Goodnight peered at the body, then back at Jones. "Why didn't you do something before they put bombs all over the dam, Jones?"

"N-no one could know. I had to w-wait until they revealed themselves. I needed to catch Hobbes or someone close to him. Harris wouldn't go down without a fight. I had suspects but he beat me, Chief. Just like he beat you." Jones grinned and spat blood. "Hobbes always wins. Always."

"We gotta book it, Chief," said Parker. "I have no idea if or when these things might go."

"Who the hell is Hobbes?" Goodnight said furiously. He grabbed Jones's collar.

Jones groaned. "The limp-dick that just sent the s-signal. No one knows his real name."

"Who does he work for? What can you tell me about Cygnus?"

Jones laughed. "If you find out, Chief, the United States government would love to kn-know. We think he's with Revelation Six. Sneaky bastards. Harris must have gotten in here and armed the bombs after we evac'd. I got him with my blade right after he did it. I tried to disarm the bombs. Helluva a worm they planted. But right before I found the fix, Hobbes s-sent the detonation signal. I missed it by seconds."

"We gotta exfil now, Chief. How can we believe anything this dude says, anyway?" Parker asked.

"We can't," said Goodnight, his face and voice grim. "But that's the second time I've heard someone talking about Revelation Six and an operation called Cygnus since I got here."

He grabbed Jones's collar and was starting to leave when a phone rang. They looked for the source. It was none of the landlines. The sound was coming from Harris's body. Goodnight moved to it and heaved the dead man over, finding what looked like a satellite phone or two-way radio tucked into his kit.

Goodnight looked at Parker, who shrugged and said, "I guess answer it, Chief."

Goodnight grabbed the phone. A light blue digital display showed an incoming number. He guessed and used the center button of the navigation pad to select it. The connection opened. He depressed the talk button on the side. "Hello?"

"Oh, thank God," a woman answered, sounding thin and far away. Static plagued the line. "Who is this?"

The phone was a push-to-talk two-way satellite radio; the woman's voice cut through to everyone in the room. "This is Glen Canyon Security Chief Fred Goodnight. Who's this?"

"Are you really fucking there?"

Goodnight gave the phone a scowl. "Yes, ma'am, I am really fu—I am really here. How do you have this number? Are you with Harris? Cygnus? If you're part of his group, you need to turn yourself in now."

"Turn myself in? The hell? I'm trying to get emergency help. How do you have this phone? Where are you?"

"Lady, I just told you who I am. I'm at Glen Canyon Dam. I don't have time for this right now. How did you get this number? If you have an emergency, hang up and call 911."

"We both have a fucking emergency! Your dam's going to blow up, Mr. Goodnight." A pause. "Look, my name is Sierra Justice. Our son and his nanny have been kidnapped. My friend is shot and bleeding to death. Some guy named Hobbes just held us hostage and killed five people. Says he sent a signal to blow up your dam—"

Goodnight hit the talk button. "Did you just say Hobbes?"

"Yes."

Goodnight looked at Parker. "What did you say your name was?"

"Sierra Justice."

"And you say he pushed a button?"

She was frantic, impatient. "What's with the twenty freaking questions? Yes, I did. He told someone on the phone he was in position.

Then after some more calls, he made a big show of pushing some button. Said it would blow up Glen Canyon Dam. Then he shot our friend. You gotta get out of there. Hobbes said it's going to be the biggest flood the world has ever seen. We need help. We need to get back to our son, his name's Benny, and I'm—I'm . . . just so scared right—"

The static became so loud that Goodnight had to hold the phone away from his face. "Ms. Justice? Ms. Justice, can you hear me?" There was nothing. He looked at the phone, with no idea how to call her back. He pocketed it as he looked at Parker.

"I don't know who to believe anymore, Parker. Let's go."

"Chief," Jones said. He grinned with bloody teeth at Goodnight and held up his watch, showing a descending timer. "We have four minutes and thirty-three seconds."

No one breathed.

Goodnight broke the silence, grabbing Jones's arm and pushing through the men. The team began yelling to exfiltrate, shouting to move and GO GO GO. They crammed into the elevator. Goodnight saw the faces of the men breathing heavily, sweating, looking up, all willing it to go faster. He had to hold Jones up. After an eternity the door opened.

Someone hollered, "Thirty seconds!"

Goodnight hobbled along with Jones's arm around his shoulders. The team outran them. Someone, maybe Parker, hit the exit door and daylight flooded the elevator room gallery. Goodnight focused on the open door and grunted.

"Almost there, Jones." A flash blinded him. A concussion turned his world to black.

CHAPTER 14

Fluvial Geomorphology

ICAN'T GET HIM BACK," SIERRA SAID. "I'VE HIT THE SPEED dial number five times now, and it's just static. No other numbers are programmed."

"911 still isn't working on Wade's sat phone either. We have to call someone else, Sierra," said Andrew.

"Who? You got a phone book?"

"Right," Andrew mumbled. He held up the other device he'd found.

"I pushed the button on this locator, but I'm not sure how that's supposed to work if our calls can't get through. We can't wait for a rescue that might never come. I hoped we had some park literature somewhere, but there's nothing."

Sierra noticed Eric listening to them, his head going back and forth as though he was watching a tennis match in slow motion.

"How many people could be down here right now on the trail? In that camp back there? What was it called? Phantom something?" she asked.

"Phantom Ranch," Andrew said. "Or Bright Angel, maybe?"

"Yes. Think about how many people we saw this morning. If the park service knows the water's coming, will they even try to get us all out?" she asked, desperate. "We have to get Eric up. Andrew, look at me."

Sierra harnessed the new-found power she'd felt in the Sandstone County courtroom. She grabbed Andrew's shoulders and spoke to him as she had addressed Judge Sumner. "We can't count on anyone else to get us back to Benny and Scarlett. Maybe this Hobbes psycho was full of it. Maybe nothing's coming. Or maybe it is. Either way, this is something we have to do ourselves. No matter what it takes. Agreed?"

"I got you."

"Then you need to get going," she said, her voice thick.

Andrew's jaw dropped.

———

Popping noises and flashes woke Goodnight. He saw a black smudge. The smudge focused into a gaping crack in the concrete above his head. Electricity sparked from snapped wires protruding from a busted conduit. He rolled over and winced. The pain in his back and legs was a deep throbbing ache, but his left arm felt scorched. A baseball-sized patch of his sleeve was burned off, a circle of raw skin pulled back. He stopped thinking about it when he saw Jones's vacant eye.

Mark Jones, or whatever his name was, was missing half his face and one arm. A pool of blood oozed toward Goodnight's leg. Now he'd be lucky to find out what Jones was doing at the dam at all, whose side he was actually on.

Parker checked on Goodnight, rolled him over, and felt for wounds.

"Nothing serious, Chief," he said. He grimaced at Jones. "Whoa. He's DRT as fuck, ain't he? Can you walk?"

Goodnight sat up, groggy, and looked at Jones. Dead right there. With Parker's help, he hobbled toward the exit.

"Watch out," Parker shouted, kicking Jones's severed arm out of Goodnight's path.

Two of Parker's men picked up the disfigured body of one of their comrades. Goodnight squinted hard against the daylight and the pain of his injuries. They escaped the concrete surface of the dam and rode the elevator up to the ivory tower, then proceeded through the parking lot to Tanaka.

"They all went off," she yelled. "We lose anyone?"

Parker gave her a grim look. "I lost Simmons. Chief here lost his XO, Jones, or whoever the hell he was. You know that guy was deep cover, General?"

Tanaka didn't answer, but the look on her face told Goodnight all he needed to know.

The Hostage Rescue Team SWAT medic examined Goodnight and told him he probably wouldn't walk normally or be able to screw anyone for a while, and he'd have a big scar on his arm. Goodnight limped to Parker and Tanaka, where Parker was talking and pointing at the monitor. Goodnight said nothing about the two-way satellite radio; he hoped Parker hadn't either. Tanaka would surely take it, and then the Justice lady wouldn't have anyone to talk to but feds who would lie to her.

"The tunnel camera's busted, but the other two still work. I see debris like we saw in the elevator room. Lots of water spraying. Must have breached one of the penstocks. With all that pressure behind it, I have to assume that thing could still fail," Parker said, pointing at the dam.

His radio crackled. "Bonsai One to Milkman, copy?" asked a voice.

Tanaka's head whipped around. "Where are they?"

"I posted men on both sides of the dam on the access roads," he said.

Goodnight admired how Parker spoke into the radio quickly and with authority.

"All Bonsai elements, this is Milkman. Bonsai Two, proceed to my position. Bonsai One, hold your position." Parker looked at Tanaka. "With Simmons gone, I'd prefer two guys with us, but I'm not letting anyone cross that dam until we clear it."

Goodnight heard helicopters over the lake. Several aircraft hovered over the boats outside the floating bomb barrier upriver. Rubberneckers jockeying for a view of whatever was happening at the dam. The choppers paused over the boats, and loudspeakers broadcast unintelligible messages. The boats cruised away in what Goodnight could only assume was a mass exodus upriver to the nearest beach. To his right was the highway bridge still covered in vehicles, but only a few warm bodies lingered to watch if the tragedy would indeed unfold.

He thought about what the Justice lady had said. How could he ignore that? The answer was simple: He couldn't. He grabbed his cell phone and hid behind a Humvee.

Judy answered almost immediately. "Give it to me, Fred."

He minded his volume.

"It's real. Start getting people out, now. And Judy . . ." He sucked in air between his gritted teeth. "Make an anonymous call to the Phoenix news. Pick a network TV station. Glen Canyon Dam is about to breach, and everyone in every city or community above or below Lake Mead needs to get out. The feds ain't gonna tell 'em in time. There'll be a panic, and they'll probably figure out I'm the one that leaked it, but dammit, we gotta let people know now. Has something to do with some secret operation called Cygnus."

He purposely left out the part about how some strange woman named Sierra Justice had influenced his decision to leak the news to the media. Same with Hobbes. After being fooled by Jones, he needed more information before he started name-dropping.

"Fred, are you—"

"Now, Judy." He hung up, walked back to the group, and noticed that Parker was watching him.

The general's radio crackled. "Ground, this is Command, do you copy?"

"This is Ground. Copy, Command," said General Tanaka.

"Engineers aren't convinced the dam is going to breach. They think the explosions might have done minor damage at best. We need to get a team in there to check before we give Washington a situation report."

Goodnight's stomach twisted into knots. What did he just say? Did he have time to call Judy back and tell her to abort? He would sure try. Just as he moved away to call her back, the two explosive ordnance disposal men comprising Bonsai Two came running from the parking lot and rejoined Parker next to Goodnight. Tanaka walked up, looking at him.

She keyed her radio. "Command, this is Ground. Interrogative: You want to send EOD back in? Is that safe, over?"

"Ground, we need to assess the damage, over."

Tanaka's face screwed up. She hesitated before raising the radio back to her lips. "Roger, Command. ETA on the engineers, over?"

"ETA your position in five, over."

"Roger, Command, out."

Tanaka looked at Parker with a long face. "You're up again, Dick. Get your people ready for another insert with the engineers."

Parker nodded. "No worries, General. This is how we pay the bills."

Tanaka looked at Goodnight. "As one of the walking wounded, you sit this one out with me."

Goodnight swore. He'd have to get somewhere alone with his phone, somehow.

Parker nudged Goodnight, who thought Parker was about to bring up the two-way satellite radio and the Justice woman and the Hobbes fella. Instead, he pulled a laminated photo out of his shirt and held it up for Goodnight to see. A pretty brunette sat next to Parker, both of them in civilian clothes in front of the ocean. Four boys of various ages surrounded them, each one the spitting image of Parker, down to the close-cropped high-and-tight haircut.

"Don't trust anything these jerk-offs on my team tell you, Chief."

"That's a beautiful family, Dick," Goodnight said, chuckling. Parker's levity eased his tension.

Parker smiled at the picture a moment, then put it back. He looked at Goodnight and turned his back to Tanaka. "Figure out who that Justice lady is, Chief. And this Hobbes person too. I'm with you—this whole thing stinks." He nodded toward Tanaka. "I've known her for years. I trust her. But if you give her that phone, and if that Justice lady and her kid or whatever really need help, she won't get it from General Foster. Get me, Chief?"

Goodnight nodded.

A Blackhawk swooped in spinning dust. The crew escorted three Board of Reclamation engineers holding clipboards and cameras to Tanaka. One's face reflected confidence, while the other two appeared terrified.

"We're ready, General," Parker said. He smiled at the engineers. "Looks like a couple of these guys might piss their pants any second, though."

"Good luck, Parker," said Tanaka. "Hopefully the news is good."

He winked at Goodnight and moved out with his team and the engineers back down to the dam.

———

"You're the runner, Andrew. I'm not as fast as you. Not even close. You have to get to Phantom Ranch and warn people and get Benny and Scarlett. He has them bound and . . . gagged." Her last word came out in a half sob. "Scarlett has asthma. She already has a hard time breathing. And Benny must be so scared."

She fought the temptation to cry again. Time to be tough.

"I'm not leaving you, Sierra. Especially not with Eric. I don't trust him."

She stood and grabbed his shoulders. "This is the only way." Together they lifted Eric to his feet. "Eric, we have to get to Benny and get you help," Sierra said.

"I can barely stand. I'm thirsty," Eric mumbled, his face white. Andrew shared a glance with her when Eric coughed up bright red blood onto the trail. "I can't walk outta here."

"Dammit, Eric, yes, you can!" Sierra shouted. "You have to. We can't leave you here, and we can't stay."

Andrew held up a finger. "I found something else in Victor's first aid kit." He pulled a handful of plastic tubes from his pack. "They're epinephrine injectors for allergic shock. Basically adrenaline. I told Victor we might need one, but he brought one for everybody."

"What will that do?" Sierra asked.

"Wake me the hell up," Eric said.

"Basically," Andrew said. "Won't last long, maybe a few minutes, but it'll at least get him moving."

She looked at the tubes and back at Eric. "What do you think? Want to give it a shot?"

"Jesus, Counselor," Eric moaned.

Sierra let out a tired laugh.

Andrew scowled at them and handed her one of the epinephrine injectors.

"Where do I stick it?" Sierra asked, trying to read the tiny writing on the label.

Eric grabbed the tube from her hands, bit the top off with his teeth, and jammed the plunger into his quadriceps. He grimaced but remained standing. "That hurt."

"What happens next?" she asked Andrew.

He shrugged.

Sierra turned to grab her pack and heard Andrew shout. At a brisk limp, Eric was headed down the trail toward the main North Kaibab intersection.

"I guess the leg works," she said. She grabbed Andrew's arm. "Please, Andrew, go. I'll keep him moving as long as I can. Please go get Benny."

"You don't have any water. There's no filter in anyone's pack. You've got food, but without water, it may be worse to eat it. It'll only dehydrate you more. Victor was a crappy guide."

"Because he was a security guard, not an outdoorsman. Please, Andrew."

"Give me time to think about it?"

"Okay. I'm going to try calling that Goodnight guy at the dam again."

"Keep trying as long as that battery lasts. When we get to the creek, we need to wash all the blood off us," Andrew said. "We look like a damn horror movie."

Sierra repeated the process with the two-way radio. This time Goodnight answered, saying "Hang on."

She waited, heard what sounded like footsteps on gravel. Then Goodnight was back, whispering. He was hard to hear with the static.

"The bombs exploded, ma'am. But we've . . . team inside right now checking out the damage. It looks . . . structure is going to hold. You said your child was kidnapped? Where?"

Sierra stopped walking.

"Yes, Benny, he was kidnapped, but, wait—no—Mr. Goodnight, they need to get out of there," she said loudly. "Hobbes told me there were big bombs in there. Hear me? Big bombs. He said the little ones were a distraction . . . or something like that."

There was a pause, more static. "What?"

"Umm . . . the little bombs were a diversion. That's what he said."

Terrible static, weird clicking sounds. "For . . . bigger bombs?"

"Yes. Big bombs in the middle of the dam," she yelled into the static. "Big bombs. Our son, Benny, is in Room—"

There was a click. Sierra pulled the phone from her ear. "Fuck! I lost him again. This is terrible, Andrew."

"All we can do is walk and keep trying."

They moved down the trail next to the creek behind a limping Eric, Sierra still trying to get Goodnight on the radio.

———

Before Sierra Justice called and dropped another static-filled revelation, Goodnight had already felt sick enough. The dam had become the world's largest sprinkler. It reminded him of the summer trip he and Blanche took to New York City years ago, when the fire department's fireboat sprayed its hoses in so many different directions during the Fourth of July show on the Hudson River. He had broken top secret protocol. Leaked the story to Judy and the media. There would be a massive panic. Runs on stores. Traffic jams. Fatalities. Terrible economic consequences. Terrified people. And all because he had to open his big fat mouth. Losing his job and tarnishing his career was bad enough, but he'd also put Judy in a dreadful situation.

Then came Sierra Justice's subsequent call. Diversion. Big bomb. His pity party and trip down memory lane erupted into full-blown terror.

"General," he shouted, trotting to her from his hiding spot behind the Humvee and slipping the radio into his pocket, "they have to get out of there, now. Call Parker back."

Tanaka frowned. "I'm under orders from General Foster to reconnoiter the dam, Chief."

Goodnight shook his head. "No, General. You have to trust me on this." He grabbed her arm, knowing he had to keep the two-way satellite radio a secret unless she refused to believe him. "You have to call them back now."

"You're not running things anymore, Chief. You need to stand down."

"Goddammit, no!" shouted Goodnight. "Call them back."

Tanaka's eyes turned troubled. The fear he felt inside must have resonated.

She raised her radio. "Milkman, this is Ground. Return to base on the double. Say again. Ground to Milkman. RTB, on the double. Do you copy?"

Parker's voice. "Copy, Ground. This is Milkman. Descending spiral staircase. We are turning around. Over."

Tanaka kept talking. "This is Ground requesting air support for immediate evac. Request two Viking ships. The EOD team will catch the second at the landing zone. Over."

The pilots wasted no time responding. "Roger, Ground. This is Viking Three, inbound. Viking Six, this is Viking Three. Request evac support at landing zone. Over."

"Roger, Three, wilco. ETA at landing zone five minutes. Over."

"I'm going to get them," Goodnight hollered.

"Negative, Chief," Tanaka yelled back. "There's nothing you can do, and you'll be one more warm body I'll have to worry about. Your feeling better be right."

Goodnight protested as another Blackhawk thundered over them, flaring and setting down in a hurry. His body felt like a live wire. Tanaka grabbed his arm, and together they ran hunched over as two helmeted crew members helped them board. The machine ascended so fast that Goodnight had to put a hand on his stomach. Soon they were high above the scene below, the dam a miniature version of itself, the vehicles in front of it on the bridge smaller still. The second Blackhawk, Viking Six, landed at the landing zone in front of the visitors' center, waiting for Parker and his team with the engineers.

That's when an impossible hand swung an impossible hammer at an impossible speed through the lake and out the front of Glen Canyon Dam.

The rupture was instant. Horrific. Violent.

Even at their altitude, Goodnight felt the swift change in air pressure, felt the helicopter shake. A plume of water, rocks, concrete chunks, steel, and dust as tall as a skyscraper projected outward from the face of the barrier and up toward them. The Highway 89 bridge was standing one second, reduced to pylons and twisted metal the next. The Viking Six Blackhawk was in burning pieces next to the severely damaged visitors' center. As Parker had predicted, the powerful explosion destroyed everything around it.

Before the blast debris finished raining down, the water was already making its violent escape.

The flood poured over the remaining base of the dam as if months of imprisonment had made it hungry for a fight. The crashing torrent, hundreds of feet high, smashed its escape from the gorge behind the now defunct dam and headed downriver, erasing what remained of the power plant and the bridge. It beat against the canyon walls, spreading out where it could, colliding where it couldn't. "Look at that," the copilot said without breaking communication tenor.

"Roger, I'm gaining altitude. There's shit flying all over the place," said the pilot.

Indeed, through his little window, Goodnight saw debris still raining down. The apex of the flood, already brown and red, grew larger still. He looked back out the other window at the water leaving the lake and regretted it. The floating aluminum bomb barrier came through like a violent string, bent and wrapped up on itself. Houseboats, pontoon boats, speedboats, and fishing boats—all unable to escape the strong current that sucked them over the shattered dam—moved like last fall's leaves in a spring flood. The loss in these first few minutes would be staggering. General Foster squawked into Goodnight's headphones, breaking him from the trance that the thrumming Blackhawk and the surreal tragedy had put him in. "Viking Three, Command requesting sitrep and ETA. Over."

"This is Viking Three, ETA twelve minutes," the copilot said, more excited than earlier. "Large ordnance explosion. Glen Canyon Dam is destroyed. Viking Six is down. Massive flooding. Over."

"This is Ground," Tanaka broke in. "Command, be advised of mass casualties. EOD team and BOR engineers presumed killed in action."

"Copy. Command, out."

Goodnight could only watch in terror.

"Jesus. Parker. His team. The engineers. Those people on the lake. They're all . . . gone," he murmured into his headset, looking at Tanaka.

The general returned his gaze. Despite the pain in her eyes, she remained stoic. "I'm sorry, Chief. Dick was a friend. But right now we have to maintain our objective." Her expression changed into a mixture of disbelief and suspicion. "How did you know, Chief?"

In the face of his grief he had to think fast, and lying was unnatural for him. "I felt it in my gut, General."

"What were you doing behind the Humvee before you told me to recall Parker?"

More fast thinking. "Relieving myself," he said, shrugging.

Tanaka nodded, although her expression still conveyed suspicion.

The helicopter eased into forward flight. Goodnight and Tanaka watched the carnage until their view was obstructed. It was a welcome end to a horror show for which Goodnight had already assumed full responsibility.

———

"I hope they got those people out," Sierra said.

"I don't mean to sound selfish, Sierra, but we've got bigger problems. Like you said, I'm the fastest. I can get to Phantom Ranch, warn them, and then save Benny and Scarlett. I can do it," Andrew said.

"We've got more adrenaline shots," she replied.

Eric had drifted off to sleep again. Their plan had been to move for as long as he could, then give him ten minutes to rest before the next shot. Progress down the trail had been slow.

"You have to make the call when the time comes, Sierra."

She rubbed her face. Nodded.

"Break's over."

"How do I weigh all these lives?" Sierra asked. "Benny. Scarlett. The three of us." She gestured at Eric. "He's dying. You claim he's part of the reason we're here. I don't know."

Andrew scoffed. "There's no maybe about it. The way Hobbes looked at him when you were passed out said a thousand things, none of them good."

Sierra studied the far reaches of the red, yellow, and white cliffs around them, unsure what to say. Benny's face pervaded her thoughts. Had Eric put their son in danger? What kind of mother was she to let someone interfere with Benny's safety? To do what she had done with him?

"We've seen seven people on the trail since everything went down," Andrew said. "Most of them took off in a hurry or acted like we were crazy."

"What would we do in that situation, out here in the middle of nowhere?"

She'd told everyone they met, "A murderer's out there somewhere with a gun. He claims to have blown Glen Canyon Dam, and he said there's a wall of water coming down the canyon. We have to get everyone safe and out, but we can't get through to the rangers. Tell everyone you see."

Two older women provided them with a full water bottle, food, and more clean gauze and wrappings from their first aid kit. They also tried to use their satellite phone but ran into the same dropped line problem with the rangers. In the end, they decided to keep heading south at a faster pace and report it at Phantom Ranch. With no way to communicate with anyone, and no way to help carry Eric, what else could they do? Others had given them looks ranging from suspicious or judgmental to terrified.

They pulled Eric's body to a sitting position against the canyon wall.

"This stuff could give him brain damage," Andrew said.

Eric cracked one eye open and trained it on Andrew.

"What difference does it make, Andy?"

A brief silence followed before they all erupted in nervous laughter, which for Eric turned into another coughing spell.

"Ready for another?" Andrew asked Eric.

"Send it, Doc. You know, Andy, we might never be bros for life, but I feel like we're bonding, don't you?"

Andrew plunged the needle into Eric's quadriceps. Eric winced but held Andrew's gaze.

When Andrew stood, Sierra sniffed and softly beat her fists against his chest. "This morning everything was okay." She gazed at him. "This is all my fault."

"No, Sierra. I'll get Benny. Then I'll come back for you."

She pushed him back, angry. "Don't you come back into this canyon. You get to our son and you stay with him, Andrew. Say it."

He wiped his eyes and nodded.

"Say it," she repeated.

"I won't come back," Andrew said, fighting his tears. "Keep trying to talk to Goodnight. I'll feel better knowing you have someone to contact."

She nodded. They embraced and kissed once more. Sierra gave him the half-full water bottle, then took off the S-shaped gold-scroll earrings with the pearl drops and held them out.

"These are for Benny. For his wife." She shrugged and smiled, her vision blurring. "Or his daughter. Just in case. Don't lose them, huh? He has to have them."

Andrew lost the battle with his tears. "You put those back on."

She grabbed his hand and put the earrings in his palm and folded his fingers over them. Then she put a finger to his lips and whispered, "Go." Just before he set off at a fast jog, Sierra called out to him.

"Hey."

He turned, waiting.

"It was ten million dollars."

Andrew seemed confused before some sort of realization dawned. He gave her a cringing yet knowing smile. "That would have been a helluva bonus, Sierra."

She shrugged and watched him until he rounded a bend and disappeared.

"Go with him," Eric said.

"If I could keep up with him, believe me, I would. I'd leave you here and go to my son. But that's not the best solution for Benny. Andrew has to move fast. Besides, there's no point in leaving you alone if I'm stuck here anyway."

She turned to find him standing. Checked her watch. "We don't know if the big bombs blew. But if they did, we'll be cutting it close. Let's go."

"Wait, Sierra."

"What? Why?"

Eric swayed a bit, focusing on her, looking like he was trying to catch his breath.

"I know what it meant for you now. What you went through. When you're stuck in something hard and it seems like it's never gonna end, you just want to be with something, somebody familiar. You wanna be with familiar people. Your people. People that will never turn their backs on you and always make you feel welcome. I felt alone all those years in the service. I had buddies, brothers that I loved. But I didn't have you. I meant what I said this morning. I'm sorry for abandoning you. I get it now. And I guess I just needed you, Sierra."

She stood quiet. Took a ragged breath. "I don't think you know how much I needed to hear that, Eric."

———

"Take us downriver. I need to see it," General Tanaka told the pilot through the intercom.

Goodnight groaned. He never wanted to see anything like it again.

"I can't, ma'am—you know that. I'm under orders to get you all back to base," said the pilot.

"Get me Command," Tanaka said.

A minute later General Foster was on the radio. "Go for Command," he said.

"Command, this is Ground. Request twenty minutes on this bird for downriver observation."

"Hang one, Ground."

The radio went silent for a bit. Foster came back. "Command with rebrief for pilot in command."

"Copy, Command. Legs here."

"Legs, take Ground to the tip of the spear, give her five minutes of observation, then return to base."

"Wilco, Command, five minutes eyes on, then RTB," said the pilot.

"Command, out."

"What the hell is the name 'Legs' about?" Tanaka asked.

"Because of my impressive height, ma'am," the pilot replied.

As the Blackhawk flew west above the South Rim, Goodnight trembled. For Parker and his wife and their beautiful family. For Parker's men and the engineers and their families. For everyone who couldn't escape the current and was sucked out of the lake. For thousands downriver who couldn't get away or would never get the warnings in time. He did his best to hide his tears.

The front of the wall of water resembled a rockslide more than a flood. The roiling mass of red rock and silt was preceded by black debris surging through the bottom of the canyon with extraordinary violence. It lurched and crashed, throwing boulders around like pebbles. Columns of dust shot up on the sides of the water as caverns and sinkholes filled.

"I wonder what that sounds like," Goodnight blurted out, surprising himself.

"Glad to hear you talking again, Chief," said Tanaka. "You disappeared for a minute. Get us a half mile ahead and put it down, Legs."

"Command didn't say anything about putting her down," the pilot said.

"He ordered you to give me five minutes of observation," she said. "Didn't say how."

"Yes, ma'am," Legs said, hesitation in his voice.

Goodnight's stomach reeled when the Blackhawk nosed down and hurtled over the canyon walls. After a few minutes the aircraft slowed as the engines unwound. Legs performed a quick deceleration and landing.

"Kill it," General Tanaka yelled, making a slashing motion across her neck. Legs hesitated again but complied. When the rotors stopped, the group stood and waited in the eerie quiet for the coming flood.

Chapter 15

Trauma

Eric peered up at the nearly two-billion-year-old Vishnu Schist, the oldest rock in the Grand Canyon, closing in over them. It was more appealing when he read about it on an exhibit than it was being trapped in it, dying. October's yellowing leaves and cooler air had forgotten this place. They sweated through their clothes.

"We need a break and you need another shot. You're pale, Eric. Andrew said we shouldn't eat without water, but as crazy as it sounds, I don't have an appetite. I've been nauseous all day."

"I'd puke if I tried to eat right now. How come you never told me you had a kid?"

She clicked her teeth and clasped her hands behind her head, staring up into the sky.

"I didn't think you deserved to know. Then I remembered the thrill of getting into that jet with you and flying to Cabo. I wanted to feel that again. So I hid him from you. Horrible mistake."

Eric didn't protest. The epinephrine had long worn off, and he held his side, grimacing.

They'd run into more people. No one had cell service or a working radio, but they had managed to push a few emergency beacons, hoping the signals wound up somewhere. Sierra started leaving out the part about the dam, only telling people that a murderer with a gun was out there to the north and they needed to get off the trail in a hurry. It worked, mostly. More people offered help, but with Eric moving so slowly they went ahead, fear or impatience getting the best of them. One man stayed to help until they got to Phantom Ranch, but he was more of a hassle than an aid, so Sierra sent him on his way. Still, there were those unbelieving few who didn't want to be troubled and simply went about their hike or run.

"People are afraid of sharks or lightning or plane crashes, things that statistically won't ever happen to them," Sierra said. "But I've looked people in the eye and told them a murderer with a gun is on the loose. We're both bloody. And some of them still looked at me like I was crazy."

Eric winced as he moved his weight on the rock he was using for a makeshift bed.

"This wound sucks major ass. Anyway, you said it back there to Andy."

"Said what?"

"You asked him what we would have done this morning if we'd been in their place. People believe based on their perception. Think about your life."

"What about it?" She searched for a spot and then stuck the epinephrine shot into Eric's leg.

Eric winced and said, "Most people haven't been through what you have. It's easier for you to accept darkness because you lived it. That's also why you love your boy so much."

Sierra sat down and stared at him. "That's like . . . exactly what my therapist said."

"I may talk like a hayseed, but I can read. And I understand those unresolved issues you mentioned this morning, too. You might think about resolving them some day."

"Is that what you were doing in Phoenix the other night? Resolving issues?"

"I thought we weren't talking about that."

"We're not. If you're such a guru, then what about Hobbes? What's his problem?"

"His existence. Fuck that guy."

Sierra grunted. "If I'm so in tune with danger, how'd I get into this situation? Lives are at stake, including my son's, and I'm literally helpless. Hobbes was right. I'm down here because I sold out. I suck as a mom. I turned out just like my mother after all."

Eric sat up, sighed heavily, and watched the creek rushing below. "No you don't, Sierra. This one's on me."

Sierra turned her head toward him. "How?"

"I never told you *when* I met Wade."

She paused. "What does that matter . . ."

Eric watched her expression change.

"Oh." Her shoulders fell. "Did you give Wade my name?"

He nodded. "I wasn't the only one, but I was the first. I took you to Cabo all those years ago for good company. Hell, Wade was still deciding on me back then. When I heard he was putting a legal team together, I told him I knew a good lawyer. Then other folks in DC told him about you." Eric swallowed. "I was in a helicopter on top of the building when you met him."

Sierra sounded angry but remained calm. "You were part of orchestrating this for years and kept it a secret from me?"

"It was a big payday for you. I didn't want you to pass up the opportunity because of me. I made sure you didn't know I worked for Wade until I wanted you to know. That's part of it, anyway."

She leaned her head back. "Dammit, Eric, why can't anything with you ever be what it seems?" He didn't answer. Gave her time to process things. His pain had subsided with the epinephrine shot.

Sierra softened. "I make my own choices. Me being down here—Hobbes, Wade—that's because I saw a way for my son to not have to live like I did. A way for me to not wind up desperate like my mother. So if I sold out like Hobbes said, then I did it for Benny, not in spite of him. I'm not down here because of you."

When he didn't respond, she prodded him. "An acknowledgement would be nice."

"I said it was part of the reason you didn't see this coming." He met Sierra's tired gaze. "Andy was right. I found out Wade was gonna fire me after this trip."

Her face bunched up. "How is that relevant? And why would he fire you?"

He rubbed his stubble and sighed. "Candi."

"Candi? Wait . . . the flight attendant?"

"That's the one. Wade had a thing for her. He found out I was, well, you know. That's why it surprised me when you brought her up in the plane. I didn't want you to know."

Sierra slowly nodded. "He found out you were screwing her. I saw how he stared at her. And I heard how she talked about you. I guess I knew but didn't want to know." She squinted. "But that still doesn't explain how you knew Wade was going to fire you."

Eric cracked a sad smile. He took in the lines of Sierra's face. The bright blue eyes that had lived in his memory and warmed his heart in faraway places. The interest she showed in him. The fact that she didn't want to leave him.

"Why are you looking at me like that?" she asked.

"Taking you in while I still can." He took a deep breath. "Back in DC Hobbes showed me an email Wade sent to Bill telling him to get a termination letter ready for me because I was having sex with one of the flight attendants. But it was really because Wade was in love with Candi."

It took Sierra a moment. But he didn't miss when her hand started to shake.

"Nobody was supposed to get hurt, Sierra. Wade was supposed to sign the documents. I didn't know anything about Hobbes shooting anyone or blowing the dam. Wade would sign, I would fly Hobbes out of the country. I didn't agree to any of—"

"You were working with Hobbes?"

"Sierra, I prom—"

"You were already working with Hobbes when you came to my room? You told him where we'd be?"

Eric swallowed. "Yes."

She stood slowly. "What was in it for you?"

He didn't answer.

Sierra grabbed her pack and moved away from him. "Tell me, Eric, you son of a bitch."

Anger ruled her face, but tears flooded her eyes. "What was in it for you? I may not make it out of this canyon to save Benny. But even if I do, I'll never see the ten million dollars I sold my soul for. Why?" she shouted.

Eric worked his way to his feet and hobbled toward her.

She backed up and put her hand out. "Get away from me. Answer the question. Why?"

He doubled over in pain, held his bloodied side, and took a moment to get his breath. "It doesn't matter."

Sierra's eyes turned skyward and her lips parted. When she focused back on him, Eric saw something in her he'd never seen before. She screamed and came for him. She lunged and swung her right hand full force into his jaw. When her fist connected with the bone, he saw a flash of light. Sierra shrieked in pain, and when he could focus, he saw her holding her hand. She wasted no time in swinging with her left, hitting Eric below his right eye, rocking his head back. She pummeled his torso and chest through angry tears.

He took the beating.

———

Goodnight and Tanaka and the four members of the Blackhawk crew stood on the edge of the rim and observed the swollen, gritty Colorado River far below. He heard the muted roar of whitewater rapids just visible to the naked eye. A cool breeze blew over the canyon into their faces. Goodnight stood next to Legs, towering over the vertically challenged pilot by at least a head. Legs? he wondered, shaking his head.

"Oh God," Legs said, pointing down.

Goodnight followed his finger and saw a line of rafts heading downriver in the shadows. Five of them, each peopled with whitewater enthusiasts, coursed down the engorged hundred-thousand-cubic-feet-per-second flow.

"That's like forty people. We have to warn them," said Legs.

"How?" Tanaka asked, staring at Legs point-blank.

The pilot looked back down at the rafters, made the sign of the cross. Goodnight saw a tiny flash from a camera, then said his own silent prayer.

"There," Tanaka said, lowering her binos, pointing east at a dust cloud.

A deep snap, mixed with what sounded like breaking ceramics, caught their attention. Upriver on the North Rim, a rock spire taller than a ten-story building had cracked at its base and broke into three immense pieces. A thousand feet down the pieces somersaulted, taking more earth and rock with each booming crash against the canyon wall.

"We better move, General," Goodnight said.

The group backed up slowly at first, watching their feet, feeling vibrations in the rock, then looking at each other. When the flood came into full view, everyone froze.

Tanaka gasped. "How can that even be real?"

The crest was now black and nearly solid with rock and debris. Goodnight saw an entire rock ledge, maybe fifty feet thick and a few city blocks long, break off into the muddy torrent. He marveled in terror at the water between the canyon walls, so high, out-of-control, and against the laws of nature that had carved the chasm over epochs.

He had heard folks describe tornados as sounding like a hundred full-speed locomotives. He'd seen a rare Arizona tornado one spring while working high-water rescues. It wasn't a big one, but as he'd watched it, he realized they were right about the sound. What was in front of him now, however, put the sound of any tornado to shame.

It was like a million freight trains, all moving at suicidal speed, all intent on slamming into whatever stood in their way, each one rumbling with power and blasting horns. Within the roar, the floodwaters popped and fizzed as the rocks tumbled against each other.

It came so damn fast. Down the canyon he watched it come. It came without a conscience, born of pressure and captivity and swollen unprovoked anger. It slammed through and over the geography without remorse or regard. It had been set free to change lives, and take them.

"We have to get farther back," Goodnight shouted over the noise.

Tanaka nodded and grabbed his arm. The Blackhawk crew moved toward their chopper.

"No, Legs, you'll never get it up in time!" Tanaka screamed.

"General, I'm not leaving the helo," Legs yelled back. "I'll get court-martialed. We're not supposed to be here."

"Stand down," Tanaka bellowed. "I'll take the heat. Get your crew another hundred meters back, or I'll be the one putting you up for court-martial."

Seconds later, the flood slammed into the canyon wall below. As he ran, Goodnight turned his head and saw the Blackhawk's tail shudder. Then the entire helicopter rolled right, snapping two of the rotors. It disappeared belly-up into the canyon with a crash when the shelf broke away and fell into the wave of black, brown, then red roiling water.

As soon as it had come, the apex was gone. Their new vantage point gave them a view of the flood moving away downstream. Goodnight found it no easier to watch, knowing everyone in those five rafts had just died a terrifying and senseless death, and more were sure to perish.

The immense debris field grew with the force of the water as it thrust its weight downstream. The sound changed to a low humming rumble, still layered with cracks and pops as boulders tumbled below the surface or were swept off the canyon walls. Goodnight's nostrils filled with the smell of dirty water and logs and the wet-hot ochre of ancient broken rock.

Tanaka tried to raise someone on the radio while she watched the flood through the binos hanging around her neck. The Blackhawk crew surrounded Legs and talked inaudibly among themselves. Goodnight pondered it all.

One man's evil deed of unrelenting and unforgiving magnitude. Hundreds, maybe thousands dead. Many more would die.

"You were right, Mr. Wilde. I made my hell today," Goodnight said, half choking. He clasped his hands on top of his head, fell to his knees, and wept. Looking through his tears above the death and chaos in the canyon, he noticed that the blue Arizona sky held little white tufts of cloud.

———

"Doesn't matter?"

Sierra screamed with each blow, her teeth gritted as she continued her barrage. "I may never see Benny again! His father might die trying to save him, and all you can say is 'Doesn't matter'? You fucking used me!" She launched into another onslaught.

This time Eric protected himself. She soon stopped. Panting. Exhausted. Their heavy breathing reminded him of when they were physically exhausted together under better circumstances back in Phoenix. "Damn. That epinephrine is great for a fight. I didn't feel a thing," he said.

Sierra left him without a word. He had a mind to sit down and let his injuries run their course, but she'd given him the shot, and for all his talk about leaving him behind, he wouldn't abandon her. He ambled down the trail as fast as the drug would allow.

He was a dumbass. He'd taken it for granted that Sierra had told him her childhood secrets years ago—a revelation he should have recognized as more than mere teenage affection. Instead of embracing her love, her trust, he had deceived himself and lost a lifetime with her. If only Old Man Traeger had been there to advise him at the beginning.

Old Man had always been obsessed with truth. They had debated it on deployments, on ship, at bars. Their one contribution to lesser academia would never be published or celebrated or peer reviewed. Old Man would quote the Bible, and he, Blue Collar, would answer with the only piece of Buddhism he knew, something he'd seen inked on a lovely Asian woman's body in the South Pacific.

"Quid est veritas?" Old Man would ask. What is truth?

"Dukkha," Blue Collar would answer. Suffering, pain, or unease.

Eric went into another coughing fit and spat out more blood onto the trail, grimacing as he pushed hard on the wound at his side. The bullet burned a hole in his lower back, and every step was pain. The heat in this part of the canyon was like it was on Bagram back in Afghanistan. Unbearable. "How can it be this hot in October?" he asked.

His eyes were burning. He searched for Sierra, but she was gone.

"Joke's on you, Sierra. I was willing to die for you, but you wouldn't let me. Now you lose. You took the epinephrine."

———

The Little Bird moved over the canyon in a grid search. Hobbes lay under a rock and watched it move north toward him. This was a restricted operations zone, so he had no doubt Senator Pace's killer was on that bird. If she had picked one from Rev Six's corps, it could be someone in the know, a double agent looking out for Hobbes's best interests. But if not, the last thing he needed right now was to engage a capable and better-armed assassin.

He was angry about losing the two-way satellite radio during his scuffle with Samuels. He was angrier about his decision not to shoot all three of them as he should have done in the first place. Samuels had gotten in some good strikes before he winged him, so it had been best to let it go and escape. If the signal had worked, they would all either die in the flood trying to get to the kid or be cut off by it and succumb to the elements in the canyon's vast wilderness. Hiding was easy here, but the longer he hid, the harder it would be to escape if by some miracle Sierra or Andrew made it out and talked. He'd forgotten to pick up the brass from the shots he fired at Samuels.

"Does it even matter at this point?" he asked.

When the Little Bird turned south, he ran north again. Every so often he stopped to make sure he could still hear or see it; it would take nothing for the small helicopter to fly around and surprise him. They'd mow him down with a minigun like SOCOM had done to those men back on the dam Saturday morning.

Samuels's rebellion had created another hitch: He'd be lucky to find a car on the North Rim. The Da Vinci was useless to him.

He removed his holster, unscrewed the suppressor, and put both items, along with the Glock, back into his fanny pack. He put the medical mask back on and trotted into the Manzanita Rest Area and filled up with water, ignoring the prying eyes of hikers at his dress and plate carrier. An attractive auburn-haired woman with nice legs stood near the fountain under a big tree next to the creek. She tried to initiate conversation. On another day Hobbes might have bit. He ignored her.

Back on the trail, he ate another energy bar and washed it down with water. The incline from Manzanita up the North Kaibab was steep and full of rocky switchbacks, but the air cooled as he ascended. The increased concentration of hikers and runners heading south confirmed his decision to conceal the pistol.

If the signal had worked, the dam explosion would be international news for a long time. What wouldn't make the headlines, however, was the deep state message from Rev Six to the US and other countries with high offices. There had long been talks between the high offices about absurd decisions made by powerful nations in the decades since Rev Six had last taken major action. It figured that Cygnus was the first operation of the new worldwide campaign.

"We just fired another shot heard around the world, didn't we, Snake Eater?" he said.

But he almost hadn't been able to push the button. Did he have the stomach anymore? Taping that kid to the chair. The nanny's whimper. Guilt, regrets—strange feelings, perhaps, but real.

Plus, another one . . . jealousy.

Jealousy of Sierra's fierce love for her son. She was willing to do anything to keep her child safe. Was he? Is that what he was doing?

Not far from Manzanita, he turned a corner and came upon a

family of four resting in the shade of two small pines on a switchback. He pulled the medical mask back over his face. The parents were young, maybe early thirties, and the two children, a girl and a boy, were small. Hobbes put his head down to move past them without conversation. As he passed, the little girl tried to jump from one rock to another but slipped and fell into his arms.

"Jenny!" her mother shouted.

Hobbes held her. She appeared mortified at first, but then she laughed, a hearty giggle that infected the rest of her family. Hobbes froze. He'd never held a child in his life. The little boy laughed hardest. He doubled over and did a slow duck walk as he caught his breath.

Sierra's voice filled Hobbes's mind: *He's not an "it". His name is Benny. He's my son.*

Hobbes set Jenny down and backed away. Their giggles subsided and soon everyone stood in silence. The little boy looked to his mother. She looked at her husband.

"Turn around and go back up," Hobbes said.

"Pardon?" the man asked.

"Go back up, now."

"Are you with the park service?" the woman asked.

"Get your kids, turn around, and go back up."

"Mister, we're not taking orders from you without some sort of ID or badge," the man said, agitation rising in his voice.

"Get your asses back up the rim," Hobbes commanded angrily.

"Hey, don't you dare talk like that in front of our children," the woman snapped.

"Or my wife," the man said, trying to sound authoritative while his voice betrayed fear. "We'll be on our way. Leave us alone."

Hobbes swore and pulled the Glock from the fanny pack. The children shrieked and ran to their mother, whose faced turned white.

The man stepped in front of them and put his hand out. "All right, we'll turn around. Just . . . put that away," he pleaded.

Hobbes watched them head back up the trail. He hollered at them, "Tell everyone you see there's a man with a gun down the trail.

Tell everyone to turn around and go back. Tell them I'm dangerous."
In a mix of confusion and fear, the dad turned and nodded and disappeared from view.

Hobbes put the pistol away. He sat on the rock Jenny had jumped from. How many kids had been on that lake? On the river? In the communities downstream? Had the dam even blown? He reached into the pouch on his plate carrier that held the map he'd drawn. It was gone. He must have lost it in the scuffle with Samuels. He remembered most of the details. That's why he'd drawn the damn thing to begin with.

He considered moving north. Grab a car, get to Washington, take care of business there. Save his own skin. Pocket a hundred million dollars, buy treatment for his cancer. Exit Rev Six as they had agreed. Start that new life with Amelia. Keep her safe.

He stared back south. Save the little boy and the nanny. Maybe die in a flood trying.

A line of busy ants moved near his feet beside the rock. He watched them crawl along the ground in their prehistoric ritual of meeting, communicating, passing each other in their searching. Hobbes stood and adjusted the plate carrier. From this height, he could see clear across the canyon to the South Rim. It was so far away.

BOOK THREE

Acceptance

Chapter 16

Apparition

IF THE BOX HAD SEEMED NEVER-ENDING THAT MORNING when she was healthy and optimistic, now it felt like a death march. Every time she rounded a corner, another long section of trail next to the stream under the cliffs stretched out before her. She kept waiting for a hiker to come through with a bottle she could keep for water. But she'd seen no one for a long time.

She imagined this was what it felt like to be meat in an oven. The gray-black canyon walls baked with solar radiation from all sides. Sierra had stripped down to her T-shirt and tied her jacket around her waist, eyeing the creek running below her. She wanted to get in, dunk her head, drink deep. But even if she could scramble down the cliff, Victor had said not to drink the water for fear of getting sick. She was getting closer and closer to ignoring the dead man's advice.

"I've hit a wall, Eric. My legs and feet are lead pipes. My back feels like raw hamburger." She bent over and stretched with a groan.

"You tried the sat phone again? Called Goodnight?" he asked.

She'd tried both. The 911 operator who had tried to transfer her calls to the park ranger service earlier was gone now too. And Goodnight never answered. Why hadn't he called her back? Probably for the same reason she couldn't call anyone else. The damn two-way satellite phone was confusing. "No answer," she said.

"Keep moving," Eric said.

"Good idea, genius. I'm so thirsty."

The dust and dehydration choked her. Screw it. It was time to drink the cold creek water. She scooted over the ledge of the trail on her butt.

"It may be full of bacteria, Sierra. What if you start puking? Then you'll never make it."

That morning she had brushed her teeth as cold water gurgled down the drain. Used the toilet. Showered, washed her hair, and shaved her legs under a stream of plentiful, clean water. She ran her tongue along her teeth and felt gritty sandpaper. She longed for the cold rapids. She could smell them, scents of musty earth and moving life in the water.

She turned a corner to find Andrew plodding along like a wrinkled old man on some pilgrimage to a holy place no one remembered. He dripped as if he'd just climbed out of the creek.

"Andrew? Are you all right?" she asked, reaching out to touch him. His eyes bulged out of his head and his open mouth revealed an ashen, swollen tongue that swung with each step. His body was bloated and gray. Sierra shrieked. He opened his mouth wider, and a fire hose-sized stream of water blasted her in the face, knocking her over on the trail. Sierra couldn't tell if the roar in her ears was from the water gushing from Andrew's mouth or his screaming. She put her hands to her ears and searched for Eric. He was nowhere.

———

Goodnight sat surrounded by the empty gray walls of an interview room across the table from two men wearing combat uniforms and sidearms. FBI Assistant Director Hayes sat between them. A video camera stared at him from a tabletop tripod. The phone next to it ran some sort of voice recorder app, the lime-green digital frequency waves dancing in reaction to their voices. He noticed a large brown moth on the wall behind his interviewers.

"Everything said in this room is classified," said Hayes. "If you share any unauthorized information, you could be charged with federal crimes including espionage, conspiracy, or treason, among others. Anderson and Jackson are in custody and have been questioned."

"What about Jones and Harris?" Goodnight asked.

Hayes exchanged glances with one of the investigators. "Harris was with Anderson and Jackson. It took some persuasion, but Anderson eventually confirmed they worked for the same actor. We haven't found anything on Jones yet," he said.

"Because that wasn't his name. He was deep cover for someone."

A flash in Hayes's eyes. "But no one has a clue which agency. The other three were tied to a secret organization that might be connected to Revelation Six, the big NGO I told you about before. We only have a description of their contact. Tall guy, possibly blond. Creepy, as Anderson put it."

"I think it was Revelation Six, Hayes. His name is Hobbes."

Hayes had that same reaction again.

"That was the name Jones—or whoever—gave me before he was killed. He mentioned Revelation Six, said he was trying to beat a guy named Hobbes. 'Hobbes always wins.' That's what he said." The two men with Hayes made notes as Goodnight spoke.

"Chief, have you been in contact with anyone downstream in advance of today's event?"

"No," Goodnight lied, then changed the subject. "Tell me about Cygnus."

Hayes and one of the investigators whispered to each other. Hayes answered, "Cygnus is classified. Our orders are straight from the president. We're evacuating all areas downstream where heavy loss of life could occur."

"Vegas?"

"Communities around Vegas, above and below Lake Mead, which is full too. But if Hoover goes, it's the other cities downstream too. Laughlin, Lake Havasu, Yuma. Might even have secondary issues in Phoenix and Tucson. They all have to be evacuated, just in case.

Hundreds of thousands of people in direct danger, millions in possible danger."

"Jesus. Is Hoover going to hold?"

"We don't know. General Tanaka said you used the phone after the initial explosions?"

So Tanaka hadn't believed his story about his gut feeling or having to piss behind the Humvee after all. Hayes had him—no point in lying—and if they already knew he'd called Judy, it might implicate her.

"I made a call."

"To whom?"

"Good grief. Lock me up, Hayes. I ain't telling you nothing."

"Who did you call?"

"Keep trying."

"What do you keep looking at?"

"That moth on the wall behind you."

Hayes craned his neck to see it and then turned back around. "Why?"

"Thinking it's the most honest creature in the room with me."

"Why did you break chain of command? Leak intel?"

"Because my frigging superior wouldn't do anything until it was too damn late," Goodnight yelled in a sudden rage, slamming his fist into the table, knocking the video camera over. "This whole damn thing is a huge screwup. Bringing me in the day after the hostage situation and not giving me a full detachment of soldiers to guard the place. You all bungled this up. But you're looking for scapegoats, ain't you?"

He took a few breaths and tried to calm down. "Cygnus isn't your disaster protocol. You knew something was coming to my facility. That's why the Joint Terrorism Task Forces weren't invited to the party, ain't it?"

"Chief, my orders are to inform the public that the dam succumbed to high water and natural forces, causing it to breach and fail." Hayes picked up the camera and pointed it back at Goodnight.

Goodnight pointed at Hayes, his voice low, and said, "Have you read any of the reports that came out decades ago, after the towers fell?

Dams are high-priority targets. A giant flood out there is killing people as we speak. I saw it. The public has a right to know."

"Do you have any other information that will assist in the evacuations, Chief Goodnight?"

"Well, Hayes . . . at least you were polite enough to let me finish my diatribe," Goodnight said, shaking his head. "The other day you were worried about another attack, but you never mentioned a word to me, the head of Glen Canyon security, about Cygnus. You had no idea they'd already breached the dam by the time the FBI and SOCOM showed up. Hell, three of their guys were on the wrong team."

"You think I don't know when I've been beat, Chief?" Hayes asked. But Goodnight caught that same odd flash in Hayes's expression.

"You want to do something about it? Send helicopters down into the canyon right now. Hundreds of people are down there."

Hayes stood and gathered up his things. Goodnight jumped up and slammed him against the wall. The two others pulled their sidearms and held them to Goodnight's temple and back.

"Let him go, Chief," one of them shouted.

"Shoot me, boys," Goodnight said with a snarl. "The love of my life is gone and my years of dedication to Arizona just ate shit. I'm not letting go until I get an answer or one of us is dead."

He was about to catch a bullet, but he didn't let go of Hayes. All four men fought for breath, the veins in their red necks and arms bulging in the standoff.

———

The white wood-framed windowpane was bordered in frost. Moonlight and snowfall behind the glass. It was open a little bit and the cold Rocky Mountain air that flowed into her room had woken her. Or was it the arguing on the other side of her door? She looked at the clock on her nightstand. Three minutes to midnight. The shouting grew louder. They were screaming now. It took all her strength to push the old window closed.

She walked to the door over the cold hardwood floor, step-by-step. She put her hand out and turned the doorknob with her eyes closed. The door swung open. Light from the den on her eyelids. The screaming. She opened her eyes. The Arizona sun blinded her, but not so much that she couldn't see the edge plummeting far below.

A sickening twist in her stomach at the long fall inches from her feet. The high cliff overlooking the creek was one step away. Death.

Her own wailing shook her from her trance. Sierra backed up several paces and sat down hard when she felt the canyon wall against her back. She was alone. Cotton filled her mouth. She'd never been so hot. So overheated. Her arms and forehead were no longer sweating. She checked to her right and her left. No one.

"Get up," she said. "Get to Benny."

She tried to push up against the hard rock but collapsed back on herself. She had no fluids and no strength.

She blinked slowly, her dry sockets grating with each movement. Sierra raised her chin to the horizon, up above the canyon walls, and looked into the sun long enough to realize what she was doing. She shut her eyes. Black spots danced across her vision.

You are my hope, Benny. I will do anything for you.

"I gave Andrew the earrings to give to Benny," she blurted out, her eyes popping open. She watched her hands open and close. Dry, cracked, dirty. She was so tired. But somehow, in her miserable state, everything became clear. Memories bubbled from the depths and rippled on the surface, the words she had spoken in that courtroom when she was twelve so clear in her mind. She had tormented herself with them for years. Now she repeated them to the canyon, to the rocks, to the water below, to no one.

"The clock said three minutes to midnight. There was frost on my window, and it was cracked open. I closed it. It was so cold. I heard voices yelling in the den. I opened the door and saw my stepdaddy screaming at Mama. Mama had something shiny. There was a loud bang and my stepdaddy's body fell. There was blood on the wall, running down. The shiny thing fell on the rug. Smoke came from it."

Sitting there under the sun, Sierra gasped.

"How far would she go?" She studied her hands again. "She knew something." But what? "She gave me Grammy's earrings after I testified. She sent *me* the earrings," Sierra croaked aloud.

One dry sob racked her. The weight of ten thousand grief-stricken hearts crushed her broken one. If she'd had the energy and the tears, she might have kicked dirt at the sun. She might have screamed at Mama and her stepdaddy and the child welfare system and Eric and Hobbes and Wade and the world. Only she had no energy. Her tear ducts were parched. She lay still, breathing.

"I couldn't face you, Mama. I'm sorry."

Bright Angel Creek ignored her. The canyon walls ignored her. The environment—this thing she'd worked for years to protect—didn't care about her or Mama or her quest to save Benny and Scarlett. It had almost just killed her. Hobbes was right.

So was Andrew. If she made it out of here alive, she'd be a better mother. She'd be better to Andrew. She would read the unopened letters from Mama. The Sandstone County courtroom had given her a glimpse of who Sierra Justice could have been. Who she should have been.

Somewhere to the south, a siren started a low moan. It increased to a howl.

She grunted and backed her way up the wall again, finding the strength to drive her legs, fighting the pain and soreness. This time she made it to her feet. She swayed, tried to focus.

"Walk, Sierra. Go, bitch!"

———

Hayes waved his hand, and the two men lowered their pistols. He straightened his shirt and tie and wheezed. "I'm sorry Chief, but a few hundred people falls short of Cygnus evacuation resource management protocol."

"What?"

"You want me to be straight? Stop asking stupid questions. We briefed NPS when you called us this morning. POTUS didn't want this going public. Department of the Interior was forced to implement radio silence long before the dam blew. To cut off all comms. The campers and hikers in the park will hear the emergency high-water siren. But . . . thanks to somebody, Chief, Cygnus is out. People downriver are leaving their homes and businesses in droves."

"I guess somebody made the right call then, didn't they? But for those people in the canyon? A siren?" Goodnight asked, shaking his head.

"Hayes, what else do you know about Revelation Six that you're not telling me? Something about them being a real-life Illuminati?"

Hayes took a deep breath, then motioned for the two investigators to leave the room. Once the door shut behind them, Hayes turned off the camera and phone recorder.

He appeared to be contemplating something. "Pretend for a minute that the CIA assassinated JFK. Took out their own president. You with me?"

"Depends where we're going."

"Nowhere good. Revelation Six is the kind of organization that would have written the script and set the stage for the CIA to think they needed to go after Kennedy—without the CIA knowing they were being played by Revelation Six to accomplish something bigger."

"Something bigger?" Goodnight asked.

Hayes whacked one hand against another. "That's just it. Revelation Six has their sights set on the world. If they were responsible for today, what does that suggest? Their network is supposedly deep and exclusive, well financed. The worst part is that no one knows if they're the bad guys, or ultimately, the good guys." He shrugged. "Glen Canyon Dam exploding is a window into their world. They're out there, Fred. In the shadows, the underground. Hell, they might even be right in front of our faces."

Goodnight looked back at the moth. It still hadn't moved.

"Some dark deals were made over the last few days," Hayes said. "Things in motion that we can't understand."

He held up a finger. "One last question. Tanaka said you told her to call the EOD team back right before the dam exploded. Why?"

"Like I told her, it was a gut feeling. I've been in law enforcement a long time. When you get a gut feeling, you act on it." He glanced at the moth again, then back at Hayes.

"Get the hell out of here before I arrest you, Fred."

Goodnight exited the building and scanned the parking lot of the police station. Troops with automatic weapons. Humvees. Several Blackhawks, Little Birds, and a Chinook idled in the desert across the street. More took off and landed every minute. His little slice of Arizona was occupied territory. He called Judy.

"It's all over the news, Fred. WRTV took our anonymous tip. It went viral. Everybody downstream is freaking out, talking about that thing you called Cygnus. They keep showing aerial footage of that monster coming downriver. I've got some pilots fueling up, spreading the word."

"Judy, I'm not supposed to be talking to you. The brass was fighting the real story from going public, but I guess we took care of that."

"Word is that Washington told the park superintendent we're on our own with evacuations. Someone set off a locator beacon down around Ribbon Falls earlier, but they wouldn't let us send a chopper down or message them back, so they're waiting on a rescue we can't send. The Army took our helicopters and our pilots. I think the bigwigs might be planning something. NPS won't just let people die."

"We're running out of time."

"What made you tell me to call the news, Fred?"

"You can't repeat this. I got a call on a radio from a woman down in the canyon named Sierra Justice. She said she was the terrorist's captive. Can you believe that? Guy named Hobbes. She's the one who told me he armed the bombs with a signal. That's when I knew it was real and we had to alert the public. Then she told me he put a big bomb in the dam. I wish she'd called me ten minutes earlier."

———

"Don't stop now, Sierra," Eric said.

"This still could just be Hobbes's terrible joke, you know," she said.

Nausea and thirst overwhelmed her. Sierra had slipped into a cycle. Andrew appeared every few minutes, stumbling with a vacant stare. His mouth would open and water would shoot out at her as he screamed. She'd scream back in terror. Then she would catch up to Eric, plodding along, coughing up blood.

"C'mon, Sierra. You big brain people think too much. Call Goodnight again."

Sierra pulled out the two-way radio, pressed the buttons. It rang and rang as it had during the last several attempts. When she was about to give up, Goodnight answered. The static was worse than before.

"Ms. Justice . . . you good?"

"I don't think so, Mr. Goodnight. I'm thirsty. I'm alone. I think I'm dying down here."

"You need to get to high ground, Ms. Justice . . . dam exploded. It's all gone . . . wall of water . . . hundreds of feet high coming . . ."

"So it is real," Sierra said. "I can't stop. I have to get to my son. I'm so thirsty. Never been this thirsty in my life. Everything hurts. My feet ache."

"You need water . . . Can you . . . creek? Water station? Anything?"

"I like talking to you. I don't like being down here alone. Can you help me find my son? He's in danger."

"You need water . . . need to get to water . . ." The static overwhelmed the phone. The connection was gone.

Victor and Eric's warnings flashed in her mind. Bacteria. Vomiting. More dehydration. What was the greater evil—taking a chance on getting sick, or dying of dehydration or heat exhaustion? Maybe Goodnight was right.

She handled it like any well-trained lawyer faced with two bad options.

"Fuck it."

She scooted down a shallow grade, sliding here, stumbling there, until she could kneel on the bank's hard round rocks. She scooped cold water in both hands, gulping it down like a madwoman. Gorged herself. Dunked her head. Felt the cold permeate the stinging pores of her scalp. She splashed it on her body and vocalized her relief between gulps. When her head cooled and her stomach was sated, she had a realization. She shivered and took in her surroundings. She wanted Benny. Andrew. Warmth. Safety. But all she had was the canyon. Eric appeared on the other side of the creek.

"I hope Andrew's not dead," she said. "He's an amazing father. I took him for granted."

"Whoop-de-doo. Get walking."

"I don't want to be out here alone in the dark."

"So get going."

She glared at him. "You broke my heart. You betrayed me. I'm going to kill you if I ever see you again."

"I'm probably already dead. You took the shots."

———

Hobbes caught Samuels stumbling along the trail in the Box. He'd picked up the blood trail miles back. The Little Bird had whizzed over a few more times before giving up the search, probably due to low fuel. It would return.

Samuels tramped along, holding his side, losing his step now and then, but otherwise making decent progress in spite of having been shot and dehydrated.

"You're hard to kill," Hobbes said.

Samuels whirled, his eyes on fire, his face a mixture of fear and anger.

"Easy," Hobbes said. "I'm not going to hurt you."

Samuels looked down at his bloodied side. "Oh, really?"

"I'm going back to make sure the kid and the nanny are safe."

"Better hurry. Hear that siren? Wall of water coming. Or is there? What's wrong—can't enjoy your blood money knowing you killed a kid and drowned both his parents?"

"Something like that."

"You don't know what to do with it, do you?"

"With what?"

"Empathy, you dick." Samuels laughed and coughed up blood. He wiped his mouth. "Is this the first time in your life you've felt it?"

Hobbes felt a tinge of anger. "I need to get across the Colorado River and make it right," he said. "I think a piece of that bullet broke off and hit your lung. That's why you're coughing blood."

Samuels smiled through rose-colored teeth. "Sierra hates me because of what I did for you. But I won't let you hurt her or her family." He shifted into an aggressive stance, flinching in pain.

"This won't end well for you, Major."

"Let's see."

Hobbes evaded Samuels's punch and muscled the pilot down onto the trail. He popped up with surprising speed and swung a right uppercut into Hobbes's gut, making him double over. Hobbes responded with a backhand across Samuels's cheek, knocking him into the gravel and dirt.

Samuels picked up a handful of it and threw it in Hobbes's face, but he saw this in time to turn his head. His ear filled with dirt, and stinging gravel peppered his scalp.

It gave Samuels an opening and he took it, throwing himself onto Hobbes. For a moment, all Hobbes could see was Samuels's fist coming at his face. He absorbed a few hits before he was able to drive his knee up and throw Samuels off.

Hobbes grabbed the Glock from the fanny pack and aimed it at Samuels. With the light trigger under his finger, he was poised to relieve Samuels of all consequences. Squeeze. End this fight. His neck lit up with fire and he lowered the pistol.

Samuels stared, surprised.

"Well, that's the way the world works, don't it? Some asshole can't win a fair fight, so he pulls a gun."

Hobbes brought the pistol back up. "The universe just gave you a second chance, Major. Don't try me again," he said, holding his neck.

"I saw that lump in your neck yesterday."

"Stand down," Hobbes said.

Samuels spat blood. "Anything else happens to Sierra or that kid, I'll never stop hunting you, here or in whatever hell is."

Hobbes was sliding the gun back into the fanny pack when another sudden, burning pain pierced his ear, snapping his head sideways. He almost fell into Samuels but kept his balance.

He touched his ear and pulled back fingers covered in blood.

"You're hit!" Samuels shouted.

Both men fell prone and wiggled behind the same rock. Hobbes touched his left ear again; the lobe was in ribbons.

"Talk about second chances," Samuels hollered. "Who's shooting?"

"An assassin," Hobbes said through gritted teeth. "Must have followed the signal from the two-way satellite radio you stole from me. Give it to me."

Samuels shook his head. "Sierra has it."

"She doesn't know to turn it off when she's not using it. We have to kill this assassin. Or she's dead."

Whipping and cracking sounds preceded tiny explosions in the canyon walls, ending in the pinging and whining of bullets ricocheting above their heads. Sitting only a foot or so off the trail, the rock they were behind provided very little cover.

"Sounds like a suppressed weapon. They're close," Samuels said, wheezing.

"Roger," answered Hobbes, checking the Glock's load and chamber.

"You go, Hobbes. Give me your piece."

Hobbes sneered and shook his head. "This is an elite assassin, most likely trained by the CIA or National Security Agency. You're injured. And you're a pilot."

Samuels grabbed Hobbes's shoulder and eyeballed him. "I'm a fucking United States Marine, asshole."

Hobbes hesitated, then pulled three full mags from their pouches and put them in front of Samuels.

Samuels took the pistol, raised himself up, and fired three shots. Hobbes ran south, anticipating being shot again. The Glock popped off in a trained cadence. A pause as Samuels reloaded, then several more shots from two different weapons. An angry whistle past his healthy ear, another loud crack over his head.

Hobbes kept running.

The Glock fell silent.

Chapter 17

Thirty Steps, Then You Can Die

I KNOW YOU'VE BEEN THROUGH A LOT, CHIEF, BUT WE need all hands on deck," Tanaka said, looking Goodnight over. "The Arizona Department of Public Safety says an experienced trooper would be welcome at a roadblock. You up to it?"

Goodnight hurt all over from the blast in the dam. He was still in his burned, dirty security uniform. "You guys trust me again?" he asked gruffly. Tanaka gave him an embarrassed smile.

"You would have done the same."

"Yeah. Still sits in my craw, though. I've never turned down an assignment in my life. A roadblock?"

"The NSA triangulated the satellite signal. The tech evidence says he's close. He planted a worm in your security system. The bombs were connected to the security system, which the tech people think was connected to an antenna on the visitors' center with a satellite uplink. They've sealed off all major roads within a two-hundred-mile radius. Multiple roadblocks. Even some dirt roads in the backcountry. They want this guy bad."

"I'll bet they're more interested in interrogating him for intel on these Revelation Six folks than they are for blowing the dam."

Tanaka flashed a knowing smirk.

"Point me in the right direction, General."

Tanaka raised her radio. "Where do you want Chief Goodnight? He's back in the fight."

As the state police chopper ascended, he worried about Sierra Justice. He messed with the two-way satellite radio to see if he could figure out how to call out. He cursed himself after ten minutes of trying. The dark, snaking canyon grew smaller as they flew away. She was down there in it. He prayed it didn't swallow her up forever.

———

Sierra entered Phantom Ranch as dusk began to fall down in the canyon. She could see bright sunlight up on the higher cliffs and the rim above. If she could only get up there and escape the coming dark. The siren had stopped a long time ago. She hadn't seen anyone since she drank from the creek. She had recovered some, was still weak, but didn't feel sick yet. She moved faster after she heard several faint gunshots behind her to the north, afraid to speculate on their origins.

Campers and hikers mingled around the canteen, lounged on camp chairs, sat in circles with beers or lemonade. Someone playing a guitar had gathered a small singing crowd. However, other groups with concerned faces were speaking in low murmurs. Two young men saw Sierra stumble in and rushed to help her sit at a picnic table. More gathered around.

Her relief at seeing people turned to panic. Her voice was thick. "I knew it. Andrew didn't make it. No one here knows what's coming. I'm so sorry." She still had no moisture available for tears. "I have to find Andrew. We have to get everybody out of here."

"This is the lady people have been talking about," someone said. "Has to be why that siren was going off. Why aren't the rangers doing anything? I'll find a medic or doctor. Stay with her."

"Got it," someone replied.

Sierra recognized a woman she had spoken to on the trail. The woman tapped someone else on the shoulder and pointed at Sierra. Mouthed the words *That's her.*

Someone handed Sierra a cold bottle of water. She guzzled it down in one take, the icy cold heading down her throat and into her stomach.

A bug-eyed older man in a brown hiking shirt and green pants moved through the crowd and asked Sierra, "Are you okay, ma'am?" He turned to the young man closest to her and asked, "Heat exhaustion?"

"My son is in danger. I need to find my boyfriend. Can you help me, please?" Sierra asked. "Are you a park ranger?"

"No, ma'am. I'm Art, camp volunteer. Do you need the medical cabin?"

Sierra grabbed Art's arm, her voice tight. "Listen to me, Art. I need to speak to the ranger in charge—now. It's an emergency."

Art's eyes bugged out even more. "Are you the lady who was with the gunshot victim? Does this have something to do with the siren?"

The young man put his face close to Art's and whispered, "It's her. I think she's Sierra Justice. She's the lawyer from TV, you know, with that fascist Canyon's Dream group? We need to get her to a doctor. She needs to be evacuated."

"We all need to be evacuated!" Sierra shouted as she stood. "What the hell do you think that siren meant?"

More people drifted over.

"Art, take me to the ranger in charge, please," Sierra said, swaying like a tall pine in the wind. Art and the young man caught her.

"I'll take you to the ranger station, but I can't promise Ranger Driscoll is there. You need medical help."

"You can't call him on a radio?" Another bottle of water appeared. Sierra drank half of it and poured the rest on her head and neck.

He shook his head. "Darndest thing. Nobody's squawking with anyone right now. The camp landline isn't working. The Wi-Fi's always loosey-goosey, but right now it's dead. Even the pay phone outside the canteen is kaput. And ten minutes ago, some of those bad actors guzzling beer over there went down to the river and ripped the wires out of the dang siren. Bunch of us are a little worried."

Sierra shook her head. "You should be a lot worried. Have you seen a tall black man in camp? Andrew Thomas. He's my boyfriend."

Art leaned back, giving a knowing nod. "I've seen him. The ranger station has your name all over it."

The faces at the Phantom Ranch Ranger Station were solemn and unkind. A tall ranger in uniform opened the door and showed Sierra in while Art waited outside. The cramped rock-walled station contained a desk with a laptop, a notepad, a phone, and a coffee cup holding pens and pencils. The coffee cup read WHO LEFT THE BOX OF IDIOTS OPEN AGAIN? Two wooden chairs sat in front of the desk. Behind the desk, the tall ranger sat in a plush chair with the National Park Service seal embossed on the headrest. An intimidating, barrel-chested female ranger, armed and in uniform, stood against the wall, arms crossed. A window AC unit hummed in the corner.

"Sit down," the tall ranger said, directing Sierra to one of the wooden chairs. He sat and crossed his arms. "I'm Ranger Hank Driscoll, and this here is Ranger Erin Horowitz."

Sierra sat. "I'm looking for my boyfriend, Andrew Thomas. Our son has been kidnapped by a murderer. Everybody in this camp—"

"Stop."

The ranger held up his hand. His voice was low and measured. A bushy black goatee speckled with gray accented his ruddy face under his flat hat. "Who are you, ma'am?" he asked.

"Sierra Justice."

"What are you doing in my station?"

"You have to—"

Ranger Driscoll's hand slammed onto the desk, rattling the contents of the Box of Idiots coffee cup. "It's Tuesday. The day I finish my eight-day stint and go back topside to my wife and kids. You, Ms. Justice, are the last thing I need. What are you doing in my station?"

That morning she might have let this big ranger dictate what she did next. Not this afternoon. She pointed at him. "You listen to me. You're here to protect and serve, right? My taxes pay your salary, right? Did you not hear that siren going off?"

Driscoll's face changed. Horowitz uncrossed her arms and moved toward Sierra. He held up his hand, stopping her.

"I was part of Wade Ford's group. You know, the billionaire the whole world hates? I'm his attorney. Everyone hates me too. We were attacked near Ribbon Falls. Three of our group were shot and killed, two hikers were killed, and another's injured back there. He might be dead. My boyfriend went ahead of us to try and warn the camp and rescue our son. I don't know where he is now."

At the mention of Wade's name, Driscoll looked at Horowitz. "I knew that preppy coming down here was bad news." He focused back on Sierra. "He wanted to warn the camp about a shooter?"

"A murderer. And a flood, but no one believes that part. There's a killer with a gun out there. Look at the blood on my clothes."

"We heard the siren. When it went off, I had no choice but to send every able-bodied and willing person in camp up the rim. But I couldn't force the rest of these folks to risk their lives going up without help. I've received no assistance or news of a flood or a storm upriver—not to mention a murderer—from anyone official." He leaned forward.

"How do I know you're not the murderer? Ask yourself that yet?"

Sierra cringed, thinking how this next part would sound. "The murderer is a psycho named Hobbes. He blew up Glen Canyon Dam. In an hour, maybe less, all that water's going to be here. And it's going to kill everyone. I have to get to my son, now."

Driscoll frowned. "As you can see out there, my ranger station has turned into Grand Central Station. I don't need some lady on the trail squawking about how some deranged killer started shooting people and blew up Glen Canyon Dam. How do you figure he accomplished that?"

Sierra pulled out the two-way satellite radio and held it up. "This was Hobbes's phone. I used it and talked to a security guy named Goodnight at the dam. He confirmed the dam exploded. There's a flood coming." She cackled in frustration. "Know what? Let me call him so you can talk to him." She tried to find the preset number, but the screen was black. She pushed the button repeatedly. Nothing. Sierra let out a howl, tossing the phone on the desk. "It's dead."

Driscoll leaned back in his chair and exchanged a dubious glance with Horowitz.

"That's your proof? A dead sat phone and a crazy story about how you called Glen Canyon Dam and talked to a man named Goodnight?" He pointed to a door in the corner of the office. "Put her in there with a cot and some food and water. Send medical in there with an IV. She's pale."

Sierra jumped up. "You can't lock me up!" she screamed. "My baby is in serious danger! Where's my boyfriend? You never answered me. Did you see him?"

"Oh yes, Ms. Justice. I saw him."

———

Eric returned fire until he had three rounds remaining. Then he did the only thing he could do.

He played dead. It wasn't hard, considering he felt dead and was covered in blood and would probably be dead soon. He stopped firing and lay there, waiting an eternity before he heard slight scuffing sounds on the trail. His debut acting performance was risky, but it was his only chance against a superior foe.

A presence blocked the light on his eyelids. A man let out his breath. Eric raised the Glock and pulled the trigger until the gun was empty.

There was a gagging, choking sound, then a heavy thud.

The assassin, an Asian man with huge arms and long hair, looked like a fish out of water as he tried to draw breath that would never come. Eric had shot him through the chest. A moment later the assassin's eyes and bloody gurgle showed that this was the end of his story. Eric struggled to his feet.

He left the M4 lying next to the dead man, deciding the juice wasn't worth the squeeze, and resumed heading south. The bullet burned in his side. The rhythm he established was manageable for about thirty steps before he had to rest.

It became a morbid game: Thirty Steps, Then You Can Die.

Over and over. Thirty steps, then you can die. He wanted to lie down for a few minutes. But he knew if he did, he would die. Brain damaging or not, the random injections of epinephrine had made him feel invincible for a few minutes at a time.

When he saw the opportunity, he ambled down to the creek, disregarded any concerns over filtering the water, and drank. He soaked for a few minutes, his face the only thing not submerged. The cold water was a shock, but it soothed the burning wound and rejuvenated him.

Thirty steps, then you can die.

Escaping the Box's narrow walls as the canyon widened gave him hope. There might be help waiting for him at Phantom Ranch. Then again, if Sierra and Andy had been successful, there might not. The thought crushed the last of his optimism.

Alone. Fighting. Dying.

This is all your fault.

For all Eric knew, Hobbes was on his way to kill Sierra and the rest of her family. Her family. Putting it like that made him realize the scope of his own selfishness.

What the hell had he been thinking? Maybe he deserved to die down here. Penance. All his efforts to help Sierra had only made her life worse. The last thing she needed was for him to walk into Phantom Ranch. He'd had his shot years ago and blown it.

Ahead near the trail, he spotted a jumble of fallen boulders that created an overhang with enough room for him to crawl under. That's where he'd finally get some rest.

———

Sierra fought Ranger Horowitz's attempt to lock her in the small room. Driscoll helped, and they muscled her into the makeshift holding cell. A metal screen door stood behind the wooden door. She beat on it, creating a racket.

"Let me out!" she shouted. "I have to get to my son."

"Sierra?"

"Andrew?" Disbelief. She ran and fell into his arms, causing him to stumble and wince. "Are you hurt?" she asked him, looking him over.

"Fine," he said. "Just locked up for no legal reason."

Sierra checked him over. His clothes and skin were covered in dirt and sweaty. There was an IV in his arm. "I thought something happened to you," she said.

"Something did. I was running along a hairy piece of the trail and my damn Achilles acted up. Lost my balance, fell into the creek. A couple hikers fished me out and helped me get back here. They probably thought I was crazy too."

"How bad are you injured?"

"Hard to walk." His ankle was iced and bandaged.

Frantic, her voice rose again. "Andrew, it's real. Goodnight confirmed that the dam blew."

He sat hard on a chair. Shook his head. "I hoped it was a bluff."

"If you can't go, then I have to get back across the river to Benny. There's no more time."

Sierra beat on the door again, screaming. She leaned her head against it. Someone began turning the handle. When Driscoll walked through, Andrew rose and hobbled to put himself between the ranger and Sierra.

Driscoll held his finger to his lips and closed the door behind him, careful to make as little sound as possible. "Keep your voices to a whisper," he said, lowering his hands to suggest silence. He was sweating. His composure had done a one-eighty. "What you're saying is actually real?"

Sierra threw up her hands. "Yes, it's real."

Driscoll softened. "I'm sorry about the tough guy act in there, but I had to play it out, and frankly, I saved your lives. You're both injured and dehydrated. You would have died trying to get up seven miles of South Kai in the heat." His face went slack. "I've had to keep it all to myself, trying not to freak out my rangers and my volunteers until I had reliable word. That horrible siren."

She put her hand on Driscoll's beefy arm. "It's coming. Is there another bridge, one that's higher? We have to get to our son."

"It's no good. The next bridge downstream is farther away and it ends in a low trail along the river. The Black Bridge, getting up the South Kai, that's it."

He shook his head. "I lost all radio contact hours ago. There's an emergency landline and a sat phone here, but I can't reach anyone on either. In all my years, it's only happened when there was bad weather. Never out of the clear blue sky would NPS leave us hanging. Then several people came into camp saying a woman was claiming that Glen Canyon Dam was blown and people were shot. When the siren went off, I had no explanation, but like I told you, I sent up everyone who was able-bodied or would leave. I've still got slow movers, people who get down here easy without any idea how hard it is to get back out. And people who think it's just a rumor. Some of them actually laughed at us."

Driscoll removed his flat hat and looked at Sierra, shaking as he gripped its brim in both hands. "A dam breach scenario has been my worst fear since I started rangering down here. They did a study back in the nineties. Said if you're down in the canyon when the dam fails, you won't survive unless you climb higher than a forty-story building. People are here or back up on the rim instead of out in the canyon or on the river because of you, Ms. Justice. But now that I know it's real, we've got to get the rest of these people out."

A shout from the main room of the ranger station turned their heads. Driscoll opened the door. Sierra gasped. Andrew, wrapped ankle and all, ripped out his IV and lunged through the doorframe.

Chapter 18

A Dimmer View of Stoicism

Despite Andrew's injury, it took both Driscoll and Art to stop him from launching himself at Hobbes.

"This is the guy!" Andrew shouted, fighting to be let loose. Driscoll grabbed his jaw and stared him down while Art and Horowitz restrained him.

"Calm down, Mr. Thomas," Driscoll commanded.

"Let me go," Andrew said, squirming.

Driscoll addressed Hobbes. "You're the one they say shot people and blew the dam?" he asked, adjusting his stance to allow him to draw his gun. "Take your mask off, sir."

Sierra found Hobbes more frightening than before. Part of his ear was missing. One of his eyes was swollen. Blood stained his neck, mask, and shirt. Horowitz shifted her stance too.

Hobbes ignored Driscoll and turned his gaze on Sierra. "I'm going across the bridge to save your son and the nanny," he said, his voice muffled. Sierra frowned and turned the words over in her mind.

"Hang on, fella," Driscoll said, putting his hand on his gun. "Take off that mask."

Hobbes looked at him.

"Why aren't you getting people out? Times almost up."

Sierra's body tensed into rigidity.

Driscoll swallowed, his voice less confident. "We haven't been able to reach anyone for hours. The fastest way out of here is by helicopter. You need to answer my questions before I detain you."

Hobbes's reacted when Driscoll mentioned a helicopter. Sierra stiffened more, felt her heart beat faster.

"You've got helicopters coming?" Hobbes asked.

Driscoll shook his head. "We don't have any kind of plan, but a helicopter would solve a lot of problems. But I need you to answer my ques—"

"You son of a bitch!" Sierra screamed, lurching forward. She pulled Driscoll's gun from its holster, fumbled with it, then swung it up toward Hobbes. Everyone in the room went into alert mode. She was terrified of the gun in her hand, but she pointed it at Hobbes. A woman screamed, but this turned out to be Art.

"Ms. Justice, put the gun down," Driscoll said in a calm voice, moving toward her.

Hobbes took a step toward Sierra.

"He caused all of this," she cried, her breath choppy and haggard. The pistol shook in her hand.

"Put it down, Ms. Justice," Driscoll said.

Sierra heard him, but she held the gun now. She kept seeing Benny's face. Hobbes took another step in her direction.

"Let me help your son, Sierra," Hobbes said, stepping closer still. "I need to do this."

Just above a whisper, she said, "I'll kill for him."

A gun fired.

———

"What you got?" Goodnight said.

"Four pilots. Four helicopters with minimal crew. We're heading down with the first one."

"Watch for rockslides, Judy. If you're on the ground, you'll feel vibrations before you hear them slide. Keep an eye out before you land."

"I have another piece of good news. The NPS and BOR bigwigs are practicing civil disobedience. They're helping with the rescue as much as they can after the military took all our helicopters and pilots."

"Where's the landing zone for the rescued folks?"

"The helipad at the visitors' center. What are you doing?"

"They finally decided I'm not a terrorist and reassigned me to my old job. I just landed out on Highway 64 just north of the park to help man a roadblock."

Judy chuckled. "An Arizona law enforcement legend stopping motorists at a roadblock?"

Goodnight chuckled himself. After the last several hours, it was good to share a laugh with her. "I'm tired, Judy. And my ass hurts from getting blown up. But I can't lie down while this is going on."

"Blown up? You okay? Fred, don't lie to me. Are you all right?"

"You can ice it for me later, if we live."

"How romantic. Watch your six, old man."

"You watch yours, too, Judy."

———

The ranger station's walls were wood paneling above concrete blocks over a wooden floor. The pistol shot was amplified to an excruciating level. Hobbes heard muffled shouts, foot scrapes. Hands went to ears. Sierra nearly dropped the gun. He'd known she would miss. She damn near yanked the trigger, and she wasn't prepared for the recoil. Even if he hadn't dropped just before the shot, she might have still missed him. His plan was to move quick and subdue her. He'd anticipated the recoil would throw her off enough that he could disarm her.

Instead, Sierra trained the gun back on him, just far enough out of reach for Hobbes to miss his chance. Her face tightened. The rangers moved toward her but didn't make it before she fired again.

This time the slug ripped through Hobbes's left sleeve. Searing pain in his upper arm. He grunted and slapped his right hand over the graze. She was about to shoot him again when he put his free hand out and dropped to a knee.

"Stop, Sierra. Just wait a fucking second!" Hobbes pleaded.

She hesitated.

"Ms. Justice, do you see that Ranger Horowitz has her weapon pointed at you?" asked Driscoll.

Hobbes glanced at the female ranger. She was in a firing stance, her pistol trained on Sierra, her eyes darting back and forth between Sierra and himself, her breathing heavy. With jumpy trigger fingers, things could fall apart in an instant.

"Art?" Driscoll said, not taking his attention off Sierra.

"Yes, sir?" the bug-eyed old man answered, terror on his face.

"Go get the doctor. We have a wounded man here."

Art shuffled out the door.

"You don't understand, man—this guy's a killer," Andrew cried out.

"Back off, son. I'm not telling you again," Driscoll said with force, and Andrew obeyed.

"Sierra," Hobbes said, hissing in pain, "I'm going up that trail faster than anyone else here can go. I'll do what I said I would."

"There's nothing good in you," she said.

Driscoll spoke again. "Ms. Justice, I'm going to give you five seconds."

Sierra didn't budge. "Give them to me."

"Give you what?"

"Five . . ." said Driscoll.

"Now." Sierra adjusted her grip on the pistol.

"You don't understand what you're asking."

"Four . . ."

"I'm not asking, Hobbes."

He unbuckled the flatpack from his plate carrier vest. "The people waiting on these documents do not play around, Sierra. You have to lis—"

"Three . . ."

"Someone's about to die here, Hobbes," Sierra said.

"Two . . ."

Hobbes pulled the slender metal box from the pack and put it on the floor.

"Pick it up, Andrew," she said.

Andrew stepped in and grabbed the box, then backed up, cradling it in both arms.

Sierra lowered the gun. "When I have my Benny back, you'll get those back."

Hobbes held his wounded arm. "How?"

Horowitz shifted and pointed her gun at Hobbes. Driscoll took the gun from Sierra, then handcuffed her behind her back.

"Figure it out," Sierra said. "And I want something else too."

"What?"

Sierra glared at him. "You know what."

He had a pretty good idea. Either way, he had to establish some goodwill.

"Samuels is still alive. At least he was when I saw him," Hobbes said.

Sierra's expression became questioning. Horowitz and Driscoll held their positions. Hobbes could tell from their faces that he was next in line for a set of bracelets or a standoff. He moved toward the door.

"Back in Washington I offered Samuels money to work with me. He said no. So I told him that if he didn't get me close to Ford, I'd kill you, your son, and him," Hobbes said, pointing at Andrew and backing up. "Keeping you all alive is the only reason he agreed to help me. I thought you should know that."

He walked out the open door and took off at a run down the trail through the crowd of confused-looking people. Behind him came shouting for him to stop but no gunfire. He was at the river in minutes, tired but not anywhere near done. His endurance and speed had made him a standout in every test the Green Berets had thrown at him, from the early days at the schoolhouse to that last rotation in Afghanistan. When he crossed the Black Bridge, he ripped off the mask and glanced upriver.

It would be here soon.

He made it across and through the tunnel and headed up the South Kaibab trail, his breathing smooth and steady, his heart rate elevated but not stressed from overexertion. He was slower than usual and his injuries hurt, but he was soon high enough that he was in full sun again. The commuter car was waiting for him up there in the parking lot. The trunk contained all the weapons he needed to fight his way out. He'd have to choose between taking the backroads or disguising himself and taking the highway. A faster escape meant more exposure.

Less exposure meant—

"What am I thinking?" he asked, panting over his knees. "I said I'd save them."

A low, croaking voice spoke in Dari around him. Hobbes looked for the source. There was no one. Not even the raven. He heard it again. He turned a corner and saw a dusty black garment hanging from a low piece of scrub along the trail, fluttering in the breeze. He didn't touch it.

His shoulders slumped. "I don't remember how to pray."

———

Handcuffed, Sierra collapsed in the nearest chair and stared into space. There were no obvious answers. Hobbes was the toughest and most capable person available to save Benny. The only faster option was a helicopter that might never come.

Eric. There'd been nothing in it for him but her life. Her child's life. A life she had endangered with her own choices.

Did she deserve to be a mother?

A vision of Benny learning to ride his bike on the sidewalk under falling leaves. Snuggling on the couch by the fire in their new house. Dropping him on his first day of school. His weird but cute obsession with dialing random numbers and talking to strangers on her cell phone. The bashful look on his face when she'd caught him—

She jumped up, her arms bound behind her. "Driscoll, take these damn things off me. Give me a sat phone and every number you have for anyone who works up on the South Rim."

He scowled. "Ms. Justice, if we could reach anyone by radio or phone, we would have. Now come on. You just shot a man. I can't let you run around here unrestrained. You forget who's in charge? I've got to get people to safety. And I'm confiscating that metal box from your boyfriend too. Now sit."

Sierra didn't sit. Her voice rose with every word. "First of all, if you take that metal box, you'll spend even more time away from your wife and kids. Second, I shot the criminal you should have shot. Third, I'm a lawyer—persistence and loopholes solve everything. Fourth?" She leaned into Driscoll's face. "I'm a fucking mom. My baby's life is just as important as the rest of these people. Get these cuffs off me."

Andrew froze. Horowitz stood as if unsure what to do. Driscoll eyeballed Sierra. He hesitated for a time before going to his desk and pulling out the ranger station satellite phone. Hesitated again. Exhaled. Tapped his cell. Sierra moved next to him.

"You gonna shoot anyone else?"

"You first, if you don't hurry," she said, turning so he could uncuff her.

Driscoll looked at Horowitz as he twisted the key in the handcuffs. "We have no time. We have to send anyone else who can move with decent speed up the South Kaibab trail now. Tell 'em they need to get as high as they can, and not to stop, just keep going. Put everyone else in groups of ten. If all else fails, we might move folks back up the North Kaibab. They'd be cut off from help in the elements for who knows how long, but at least they might be far enough from the flood. Keep everyone calm. Go, Horowitz."

Art entered with a confused-looking man Sierra assumed was a doctor.

"You're too late, Art. Don't need him anymore. Go help Ranger Horowitz," said Driscoll.

Art's goggle eyes reflected disappointment. Murmuring, he and the man walked back out of the station.

Sierra rubbed her wrists and picked up the phone.

Driscoll rattled off the first number as if it was painful. "Damn waste of time, Ms. Justice," he mumbled.

The satellite phone was clumsy and slow to use. She put it on speaker mode. The line rang several times, then gave three beeps and clicked into dead air. There wasn't time to try any number twice.

After five minutes, Driscoll stood. "Enough."

"He's right, Sierra," Andrew said.

"I have five more minutes. I have to know if my baby's safe, even if trying to save his life is my last act on earth. Keep going." She heard Horowitz outside yelling on a bullhorn, heard people shouting. The remaining five minutes passed. Maybe Driscoll was right. Hundreds of feet of water. The canyon breaking apart. Everyone dying an awful death—

"Hello?" A woman's voice came through loud on the phone's speaker.

Sierra lit up. "Who is this?"

"Should be Christy Garrett," Driscoll said. "She runs the laundry service."

"Christy?" Sierra asked.

"Yes . . . Who's this?"

"My name is Sierra Justice. I'm in Phantom Ranch with Ranger Driscoll." She held the phone out to him. "She needs to hear it from you. Tell her to go to the Coconino Lodge and open the door to room 713, by force if they have to. My six-year-old son, Benny, and his nanny, Scarlett, are bound and gagged in there."

Driscoll took the phone. "Christy, this is Hank down in Phantom Ranch. This will sound crazy, but I'm begging you to help us." He repeated Sierra's instructions to Christy.

"Don't let her hang up," Sierra said.

Christy's excited voice came back. "No kidding there's an emergency, Hank. A flood's coming down the canyon. What are you still doing down there? They're evacuating everyone. Someone tied up a kid?"

"And a woman. We just confirmed the flood down here. We've

been in the dark for hours," said Driscoll. Minutes passed. Andrew hobbled over and watched in anticipation.

Christy came back on the line. "Hank, the lodge manager's on another line. They'll meet us at the room with a master key. I'm with two rangers, Jim Bush and Lilli Bianchi. You're awful lucky you called when you did. NPS ordered everyone out. Glen Canyon Dam exploded. It's all over the news."

Sierra watched Driscoll's face drop at this confirmation that he'd been intentionally kept in the dark. He looked at her and said, "If not for you, we might all have died down here without a clue of what was coming."

Sierra didn't know what to say.

Through the phone came the sound of a vehicle accelerating and shifting fast, the rangers murmuring with Christy. "Hank, we're not far from the lodge. Whoa, look out, Bush. Sorry, Driscoll, people are driving like idiots up here," Christy said.

Driscoll gave Sierra and Andrew a sober look. "I hope for the best on every search and rescue, but maybe you two shouldn't be listening."

Sierra snapped, "I saw five people get murdered today. I can handle this."

"Same," Andrew said.

Driscoll put up a hand and nodded.

"Okay, Hank, we're in the lot. Getting out of the car," said Christy.

Sierra heard running footsteps and people panting.

"Headed to the room. We're in the hall. The manager's opening the door."

Several moments passed. Sounds of people yelling. Scuffling.

"What the hell?" Sierra shouted. "What's going on? Is Benny okay?"

Christy's confused voice said, "There's no one in here."

———

Goodnight had listened to the radio during the helicopter ride. The National Guard for Arizona, Nevada, New Mexico, Utah, and even

California were deployed to handle evacuations and render aid. Lake Mead was on full emergency release, as were the dams below it. The Flaming Gorge Reservoir above Lake Powell was shut off completely, but that wouldn't last long, as the swollen Green River was filling it quick.

Widespread panic was afoot. Law enforcement agencies in multiple cities and communities throughout the Southwest were in full emergency evacuation mode. A National Park Service official said it would be a little more than a half hour before the Phantom Ranch area was hit. With the unfolding disaster washing down the canyon, there were no officers to spare. They were down to rookies and has-beens like Goodnight to man roadblocks.

His job was to check every soul who passed through his checkpoint. If the man who'd spearheaded all this showed, Goodnight had no intention of calling it in. Anderson had described him in detail when the feds interrogated him earlier that day—Goodnight had it memorized.

He had to survive this. He thought of his children. His grandchildren. Judy.

Ranger Judy Moore was a keeper. But if he were to get hitched to her, what would Blanche say one day when they met in heaven? Would be a weird meeting, he thought. Blanche would understand.

He was posted with a trooper fresh out of the academy. An athletically built fellow, early twenties at most. His uniform was crisp. His duty belt shone. Goodnight noticed his service weapon was equally clean.

"What's your name, trooper?" Goodnight asked.

The young man turned, and his clean-shaven face lit up. "Deadass? No way, bro. Commander Goodnight?" He saluted.

Goodnight half-heartedly returned it.

Then the trooper bowed and offered his hand. "Trooper Mike Garcia, sir. You're a legend, Commander. I saw your photo at the academy. Heard the stories, bro." He looked Goodnight up and down. "Your uniform has seen better days, though. What happened to you? I gotta get a pic. Can I?"

"I guess," Goodnight stammered.

Garcia held out his phone and leaned in next to Goodnight and took a selfie, his other hand in a hard-rock V.

"You saw my picture at the academy?"

"Yes, sir. Lots of 'em. You're the man, Commander Goodnight."

"When did the Arizona Department of Public Safety Academy curate a dinosaur exhibit?"

Garcia smiled as the joke dawned. "That's funny, Commander," he said with a nod.

"It's just Chief now, Garcia. Let's get ready for our first customers. We're looking for a—"

"White male. Tall, approximately six foot four. Thin build. Close-cropped blond hair. Blue eyes. One ninety-five. Definitely clutchin' glizzies. Goes by Hobbes, which is likely an alias."

Goodnight scowled. "Clutching what?"

"Armed and dangerous, Commander. I mean Chief."

They leaned against Garcia's cruiser and gazed out at the valley surrounded by pine forests that gradually opened up into the desert to the south. They still had some decent daylight. Goodnight hoped this posting would distract him from the explosions and flooding and horrors repeating in his mind.

———

"There's no one in there?" Sierra cried out. Andrew put his hand on her shoulder. She threw it off.

"Driscoll, this is Bush. We'll keep searching," a male's voice said. "It's pandemonium up here right now."

"Wait, this is an adjoining room," Christy said to someone.

There were scuffling sounds and a bang. Then a shout. More scuffling and more shouts.

"What's happening? Tell me Benny's okay!" Sierra screamed into the phone. More thumping and scuffling sounds.

"We got him!" Christy exclaimed. "He's taped up and scared and crying. He's a mess but he's fine."

Sierra and Andrew fell on the floor weeping, gripping each other. She sat up. "And Scarlett?"

Bush's voice came back. "The woman's unresponsive. I'll try and get a chopper from the hospital in Flagstaff. It's going to be tough with this evacuation, but we'll get them to an ICU ASAP."

"Scarlett has asthma. She needs oxygen. Let me talk to Benny," Sierra demanded.

"Ma'am, I'm not sure he's in a place to—"

"Put my son on the phone, dammit!"

More scuffling sounds, then Benny's small voice crying and asking for his mama.

"I'm here, Benny," Sierra said, hysterical. "Mama's here, baby. So is Daddy. Are you okay?"

"Mama? My mouth had tape on it. Mama . . ." Benny trailed off into a wail.

Driscoll grabbed the phone and spoke in soothing tones. "Benny, your mom and dad will see you real soon, buddy. Bush, Bianchi, don't let anything happen to that boy or that woman."

"Ten-four, Driscoll. We're on it."

Driscoll addressed Sierra and Andrew. "Tell him you love him and you'll see him soon. We have to go. Sounds like people are losing their minds outside."

"Mama loves you, baby," Sierra sobbed.

"Daddy loves you, too," Andrew said, sniffling.

In a muffled, crying voice, Benny said, "I want Mama."

"Please," Sierra begged.

Driscoll took the phone. "It's time to go if you ever want to see him again. Christy, bless you, bless you, bless you, for answering the phone. Be safe up there."

"How are you getting out of there, Hank?" Christy asked.

"Working on it. Bush?"

"Here, Driscoll."

"Put a bulletin out for our suspect. Tall fella, maybe six foot five. Thin, probably less than two hundred pounds. Has blond hair, blue eyes. Calls himself Hobbes. Armed and dangerous. Wears a black mask. From what I understand, he blew up Glen Canyon."

"That matches what I heard earlier. I'll put it out again."

Driscoll hung up the phone. Sierra embraced Andrew, and they wept.

CHAPTER 19

The Black Bridge

HOW CAN YOU BELIEVE ERIC'S STILL ALIVE?" SIERRA WAS unsure. Every time the knowledge that Benny was safe hit her, she broke down in another grateful sob. All she wanted was to be with Benny. But Eric might be alive, trying to get back to her. Andrew rubbed his hand across his forehead. "Say you make it out of here with Eric alive. What sort of future is that?"

"What? No, Andrew." She shook her head. "Eric and I weren't meant to be together."

That was harder to say than she thought it would be. Andrew seemed to notice. She touched his arm, "Everything with Eric ends in disaster." She laughed at herself. "How apropos is that?"

She rose and touched Andrew's cheek.

"I'm sorry I wasn't more forthcoming with you about Eric. But you heard Hobbes—Eric cooperated to keep Hobbes from killing me and my family. He kept us safe. What kind of people would we be if we ignored that?"

Andrew took her hand. "What does Eric have that you need? I'll give it to you. Anything, Sierra—whatever it is. Let me give it to you."

Sierra soaked in his honesty and yearning. She'd tried to answer that very question for years. Why would she risk so much for Eric?

"Closure."

"Closure?"

"Yes. That's what Eric has that you can't give me." She pointed at the top of the South Rim. "If I could go up there right now to our son and never think about any of this or Eric again, don't you know I would?"

Andrew motioned with his hands for Sierra to lower her voice. She didn't.

"Eric saved our lives, Andrew. He didn't bring us down here. Wade brought me and you volunteered. All Eric tried to do was keep us alive. We could all be dead in DC right now."

With every cathartic word, her voice grew louder, more intense. Driscoll left the room.

"This is so unfair," said Andrew.

Sierra recalled Victor's words.

"Fair isn't part of the equation. I have to make up for my sins."

"Never heard you talk like that before. What sins?"

"I should have kept my mouth shut in that courtroom."

"What are you talking about?"

"Nothing. Look, Andrew, Eric was there for me long before you. For years he was the closest thing I had to family. If I leave this canyon knowing I could have saved his life but didn't try, I'll never be the best mother I can be to our son. I don't want to do this, Andrew, but I have to . . . Wait. Hear that?"

They stepped outside next to Driscoll and watched a helicopter land down by the Colorado River. Several minutes later, an older female ranger and two crew members jogged toward them. Sierra was already formulating her plan to get Andrew on the helicopter.

Driscoll shouted, "Judy Moore, am I glad to see you. How'd you manage this?"

"A lady ranger never reveals her secrets, Hank," Judy hollered back. "Thank God you rounded people up. Pilot says he can get eight each trip."

Driscoll nodded. "I've got people crying, screaming, or dazed that need outta here quick. Got one group in purple unicorn costumes sitting around drinking whiskey, and they don't believe the flood's coming. Another group's locked in a cabin and they're going at each other like rabbits—said they're going out with a bang. That's an exact quote. You got more helicopters?"

"Four total. Military came through and ordered almost every pilot and machine to the west for evacuations."

Driscoll nodded. "We got about sixty people here. I sent all the faster people up a while ago. Most of the ones still here, I don't know that they'd make it up high enough in time. Besides the drunks and fornicators, it's mostly older folks, a few partially disabled people, hikers with heart issues."

Judy turned and motioned for the two crew members to get moving. "Grab the first eight and let's go. Try to keep family and friends together. We need to get these people closer to the river for faster evac, Driscoll. It's almost a ten-minute walk from the helipad to here. I know that seems counterintuitive, but what choice do we have? Who are these two?" She gestured at Sierra and Andrew.

"They were hostages of the guy who blew the dam. This is Sierra, the woman who got all these folks here. This is her boyfriend, Andrew."

Judy looked at Sierra. "Sierra Justice?"

Sierra stopped. "How do you know that?"

"I'm not at liberty to say," Judy replied. "I don't think you realize what all you've done here, ma'am." She shifted to Driscoll. "Why didn't you arrest that bastard?"

"It's a long story."

"Aw, but I love stories. Ms. Justice, we'll take all the help we can get. I need to hurry up and get home to my fur babies."

She winked and smiled.

"I'm headed back up the trail," Sierra said, realizing Judy was trying to lighten the mood. She pointed at Andrew. "But he needs to be on this helicopter." She faced him. "You're going straight to the hospital to Benny. I can't leave here without knowing you'll be with him."

Judy lost her smile and shook her head at Sierra. "You got a death wish?"

"It's a—"

"Long story. Yeah, I got it," Judy said with a wave. She shouted at the two crew members, "Make this first group seven. We got another passenger here."

"We can't wait for you," Driscoll said to Sierra.

"I know."

She pulled Andrew aside and whispered, "Keep the box hidden in your shirt. Don't tell anyone you have it."

"Benny's safe now. Why do you still want it?"

"Just do it, Andrew."

Before he could respond, she embraced him. Shut her eyes. Listened.

She absorbed the sounds of the creek falling over the rocks. Birds calling. Leaves fluttering in the breeze through the cottonwoods. A surge of life through her heart. Andrew's warm smell filling her nose. His uneven breathing. This man with whom she'd created life and shared it with. This man she had betrayed.

Driscoll's deep voice. "If he's going on this bird, he's going now."

Sierra cinched up her pack. "Get to our baby. Tell him I love him. Still got Mama's earrings?"

Andrew patted his shorts pocket. "I love you," he said.

She kissed her fingers and put them on his lips, then headed up the North Kaibab trail.

———

Despite all Sierra had been through since early that morning, she was still moving. Thank God for her fitness regimen. Everything hurt, she was exhausted and going slow, but at least she could still move. What if Eric had fallen over the edge like she almost did? Like Andrew had? Became delirious and disoriented and headed back north? How far would she go before she turned around and went back to Benny? Her imagination and conscience taunted her. A gauntlet of vaporous mothers materialized around the canyon, uttering awful things and jeering.

"You stupid, selfish bitch. Your son needs you, but you chose to stay out here?"

"So what if his father's with him? You aren't. Go chase your ex-boyfriend's ghost, whore!" shouted another.

"Whose life is more important, *prossy-toot*?"

Sierra shook her head to make them disappear. She had told Andrew she needed closure, that she and Eric were never meant to be together. But did she really believe that? Was her reason for being down here now looking for Eric much deeper than finishing a chapter? Could she turn around now and live with herself? In fifty feet? Another mile?

The sun had passed over the canyon wall; it was dusk in the depths when she spotted hiking boots jutting out from under a rock fifty yards away. She jogged as fast as she could until she noticed how the boots were splayed. No movement. She stopped and watched. She put her hand against the Vishnu Schist and lost track of time.

Another sneering mother manifested from behind the rock. She pointed down. "Is that what you betrayed Benny and Andrew for, slut?"

Sierra walked to the rock and put her hand on it. Peeked under and watched his chest to see it rise and fall. It didn't. His bloody hand lay by his side. She squatted lower and could see his neck, his face still hidden. No movement.

"If we had only had more time. A little more time," she said. She turned a slow circle and slid down against the rock.

"Maybe enough time to get back to those helicopters I heard?" Eric's voice rasped.

Sierra shook her head. "I'm done talking to ghosts."

"If I'm a ghost, I guess I'm in hell."

"I guess so. Leave me alone."

"I thought you were upset with me for leaving you alone all these years."

She tensed. "Is that really you, Eric?"

"Are you serious?"

She peered under the rock, saw his face. He gave her a weak wave. She cried out, crawled to him, shook her head, and hugged him. She reached into her pack and pulled out one of two remaining epinephrine shots. She popped the top and jammed it into Eric's leg.

"We have a helicopter to catch," she said.

"I knew I heard choppers. Why aren't you on one?"

"If you knew how many times I've asked myself that question," she said, pulling him up and ignoring his cries.

"Hobbes came back," Eric said, shuffling, one arm over her shoulders. "We gotta watch out for him."

"No, we don't. He's headed back up the rim."

"Don't reckon you'll tell me why?"

"We'll talk about it later."

"Yeah, well, I hope he falls off a cliff and busts into a million juicy watermelon pieces."

Sierra stopped, Eric's impression of Mel the Mule Wrangler overcoming her with wheezing laughter. When she could finally breathe again, she said, "Dammit ta hell."

"All right, Counselor, enough giggling. Hear?"

They exited the vestiges of the Box and crossed the last bridge before Phantom Ranch. Although Eric's wound had caked over with dried blood and dirt, it still seeped bright red. Sierra eyed it closely. "Why'd you come back?" he asked.

"Hobbes told me what you did for me, Benny, Andrew. Why didn't you tell me that when I beat the hell out of you?"

"Would you have believed me?"

"No."

"Well, there you go. Where the hell did you learn to punch like that?"

"Andrew bought me a heavy bag a few years ago."

"Of course he did."

Sierra heard the sound of a helicopter.

Eric's energy flagged more as the epinephrine wore off. "I'm done, Sierra. Get to that chopper."

She pulled the last shot from the bag and jabbed his leg. "Move or I'll stick my finger in your bullet hole."

"Stick it where?"

"Stop," she said, fighting tears and a giggle.

They kept moving. She could still hear the helicopter. She screamed for help over and over as it grew closer. The aircraft's engine whined harder, and its slapping blades grew faster. It was airborne over the canyon. Sierra let go of Eric and waved her arms and jumped and screamed.

Gone.

Eric again clung to her shoulder. If they turned north to escape the flood, they'd die. Eric would bleed out. The bridge would be gone and the river flooded. Exposure or dehydration would get her.

There was only south. Across the bridge before it was gone.

"We have to keep going."

"Whatever . . . you . . . say . . ."

He slipped off her shoulder.

She caught him and grunted, forcing him back up. "Move your ass, Marine!" she shouted.

He jerked as if awakened from a deep sleep. They moved through the campground down the long straight path near the creek under the tall cottonwoods that had been so welcoming that morning, descended the trail, and came to the rock masonry water spigot near the swift, swollen river. A thin corridor of sunlight survived in this part of the canyon.

"The bridge," she shouted, pointing. "We're almost there, Eric. Let's get some water."

They drank from the spigot before trudging up the incline and past the plastic information podiums boasting Centuries of History and The Mighty Colorado River. The bridge seemed longer than it had that morning.

"Catch your breath," she said. "We're crossing in one push, okay?" A sound like a crackling gunshot echoed down the canyon, making Sierra's head jerk.

"The hell was that?" Eric exclaimed.

Sierra put her hand on one of the bridge's steel rails. A thrumming under the flesh of her palm.

It increased in intensity with each passing second.

"Run!" she screamed.

———

Hobbes exited his room after treating his wounds and walked to the commuter vehicle. His run up the rim had exhausted him more than it should have. Bags and clothes were strewn throughout the hall and out into the parking lots around Grand Canyon Village. National Park Service officials on loudspeakers repeated evacuation orders. Few people remained and the light would soon fade. He'd been fortunate that more tourists and hikers were milling around the South Kaibab trailhead when he returned. A few young thrill-seekers had fought off the rangers' attempts to get them to leave the canyon's precarious edge, coveting their front row seats to the greatest frigging show on earth, dude.

He kept on the medical mask, using the distraction and panic to get into the commuter for the drive back. In Grand Canyon Village, mothers yelled at straggling children. Rangers and park volunteers barked commands at people taking too long to get the hell out. No one paid any attention when Hobbes opened the trunk, put on the thigh holster, and slid the Glock 19 into it.

When he discovered the adjoining door open and his hostages gone, he drew his weapon and moved slow, anticipating an ambush. When he realized there wouldn't be one, he kicked open the door to Sierra's room and searched for something he could use. After rifling through their bags, he saw something that gave him a thought: This could work.

He took the small shoes. They weren't a hostage, but they were better than nothing. The bigger question was how to get the documents back from Sierra? Rev Six wouldn't wait long before making good on their threat.

He grabbed the street clothes from his just-in-case bag in the commuter's trunk. Changed right there in the lot. He had considered an under-the-shirt bulletproof vest, but if he got into a fight, he'd need the plate carrier for the extra mags anyway. He slid the hard armor plates back into the carrier.

With a heavy thwocking sound, the helicopter crested the rim and flew south. That meant that any of the people from down in the canyon—Sierra, Andrew, maybe even the big ranger—might be able to point him out.

He moved all the other weapons from the trunk into the front passenger seat and floorboard. He slid extra full mags for the SCAR and the Glock into the pouches on the plate carrier and put it in the passenger seat. Checked the loads and chambered rounds in each gun. He put the paper bag with the C-4 and the detonators on the front seat with the plate carrier, then covered it all up under the black towel.

A Rev Six assassin. One of Senator Pace's killers. Law enforcement. The Army. "Gotta be ready for anything now," he said.

An ominous noise rose from the canyon.

He couldn't see anything from where he stood, but there was no denying the rumble. At first people stopped and turned toward it, as if it had control over them. Then they broke and screamed louder and ran faster around him. Hobbes laughed. The flood wasn't funny. Watching them come unglued a mile above it, however, was hysterical.

Hobbes squealed out of the lot. Two NPS rangers, one male and one female, were setting up a roadblock when he drifted around the next corner, veered off the roadway, came back onto it, and skidded to a dusty stop. He'd throw them off with his disguise: a terrified, out-of-style, grunge-loving tourist escaping impending doom.

No dice.

They put their hands on their pistols and waited for him to approach. Who'd talked? Senator Pace? The big ranger? Sierra? He put the commuter in park, threw off the black towel, grabbed the plate carrier, and wrestled it on inside the small car. Watched. "Don't do it, you stupid bastards," Hobbes whispered. The male ranger pulled his pistol.

Hobbes swore and became a machine.

Gunshots made him duck. He flung open the driver's door. The left front tire exploded as he grabbed the SCAR. He knelt behind the open door. Brought the machine gun up between the open door and the jamb. Hot, stale air from the shot-out rubber tire filled his nostrils.

He aimed and squeezed the SCAR's trigger, holding the weapon firm as his shoulder absorbed the rhythmic pounding of a twenty-round magazine full auto dump. He shot half the mag at each ranger. Sweat stung his eyes.

The SCAR hammered out the six hundred-round-per-minute stream with little rise. The male ranger went down. The small dark-haired female ranger to his right screamed something that sounded like the word "bush."

As he released his mag and pulled another from the pouch, she continued firing. Hobbes heard a buzzing near his face and ducked, giving her a second longer to release her mag. She beat him on the reload. He lined her up in his sights.

Shocking white light. A home run swing to his chest.

The white light turned into blue sky. He only heard the ringing in his ears. Smelled burning skin. His right forearm sizzled—the SCAR's hot barrel.

He threw it off and shook his head, gasping. Jammed his hand under his shirt. No blood. The plate had absorbed the bullet, but not the impact. He'd been hit before, but never square in the sternum.

Dizziness gripped him. "My God, that hurts."

Movement to his right. He had no time to get the SCAR up.

Sucking air, he pulled the Glock and fired six blind shots toward the footsteps. Muffled sounds as she grunted and scrambled for cover. Hobbes struggled into the commuter, shifted, and slammed on the accelerator, his left leg still hanging out the door. The rim of the blown tire threw sparks and thumped in protest on the asphalt.

He muscled his leg inside just before the door clipped the ranger's

SUV and slammed shut. The rear window shattered behind him. Another bullet blew a hole through the windshield right next to his head. Yet another fragmented the rearview mirror.

"Fuck, she can shoot," Hobbes yelled, trying to stay low as he tried to create space between them.

He made it a few hundred meters and stopped. She'd either chase him or call reinforcements. He yanked the wheel and brought the car to a broadside standstill. Fighting an elephant on his chest, Hobbes changed mags in the Glock and holstered it. He took the M24 rifle out and used the commuter's hood and his burned arm to steady it. She was running toward one of the National Park Service SUVs when he put the reticle on her sternum and followed her movements.

Exhale.

Squeeze.

Fire.

Miss.

He was shaking, wheezing for air. He worked the bolt, ejected the shell. Chambered the next. Felt his body rock with each heartbeat.

Exhale.

Squeeze.

Fire.

The rifle bucked again.

Hobbes squinted through the glass. She lay facedown on the road. He checked his surroundings for any other threats. Nothing.

The jet-black raven landed in a pine tree next to the road. It raised its wings and let out an angry, guttural caw. Hobbes looked away from it.

He set the rifle barrel down on the passenger seat and gunned the engine. It was time to find a car that wasn't shot full of holes or missing a tire. No point in being picky anymore; they were on him. Grand Canyon Village was empty now, so he wouldn't be carjacking anyone or stealing keys.

Looking through busted glass, he fought the clunking commuter's steering wheel for a few hundred meters down the road around the railroad tracks. He saw a sign: EMPLOYEE AND RESIDENT PARKING

ONLY. He pulled into the near-empty lot, searching for something older that he could hot-wire. "C'mon, gotta be one damn car here."

He'd made almost a full loop when he saw a vehicle parked next to a dumpster.

For the first time that day, Hobbes managed a grin.

———

Every so often, a motorist drove like a crazed animal on the shoulder around the roadblock. They had no choice but to let them go and radio the vehicle's plates and description to a dispatcher, even though there were no available officers in the entire Southwest to take the call. As the sun dipped nearer the horizon, they stopped bothering. Goodnight and Garcia used cones to funnel both lines of traffic into one. It was only a matter of time before some wackadoodle ran them over. Goodnight ordered Garcia to get his M4 out of his cruiser and sling it over his shoulder. Goodnight did the same with the trooper's 12-gauge shotgun.

They took everyone out as ordered, even children. Garcia worked each car with precision and courtesy, and they bantered back and forth between searches.

"Crazy to think the park is getting hit with that flood, Chief," Garcia said. "I wish I could have seen that. On God, bro."

"No, trooper, you don't."

"You saw it?"

Goodnight squinted at the traffic clogging both lanes of Highway 64. A minivan full of college-aged girls rolled to a stop. The windows were shoe-polished with RIM-TO-RIM-TO-RIM HOTTIES and UNIVERSITY OF ARIZONA BADDIES.

Garcia whirled on Goodnight with bulging eyes and a grin.

"Trooper, they're just women. Came to run across the canyon and back. I think that's what rim-to-rim-to-rim means, anyhow. Nuts."

In spite of their fear, or perhaps because of it, the girls in the van flirted with Garcia. The handsome young man devoured their attention like a five-course meal.

"All right, move 'em along," Goodnight ordered.

Garcia shot a pleading and embarrassed look at him. "Ladies, thank you for your cooperation . . ." More vehicles came and were searched and went.

"How we supposed to move all these people, Chief? We need backup, yo," observed Garcia.

"You're an Arizona state trooper, Garcia. We are the backup."

"Yeah, Chief, but damn. We can't process people fast enough to get them to safety."

The kid was right. They needed to shift gears, especially with the sun sinking behind the desert.

"All right. No more taking 'em out of cars. You take one line, I'll take the other. Watch yourself. Might be someone in your line who's decided they're never going back to prison. And it ain't likely, but our guy might be here."

"Word, Chief. Whoa. See that?" Garcia asked, pointing north at the big dust cloud.

Goodnight said a silent prayer for Judy.

———

Sierra pulled hard on Eric, running with all her strength to get him across the elongated bridge. The sound of the flood grew.

"Faster!" she shrieked.

"Giving it all I got, for a dead man," Eric shouted back.

They made it across the bridge and into the tunnel. They caught their breath and rested against the dark walls.

"We can't stay in here!" Sierra yelled.

They pushed through and made it out the other side. But Eric couldn't ascend the water bars. A boulder the size of a truck clonked down and just missed turning them into flat red splotches, then bounced and tumbled into the river.

"Sierra, I can't anymore. Please, just run," Eric growled as he lay down on the trail and coughed up blood.

She heard a dull liquid roar peppered with things breaking and roiling. Popping. Crashing and swooshing. Her shoulders at first dropped, but then she raised her fists and screamed at the darkening sky. She raged until her air left her.

She fell upon him, sobbing. "I don't know how to live this life without knowing you're still out there somewhere in it. That maybe there's a chance I might see you again. Please don't go." She clung to his neck. "I . . . I love you, Eric." She felt him reach up and feebly run his fingers through her hair.

"I just wanted you to love me back," she cried.

"I did, Sierra. All this time." He cradled her head on his chest. "I wish you could stay here with me forever," he mumbled.

The roaring sound loomed closer.

"Forever doesn't pay the bills." There was no humor in her voice.

"That's not how that saying goes," Eric said. She saw the Eric she had fallen in love with. Shared her body and memories with. She cupped his cheek, caked with sweat and the red dust from the trail underneath his failing body. In those final seconds, time seemed to freeze the connection between his eyes and her own. Time. So much they had lost, and now there was none left to be had.

He pushed her away. "Don't look back, Sierra. Go!"

She sobbed again and kissed his lips one last time, hard. Then she rose and ran. The adrenaline dump made her feel superhuman until she clipped a water bar with her right foot and fell flat on her face. Dirt and dust clogged her vision and breathing.

Thundering water approached.

Chapter 20

Hotel Oscar Bravo Bravo Echo Sierra

ERIC DRAGGED HIMSELF AGAINST THE TRAIL WALL. THE earth under his body shuddered. When the flood was still behind the upstream canyon walls, it had sounded muffled, like a speaker behind a mattress. Now that the mattress had been pulled away, it was earsplitting.

"Holy God," Eric whispered. "This is it."

He saw a group of people running across the bridge, a few of them in purple costumes. They were halfway. "Are those unicorns or am I already dead?" Eric murmured.

Something—an errant boulder or the earth shuddering around the structure—caused the east cable anchor to crack, adding slack. The bridge dropped on the that side, throwing the runners off balance. A second later, the anchor broke free. The three conjoined steel cables collapsed on the flailing figures, knocking two of the unicorn people into the river.

That's when a towering, horrifying wave resembling scrambling giant black spiders blew the bridge apart. The brunt of the reddish-chocolate-milk surge rolled in behind it so fast, it looked like a film someone had sped up to make it appear unnatural.

"I thought I'd buy it in the air," Eric said.

He let out a ragged laugh. Pushed himself against the rock behind him.

The sounds faded. He turned away from the flood toward the setting sun.

Silence. He hoped Sierra made it.

The sun morphed into the moon. The square-jawed man in the moon wore a forward-tilted Smokey Bear hat. He saluted Eric. Semper fi, Marine.

The moon disappeared in the waters.

————

Don't look back.

The adrenaline turned Sierra's body and brain into a survival machine running in overdrive at ten thousand RPMs. Up she ran on the gravel trail, leaping over water bars, grunting. Blood flowed through her body and ears: depleted, reoxygenated, depleted, reoxygenated.

Don't look back.

Two running steps, then a jump up onto a water bar. Three steps, then another running jump up a water bar. Turn the switchback. Run, run, run. Precious seconds when she needed mere inches to survive.

Don't look back.

She pushed. Her lungs burned. Her quads screamed. Forty stories, Driscoll had said.

When the earth rolled under her feet, the impulse was too great: She turned to face her attacker.

————

Faces ran together. Goodnight watched Garcia wipe his brow, noticed he was talking less. It was dusk, they were tired, and they were out of water. The repetition and thirst exhausted their brains, opened them to threats like missed movements, unseen weapons. End of watch.

"Trooper, stay alert over there," Goodnight said.

"Roger that, Chief, I'm frosty."

Garcia waved through a pickup holding three twenty-something men with scrappy beards and trucker hats, all raising open canned beers. "Cheers," they shouted.

A female dispatcher's voice came over the radio. "All units be advised, suspect is still at large. Witnesses report he's armed with a full auto machine gun and killed an NPS ranger and wounded another in Grand Canyon Village. Sources in the canyon report his name or alias may be Hobbes. Hotel Oscar Bravo Bravo Echo Sierra. Armed and extremely dangerous."

Hobbes always wins. That's what Jones had said.

Goodnight alerted to an early model muscle car five vehicles back. It was light green, squatty in the rear and rising in the front, the twin air scoops on the hood surrounded by splotches of primer gray, the driver's door sporting a big dent. The driver side vertical grille was gone, and the dark, aftermarket window tint had bubbled. Yet it had new street tires and a gasoline engine that sounded well maintained.

Something about that car.

It was the gut feeling he'd told Tanaka and Hayes about. Only this time it was real. The feeling a cop gets after years working the streets. Instinct was only half of it. Experienced cops trusted their instincts. They didn't give countenance to hurt feelings.

"Garcia," he said.

"Sir?"

"That old green muscle car back there. Primer on the hood. See it? Not passing my smell test."

"Damn, Chief. Gotta be some stank up in there for you to smell it from here. I'm on it."

When Sierra turned, the limits of what was possible in this world expanded inside her mind in an instant. She thought the massive

Colorado River had been intimidating, loud, and surging. It had been a babbling brook compared to this. A towering mass of rocks, logs, boulders, and unidentifiable things hurtled toward her in fast-forward. The sound was like TV or radio static turned up loud enough to damage eardrums.

When it hit her, the overspray from wet, smashing boulders soaked her in muddy red silt. Rocks rolled and thumped up the bank and sailed through the air. A good-sized one slammed into her torso and left her breathless. A colossal log danced end over end out of the water and debris, only to get sucked back in.

The muddy, rock-filled meat grinder of a flood roared past, missing her by inches. If she'd spent one more second with Eric, she'd be caught up in it, broken and dead.

She was in the widening slot canyon above the tunnel. The water had to spread out there, roiling within the concave area. A giant whirlpool formed instantly in front of her, sucking in and spitting out huge pieces of debris, gurgling, and crashing. A giant toilet—it climbed toward her, threatening to take her down into its vortex. Sierra whimpered and cried and fought to get away from it all.

Across the canyon the debris field obliterated the vegetation leading into Phantom Ranch. A truck rolled up from the reddish-brown torrent, turned over to reveal a drive shaft and exhaust piping, then disappeared into hundreds of feet of water. A wooden building floated past, tumbling end over end and breaking apart. Once Sierra knew she was high enough, she lay on the trail, wheezing, sobbing, watching the flood in the waning light.

————

Goodnight put up a hand to stop his lane. He moved a cone and directed the muscle car in between himself and Garcia. The driver hand-cranked his window open. The engine's rumble vibrated through Goodnight's boots. Gasoline vapor from the vehicle's carburetor filled his nose. Garcia circled the car, inspecting it, the M4 at arms.

"Turn off your engine, please, sir," Goodnight said. He leaned down and saw a slim man with long hair and a black baseball cap. The man's legs were pushed up from lack of space. He wore sunglasses, a T-shirt the color of ultraviolet light that said TEN on it, blue jeans, and a black medical mask. Rock music played at low volume from the car's stereo. The driver turned the key and the car's growl glugged to a stop. The music died.

"Garcia, cover me," said Goodnight.

Garcia stood outside the passenger door, pointing the M4.

"Need to see your ID, please, sir. Please remove your sunglasses and cap," Goodnight said. "And the face covering. Keep your hands where I can see them."

The man removed the hat, revealing a head of thick, long brown hair. The sunglasses and mask stayed on. Goodnight saw a paper bag on the front passenger seat and a black towel covering something on the floorboard.

"This your car?" Goodnight asked.

"Yes, sir."

"Looks like you're a bit cramped in there, fella."

"This is as far back as the seat goes."

Goodnight grunted. "I need your driver's license, sir. Remove your eyewear and the face covering. You get hurt in the park?" he asked, motioning at the bandage on the man's ear. The man pulled the sunglasses off. Ice-blue eyes. Goodnight kept calm. Lots of folks had blue eyes.

"I'm not going to cooperate," the man said.

Goodnight's neck tingled. "You won't?"

"There's only two of you. Lots of traffic back there."

Without looking away from the driver, Goodnight addressed Garcia. "How are the cars behind us, Trooper?"

"Hooah, Chief," Garcia replied.

"You gonna change your mind, Hoss?" Goodnight asked the driver, placing his finger on the shotgun's trigger.

The man's face turned dark. "I have something valuable in the trunk." He held up a pair of child's shoes.

Goodnight's insides turned to water.

"I also have this." The driver pointed at the brown bag.

"That your lunch?" Goodnight regulated his breathing.

Terrible things swam in the driver's eyes. "It's the end of you and me. The end of what's in the trunk. That kid with the M4. The five or six cars behind me too. You really wanna do this?"

They held each other's gaze. Goodnight felt his legs trembling. The driver turned the key. The muscle car coughed and growled in slow cycles again. The music came back.

Goodnight heard a soaring electric guitar, something he remembered from long ago. Before Blanche. Before children. Before bad guys. Before Judy and dams and floods and some little kid's shoes. He hated to let this guy go. Said he wouldn't. He needed to tell Judy how he really felt about her.

"Chief?" Garcia shouted.

"Shame for something to happen here," the man said.

"What are we doing with this guy, Chief?" Garcia hollered.

Goodnight heard horns. Shouting from impatient motorists. They sounded far away. He strangled the 12-gauge. Could he take him? Something valuable in the trunk. The boxy car idled heavily as the setting sun bathed the men in a golden glow.

He had to trust his instincts. Hobbes always wins. But Goodnight had to know how he'd done it. "Where'd you hide the big bombs? How'd you pull that off?"

The driver's eyes came alive from what Goodnight could only assume was a grin behind the mask, but he offered nothing else.

"Had to be the dungeon floor. In the electrical access panels? The elevator shafts?"

The driver shrugged.

Goodnight wanted to swing the shotgun up and blow his head apart. But he'd had enough of bombs for one day. Even the threat of one. Maybe there was a kid in the trunk. Maybe not. Did he want to gamble on maybe? Garcia had his whole life in front of him. And lots of innocent people were sitting back there, waiting.

Damn it all. Not today. He had to let him go.

Goodnight forced himself to back away from the muscle car.

The man dropped the little shoes onto the pavement at Goodnight's feet as the car idled forward.

"Give those to Sierra Justice."

Chapter 21

Shimmering Bubble

DOWN THERE IN THE DARK, A MILE BELOW WHERE SHE stood, it rumbled like a far-off locomotive. Sierra's hips and knees and lower back ached, the joints and muscles and connective tissue wound up so tight that they felt they might rupture or shatter like glass. Her feet burned with hot spots and blisters. Her exposed skin had bubbled in places. Her lips cracked. The cooler night air helped. She sat when she needed to rest, then she'd fight her way back up, then shuffle, then walk.

She saw the stars overhead. A deep obsidian black dotted with every size of burning history, so many tiny lamps pitted around larger lights. The Milky Way's purplish presence. And the only other constellation she knew, the Great Bear, the one Mama had shown her, more clear than she'd ever seen, low in the north, across the canyon she had just escaped, over the torrent that had destroyed worlds, out into the universe.

A compassionate park ranger's headlamp beam met her at Ooh Aah Point. He wore a helmet and was equipped with ropes, jangling metal carabiners, and a large pack. He gave her water. Listened to her story. Nodded. Nothing, not even violent murder, surprised anyone today. "There's a command post and first responders at the trailhead. They'll get you to the hospital. They're waiting on my report by radio before they send anyone down for survivors."

"Survivors?" Sierra asked, incredulous. She put her hand on his shoulder. "There are no survivors. Not even bugs."

In the last quarter mile up the steep trail next to the deep, dark cliffs, the last thing Sierra saw were several headlamps approaching. She fainted. She woke in an ambulance hooked to an IV with ice bags between her legs and under her arms. "I have to get to my son," she said, frantic. "His name is Benjamin Thomas. His father should be with him. Andrew Thomas. They're at the hospital."

"Rest," said a female EMT. "Your son's fine. It'll keep." She slid a needle into Sierra's IV port.

Sierra found herself back in the canyon. Eric telling her to leave him. The roar of the flood. Kissing his lips. Letting his hand go. The rocks hitting her. The whirlpool threatening to suck her inside.

Don't look back.

She woke, panting. The ambulance had stopped. The back doors opened. Several people exited other vehicles amid flashing lights, including two men in suits, an older man wearing a burned security uniform and a gun belt, and a woman. It was the red-headed ranger from Phantom Ranch.

Jamie? Julia?

Judy.

Sierra ripped the IV from the port in her wrist. She climbed out of the ambulance with screaming joints and tight muscles. The two men in suits held up FBI badges. "Ms. Justice. We need to ask you some questions, ma'am."

Judy positioned herself in front of Sierra. "You'll wait to ask your questions, gentlemen. I don't care what your damn badges say." She hugged Sierra.

"I'm taking you to Benny. I brought along my good friend, Chief Goodnight. He told me you two know each other a little bit already. He's been worried sick about you."

The older man in the security uniform nodded at Sierra and removed his hat. "It's nice to finally meet you in person, Ms. Justice."

It was in some other lifetime when she heard the same distant yet comforting voice.

"I had him, Ms. Justice. I could have . . . taken him. But he . . ." The man choked up. "Oh, hell it doesn't matter now. Anyway, I have these." Chief Goodnight held up Benny's shoes, still tied together.

Sierra gasped, snatched them, held them close to her chest. "Thank you," she whispered, unable to control her sobs.

"Your information saved countless lives," he said. "If it hadn't been for you . . ." He stammered again and reached out to hug her tight. Sierra let him. She found the strength to run to Benny, who was lying in the ICU bed, and blew past the nurse who tried to stop her. He was groggy but awake. Sierra climbed into the bed on top of him, covering him with kisses, apologizing, crying, laughing, checking him all over.

"Let him breathe, Sierra," Andrew said in a voice somewhere between jest and concern.

"Are you okay, baby? Mama's here, Mama's here." She sat back, examining him. "I'm sorry about all of this, baby. Mama's so sorry."

"He knows it's not your fault, Sierra," Andrew said. He grabbed Benny's hand. "We've been talking about it. Right, Big B?"

Benny panned from Sierra to Andrew, then back to Sierra. "The bad man got me and Aunt Scarlett because I dialed the numbers," he said, his little voice trembling, tears welling in his eyes.

Andrew rubbed her back as Sierra squeezed Benny as if she were trying to pull him into her, to make them one again, to make him safe. After a few moments, she cupped his face in her hands. "No, baby. It's not your fault." Sierra smiled, sniffling. "Do you want to know how we found you?"

Benny's big browns held her gaze.

"I used your trick. I dialed numbers on the phone until someone answered. You're so smart, Benny, and you're such a brave boy. I'm so proud of you." She kept his face framed in her hands. "You are my hope, Benny. I will do anything for you."

Benny held her gaze a moment longer, the slightest hint of a smile on his face. He drifted off to sleep.

"He hasn't slept until now," Andrew said.

"He knew, Andrew. Remember? He didn't want me going on this trip. He knew there was a bad man out there." She leaned back, took a deep breath. "Scarlett?"

Andrew shook his head. He walked her to the plush chair and sat her in his lap. Pulled her close.

"Her asthma." She lay in Andrew's arms, crying for their family friend—her kindred sister—and for Benny.

Andrew rocked and soothed her. He took her hand and put something in it. The earrings. She fell into a darkness she recognized from long ago, but this time she wasn't alone.

——

She woke in Andrew's lap, taking a minute to bring her world into focus. "What's going on?"

"You and Benny have been out. It's two a.m. They want to transport him to Phoenix for tests and observation at the children's hospital."

"The last time the three of us were together in a hospital room at two a.m. was his birth."

"Yep."

"I remember something Hobbes said."

"You need to forget that psycho."

She sat up, wincing. "No, Andrew. We need to remember. He said that people who escape crisis situations go back to living the same lives. Promise me we'll be different."

He took a deep breath. Exhaled. "Okay. I promise."

She grabbed his hands. "I'm sorry about everything that happened with Eric." She stared through the window at the dark. She'd tell Andrew the rest back in Washington. They needed to be strong as a couple for Benny right now. "He's gone. I don't know why I held on for so long. I'm scared."

"Back in DC, you said you needed a change. Change is scary."

Sierra nodded, then saw Benny's shoes, still tied together, on the floor by their chair. She picked them up, examined them. "How did Mr. Goodnight get these?"

Andrew shrugged. Then he leaned over and pulled something out from under the chair. The slim metal box. A relic from another life. Holding the documents gave her power, leverage. It also meant something else.

Hobbes was coming for her.

———

He watched the modern brick building from his car, parked two blocks down, as a male voice reported the news through the car's radio.

"Official reports are that the Hoover Dam, although it has sustained heavy damage, will hold and can be repaired. Loss of life is estimated in the several thousands, and millions are without power and water. However, Sierra Justice, the once despised attorney for the late Wade Ford, has been lauded by officials and credited with saving innumerable lives after she reportedly provided a tip to authorities about the impending disaster. Damage is estimated in the hundreds of billions of dollars and will take years to repair."

The talking heads were already stirring up conspiracy theories and pointing fingers. Congresspeople demanded inquiries into a government cover-up. Every affected state in the Southwest was declared a disaster area. Lake Powell was gone. Despite the Flaming Gorge Reservoir, the Colorado River was once again wild and unpredictable through the Grand Canyon.

Nothing, however—not even a mere suggestion—of Rev Six.

The newsman continued. "The FBI and most local law enforcement agencies have a police sketch of Hobbes on their website and are encouraging Americans to view it and be on the lookout. If you see anyone matching his description, report it to authorities immediately. Hobbes is number one on the FBI's Ten Most Wanted List."

Hobbes. An alias finished in both name and purpose. But the man himself still had work to do.

The FBI had found Samuels's poorly-destroyed burner phone and pulled the pings. The heat was all over Arizona, especially in Phoenix and the Sky Harbor International Airport. Rev Six would be looking for Hobbes with malintent until he delivered the documents and completed Cygnus. For her own reasons, Senator Pace would send another assassin to take him out if he popped up on the radar.

"Time's running out," he observed.

He had switched cars twice since stealing the muscle car in Grand Canyon Village. His latest ride was an aging black four-door midsize sedan that smelled like stale beer and pot, but it had contained a full tank of gas when he found it running outside a truck stop on the I-17.

He was grateful he had exchanged the cash prior to going to Grand Canyon. He bought some things from a drugstore. Dyed his hair black. Dyed the emerging scruff on his chin black too. His height was the issue; he couldn't cut a foot off it.

Movement in his binos.

From the hotel, Andrew limped out wearing a medical boot and holding Benny's hand. They got into a car and drove away, just like yesterday. A trip out for food or entertainment. He had perhaps an hour window, tops. Hobbes was down the street, through the alley, and inside the hotel in three minutes, hoping his disguise—a green ball cap, apron, and a bouquet of flowers— held up.

He walked stooped and with a fake limp.

"Delivery for Sierra Justice," he said, holding up the bouquet of flowers, complete with a card. No law enforcement in the lobby, which wasn't necessarily good. He scanned for signs of an ambush.

The clerk was a middle-aged white man with a name tag that said ALBERT. "We're very proud to have a national hero in our hotel," he said, beaming. "Just need an ID, please, sir."

Hobbes smiled and held up the Arizona fake.

"Perfect, Mr. Woods. Let's see . . . ah, room 642. Hold on a sec while I give her a call." He dialed. "Uh, Ms. Justice? Sorry to bother you, but there's a flower delivery man here for you. May I send him up?" He hung up and smiled. "She's waiting for you, sir."

Two more potential obstacles: security guards and cameras. Using the bouquet and his hat pulled low, he did his best to shield his face from the digital lenses and took the stairs. On the sixth floor he peeked around the corner, pulled the Glock. The security guards he had wondered about weren't there. If it was an ambush, he'd have to risk it. Time wasn't on his side. He pulled his lock-picking kit from his apron but saw that the door was already propped open with the safety lock. He tapped three times with the end of the suppressor.

"Come in."

She sat on the bed in jeans and a black T-shirt. Her feet bare, her face peeling. Soft music played from her phone. Hobbes listened a moment. Smiled. He knew the song.

"No security?"

"I told them to leave yesterday. It's been days. You had until today. We leave tomorrow, and I don't need you coming to our home."

"Wasn't easy to find you. Give me the documents and I'm gone. Someone's watching this hotel. Probably already on their way."

She nodded toward the drawer under the television. "I'll give you ten minutes before I have to call it in. If they don't get you first."

"I was prepared for this to go another way. But you already found the information in the shoes, didn't you?"

Sierra didn't react.

"What's mentioned there is only a fraction of what you'll get if I can deliver the documents." He watched her turn it over in her mind. "It's clean money, Sierra. I took all the steps."

Hobbes opened the drawer and retrieved the box and took out the documents. Inspected them. "Tell them I must have slipped in when you were sleeping."

"Who's Amelia?"

Hobbes turned, puzzled.

"When you pressed the button, you said, 'I'm sorry, Amelia.' Who is she?"

He didn't remember saying Amelia's name aloud. "My daughter. I met her a few weeks ago."

Sierra's gaze made him uncomfortable.

"Your turn," he said. "You said something about a clock. Three minutes to midnight."

"That's about the time Mama shot my stepdad in the face in front of me. I was twelve. They made me testify against her. I've never spoken to her since that night. She knew something. I'm still trying to figure out what. Or remember, maybe."

"That's a lot to carry, Sierra."

She shook her head. "I had a lot of time to think down there. That thing in your neck . . . Have you got months? Years?"

He shrugged. "Depends on what this money will buy." Hobbes took a deep breath. "I never said a prayer when I made it out of the canyon."

"What does that have to do with anything?"

He sat on the other bed. "Our target was a Taliban lieutenant who was especially creative with improvised explosive devices. The intel put the local fighting force at ten to twelve experienced fighters. No civilians. Everything went off without a hitch from insertion to killing the target. On our way out, we learned the local fighting force was nearly double in size."

Sierra face changed expression enough for him to continue.

"I kicked down a door to this little outbuilding during the firefight to take cover. An old woman was hiding in there. I was so amped up, I almost shot her. She had these dark brown eyes. She never made a sound or moved, just watched me reload. Then I took off to the landing zone."

"You were one of the good guys once, then?" Sierra asked.

Hobbes smirked. "We were nearly out of ammo when the helos flew over the mountain to the landing zone. Me and Johnson covered each other on our way back. I heard him banging away behind me. I turned to take over covering fire just as he took one to the leg. His blood was so hot through my glove. He was screaming. I kept firing . . . dragging him . . ."

"What happened?" Sierra asked.

"That old woman peeked around the corner of her little building right into one of my 7.62 rounds. I had to get Johnson to the chopper. I pulled off my glove and stuck my finger in his leg. In my nightmare, I still see the ground falling away. I feel Johnson's body going limp. And I see that old woman lying there dead."

A silence held until Sierra broke it. "What's Revelation Six?" Her expression was fixed.

"We're the good guys."

"Seven minutes, Hobbes."

He pointed at her phone "You have good taste in music, Sierra."

To switch it up, he took the elevator down. When he stepped into the car, he grabbed his neck and winced.

An elderly matron watched him. "Are you all right, sir?" she asked.

"Yes, ma'am, thank you."

"Such a shame about this awful tragedy, isn't it? Do you deliver flowers?"

"Yes, ma'am. I'm on my way to visit a United States senator right now."

"To deliver flowers? How marvelous," she said, her face aglow.

"Yes," Hobbes said. "How marvelous."

———

Hobbes had two days to think as he drove east on back roads. After he'd turned over the documents and wire transfer receipts, the Second Seal gave him location intel and told him that Senator Pace still didn't know she was compromised.

He took Ichabod outside a Fisher Heights grocery store. Hobbes swung an expandable baton into Ichabod's right knee when the tall man was opening his car door. He heard a crunch, Ichabod mewling. Hobbes zip-tied his hands behind his back, then threw a bag over his head and zip-tied it around his neck. Shoved him in the car's front seat. Locked the door and shut it. Watched until it was over.

"Sorry, Ichabod."

He found Philly in a hotel. After the struggle they sat eye to eye on cheap wooden chairs at the kitchenette's table. Only it was Hobbes questioning Philly this time, and Philly was down to one working eye. Hobbes watched him like he would a bug in a jar.

"She promised to appoint you as part of her cabinet—an office, something like that, right?"

"I don't know," Philly said, his tough facade gone. Tears and bloody drool fell onto his naked stomach and legs, his white briefs around his chubby hips. He'd been reduced to blubbering and words of sorrow and regret.

"You had no idea she couldn't deliver, did you?"

"I . . . no . . ." Philly said in a whisper.

Hobbes clicked his tongue. "But you knew Pace killed innocent people out of greed." He sighed. "It might surprise you that I really don't want to do this." Plastic bag. Zip tie. The bag pumped in and out, condensation droplets accumulating on the inside until Philly stopped convulsing on the kitchenette floor. Hobbes sat in the cheap wooden chair and watched. It took a long time.

———

Senator Pace looked up from her book and removed her reading glasses. Between the fire and the lamplight, Hobbes saw a glass of red wine in her left hand. A revolver, maybe a .38, on the couch near her right. Hobbes shook his head and pointed the Glock at her when she reached for it. He breathed in the smell of a clean home and woodsmoke.

"My security detail were pushovers, huh?" Senator Pace asked.

"They're Rev Six soldiers, not traitors."

Her brow furrowed. "Aren't we all traitors, Hobbes?"

"Our oath to Rev Six supersedes any other," he said, clearing the room.

She cocked her head. "You honestly believe that Rev Six wants what's best for the world?"

He again recognized Senator Pace's elegant beauty. Something about her reminded him of Sierra. Except that Sierra was still young and pure of heart. For a moment he considered possibilities.

No.

Sierra would never go for it. Besides, he was getting out.

Senator Pace's eyes darted toward the revolver. Hobbes pretended not to notice. Let her believe she had a chance; it would be easier. He walked around the couch and sat on the rock hearth bench behind her.

"You knew something was off back in Phoenix. You knew something about Cygnus."

"I did."

"You ignored your instincts."

"Biggest mistake of my life, I'm gathering. My staff?"

"Dead."

"That's too bad. Richard had a nice family."

"The tall, gangly one?"

"Yes."

"Maybe I should have done him in quick."

"Why, Hobbes?"

"I don't know. Because he wasn't as much of an asshole as I thought."

"No, Hobbes. The dam, the extortion . . . Obviously I've inferred by now that Rev Six learned of my plans. That's why I'm hiding here like a damn fugitive. But if my gig was up, why blow the dam? Why demand a measly hundred million, then kill all those people anyway?"

"You know I was Special Forces?"

"I know everything. I selected you."

He nodded. "It was never put in writing, but when my unit took out a terrorist target, we made it count. Made it messy. Made it look like terrorism."

"Ah," she said. "So Rev Six wanted to send a message." Her right shoulder dipped. He knew she had the pistol in her hand. Probably curling her finger around the trigger.

"Senator, how do we keep humanity from destroying itself if we let high-level corruption slide? You think I ratted you out?"

"Did you?"

"You implicated me in things I never knew about. They almost killed me. You were a high office director. Your elimination had to go before the International High Office. You know what the bylaws say. They used me to get it done."

"I *was* a high office director?"

"The international vote took place this morning. With my evidence. The money. The documents."

"So the Second Seal turned my best assassin against me." She shook her head.

"I should have trusted my instincts." She took another sip of wine. "What do you get for it all?"

He raised his eyebrows. "The money I took from you. The entire hundred million. Rev Six is going to let me out."

"Alive? That's a first."

"They gave me one last job before they'll clear me."

Her shoulder moved with more purpose this time. "Me."

"Rev Six negotiated a secret deal with the United States this morning after the international vote. Your cronies in DC didn't hesitate to use you as the scapegoat for the dead hostages and the blown dam. This morning the DOJ got warrants and seized everything you own. They're coming."

Her shoulder was still. "What's the plan after this Cygnus nonsense?"

"You know the drill. Rev Six has watched nations kill each other over petty issues or greed for generations. We step in when redirection is needed. Things are getting scary out there. Rev Six decided it was time to step in again. They charged me with the first mission." He chuckled. "Of course, they left out a few minor details. But I achieved my objective anyway."

"Hobbes, Rev Six was saying the same damn kind of things when my hair had no gray in it."

"Fair enough. But these days we're talking about fighting an infiltration of the human mind, threatening the safety and sovereignty of entire future generations. There are bigger stakes for all of humanity, not just individual nations. Rev Six is mustered—loaded and locked."

"Sounds like beating a drum for war," Pace observed.

"It is war."

They listened to the fire crackle.

He cleared his throat. "When I walked into the power plant and saw all those dead people, that little girl dying, I wondered who gave the order."

He raised the Glock to the back of her head.

He continued, "I was never supposed to walk out of that dam. You heard the rumors about Cygnus. You wanted no witnesses for Rev Six to interrogate. You knew your shitty mercenaries would die. But you didn't know they'd sniffed you out a long time ago. Anything else?"

"I should have hired better mercenaries," said Senator Pace.

She whirled and tried to raise the revolver, but Hobbes already had the Glock trained on her face. He fired once. In the dimly lit room, the muzzle flash revealed split-second horror in her eyes.

———

When he made his way out to his geriatric midsize SUV parked in the backyard drive, the raven screamed above in the quiet snowfall, knocking white powder from the tree. Hobbes squeezed his eyelids shut. Waited for the bird to stop. When it quieted down, he opened up.

She stood in the cold, her bare feet covered in snow. She no longer wore the hijab, just a long black linen dress. Half her head was missing. Only one graying braid remained. Only one dark brown eye stared back. There was no vapor from her distorted mouth.

"I'm sorry," he said.

She watched him a moment. He repeated the process of closing and opening his eyes. She was gone.

He got into the SUV and pulled out his burner. Dialed her number. Voice mail. He called again and she picked up.

"What do you want?" Her voice was cold.

"Hey." The pit of his stomach turned. I was calling—"

"What do you want?"

"I-I . . . want what we talked about that day over coffee. To see you again. To catch up."

Her deep breath. "I wasn't sure about the sketch. I had to check the pic I took of you against the TV to be sure. But when they showed the still of you from that hotel, even with the dark hair, I knew it was you. You said you'd be out of town for a while. Then nothing for a week after the dam exploded. I didn't want to believe it, but it made sense. I don't want to know anything else. Whatever you did, you have to live with."

"I have cancer, Amelia. I don't know how much time I have. I have to get treatment and—"

"I tried to find you for five years. That's after eighteen without a father. If it hadn't been for the file I found in my mom's desk after she died, I never would have known anything about you. I paid a private investigator twenty grand to find you. He said it was like finding a ghost. A week after I worked up the courage to meet you, I found out you might be a mass murderer. I can't take this. I won't."

"If I told you why, would it make a difference?" His voice sounded thin again.

"No."

"Amelia, please—"

The line went dead. He lost track of time gazing at the flip phone. He eventually grabbed the cigarettes he'd been avoiding, rolled down the window, and lit one. Timeless snowflakes melted on the arm of his black coat. When the first cigarette was gone, he lit another. He dialed the Second Seal. The director answered. Shark Eyes. "Code in."

Hobbes considered the date. English today. "Deceit may bleed the moon."

"And cause the stars to fall. Go."

"This is 451588. 009853 is eliminated. Is my daughter safe?"

"Affirmative."

Hobbes exhaled. "And my status?"

"Cleared as agreed. You have full payment for your service."

"What if I want back in?"

———

Sierra beat the hell out of the heavy bag. Took a shower. She touched herself, more with care than utility. No tears anymore, but still that strange, compulsive feeling. She dried off and styled her hair. Put on her makeup and the S-shaped gold scroll antique earrings with the pearl drops. Brushed her teeth and smirked at that crooked tooth still staring back at her. Helped Benny dress for school. Downstairs, she had coffee and watched Andrew scramble eggs. Wondered if she'd ever have the courage to tell him about that night with Eric. She'd already waited almost a year. Sometimes the truth did more damage than good. With Eric gone, maybe this was a situation where their secret stayed a secret.

Andrew turned to her. "I put the box back under our bed. You left it out," he said, smiling. "How's that going?"

"Slow. Even with what I already know, it's still a lot. Mama's a good writer. But it's like there's something she wants to tell me in it all. Every letter seems to drop a hint. Ever since the canyon, I've felt like there is . . . something, somewhere deep down, you know? But no matter how hard I try, I can't remember. I had hoped reading the letters might open some doors."

"Still thinking about a visit? You could ask her."

"Maybe." Sierra paused.

"Oh, did you look at the trunk-or-treat flyer I put on the fridge?" she asked. I want to make this Halloween fun for Benny, considering . . . last year."

"I'll get on it," said Andrew.

"Don't forget, we need to book flights for Judy and Fred's wedding next month." She walked to him for a hug. "See you this evening, Dr. Thomas."

He held up a finger. "Doctor-in-training. I love you."

She hesitated. "I love you too."

After almost a year of experimenting with that word, it still didn't fit. Maybe Andrew had noticed, or maybe he hadn't. She touched Scarlett's photograph by the front door as she ushered Benny to the car. She could never pair it with one of Eric, even if she had a photo of him, but Scarlett's image somehow brought his to mind each day. She'd take what she could. Fifteen minutes later she walked Benny up the steps of his school, ignoring the gawking faces. There were fewer with every passing month. Sierra helped him remove his parka and gloves.

"You're safe at school now, Benny."

He nodded. She cradled his face. He'd come so far in the past year with the therapy and more quality time. "I'll be here at three o'clock this afternoon to get you. You are my hope, Benny. I will do anything for you. I love you."

"I know, Mama, love you."

Traffic was the usual Washington drag, but she found a space in the parking garage without much trouble. Grabbed her purse. Extended the handle on her tote. Rolled it to the elevator.

"Wow. I get to share the elevator with the one and only Sierra Justice, Savior of the Southwest," said Matt, a lawyer from her building.

"Shut it, Matt. Whatcha got today?"

"Divorce prove-up and a temporary restraining order," Matt said. He pushed the button for the fourth floor. "My assistant double-booked me. But that's why I make the big bucks," he said with an eye roll.

"I don't know how you family law attorneys do it," Sierra replied.

"Job security, Ms. Justice. No one fights more than family. Hey, I've been meaning to ask you. You'd never argued in a courtroom until a year ago?"

She nodded.

"I saw you argue a summary judgment last month in front of Judge Prabakharan. Do me a favor—don't take any family cases." He chuckled. "Media still messing with you?"

Sierra shook her head. "People forget."

From the elevator she negotiated the vast hallways to find her assigned courtroom, one of the older ones that still had windows, empty. It smelled like an old library. Books and wood polish. A comforting and musty tone. She set up her laptop and laid out her file. A few things were in the wrong place, but she'd take that up with Lauren, her new paralegal, later during their daily call. Lauren was no Scarlett.

A portly whistling bailiff entered and bid Sierra good morning. The court reporter checked her equipment. Litigants, their family, and friends filled the gallery. The clerk took her seat. Lawyers on other cases filed in and took seats in the well or jury box. Sierra's opposing counsel set up on the other table and exchanged banter with her. The judge entered and they all stood. He called Sierra's case first and she went to work.

That afternoon she sat on the stoop watching Benny play with his bubble machine on the sidewalk. As he chased the bubbles and shrieked with joy, Sierra knew it wouldn't be long before he'd outgrow it. A simple diversion, magical only for a time.

Her phone buzzed. With Andrew working the ER, she never ignored a call. She removed the S-shaped gold scroll antique earring from that ear and tapped the green button.

"Hello?"

"Sierra."

The voice was unmistakable.

"I didn't have time in the hotel last year to tell you I was impressed at how fast you found the account funding information in Benny's shoes. That new DC brownstone didn't come cheap, did it?"

Sierra stood and checked their surroundings, then walked to where Benny played, touching his shoulder, swiveling her head. After a few beats she cleared her throat and found her voice. "Why call? I helped you. You helped me. I changed everything—my phone number, my address, our neighborhood, all of it. I started over. We're clear."

She refused him the satisfaction of upsetting her. "You're cured, I presume?"

"Depends on what you mean. Have you found the law to be boring after our adventure?"

In a life long gone, this might have shocked her. Her words came out slow.

"I've been watching the news over the last year," she said. "The huge reversal the public doesn't understand. But somehow they still accept this crazy story from some unknown source about the mysterious man who actually tried to stop the dam explosion. Your sketch."

"I'm just like you now, Sierra. We're heroes."

"It's not all it's cracked up to be. Don't call me again," she whispered.

"You realize because of me you got everything you wanted?"

"What did you just say?" Her face felt hot. "Do you even realize what you put my son through? What it did to him? It's taken a year for him to stop screaming at night. I lost people I loved."

"I won't spell it out for you, Sierra. I'm recruiting for the next operation. Rev Six needs someone tough who can keep a secret. Someone with a legal mind who's already proved capable." He chuckled. "Someone who clearly needs another adventure."

Sierra pulled Benny closer.

"I saw it when you shot me, Sierra. We'll work on your aim, but the fire was in your eyes," Hobbes said. "We started a discussion in the canyon, remember? You still have questions, don't you?"

Benny moved away from her leg when his battery-operated bubble machine blew a fresh stream of floating, soapy orbs.

"We started a war. It's going to happen with or without you, Sierra. What are we willing to do for our children? For their future?" asked Hobbes.

A bubble graced its way in front of Sierra's face. She watched its surface dance as she pondered Hobbes's words. Shimmering continents and oceans. Clouds of purples and blues. The bubble shimmered faster and faster.

"Sierra? Are you ready for answers?"

Benny laughed and jumped, grasping at bubbles.

When the air pressure inside the bubble ruptured the thin film of its existence into mist, Sierra stared at the empty space. She sat on the concrete stoop, still warm from the day's sun, the phone against her ear. She'd let Benny play a little longer.

"I'm listening," she said.

Acknowledgments and Author's Note

No one writes and publishes a novel alone.

To my readers, fans, and supporters—I wanted to entertain and inspire you. I hope I did. Stay tuned for more Sierra Justice.

My wife, Faith, endured countless nights, weekends, and early mornings listening to me clack away as she made lunches or ferried children without my help and went to bed alone while I typed. Our five children put up with my eyes entranced by a screen or my hands super-glued to a keyboard when they needed their dad.

Thank you to my parents, George and Patty, for always supporting my endeavors and encouraging me to work hard and strive for success.

My readers: Faith Falkenberg, Sarah Burrell, Julie Rich, Laurence Parent, Rebecca Lively, Brian Powers, Brandon Bonser, Slade Falkenberg, Robert McManus, Rick Dillenbeck, Chad Tiller, and Luke Allison. All of you provided invaluable feedback that helped me eventually hammer raw iron into a workable tool.

Regarding the technical aspects, certainly I screwed something up somewhere, and I intentionally changed some things. I'm not an expert in anything but maybe the law, and that's debatable. But it would have been worse without the help of several people:

Chad Tiller, an ex-Green Beret, who helped me with Hobbes and tactical scenes; Robert McManus, a Marine and helicopter pilot who provided endless and fast technical advice on everything from helicopter piloting to weaponry and plate carriers and radios; Rick Dillenbeck, for providing further support on the helicopters (he's an exceptional helicopter pilot too) and radio speak; Sarah Burrell, a former Air Force JAG lawyer, law school classmate, mock trial partner, and one of my closest friends during law school and today, for also pointing out flaws within my radio speak and military customs, and for reading this thing more than anyone; Sarah, along with her mother, Julie Rich, threw all sorts of literary goodies my way in the form of critique and suggestions; Ron Anderson with the Bureau of Reclamation for his insight on Glen Canyon Dam, the terminology, and the layout and specs of the dam itself; and Joëlle Baird, a National Park Service ranger at Grand Canyon National Park who handles media relations, and who helped me understand how operating procedures and emergencies and protocol work within NPS. Any technical mistakes or inaccuracies are mine, and mine alone.

My editor, Caroline Kaiser, for her attention to detail, patience, and willingness to go above and beyond for a new author. My cover designer, Agata with Bukovero—I sent her a rough sketch and synopsis, she turned it into a terrific, eye-catching cover.

Thanks to Laurence Parent, author of *Death in Big Bend* and many other non-fiction titles, for answering my out-of-the-blue fan email twelve years ago, meeting me for lunch in Wimberly, TX, for giving me tips on backpacking, inspiration to write a novel, ideas on publishing, and explaining what it takes to get the book marketed.

Thanks to Jeffrey Boldt, a writer and an administrative judge who authored *Blue Lake* and *Big Lake Troubles*, and who graciously answered my rookie novelist questions.

Thanks to Michael P. Ghiglieri and Thomas M. Myers for writing *Over the Edge: Death in Grand Canyon*, a terrific anecdotal and forensic read on what'll kill you in the Grand Canyon. Their stories helped me not only research for my book, but also kept me healthy in my treks across the canyon. To the authors of an insane amount of web pages and photos that I could never fully list here, answering more questions than any one person could ever entertain. To all those websites, bloggers, and article writers—please know you helped me.

To Grand Canyon National Park: I first gazed upon it when I was eight years old on an RV trip with my family. I've brought my own children to see this wonder, and I've crossed it three times on foot, from the South Kaibab Trailhead to the North Kaibab Trailhead and back to Bright Angel Trailhead, nonstop, including the very trail that Sierra and Hobbes and company traversed.

To the Black Suspension Bridge: I conceived the initial concept for this novel when I stood alone upon its planks over the massive Colorado River and had the inception for Sierra Justice's adventure. To the builder John Lawrence and the workers, including 42 Havasupai tribesmen, who built the Black Bridge in such a precarious, wild place almost a hundred years ago, I tip my hat.

Thank you all.

Deceit Runs Red
May 2022
August 2024
Spring Branch, Texas

About the Author

ROBERT FALKENBERG WAS BORN IN WEST TEXAS AND HAS A love for mountains and big skies and books. He received his BA in English from Texas State University where he began writing short stories. He was later an editor and staff writer for the St. Mary's Law Journal. In his time as a judge, he has created in collaboration with other legal professionals on various projects and has also worked as a freelance ghostwriter. His current work-in-progress is Volume II of the *Sierra Justice Series*. He lives in Texas with his wife and children.

Learn more at www.robertfalkenberg.com